S. A. HUNT

I COME WITH KNIVES

TOR

A TOM DOHERTY ASSOCIATES BOOK

NEW YORK

I COME WITH KNIVES

Copyright © 2020 by S. A. Hunt

A Tor Book
Published by Tom Doherty Associates
120 Broadway
New York, NY 10271

www.tor-forge.com

Tor® is a registered trademark of Macmillan Publishing Group, LLC.

The Library of Congress Cataloging-in-Publication Data
is available upon request.

ISBN 978-1-250-30646-3 (trade paperback)
ISBN 978-1-250-30645-6 (hardcover)
ISBN 978-1-250-30644-9 (ebook)

Our books may be purchased in bulk for promotional, educational, or business use. Please contact your local bookseller or the Macmillan Corporate and Premium Sales Department at 1-800-221-7945, extension 5442, or by email at MacmillanSpecialMarkets@macmillan.com.

First Edition: 2020

Printed in the United States of America

0 9 8 7 6 5 4 3 2 1

This book is dedicated to my agent, Leon, the first one to give me a chance. It is also dedicated to my editor, Diana, who kept me in line both structurally and culturally. When there was one set of footprints in the sand, it was you who carried me.

<u>Content Warning</u>
intense scenes
animal abuse
police brutality

I COME WITH KNIVES

Then

Knock, knock, knock. The teenager stood in Marilyn Cutty's driveway.

It'd been a few years since Robin last fled to Marilyn's house to escape her feuding parents. Jason and Annie didn't fight much anymore—their relationship had cooled from a forge-like heat to a cordial deference—so Robin hadn't had much occasion to get away from their shouting, instead opting to sequester herself in the cupola. But today was a special case.

The screen door eased open, and Theresa LaQuices peered out. Her oval face was framed with wispy waves of black and gray.

"Yeah?" asked Theresa. "Can I help ye?"

"Hi," said Robin. She'd never grown as close to the other two women as she had to Marilyn. Theresa and Karen spent a lot of time traveling—in fact, this was probably the first time she'd seen Theresa since early middle school. "Is Marilyn at home?"

"Maybe. Who's askin'?"

"Uhh . . . Annie's daughter."

Theresa pushed the screen door open as far as it would allow her bulk through the frame, until the piston interrupted her with a tortured creak, and she stepped out onto the cement carport. The middlest sister of the Lazenbury three was an enormous brick of a woman, all shoulders and forearms, her hair piled on top of her head in a messy bun. Billowing around her legs was a ruffled cotton sundress in bridal white.

"Annie's kid?" Theresa squinted at her. "What you doin' up here?"

As always, she was barefoot. Robin thought of that rhyme from Stephen King's clown novel: *He thrusts his fists against the posts and still insists he sees the ghosts.* When Theresa walked, her blunt, stony-looking feet pressed themselves against the cement like dirty fists.

"Mom and I had an argument and I didn't really have anywhere else to go. I was gonna go to town, but I don't have any money or a car."

"So, you figured you'd toddle your little ass out here like you did when you was a kid, hmm?" Theresa nodded thoughtfully, staring at the evening sky. "Yeah, I remember. You'd wander out here and sit on the stoop, and you wouldn't knock on the door or anything, you'd sit there and cry until one of us happened to hear it and come to see what was goin' on."

The two women stood there in the driveway for a moment, one young and indignant, one ancient and surly, as the sun gingerly eased itself onto the horizon behind them. Finally, the old woman said in her Cajunesque accent, "Your daddy always did mistreat you and Annie. I guess I can't say I blame you for ending up out here the way you did. I could hear them hollerin' at each other all the way up here."

Robin nodded without looking up.

Heavy sigh. "Well, no sense in standin' out here lettin' the mosquitoes suck out your blood." Theresa opened the door and waved the girl in. "Get on in here. Marilyn's upstairs taking a nap, but I expect she'll be down presently. It's almost time for dinner and all."

Being a lifelong gourmand, Theresa kept a clean workspace. The Lazenburg House's kitchen was spotless, as always. "I made some banana bread this morning, if you want some," she said, as they entered the house. One bearclaw finger directed Robin to a little yellow-brown loaf sitting on a cutting board on the island. "Help yourself. If you'll excuse me, I'm goin' to get back to my stories." With that, she trundled back into the living room.

Hushed voices and subtle music came drifting back. Robin cut a piece of banana bread with a nearby bread knife, then sat eating it and staring out the huge bay window at the vineyard out back. This time of year, the grapes were still a couple months out from being harvested, so the vines drooped with clusters of tiny green and purple marbles, the lush trellis frosted with fire from the sunset above.

The bread was pretty good. She cut another piece and found a stick of butter in a covered dish, smeared that on it.

As she ate it, her mind slipped back into her bedroom, back into the lingering sensation of the other girl's rough softballer hands on her hips, the floral smell of her hair. *Second base in girls' softball, four inches taller and an Amazon of a sophomore. Under her hands, Brianna's soft skin was cold and hot in turns: gooseflesh from the cool spring air and warm under the hoodie.*

"Hi, littlebird."

Snatched out of her reverie, Robin suppressed a jump and looked over her shoulder. Marilyn Cutty stood at the kitchen door that led beyond the fridge into the rear hallway with its wet-looking tomato-soup paint job.

"Hi, Grandma."

The old woman sauntered behind the island and pushed up the wizard sleeves of her gigantic sweater. "What brings you to my neck of the woods?" Cutty asked, washing her hands. She was as tall as ever, a heron in cable-knit wool, and so towered over the counter it seemed as if the kitchen were made for a shorter species. She looked like an ancient sorceress or a high priestess of some long-dead tribe, regal and well composed. "Been a long time since you found your way over here. Could I assume your parents have taken up that time-honored pastime of yelling at each other once again?"

"No," said Robin, hunched over, clutching her piece of banana bread like a squirrel with an acorn. "No, they hung up their gloves. Looks like I picked up where my dad left off."

"Ahh, now you and Annabelle are getting into it."

"Yep."

"What about, if I may be so bold?"

Insides wound as tight as a bowstring, Robin searched for tactful words. "She keeps me all chained up in her house and in her—in her philosophy?" No, that wasn't quite right. "I don't know what to call it—she's really religious, you know? More and more ever since I was little. And she's always trying to push those ideas onto me and, I dunno, 'keep me on the straight and narrow,' or something. She used to drag me to church, but back then she was all right. Just a Sunday thing. We don't go anymore, but—"

"Feels kind of like you live with a nun?"

"A little bit, yeah."

"Feels like you don't go to church anymore because she brought church home?"

"Yeah." A tiny thrill of adrenaline arced up Robin's insides at how spot-on Cutty had gotten it. Never thought of it that way before, but hearing it out loud was like being slapped. "Yeah. I mean, she didn't really launch into it today, but sometimes she'll see me looking all messed up 'cause I had a bad day, and then she'll come into my room with 'words of wisdom,' and quote scripture and shit. Proverbs this, Matthew that. And sometimes we'll be sittin' and eatin' dinner at the kitchen table, and she'll get on a kick of talking about Jesus, and about how Jesus loves me, and how it's okay if I think this or that, because Jesus loves me anyway, and we're all sinners. Today, Mom caught me making out with Brianna Wilson in my cupola bedroom. Came creeping up the stairwell and saw us. Now she's giving me shit about being a lesbian. And I'm not even a lesbian."

"Not that there's anything wrong with that."

"I mean, no. No—but I don't appreciate the assumption. I like dudes, too."

Did you forget how to knock?

You must not have heard me, her mother had said. *I guess you were busy.*

"She's always sneaking up on me like some kind of ninja, trying to catch me doing . . . something. What, I don't know."

"Living your life?" asked Cutty.

Why are you always interrupting my life? I finally manage to make friends, even though you hardly ever let me go anywhere other than school, and you're still hovering over me with your Flowers in the Attic *crap.*

"It's not like I ever do anything that would justify her paranoia—"

I'm not imprisoning you up here. You're free to leave whenever you want.

"—I don't do drugs. I'm not out there slutting it up, you know? What is she going to catch me doing? I mean, besides making out with my girlfriend." In a smaller voice: "I guess."

Is that right? Robin had retorted. *So, you're not going to stop me if I walk out of this house and go wherever?*

Mom: *Where is 'wherever'?*

That's the problem! You don't need to know!

'Wherever' turned out to be Grandma's house. Cutty busied herself over the stove, filling a kettle with water and putting it on to boil. While she waited, she shoveled a couple scoopfuls of sugar into a pitcher. As she did, she chuckled to herself.

"Hmm?" Robin made an inquisitive noise. "What's funny?"

"You'd never believe the kind of person your mother used to be." Cutty turned and folded her arms, leaning against the counter. "She wasn't always a Southern Baptist. She was a pagan, like us. And may I say, one hell of a hippie. So, it's funny to hear about how she's buttoned up her past and you along with it. She has *no* room to talk."

"What do you mean? Was she a flower child?"

"Well, she was born in the last couple years of the seventies, so she didn't get to . . . partake of the 'cultural revolution,'" said Cutty, air-quoting with her fingers. "All her development took place in the eighties. The Me Decade. She was into Madonna, and Loreena McKennitt, and Nirvana, and she burned so much dope, the fire chief could have put out a warrant on her."

Robin blinked. "Really?"

"Oh, yes. Wild child." Cutty shrugged. "Perhaps she felt a certain measure of guilt at her freewheeling ways when you were born. Renounced them to become a better mother to you. Maybe in the intervening years she's burrowed a little too deep, spent a little too much time in that house, in her own head, and all that scripture's rotting her brain." Robin made a face and Cutty half-turned to stare out the window. "It happens. People seek shelter in religion. For some, it slowly transforms from a shelter into a cage. If you hold on to something too tightly for too long without giving any of it away—religion, love, hatred, knowledge, many things—it turns bitter and thorny and useless inside of you. Anything can torture you, if you let it."

They sat quietly as the kettle huffed and chuckled on the stove.

Uhhm, Mom had asked, *so does this mean you're gay?*

What? No. What would it matter if I was? God doesn't give a shit.

Don't matter to me. Just wanted to ask. And don't take the Lord's name in vain, please.

If it don't matter, why ask?

Her mother had ignored the question. *You go out there and I can't protect you!*

Protect me from what? Does it have something to do with the hoodoo carved into the windowsills? Yeah, I noticed it, even though you painted over it. You know you're crazy, right? It's been there for years and years. What even is that? Some kind of Catholic exorcism shit? It looks like chicken scratch. Robin's hands had naturally, easily, scrunched up into fists, and she'd fully faced her mother down for the first time in her life. *You know everybody in town thinks you're fucked up, right? They call you Hocus Pocus, call you the Blair Witch. Last week, I was walking out of fifth period. Some cheerleader bitch out in the hallway said, 'I'll get you, my pretty, and your little dog, too.' Last year, somebody scratched a pentagram into my locker door and pushed a dead mouse through the front vent.*

At the time, the hurt and surprise on her mother's face had bounced right off of Robin's angry mind, but as she thought back on it an hour later, guilt lay on her like a hot, heavy quilt. *God, if only they knew how wrong they were,* she had continued, laying in to her mother. *You're about as far from a witch as a woman can get, with your Bible crap, and saying grace over lunch at Taco fucking Bell. You look like you should be out back milking goats, not sacrificing them. You're sick in the head. I can't stand being around you.*

A cannonball of shame rested in her guts.

"Marilyn?" Robin asked, here, now.

"Yes, dear?"

"I been wanting to ask you a question for a really long time. It's kind of a weird one. I'm sorry if it's super awkward."

"Absolutely fine. Fire away. I am nothing if not weird."

"Are . . ." The girl looked down at her hands; they'd found their way to the drawstring of her hoodie and were meticulously braiding the ends together. "Are you my real grandma?"

A genuine smile spread across the old woman's face. "No, little-bird, I am not. I'm afraid I can't claim that particular distinction."

"Mom says my grandmother disappeared after her parents split up, when she was a kid. She didn't want custody, and she moved away, but Mom doesn't know where she moved away to."

"Yes, that's right. Your mother was raised by your grandfather John in Virginia. John Reynolds, I think his name was. Reynolds was your mother Annie's maiden name."

"I always wondered if you were my real grandmother." Robin finished off the banana bread and contemplated another piece. "I wondered if there was some awful family secret keeping my mom from telling me about you."

"No, dear." Sly amusement spread across Cutty's face. "I'm a foolish, sentimental old woman. I love to help people. I have the compulsion to save everybody, whether I have the means or not. When your family moved out here, I saw your mother out there mowing the lawn by herself." She busied herself tidying the kitchen. "While I am normally an advocate for women doing whatever the hell they please, up to and including their own yard work, I found it inconceivable she should have to do *all* the housework *and* paint the house—that house was a real fixer-upper when you all moved in—*and* do the yard work. Well, my friends and I went down there to introduce ourselves, and we ended up helping her do that huge lawn and paint the house while your father was at work."

The kettle whistled. "And so we've been friends ever since. A little surrogate family, I suppose, and Karen and Theresa your mother's de facto aunts. I guess that makes me her surrogate mother." Marilyn sighed and poured the hot water into the pitcher of sugar and added two teabags. There was a brief pause where she seemed as if she were about to say something else, but then she fished in a drawer for a wooden spoon and stirred the pitcher with it. "So, when your mother had you, I suppose I naturally slipped into the role of surrogate grandmother as well."

"You're good at it," murmured Robin.

"Thank you, littlebird," said Cutty. "I appreciate that. Never got the chance to be a real grandmother in my own right, so it was nice I could do that for you. I hope you derived some measure of comfort and guidance under my watch."

Robin shrugged, overcome with a sudden awkward shyness. "I guess so."

"I could, though." The old woman rinsed the spoon and put it in the dish drain, coming around the island to sit next to the girl. "Be your grandmother. If you wanted. You're still welcome here. You could stay here. At least, for a while. Until you graduate high school."

"I don't know . . . I wouldn't want to impose."

"It would be no imposition at all. Love to have you around. And I'm sure that now you're a young lady with a little maturity, no longer a squalling babe, the other two would come around to the idea. We could teach you so many things, littlebird, about the woods out there, and about wine, and gardening, and about love, and the world. I would very much like to have a fresh new face around here—you know, I love my sisters, but sometimes I see so much of them, I want to wring their necks. We can even learn from each other. You can teach me about the internet and help me set up one of those Facebook things. Got some friends out in Arizona and Maine I should be keeping up with."

"Sounds nice, actually," said Robin. "But I don't know." She couldn't quite put her finger on why that sounded both so enticing and also so . . . *weird,* for lack of a better word. Maybe it was because she had become so unfamiliar with them in the intervening years, especially Theresa and Karen. Or maybe it was the idea of suddenly sharing a living space with people who were so much older, their age making their routines and the house's atmosphere so fundamentally foreign to her. Living with a house full of spinsters from another time just seemed to rub her the wrong way.

"We could learn so much from each other," said Cutty, bumping shoulders with the girl. "I know things that would *blow your mind,* kiddo. Secrets."

"Secrets?"

"Like the book cover says, *Things They Don't Want You to Know.*

Know what I mean? Things a lady of your age and demeanor would be served well to know. Things your mother knows, and stuff she has . . . chosen not to accept in her new life as a God-fearing woman. High time you step out of your childhood and consider your options as a young woman. We can help you in ways your mother no longer has the tools or wherewithal for."

Okay, this had gone from weird to unnerving.

As if on cue, the screen door opened and Annie Martine stepped into the Lazenbury's kitchen, out of breath, in a jacket and sundress. Ancient dollar-store flip-flops tried their best to stay on her feet.

"Hello, Annabelle," Cutty said sharply, casually, an assassin's dagger.

To Robin's surprise, her mother's eyes were glazed with alarm. "What are you doing in here?" she asked, without preamble.

"Eating banana bread and talking to my grandmother?"

Annie blinked, her eyes going wide. "Marilyn Cutty is *not* your grandmother, and how many times have I told you not to come up here?" She half-lunged toward her daughter, taking the teenager's wrist and almost dragging her backward off the stool.

"*Hey!*" Robin twisted to catch herself as she stumbled to her feet. "The hell you trying to do, break my neck?"

"We need to get home," said Annie. "We need to get home *now*."

"No." Robin wrenched her hand out of Annie's grasp, her mother's fingernails whipping painfully down the back of her thumb. "No, I don't need to go home. I *am* home."

"This is *not* your home."

"It's more of a home than *that* house has ever been," said Robin, pointing vaguely in the direction of the Victorian. "Between you and Dad screaming at each other and this Jesus-freak shit the past few years—you know, you were right, it *has* turned into a boxing ring. And I'm done fighting for my life."

"What?" said Annie.

"I told you, you keep me cooped up in that place like you're afraid somebody's gonna hurt me. Or kidnap me or something. Have you been watching too much *Forensic Files* or something?"

She caught Annie's eyes flicking toward the old woman.

"Her?" asked Robin, pointing at Cutty. "You're afraid of *her*?"

"No," said Annie.

She reached for her daughter's hand again, but Robin snatched it away.

"She's not afraid of me." Cutty said it blandly, but her eyes were flecks of hot steel. "She's afraid of Karen."

"Karen?" Robin drew a blank for a second. Her mind reeled through a Rolodex of faces. "The one that dresses like a horse thief and spends all her time making her own clothes and looking for mushrooms in the woods?" She looked at her mother. "Why are you scared of *her*?"

"I'm not."

"She is afraid of Karen," said Cutty, "because your mother is the reason why Karen's husband is no longer in Slade Township. It is a blood feud from before you were born, and your mother is terrified of participating in it, because Karen Weaver can be a terrifying woman to antagonize. But what she fails to acknowledge is that I am the Dutch dam between your mama and the ass-whooping she deserves. Whatever measures she's taken to protect herself—and you—are entirely unnecessary right now. As long as I am here, she—and you—are safe."

"I think we've done enough talking," said Annie, fully lunging for Robin. She tangled a fist in the girl's T-shirt and hauled her toward the screen door. Robin banged through it and stumbled out into the driveway, her mother right behind her.

Continuing the theme of surprise, Annie grabbed her again. But this time, instead of anger, there was a panicked protectiveness. Annie clutched the girl's head against her chest, even though Robin was a couple of inches taller.

"Mom! What are you doing?"

Her mother's eyes were full of fear, darting in every direction, searching the horizon. "Gotta get you home, okay, baby? I need you to trust me and shut up and start walking. We need to get the fuck out of here and back to the house. I'll leave you alone, you can do whatever you want, and I won't say a word. But we need to go."

It was the first F-bomb she'd heard her mother drop in . . . a very long time. If ever. "What is so important about the house? Why do you look so scared?"

"I'll tell you some other time. Right now, we need to move."

"No," said Robin. "Not until you tell me what's going on."

With a soft slap, the screen door closed. Marilyn Cutty had joined them outside and stood there watching quietly, her arms motionless but subtly tense at her sides.

Annie watched the old woman. "We don't have time for this."

"This is Dixieland, Annabelle." Cutty's thumbs and forefingers rasped together in the stillness of the evening, like a gunslinger getting ready to draw down on a desperado in front of the town saloon. "The days run slow here."

"What did you do?" asked Robin. The three of them formed an acute triangle in the driveway. "Why is Karen mad at you?"

Cutty's eyes softened. Her head tilted in anticipation.

"I had him arrested," said Annie. "Karen's husband. He . . . I caught him touching kids out there in that old amusement park. *His* amusement park. And he was hurting them." Her eyes cut over to Robin's, and her face hardened. "I called the police, and they didn't do shit."

"Oh, they arrested him." Taking languid, lawyerly steps, Cutty paced around them. "They took Edgar away, and they did their little investigation. But they didn't find anything, did they, Annabelle? So, they had to let him go. They let him come back home, and that's not the whole story, is it, hon?"

Annie said nothing, just stood there, breathing hard, her hands shaking. Robin couldn't tell if she was furious or terrified.

"Because he didn't stay home, did he?" continued the old woman.

"A year or so later, he just, hell, I don't know, he wandered off, didn't he? Slipped into the ether, like Amelia Earhart. Couldn't nobody find him. Didn't nobody know anything about where he went."

"We need to go home," said Annie through gritted teeth.

"What is she talking about?" asked Robin.

This time, Annie bulldozed her daughter down the driveway from behind, almost powerwalking her, muttering Bible verses under her breath. "The Lord himself goes before you and will be with you. He will never leave you nor forsake you."

"Karen seems to think you know." Cutty lingered somewhere far behind them at the top of the driveway some thirty or forty feet back. Her voice echoed off the side of the Lazenbury as she spoke. "Karen thinks you know where her husband went."

"Oh God," Annie murmured in the girl's ear. "Don't turn around, okay, baby?" Chills ran up the girl's arms at the panic in her mother's voice. "Don't look back. Don't look back at her. Don't look her in the eyes. Walk. Keep walking until we're home. Even though I walk through the darkest valley, I will fear no evil, for you are with me." Robin twisted, trying to see the expression on her mother's face. Annie manhandled her. "Thy rod and thy staff, they comfort me. Eyes front, baby girl. Jesus loves you."

"Oh, people liked to talk," Cutty called from the gathering darkness beside the hacienda. She was almost shouting now, but her voice remained casual, as if she were trying to carry on a conversation across a baseball field. "People said he ran off because he was embezzling from the city. Somebody allegedly found dead babies in a dumpster on his property. They even said he was putting LSD in the Wonderland Slush Puppie machines. People, *people,* my God, they can say such mean things, they can get you in so much trouble, can't they? They can get folks put in jail. They can get folks burned, get good women drowned in the river."

"What is she talking about?"

The girl's eyes managed to lock on the distant figure at the top of the driveway, an elderly Q-tip in a big slouchy sweater. Cutty stood stock-still, hands clasped behind her back.

"Don't look," said Annie, forcing her head forward again. "Don't listen. She can't do nothing if you ain't listening and you ain't looking. The Lord is my light and my salvation. The Lord is the stronghold of my life—"

"I just don't—" Robin glanced over her shoulder.

All she saw behind them was beige cable-knit. Marilyn Cutty was inches from her mother's back, right behind them, gliding effortlessly, close enough to touch, still motionless at parade rest, her hands behind her back. She loomed over them, a suddenly mythic shape, not walking yet still somehow advancing on them, as if she were standing in a toy wagon that her mother was pulling like a sled dog. "Cast your cares on the Lord and he will sustain you," Annie was saying, her voice growing hoarser with every word. "He will never let the righteous be shaken."

In a voice like the buzzing, sleepy drone of a hornet, Cutty said, *"Go ahead and look."*

Despite her dread, Robin's eyes traveled the Celtic knotwork of the sweater, passing over the drooping cowlneck, and she peered up into Cutty's face. Only, there *was* no face. Cutty's hair had been reduced to lifeless gray moss on a parched skull. The old woman's own eyes were not eyes; they were one puckered, misshapen socket that gaped asymmetrically across her face like an old shotgun wound. Her skin was pale book-leather, pebbled and cracked. Her lips were pulled taut against driftwood teeth, her stretched mouth almost combining with the eye socket into one amorphous C-shaped hole.

"Go home, littlebird," something buzzed from deep in Cutty's throat.

Inside those nightmare face-holes, flesh that should have been wet and pink was dry yellow rawhide. Robin's skin flashed as cold as frozen nitrogen. A scream tried to climb out of her throat, but she could only produce a wheeze. "Lord God in Heaven," Annie was saying, "hallowed be thy name. Please let us get home safe and sound." Then she muttered something in her daughter's ear like a record being played backward underwater—

• • •

Night had arrived in earnest. Soft light fell in from the Martines' living room as Robin and her mother moved through the shadows in the foyer, Robin's hand clutched in Annie's. "Come on, let's fix you something to eat."

"What happened? How did we get here so fast?"

"You 'bout passed out in the driveway."

"Passed out?"

"Yeah. Have you eaten today, baby?" asked Annie, leading her down the hallway toward the kitchen. Her mother seemed to have lost all her fear and was now almost . . . *chipper.* "Did you eat lunch?"

"I had some cheese crackers. And a cup of yogurt, I think."

"One cannot live on cheese crackers alone."

They filed into the dark kitchen and Annie deposited her daughter at the table, pulling out a chair for her. She turned on the hood light over the range, which cast a dim greenish glow over the table. "Still got some of that chicken. I'll make you a sandwich. Want some french fries?"

"French fries?" The words tumbled out of her mouth rusty and ill-used.

"Yeah, I got some Ore-Ida in the icebox."

Annie set the oven to preheat and rummaged in the freezer. "Maybe that fight we had did something to your blood pressure or something, I don't know. But it ain't gonna hurt to get some food in your belly." She pulled out a bag, got a cookie sheet out of the drawer under the oven, and poured a heap of crinkle fries on top of it. As she scattered them on the sheet, Annie kept talking. "Look . . . I'm sorry I walked in on you, baby. Hey, from now on

I'll—I'll flash the lights in the stairwell, all right? There's a light switch at the bottom, I'll flick that a few times. How about that?"

"Yeah, that's—" Robin blinked, examining the kitchen from her seat. Everything looked dark and new in the lamplight, thrumming with some ominous note she could feel but not quite hear. "Did we— Were we just on the other side of the highway?"

Annie stared at her. "Dunno what you mean."

"Did we go to Grandma Marilyn's house?"

"Not that I know of. I found you down by our mailbox, sittin' in the grass, talkin' nonsense."

Robin searched her mother's face. "What was I saying?"

"Oh, I don't know. You were mumbling something, I couldn't hear it. You didn't fall and hurt yourself today, did you?"

"No."

As if by instinct, the girl reached up and ran fingers through her hair, feeling for a bruise. There were none.

"So," Annie said.

"So."

"You're not batting for the home team, then?"

"I play for both teams, Mom. I like boys and girls both. Not that—" *Not that it's any of your business,* she started to say, but it turned to ashes in her mouth.

"There's a lot of love in your heart. I guess it makes sense you'll give it to anybody that'll take it. It's all gotta go *somewhere.*" Annie huffed a cool laugh. "Just a surprise, is all."

Ice tinkled. Mom was pouring tea into one of the glasses with lemon wedges painted all over. Robin sipped at it, staring down into the dark kaleidoscope of ice and tea, then she put it down on the table without letting go. Something about the weight of the glass, and the liquid inside, reassured her—as if some voice in the back of her mind said that if something happened, something that justified defending herself, she could throw it.

"Did you do something to me?" she asked.

Dirty dishes thunked slowly against the basin. Her mother had turned to the sink, elbow-deep in hot water. "I don't know what you mean." Annie rinsed a plate, putting it in the dish drain rack.

You know what I mean, Robin started to say, but it was as if the words had been typed onto a sheet of paper in front of her and some unseen hand had snatched it off the table before she could read it. Instead, she found only silence on her tongue. So, she thought of something else to say. "What was Marilyn talking about?"

Looking over her shoulder with a guileless expression, Annie said, "I don't know. I haven't talked to old Mary Cutty in a long time. Did you run into her today?"

We just talked to her, Robin wanted to say, but the words vanished into the dark again. Her lips parted as if to speak, but her tongue pressed uselessly against her teeth. *Did you do something to Karen Weaver's husband?* she subvocalized, trying to push the words, to birth the words, but nothing came out.

"I heard he ran off with some hussy," said Annie.

"What?"

Cold surprise flickered across Annie's face. Before either of them could say anything else, the oven chimed to let her know it was done preheating, and she put the baking sheet inside with a bang, setting the timer for twenty minutes. Wiping her hands on the towel that forever hung from the oven door handle, Annie marched out of the room. "I'm going to go see what your father's up to. Keep an eye on those french fries, hmm? I put enough in there for both of us."

Minutes crawled past. A clock ticked softly on the wall, but the time on it was senseless, the hands splayed in random directions. Robin couldn't focus well enough to divine its meaning, no matter how hard she stared at it, as though she could anchor her mind in the solid contrast of black numbers on white, black hands on white.

After an eternity of trying to tell the time, her eyes wandered away and settled on the kitchen door framing a narrow glimpse of the hallway: the right end of the sideboard table, on which stood a portrait of the three of them together—her father Jason, her mother Annie, and herself. Taken in Gatlinburg almost a decade earlier, everybody in cowboy gear. Dad still had his horrible goatee, Mom still had her cutesy bangs, and Robin herself was a little girl with glittering eyes and a sullen expression.

Mom. Fear shot an arrow through her chest. Suddenly, she didn't want her mother coming back through that doorway. If Annie Martine came walking through that door, she thought she would scream and run like hell. *Mom made me forget something. She's still making me forget something.*

How?

She's a w—a wuh

She's—wwwwh

A w—

She's a www-wwuh—

Robin got up and spat into the kitchen sink, as if she could spit out the words. As she stood there gazing into the drain, with its mesh drain-trap full of soggy bits of food, she remembered the french fries. She opened the oven door and looked at them. After half a minute of staring, she realized they weren't even remotely done, so she closed the door and stared at the range.

What was I doing? She scanned the kitchen the way you do when you've walked into another room and forgotten what errand brought you there.

I need to protect myself.

From what? How?

Creeping cautiously but quickly up the stairs without knowing quite why she was creeping, she went up to her room, where she pulled her laptop out of the drawer underneath the north windowsill in her cupola. She sat there staring at the screen for a long moment, trying to recollect why she'd come up here and connected to the Wi-Fi.

On the windowsill, the carvings under the paint were thrown into sharp relief by the screen's stark light.

A nail file in her backpack. With it she dug at the paint as if it were a lottery ticket, trying to reveal the symbols her mother had scratched into the window frames, looking for some kind of revelation or inspiration that could help her figure out what was going on in her head. Underneath were symbols that almost looked like English letters—*F, N, S, R,* some odd combination of lowercase *b* and uppercase *P,* all manner of symbols composed of straight lines and right angles. Looking back at the screen, she did a few Google searches and finally found something resembling her mother's carvings. According to the website in front of her, they were Nordic runes. Something called Elder Futhark—

Reality jumped like a broken film reel and Robin blinked, startled.

She was no longer sitting on her bed; she and her mother were standing in the bathroom, and her mother was scrubbing at the back of Robin's left hand with a washrag and scalding-hot water. "What did you think you were doing?" asked Annie. "What is this, some kind of Satanic thing?" Half-obscured by suds and the rag in Annie's hand, there was something written on Robin's skin with a Sharpie marker, some strange smeared symbol that looked like a chicken's footprint. "Are you writing evil things on yourself? What is this?"

A greasy stink lay on the air. The french fries had burned.

"This isn't evil." Robin's words were heavy and slurred, as if she were having to lift them over the wall of her tongue. She expected her mother to ask her if she'd been drinking, but she didn't say anything, just kept scrubbing. "It's . . . Mama, it's the stuff, like you scratched in the windowsills."

"I don't know what you're talking about." Annie glared up at her and kept scrubbing.

"Yes, you *do.* Are you doing something to me?"

"No!" cried Annie. "You trying to fight with me again? I thought we were okay now, thought we were cool. I wish you would sit down and eat your supper. You're not well. Your blood sugar is low."

Robin shook her head, slow at first, and then wildly, her ponytail sweeping across the back of her neck in a growing panic. "My blood sugar is fine, Mama."

"Then what the hell?"

"I feel like I'm forgetting things. Some*thing*." She reached up with her free hand and ground the heel of her palm into her eyebrow. "Something happened and I can't remember what. I went somewhere and something happened, Mama. Something happened and I need to do something and I can't remember what."

"Do I need to take you to the doctor?" Annie's eyes were glittering black pools in the dim bathroom light.

Not a medical doctor—a psychiatric doctor. Robin could read between the lines well enough. A shrink. "No, I don't need to go to a doctor. I need you to stop doing whatever you're doing to me. We went to—" Robin blanked, staring at the wall. The words had been there, *just there*; she was about to say them, and they flitted away like a housefly. Some sensation like a smooth wall had set itself up between her brain and her mouth, the same feeling like when you're trying to do math but you're too tired to focus.

Out of the corner of her eye, she could see her mother's lips were moving, like a ventriloquist's. Subtly, silently, almost a trick of the light.

Summoning all of her will, Robin closed her eyes and fought the wall in her head, pushing, punching, pressing. She felt like she had to sneeze, but with her brain—that same kind of high, half-painful anticipation.

just walk

even though I walk through the darkest valley, I will fear no evil

Terrible black eyes. Eyes reaching into her and scooping her clean.

keep walking until we're home

But there were words in there, thoughts, crusted in the darker corners of her brain, that her mother's spoon couldn't reach, if it was indeed her mother doing this, whatever it was, this creeping assassin dementia. "Wwwee www—wwwennt," Robin tried to say. "Wwweee went. To Gramma Mmm-mmary's houuuse." The words came out like meat processing through a grinder, tortured and crushed, almost in the same slow, buzzing hornet-voice Cutty had spoken to her earlier that evening.

Alarm spread across Annie's face.

To her horror, Robin glanced away from her mother. The bathtub was full of dark water, silty with blackness.

the Lord himself goes before you and will be with—

"We went to Grandma Mary's house," she said, and the lights went out.

Arms reached for her from the darkness, water clattering across bathroom tile, as something stood up out of the bathtub and clutched at her.

Ragged fingernails chiseled cold fire into her wrists. She opened her eyes and saw a drowned woman, mouth gaping low and full of black teeth, eyes shrunken to hard pits, sockets cavernous. Her skin was clammy, glistening, almost gelatinous. Hair streamered black down the corpse's shoulders—

That film-hiccup effect again. She was no longer in the bathroom.

A half-moon perched high in the sky, bathing her in monochrome light. She sat in her bed, quilt pooled around her hips. Her wrists thrummed with pain, hot now instead of the cold of the thing in the bathtub. Leaning across the bed, she turned on the nightstand lamp.

Blood streaked the sheets.

One of her hands was a tight fist around the nail file, the one she'd been scraping paint off the windowsill with, and it was smeared with blood. Still wet, fresh.

Inside her wrists were a pair of lines burning with hot agony, cut deep with the file, but not deep enough to pierce the vessels. Scary, but not suicide-scary—they had made a mess, but they weren't bad enough to justify calling an ambulance. Had she tried to slit her own wrists in her sleep?

No . . . they weren't just "lines." Splaying toward the crooks of her elbows were three lobes where she had cut the Elder Futhark chicken-foot symbol into her skin.

She pulled a T-shirt out of her dresser and tore it into strips, winding them around the cuts on her arms, then stripped her top sheet and retrieved her laptop. She checked her browser history, but there were reams and reams of research there, probably fifty or sixty links to pages about ancient symbols. Too many to suss out the meaning of the drawing she'd carved into her own arms. More than she remembered seeing earlier.

How long has Mom been doing this? she wondered, eyes welling. *What is she even doing? What was she saying in the bathroom?*

In her bookmarks, she didn't see anything out of the ordinary. Webcomics, links to Etsy shops, YouTube channels, Wattpad stories, DeviantArt galleries, Facebook groups, history websites for homework. She scrolled to the bottom: an online order form for Miguel's Pizza and a link to the first season of a show on a pirated-anime website.

Going back to the history, she got an idea. Maybe she'd carved her arms as soon as she'd found the symbol, which meant the page with the symbol would be at the bottom.

Click. *RuneSecrets.* There it was. The three-lobed Y.

"*Algiz,*" she mouthed silently. "Represents the divine might of the universe. A Norse symbol of divine blessing and protection." It also stood for the elk. Below was a large picture of the *algiz* rune. "Alignment with the divine makes a person sacred, set apart from the mundane."

Past-Me knew what was going on. Dots of blood pierced the gray cotton around her wrists. Maybe these blood sacrifices would protect her from them—from the gap-faced ghoul, whoever or whatever it was. *God, how long? How long has she been making me forget? Is this the first time I've tried to push back?*

Maybe this symbol, this "*algiz*" would protect her. Protect her from her mother—from the woman who imprisoned her and made her forget.

You can't wash away a scar.

1

Present Day

Forty yards back, a steel pole as big around as Michael DePalatis's arm stretched across the overgrown dirt road. Pulling the police cruiser up to the gate, he unbuckled his seat belt and started to open the door.

"I got it." Owen checked the gate and found there was, indeed, a chain confining the gate to its mount, and a padlock secured it. Two of them, in fact.

Hypothetically, they could go around it, if not for the impenetrable forest on either side. "Shit." Mike got out of the car anyway. "Looks like we're walking." He hopped over the gate, his keys jingling. The grass beat against Mike's shins, and hidden briars plucked at his socks. "When we get out of here, you might want to check yourself for ticks. Few years ago, I was part of a search effort out in woods like this, and when I got home, I found one on my dick."

"Oh, that's nasty," said Owen. He laughed like a kookaburra.

Conversation slipped into silence. The two men walked for what felt like a half an hour, forging through tall wheatgrass and briars. Mike glanced at his partner as they walked. Officer Owen Euchiss was a scarecrow with an angular van Gogh face. The black police uniform looked like a Halloween costume on him.

They called him Opie after the sheriff's son on *The Andy Griffith Show* because of his first two initials, which he signed on all of his traffic citations. His constant sly grin reminded Mike of kids he'd gone to school with, the little white-trash hobgoblins who would snort chalk dust on a dare and brag about tying bottle rockets to cats' tails. Middle age had refined him a little, but the Scut Farkus was still visible under Opie's mask of dignified wrinkles.

"Ferris wheel," said Owen, snapping Mike out of his reverie. He straightened, peering into the trees.

The track they were walking down widened, grass giving way to gravel, and skeletal machines materialized through the pine boughs. They emerged into a huge clearing that was once a parking lot, and on the other side of that was an arcade lined with tumble-down amusement park rides, the frames and tracks choked with foliage.

Had to admit, the place had a sort of postapocalyptic *Logan's Run* grandeur about it. A carnival lost in time.

The two policemen walked aimlessly down the central avenue, heels crunching on the gravel. "What did Bowker say we're supposed to be looking for?" asked Owen.

"You heard the same thing I heard."

"'Something shady.'"

They came to a split, facing a concession stand. Owen took out his flashlight and broke off to the left, heading toward a funhouse. "I'll check over here."

Mike went right. A purple-and-gray Gravitron bulged from the woodline like an ancient UFO. Across the way was a tall umbrella-framed ride, chains dangling from the ends of each spoke like something out of *Hellraiser*. He contemplated this towering contraption and decided it had been a swing for kids, but without the seats, it could have been a centrifuge where you hung slabs of beef from the chains and spun the cow blood out of them. Or maybe it was some kind of giant flogging-machine that just turned and turned and whipped and whipped.

When the rides had been damaged enough and lost so much of what identified them, they became alien and monstrous.

Third-wheel mobile homes made a village in the back, caved in by the elements. Bushes cloaked their flanks and bristled from inside. He slapped a whiny mosquito on his face.

Blood on his fingers. He wiped it on his uniform pants.

After wandering in and out of the carnie village, Mike decided none of them were in good enough shape to sustain life. He headed back into the main arcade.

At this point, he had developed an idea of what Wonderland looked like from above: an elongated *I* like a cartoon dog-bone, the arcade forming the long straight part down the middle. Mike stood at the west end of the dog-bone, staring at the concession stand, and took his hat off to scratch his head.

He took the left-hand path, walking toward the funhouse. Behind the concession stand to his right was a series of roach-coaches: food trucks with busted, cloudy windows, wreathed in tall grass. A Tilt-A-Whirl, an honest-to-God Tilt-A-Whirl. Bushes and a tree thrust up through the ride, dislodging plates of metal and upending the seashell-shaped cars. A wooden shed with two doors stood behind the Tilt-A-Whirl, quite obviously an improvised latrine.

Here, the tree line marked the end of Wonderland. A chain-link fence tried to separate fun from forest, but sagged over, trampled by some long-gone woodland animal. Tucked between the Tilt-A-Whirl and the smashed fence was a pair of gray-green military Quonset huts. At the end of one of them stood a door with no window in it, secured with a padlock. NO ADMITTANCE—EMPLOYEES ONLY!

"The hell?" Mike lifted the padlock. No more than a couple of years old. Schlage. As he tried the doorknob, the entire wall flexed subtly with a muffled creak. Old plywood? He pressed his palms against the door and pushed. The striker plate crackled and the wall bowed inward several inches.

"Geronimo," he grunted, and stomp-kicked the door. The entire wall shook.

Another kick set the door crooked in the frame. The third kick ripped the striker out and the whole door twisted to the inside, the hinge breaking loose.

Inside was pure, jet-black, car-full-of-assholes darkness. Dust made soup of the air. Mike took out his flashlight and turned it on, holding it by his temple, and stepped into the hut. A workbench stood against the wall to his right, and a dozen buckets and empty milk jugs were piled in the corner, all of them stained pink. Wooden signs and pictures were stacked against the walls:

VISIT HOOT'S FUNHOUSE!

ARE YOU TOO COOL FOR SCHOOL? DRINK FIRE-
    WATER SARSAPARILLA!

GET LOST IN OUR HALL OF MIRRORS!

Three hooks jutted up from the bare cement floor in the middle of the room. Chains were attached to them, and the chains led up to three pulleys.

Old blood stained the floor around the hooks.

"Ah, hell," said Mike, drawing his pistol.

On the other side of the workbench was a door. He gave the stains a wide berth, sidling along the wall.

Flashlight in one hand and pistol in the other, he crossed his wrists Hollywood-style and pushed the door open with his elbow. Beyond, the polished black body of a Monte Carlo reflected his Maglite beam.

POW! Something exploded in the eerie stillness.

A bolt of lightning hit Mike in the ass. Electricity crackled down the Taser's flimsy wires, *tak-tak-tak-tak,* racing down the backs of his thighs, and he hit the floor bleating like a goat. The pistol in his hand fired into the wall between his jitterbugging feet, blinding him with a white flash.

"You *had* to come in here, didn't you?" asked the silhouette in the doorway, tossing the Taser aside and plucking the pistol out of Mike's hands. Chains rattled through a pulley and coiled around his ankles. Strong, sinewy hands hauled him up by the feet and suspended him above the floor. One of those white five-gallon buckets slid into view underneath his forehead, knocking his useless arms out of the way, and then his hands were jerked up behind his back and he was locked up in his own cuffs, dangling like Houdini about to be lowered into a glass booth full of water. "This is what I should have done to that faggot, instead of lettin' him hang around," said a man's voice, reminiscent of Opie but growlier, deeper, more articulate. "But I got his fuckin' car now. Sweet ride, ain't it? Did you see it in there?"

Mike's heart lunged at the *snick* of a blade being flicked out of a box cutter.

"No, *please!*" he managed to grunt.

"You live, you learn, I guess." The man cut a deep fish-gill *V* in Mike's neck, two quick slashes from his collarbone to his chin.

Both his carotid and his jugular squirted up his cheeks and over his eyes, beading in his hair. The pain came a full second later, a searing cattle-brand pincering his throat. Mike gurgled, sputtered, trying to ask questions, deliver threats and pleas, but there was nobody in the garage to hear him.

The door slammed shut, leaving Mike in musty darkness.

Heinrich's eyes were intense—not wide and starey eyes, but small, flinty. He'd grown a beard at some point, and it was as gray as brushed steel. He was a big man—not burly or stocky, but long-trunked and long-limbed, with a commanding, arboreal presence. Robin's witch-hunting mentor looked like a bounty hunter from the Civil War.

To her eternal surprise, the old man took his coffee as sweet as a granny. She studied his face as he folded his sunglasses neatly, hanging them from the collar of his shirt.

"I watched the video you posted the other day and knew you were heading back to Georgia. Hopped in the car and hauled ass out here. That's why I haven't been answering the phone—I've been on the road." They all sat around the kitchen table in the Victorian house at 1168 Underwood, nursing cups of Folger's and listening to Heinrich recount how he caught up to his protégée. Robin was still a bit dazed from the previous night's encounter with what the kids called "Owlhead," the ensuing vision she'd had of her much younger mother summoning it, and the antipsychotic meds she'd overdosed on in an attempt to dispel what she'd thought was a hallucination.

Her GoPro camera lay on the counter next to the coffeemaker, recording their impromptu palaver. "Did you come out here to help me," Robin asked, "or stop me?"

Taking off his gambler hat with a measured motion, Heinrich placed it in the center of the table, revealing his glossy brown head. He regarded her with a flat stare, Kenway and Leon sitting quietly to either side, and ignored the question. Instead, he asked, "What are the side effects?"

"Ischemic stroke. Anaphylactic shock." She looked out the window at a slate-gray sky. ". . . Seizures."

Heinrich rolled his head in wry agreement. "Where there's smoke, there's fire. You had a seizure last night, according to these men," he said, giving the eyeshadowed Joel an assessing up-and-down. The pizza-man eyeballed him right back, folding his arms indignantly. "Maybe you *do* need to ease off."

"I don't think you need any more," Kenway said in a flat growl.

"I *have* been cutting back." Robin frowned. "But I need them to stop the hallucinations."

"No, you don't."

"Hallucinations?" asked Leon. "You mean this kind of thing has happened before?" He glanced toward the hallway door, as if his son Wayne were standing there. She could see the protectiveness written all over his face. Embarrassment she hadn't experienced in a long time made her face burn. She probably wouldn't have felt this way if Wayne weren't involved; she could almost hear Leon thinking of ways to keep him away from her.

"On top of the illusions that the witches can plant in your mind, I've been seeing strange things for a very long time," she told him. "Night terrors. Nightmares that might be memories—"

(*Go ahead and look,* buzzed a stretched-out face.)

She visibly flinched, and a little coffee spilled on the table. Robin mopped at it with the sleeve of her hoodie. "—memories that might be nightmares. And the owl-headed thing."

"Well, I think we proved Owlhead ain't a hallucination. I saw it with my own eyes. Maybe all that other shit is real too." Leon's taut expression loosened a little. "Maybe you're not crazy after all."

"We'll discuss your meds later." Heinrich took out a cigar and leaned forward with his elbows on the table, examining it at length as if it were the bullet destined to end his life. "I'm sure there's some other antipsychotic that won't fuck you up so much." He didn't offer one to anybody else, even though he knew Robin was a smoker. "Anyway. I ain't here to be your pharmacist, and I sure as hell ain't here to stop you. I ain't never been able to stop you before."

"Speaking of psychotic, we talked to a member of the coven. The young third one, Weaver."

"What about?" He stuck the slender cigar between his lips and dug a matchbook out of his shirt pocket, the Royal Hawaiian wagging as he spoke. Robin knew what it would be before she even saw the label: *Vanilla Coconut.* He cupped the cigar with a hand and lit it, shook the match out, and dropped it into the dregs of his coffee. "You two catch up on life 'n shit? Quiche recipes, grandkids, who's fuckin' who on *The Young and the Restless*?"

"She put an illusion on me and left me in a hospital laundry, hallucinating bugs crawling out of my skin. How did you get in without her seeing you?"

Disgust passed across Leon's face, tinged with sympathy.

"I parked in the trailer park and hung out there for a while to watch the house." Heinrich took a deep draw, the cherry flaring, and blew it at the ceiling. The rich smell of coconuts floated in a dragon of blue smoke, turning the kitchen into a dingy cabana. "Waited for her to go in the house, went around the side."

Robin started to take a sip and put the mug back down. "Weaver told me I'm a puppet. Your henchman, your human shield." *Your personal Jesus,* interjected some weird neuron in her brain. "Said you groomed me to be a witch-hunter so you could quit the game and pull a D. B. Cooper." She leaned over her coffee. "You didn't teach me how to fight so I could avenge my mother, did you? You did it so you could hide in your fortress in Texas, and let *me* do all your dirty work."

"I'm turning sixty-six this year." Heinrich ashed the cigar into his coffee mug. It was white and had a picture of Snoopy on it, fast asleep on the roof of his doghouse. "I can't fight the good fight forever. Somebody's gotta take over, and you were ready to be sculpted, a block of marble ready for Michelangelo's chisel."

Robin battled the urge to throw her coffee in his face. "I'm not your bitch." She took a deep, shaky breath and let it out in a sigh.

"She told *your* tall dusty ass," interjected Joel, clutching a cup of coffee.

"You were never meant to be." Heinrich ashed his cigar again and leaned back. "They're turning you against me, Robin. Fragmenting the opposition. If you're gonna make the decision to come back here and fight, you're gonna have to keep your head together. Don't let Weaver tie you up in knots. That's what she's good at. They've all three of them got specialties, and hers is getting inside that dyed-up volleyball you call a head. Remember how I told you back in the day how they'll use tricks and lies to keep you from getting close? Well, this is it."

"Maybe." She sipped coffee, trying to read the expression on Kenway's face. The anger over the Abilify was new. It wasn't scary, but it left her feeling cold and hollow inside.

Heinrich stared at the table, woolgathering.

"I saw a little girl with a lot of hurt and hate in her heart." The old man's voice was torn between defensiveness, compassion, and anger. "I seen good people turn to shit trying to burn it all out with drugs. When I found out Annie had a daughter and she was in the mental hospital, I knew I had to get to you before the streets did. Or, worse, you tried to fight Cutty with no preparation." He took another draw and talked the smoke out. "Bein' homeless ain't no joke. The hell you think you'd be if I hadn't taken you in?"

Reaching across the table as quick as a cobra, he grabbed Robin's wrist and turned it, held it up to the dim morning light. The pink rope of scar tissue running down the inside of her wrist shimmered with a faint opalescence.

Fresh concern came over Joel's face at the sight of the scars. She wrenched her arm out of the old man's hand, his fingertips slipping shut on empty air.

"You'd be dead in a gutter," said Heinrich, pointing at her with the two fingers pincering the cigar, "*that's* where your skinny white-girl ass would be. So, listen to your heart and use your head, Robin Hood. Ain't nobody against you but them. Don't let 'em talk you in circles. That's their first trick. You know that. You know better. I didn't take you in and teach you what I know for you to fall for their bullshit."

The sun continued to fill the kitchen with morning light. "I saw my mother," Robin said eventually. "In a dream, when I had my seizure."

She recounted the contact with Owlhead and the demon's stolen vision from start to finish, from the ritual Annie performed on Weaver's husband to the demon crawling out of the hole. Leon choked on his coffee and got up to fetch a paper towel to mop it up off his shirt. "There's a hellhole in my goddamn basement?"

"I don't know what it is, specifically, but—" Robin started to say.

"No, that's exactly what it is," said Heinrich. "Sounds like what happened was Annie thought she had sacrificed Edgar Weaver to draw a demon into our world to kill Cutty, but what she did was sign a blood contract that allowed Hell to annex the house."

"In plain English, please," said Kenway.

Heinrich swept a hand down his face, pulling at his cheeks. His lower eyelids were rimmed in red; he obviously hadn't slept. "Basically, like Puerto Rico is a territory of the United States, this house is now a territory of Hell. It has been for about two decades. I imagine it's why ain't nobody lived in it since Annie died." He pointed toward the living room. "The dark version of it that little boy in there found with his mama's ring? That's the Hell-side of this house."

Everyone stared at Robin, making her want to shrivel up. "I thought you said there wasn't a Hell," said Kenway.

The old witch-hunter grimaced, tossing a hand. Ashes dusted the tabletop. "Of *course* there's a Hell." Heinrich swept them off onto the floor. "Is she filling y'all's heads with her Dalai Lama God-is-love-and-Hell-is-regret bullshit?"

They smirked at him. Robin gave him the finger.

"There for a while last year, she got real deep into Nichiren Buddhism," said Heinrich. "She even had me chanting *Nam Myōhō Renge Kyō* over and over again, doin' yoga and shit and eatin' rabbit food. *Me—!* The last time *I* did the Downward Dog, I got crabs and a night in jail."

"Y'all nasty," said Joel.

"The demon," said Heinrich, getting up from the table. "The hallucinations. Owlhead was drawing you here." He paced slowly up and down the foyer hallway, one hand in his pocket, the other holding the cigar to his mouth. "He wants you here for some reason."

"But why *now*?" asked Robin. "I've always seen him, but it's only been every now and then. The first nineteen years of my life, I saw him four times. Once when I was as young as that little girl in there, once in middle school, and twice in the mental hospital. The last two years, I've seen him at least fifteen times. It's like he's leading me here. What's special about now?"

"You turned eighteen. Came of age. Maybe he thinks you've passed some kind of threshold that would make it possible for you to let him manifest in our world? You are the daughter of the woman that summoned him, after all. Maybe there's a link somewhere."

"If he's looking for a virgin, he's barking up the wrong girl."

Heinrich laughed.

"And if he wants me to let him loose, I ain't doing that. I wouldn't even know how." She eyed the cigar smoke in the air. "You're the research wonk—do you know if there's another part to that ritual beyond cleaving off a shadow-clone of the house to imprison him in?"

The old man shrugged. "Hell, I don't know, I'd have to look at the materials she used."

"What *are* demons, anyway?" asked Joel. "That thing with the owl-head didn't look like any demon *I've* ever seen. I would've expected, y'know, the usual—cloven hooves, pitchfork, horns, the whole nine yards. Not a dilapidated animatronic owl from a haunted pizzeria."

"Demons, at their simplest," explained Heinrich, "are viruses."

"I ain't pickin' up what you're throwin' down."

"All right, a virus is basically a piece of DNA wrapped in protein. You could say it's dead, but it would have to have lived to be dead, and it's never been alive. But it *wants* to be alive. And the only way a virus can assume some semblance of life is by infecting a living being. I like to think of it as a Terminator—a facsimile of life that's never been alive itself, wrapped in meat." He sighed and took the cigar out of his mouth, staring at it as he rolled it in his fingers. "The way it's been explained to me is, there are two kinds of souls. The souls that come out of Creation's oven well formed and functioning find their way into a living body at some point. The souls that come out deformed don't get a body. They sorta float around out there in the dark, in the void of Purgatory. Demons are those two-faced, water-headed, heart-on-the-outside, too-fucked-up-to-live souls. And the only way they can reach the same level of life *we* enjoy is to possess a living body, the same way a virus possesses a living cell."

"You say 'Creation's oven,'" said Leon, wiping his hands dry with a towel as he came back to the foyer. "So, you're tellin' me there's an actual God up there, cranking out souls in His spiritual bakery?"

Heinrich guffawed, leaning back to laugh at the ceiling.

"That's the million-dollar question, ain't it?" He stubbed the cigar out on the sole of his boot. "Welcome to the clergy."

3

The Parkins didn't have any of the ingredients for breakfast, but Leon needed to make a trip to the grocery store anyway to get the steaks, leaving the kids with Kenway and Robin.

"I'm gonna go with you, if you don't mind," said Joel as the Parkin patriarch headed for the door. "You can drop me off at my house. After bein' face-to-face with Granny Clampett out there, I think I've had my fill of witch shit for today. I don't have to go in to Miguel's tonight, so I'm gonna take a long nap, sleep all afternoon, then take a long, hot shower and get drunk as a skunk and watch Netflix."

"I don't blame you one bit."

Robin gave him a hug. "Much love, brother."

He returned it. "Love you too, sister. Good luck with your thing. Don't let 'em get you. I expect to see your tiny ass in one piece tomorrow."

To the boys' surprise, the veteran Kenway was quite a gamer, and they geeked out with him over Wayne's PlayStation. Heinrich spent most of the morning sitting on the back stoop smoking his cigars and staring at the forest out back. Wayne kinda liked that dude—he was standoffish and creepy, but in a cool, self-aware way, as if it were a façade he'd developed over the years.

"You *will* tell us how it went, won't you?" asked Amanda, as the kids got ready to head home to Chevalier Village. They were standing on the front porch of the Victorian. The day had grown cool, and the overcast sky was the blank, featureless white of an unwritten story. "You know, dinner with the witches? And don't leave anything out, no matter how gross."

"Why don't you go with us?" Wayne offered.

Both Pete and Amanda visibly blanched at the thought.

"What, are you scared?"

"Hell, yeah," said Pete.

"They're super creepy." Amanda folded her arms and glanced at Pete as if seeking reassurance. "I don't think you understand, Wayne. We've been living down the hill from those women our entire lives. Our parents—I don't know if they're *afraid* of them, but . . . nobody in Chevalier Village goes outside much after dark unless it's an emergency, you know? The women don't talk to *us*; we don't talk to *them*." Her eyes found their way up to the hacienda. "This morning was the first time I've ever heard Karen Weaver speak."

"They're kinda like you guys' Dracula, huh?" asked Wayne.

Pete's head tilted. "What do you mean?"

"The mysterious Count Dracula, living up on the hill overlooking the town. Nobody goes up there, and the village warns away anybody that comes snooping. Chevalier is kind of a mini-Transylvania, ain't it? They got you spooked like a vampire."

Amanda nodded but didn't say anything.

"Astute observation," said Robin, startling Wayne. She was sitting in the swing at the end of the porch.

"We'd better get out of here, I guess," said Amanda, bouncing down the front steps. As she stepped into the grass, she turned back to him. "Be careful. If they really *are* witches, they're dangerous. Take care of your dad, okay?"

"I'll try. I don't think they're gonna do anything. We're just eating steak, right? We're going to dinner there. They can't violate guest right."

"Real life isn't *Game of Thrones*."

Wayne swallowed anxiously and sat down on the steps to watch his new friends trudge back to the trailer park.

The woman who called herself Malus Domestica came down to his end of the porch. She wasn't wearing her chest harness, but she carried the little camera in her hand. Her messenger bag was slung around her shoulder. Robin put the camera on top of the newel post at the end of the porch railing, facing them, and the red light on it told him it was recording.

"So, you got a YouTube channel?" he asked her.

"Yup. It's got all my detective work and encounters on it. All my fights this far. Well, almost all of them. I've been ambushed a couple of times." She sat down next to him, leaning over with her elbows on her knees. "You and your dad should watch a couple of them. So you can—I don't know, maybe it'll help you trust me."

"I think after showing him the monster in the doorway, he believes," said Wayne.

The woman's eyes sparkled even in the dim light of the overcast day. She was intensely pretty, he thought, fine-featured and pale, but her eyes were old. Or maybe tired. There was a sharp, almost unsettling intelligence in them, like a crocodile.

He sighed. "I know *I* believe."

"I have a plan," she told him.

"A plan for what?"

"I want to use your ring to get into their house without having to walk through the front door. Take 'em by surprise."

"Why would you want to do that?"

"There's a fourth witch, somewhere on the property," she said, looking up at the Lazenbury. "I'm pretty sure she lives upstairs, in the attic. She's much older than the other three. That fourth witch is the one augmenting the power of the rest of the coven. Witches can band together and draw on each other's power—that's the whole point of a coven."

Delving into her messenger bag, Robin took out a beautiful dagger. "Made of silver. The entire thing, from point to pommel. This is what we're going to use to kill them."

"I thought silver was for werewolves."

"This silver . . . ." She turned it so the stiletto caught the white sky, and ivory shimmered down the mirrored metal blade. "To use a comic book analogy, it's spiritual adamantine. Witches can't change it or defend against it. It's magically inert. Energy-neutral. If you had enough of these, you could pin a whole coven of witches to the floor and there's nothing they could do about it. Only lay there cussing at you."

"*Do* you?" He lifted the dagger out of her hands and examined it. "Do you have enough?"

"Heinrich says there are two others in the world, but this is the only one of these I've ever seen."

"Can't you make more?"

"According to him, they were made with the nails the Romans used to pin Jesus Christ to the cross on Golgotha. The nail is the core of the blade. Whether that's total bullshit or not, I have no idea. Heinrich *says* a lot of things. Half the time he could be full of shit—for all I know, they're made with Elvis Presley's melted-down fillings. But I'll tell you right now, this one works. It's helped me kill a lot of witches."

"What do you do, stab 'em in the heart?"

"Witches don't have hearts to stab." Robin explained the ritual of Ereshkigal's sacrifice, how they offer their hearts to the goddess of death in exchange for a direct line to her power. "You pin her down with it and set her on fire while she's immobilized. Guns can slow them down, but fire is the only thing that can stop a witch.

You can't kill them, you can only destroy them. And if I can get to the fourth witch and pin her down with this, I can burn her. With her out of the picture, the other three will be a lot easier to handle. Hopefully, if I play my cards right, I can take them out one at a time."

• • •

Leon brought back lunch from his trip into town, so the two witch-hunters talked shop with everybody at the kitchen table eating Taco Bell. The GoPro sat on the table, dark and deactivated, staring straight up at the ceiling as everybody talked over it. Leon sat by himself in the living room, getting ready for the coming week, going over lesson plans and grading a pop test he'd given Friday. He hadn't gotten around to it, with Wayne's emergency hospital visit. "Witches and monsters can't make your job disappear," he said, and dived into his homework.

Something else was eating at Dad, that much Wayne could tell, at least. Leon didn't seem amenable to talking about it, though. Wayne left him to his own devices and sat in the kitchen, nibbling on a burrito, eavesdropping on the witch-hunters' conversation.

The table was piled with a dozen old books bound in choppy chunks of thick, yellowed pages. Titles in obscure Latin and insignia that looked like geometry diagrams were etched on their covers in faded gold. The ones in English had pretentious or boring titles like *Chronology of Cabbalistic Philosophy, Essential Demonic Taxonomy, Invisible Science, Western Applied Invocation*. If he didn't know any better, he'd think they were college textbooks. They certainly sounded like the ones Dad had stacks of, boxed away in his bedroom.

Robin told Heinrich about her plan to use Wayne's ring to get upstairs to the fourth witch without Cutty seeing her.

"Dangerous," he said. "That demon's waiting for us to wander back in there."

"What do you think about the ring, anyway? Have you ever seen anything like this?" asked Robin. "I've heard of relics with symbolic importance and holy character—like the Shroud of Turin, the Spear of Longinus, the Sacred Cloak of the Prophet, the Osdath-regar. And I know you can alter the properties of witch-magic by inscribing runes and other symbols like the *algiz* on yourself, your car, your house. But this is the first time I've seen a contemporary object that isn't the Osdathregar created for, and dedicated to, a specific purpose."

"I have an idea about that," said Heinrich. He picked up a book, *Western Applied Invocation*, and leafed through it.

"Well?"

Heinrich eyed her. He shut the book with a dusty *clap!* and glanced at Wayne, and said, "I didn't want to get anyone's dander up, or lead the boy here down a deep, dark rabbit hole. But there is a precedence for this sort of thing. The organization I used to be a part of creates, collects, and uses relics like the Osdathregar and Wayne's ring in their work, and the people who curate that collection are referred to as the Origo. They're specialists in a technical discipline called 'conductive semantics,' and they're a kind of esoteric quartermaster."

"Are you saying the person that made this ring was an Origo?"

Chills ran down Wayne's arms at the idea that his mother, Haruko, could have been involved with these people and this secret war against witches and demons.

"What I'm saying is, becoming one of the Origo requires decades of training, meditation, attunement, research. But some Origo are recruited because of a natural talent for handling and crafting magical conduits like this ring. Whoever made this ring might have possessed this latent ability for crafting objects capable of manipulating paranormal energies. And going on how powerful those two wedding rings are, I'd say they could have made one hell of an Origo."

"It's dawning on me there's something you're not telling me," said Robin. She'd put on a heavy-looking hoodie and now sat slumped back in a chair, one hand bundled into a pocket and the other clutching a burrito.

"It's a long story, and we've got a long road trip to get back to

Texas." Heinrich picked up another book and opened it to the middle. "Right now, it isn't important. What you need to focus on is getting into that house and ending that coven, and then figuring out what to do with the green-eyed monster. We can worry about the past when we're done with the present."

"No, I think I want to know now." It was the one dark spot in Robin's mental picture of Heinrich Hammer, the renegade witch-hunter and thief of esoterica—the cult he'd escaped from almost twenty years before. He'd never told her anything about them, only that they were bad business.

"They were incredibly dangerous people," said Heinrich, becoming visibly agitated. "I've told you a hundred times, I barely got away from them by the skin of my teeth. I don't want you getting caught up in their ways, and the less you know, the better. I've bent over backwards these past several years, keeping you off their radar—if I start giving you specifics, I know for a fact you're going to go looking for 'em, 'cause that's the kind of girl you are, and that way lies trouble."

"Maybe before!" Robin was almost shouting, gesturing wildly. "But now we've got things like Wayne's ring, which was made by his mom, who may or may not have been something from this cult called an Oregano, and you're still telling me this isn't important?"

"Yes!"

"Too bad! How about I kick you in the fuckin' balls until you start talking?"

Heinrich laughed, which earned him a boot in the shin under the table. "Ow!"

"Hey, ease up on the cussing, please," said Leon from the other room.

"Look," said Heinrich, "like I said, we'll worry about Origo and rings later. Right now, we know it works as intended, and we know we have a dangerous coven on our hands. How the ring was made and why aren't salient to this. Look, I'll tell you the story about the cult on the way home. And when we get back to our books in Texas, we'll investigate this shenanigan with the ring."

• • •

Opening one of the books on the table, Robin pressed a fingertip to a grotesque picture at the top of the page. "I've been researching the demon," said Robin. "Okay, Wayne here calls it Owlhead."

He peered over his shoulder at the picture. The left-hand page had a detailed but primitive drawing of a man with a bird's head and huge staring eyes. His right hand clenched a broadsword, and his left hand was up in the air as if trying to get someone's attention. It didn't quite look like the thing in the Darkhouse, but Wayne could see how somebody could extrapolate this drawing from what he'd seen in there.

"This guy right here is the closest I can find to what we're dealing with," she said, holding up the book so they could all see it. "He's a killer spirit, a chaos-maker."

"A cacodemon," said Heinrich.

On the right-hand side was a long passage. "The sixty-third spirit is Andras," she said, reading from the book. "He is a great Marquis of Hell, appearing in the form of an angel with a head like a wood-owl, riding upon a strong black wolf, and having a sharp and bright sword flourished aloft in his hand."

"If that was the body of an angel," said Wayne in disgust, "angels are freakin' hairy."

"His office is to sow discord. If the exorcist have not a care, he will slay both him and his fellows. He governeth thirty legions of spirits. The *Ars Goetia*. And this is his seal," added Robin, holding up the book to show them a convoluted pentagram full of angles and squiggles.

"What's the *Ars Goetia*?" asked Wayne.

"One part of a very old spellbook called *The Lesser Key of Solomon*. Basically a demonic encyclopedia. Not the original, of course. This one is four transcriptions removed from that one."

"So, Owlhead's real name is Andras?"

"I don't know," said Robin. "Maybe."

She stared meaningfully at the corner of the kitchen next to the back door. Heinrich shifted in his seat to look, and a thrill of adrenaline buzzed through Wayne's system. "Is he there?" asked the boy, his voice barely above a whisper. "Can you see him?"

"No, but I can feel him. You know when we were in the bathroom? I could *feel* him in the house. Like heat coming off an oven."

"I have a theory," said Heinrich. For the last few minutes, he had been folding a piece of paper into what had turned out to be a tiny figure of a dog.

"Lay it on me."

"It explains why Cutty used a familiar to murder your mother, and why they haven't preemptively attacked you." As if to illustrate his point, he thumped the paper dog across the room. It landed in the sink, settling into the drain. "They're afraid of the demon."

"Weaver came into the house, though. She wasn't afraid of him. And I could feel him in here, looking at her like she was a cheap piece of meat."

He gathered up a fist with an elaborate gesture. "Demons eat their energy. They're psychic vampires. Like a poltergeist feeds on emotional energy, demons feed on paranormal energy."

"They don't eat the witch herself?"

"Not that I can tell. I'd have to see what Andras would do if he and the witches were in the same physical space, but unless she uses her magic in the house, he can't get to her from where he is. Which I'm calling the Dreamlands, by the way. From the old H. P. Lovecraft books." Heinrich picked up a book and studied the cover. "Anyway, the demon is keeping us safe. I don't think Andras can see us on this side—he can only detect you if you're expending spectral energy, like some kinda heat-seeking missile. Weaver didn't use it here, so he couldn't see her. I think if any of them deadheads up there try to use their power here in the house, Andras will tear into their heart-roads. And they know it."

"If only we could get Andras out of there," Kenway said through a mouthful of food. "Maybe we could lead him up to their house and let him go to town on 'em. Sic him on 'em like a dog."

Robin smirked. "You want to let a 'Marquis of Hell' loose in the material world?"

He paused. ". . . Yeah, now that you put it that way, maybe it's not such a good idea after all. Maybe we could trick the witch into going into one of Wayne's doorways."

Robin gave Heinrich a sidelong look. "There's a thought."

"Maybe." A distant look came over his eyes.

"What is a heart-road?" asked Wayne. "You guys keep saying that and I don't know what it is."

"It's where the witches get their power." Heinrich clutched his chest as if he were having a heart attack. "When they become witches, they undergo a ritual where they sacrifice their heart, *Kali-Mah!*, to the goddess of death, Ereshkigal, and she replaces it with a direct line to her power."

"What does *she* get out of it, though? Why?"

"That's a good question," said Robin. "I never bought the hearts thing. Like, does she have a big box of hearts out there in Purgatory, or something?"

Heinrich crumpled a taco wrapper into a ball. "The more power Ereshkigal can put into the real world, the easier it will be for her to manifest here. She's always trying to lay the groundwork for her return to the physical plane. The stronger her network here, the stronger she'll be when she finds a way back. And her coming back is not something you want—all those witches, all those Gifts they have? Illusion, healing, telekinesis, transforming, scrying, body-hopping, elemental manipulation . . . each one is a fraction, a splinter, of Ereshkigal's power. She's all those witches combined into one. She's the Mega-Witch. An actual god.

"And believe me," he said, free-throwing the wrapper into the garbage, "we don't want *that* on our hands."

4

A half an hour to six, Robin took Wayne into the cupola to have him open the way to the Darkhouse again. But before she could close the stairwell door, Leon put his hand against it, holding it open. "For the record, I want to vote against this."

"Vote against what?" Robin and Wayne sat on the stairs, and her camera was attached to her chest harness, ready to record her foray into the strange other-version of the house. "Opening this door?"

"That too, but I'm talking about attacking those women. I haven't seen any hard proof they're . . ." Wayne could tell Leon hated even saying the word. ". . . witches. Hell, even if they are, what's to say they aren't *good* witches?"

"There's no such thing as good witches, Mr. Parkin."

"What about your mother?"

Robin bit back any further words.

mom made me forget something

words in there, thoughts, crusted in the darker corners of her brain, that her mother's spoon couldn't reach

She had a toothpick in her mouth in that Sly Stallone *takin' care of business* way, and as she let Leon's admonishment slide unanswered, the toothpick rolled around in her teeth.

"They paid my son's medical bills." Leon gestured to Wayne, beckoning him down off the steps. "Paid 'em off, every red cent. Even if they *were* bad people—and I haven't seen a bit of evidence to support that claim—I don't know if I can condone this." Leon rubbed his scruffy chin and folded his arms. "I'm sorry . . . but if you do this, you're gonna have to do it without me or Wayne."

With a heavy heart, the boy stood next to his father, pushing his glasses up his nose. He tried to apologize to Robin with his eyes. *I'm sorry, lady. I got to do what my dad says.* She was crestfallen, but only briefly. Robin's face hardened and she stared at the steps between her knees. "I understand." Getting up, she sidled past them and went downstairs.

They found her in the living room with Heinrich and Kenway. "Change of plans," she told them, standing in the doorway. "I'm going to dinner with Parkin and his son."

Heinrich put down the book he was reading. "What? Why?"

"Because I want to talk to Marilyn Cutty face-to-face. I used to consider her a grandmother, and I want to see the evil in her eyes before I go through with what I came here to do. And . . ." She took the toothpick out of her mouth and glanced at Leon. "Mr. Parkin has reservations about what we're planning on doing. He's not going to let me use Wayne's ring to traverse into the Lazenbury."

The old witch-hunter got up off the couch and came in close, talking in a low, venomous tone everybody could hear. "What Parkin thinks don't matter. They been killing children for years. You *know*. Andras showed you. That run-down amusement park out there wasn't no fun-joy-happy-happy place—it was a goddamn slaughterhouse. Those women are singlehandedly responsible for nearly every missing-persons poster and cold case in the Blackfield

I COME WITH KNIVES · 55

Police Department. And when your mother tried to stop them, they killed her and imprisoned her soul in a fucking tree."

"You seem awfully ready to put boots on the ground when this morning you were ready to call the game on account of rain."

"I didn't think you were ready," said the old man, picking lint off of his black cowboy hat. "In light of what you just said, I'm not sure. A parley? Really? What's next, a knitting circle? Necromancy book club? 'Come and kick back with a cold one'?"

"Parkin deserves to see proof before I enlist his son into being my secret weapon. I want to show him the dryad. They've been through a lot, and I owe them that much. They deserve to see the truth. And *I* deserve—"

"You're lettin' them use him against you. You think Weaver bein' out there in them woods was an accident? I wouldn't be surprised if she's the one that planted that snake out there for the boy to find in the first place." He threw a hand toward the window, toward the mission house. "You know what this tells me? This tells me they're *afraid* of you."

"Why on Earth would *they* be afraid of *me*? And why don't you want me to talk to them?" Then something occurred to her, something so staggering she actually recoiled. He was trying to keep *them* from talking to *her*. And he had been trying to keep them from fraternizing ever since her mother's death, taking her out to Texas and steering her away from Blackfield, everywhere in North America but here. All her fervor faded and her guts solidified into ice cubes. He knew something he didn't want her to discover. But what was it? What was the biggest remaining secret she had left to sniff out here?

She now knew what the monster was.

A demon.

Who brought it out here?

Her mother.

She knew why—to protect the house, and by extension, Annie, against retribution from Karen Weaver and possibly the whole coven, and how—a Germanic cacodemon-summoning ritual. The only item she had left to suss out was how Annie had paid her end of the bargain to get Andras to stick around and be her guard dog. And to her horror, she realized, her mother had been hiding something from her, using her Gift to make Robin forget—forget the things she'd seen, forget what Cutty had told her, forget to ask questions.

Was it the price her mother paid? Was that the secret at the bottom of it all?

"You *know,* don't you?" she said.

"Know what?" Heinrich stepped away and went to the window to stare out at the early evening, as if he were running away from the interrogation.

"What happened to my mother after she summoned Andras," Robin said in a leading tone. "I told you what happened in the vision the demon gave me. She opened the house to possession and invoked Andras into it, but he caught her before she could escape. But he didn't kill her. She made a bargain with him. You know what happened down there, don't you?"

Heinrich said nothing, his hands clasped behind his back, turned away from them.

"What did she trade for his protection?"

"I think you know already." The old man sighed, his shoulders rolling. Robin's accusatory finger sank to her side and she stared at his back.

Oh, God.

Her face gradually twisted into a mixture of disgust, horror, and . . . relief? She went to the couch and sat down, staring at the TV as if it were on.

"I am completely lost," said Kenway.

Leon put his hands in his pockets. "You ain't the only one."

Clearing his throat, Heinrich spoke to the window, quoting the *Ars Goetia*. "He is a great Marquis of Hell, appearing in the form of an angel with a head like a wood-owl. His office is to sow discord, and if the exorcist have not a care, he will slay both him and his fellows." He glanced over his shoulder.

"I know that much," growled Robin, glaring.

Heinrich didn't return the glare. "What the *Ars Goetia* doesn't include is that in addition to being a cacodemon, Andras is known to some demonologists to also be an incubus. He doesn't always slay the exorcists tasked to remove him, or the individuals complicit in his invocation. He can be persuaded to serve the invokers, but they must pay a heavy price for his service."

"What's an incubus?" asked Kenway.

"I know at least this much about demons, being a literature teacher," said Leon. "A succubus is a female demon that ambushes sleeping men and has sex with them." Leon's face darkened and his chest heaved as if thinking about it winded him. "An incubus is a male demon that preys on women the same way."

"The demon took advantage of my mother." Robin was staring at her hands as if she were on a bad acid trip. Realizing she had the GoPro attached to her chest, she turned it off. She drew her legs up under her, boots and all. "She gave herself to a demon to protect us. To protect me."

Sympathy and dismay gave Kenway the expression of a man visiting someone in the cancer ward. Heinrich, in comparison, observed her impassively—coldly, even.

"Must have happened when I was a baby," said Robin. "Witches can't have children, because they're undead and barren. She's had that scarred-up tongue as long as I can remember." Tears stood in her eyes. "Now I know why my mama turned her back on magic and went to religion the way she did. She was scared straight."

"Yeah," said Heinrich. He hesitated. "Yeah . . . when you were a baby."

"Are *you* the one that gave her the Germanic invocation?"

His head bowed and he spoke to the windowsill. "Yes."

"Why?"

"Because I thought it would be the only way to finally destroy

Cutty." Taking out one of his coconut cigars, Heinrich studied it in the last light of the day. "*She's* the one that came to *me*, you know. I mean, when I found Cutty's coven here in Blackfield, your mother was the one I approached because she was the youngest, and I knew she would be the easiest to influence. To turn against them. But back then, I didn't know about Edgar Weaver and his carnival. She came to tell me about them, to ask me for help making Edgar pay for killing those kids. She didn't want anything to do with the coven anymore. That's when I knew I had the sacrifice I needed to complete the ritual: Edgar." He sighed. "I had no idea the house itself would be possessed, and that she would get trapped in it with Andras. I only found out after the fact he's an incubus."

Robin sneered. "And you call *me* impetuous. You almost got my mother killed. You knew he would make her pay dearly for the deal they made to protect the house. You knew it, and you gave her that ritual anyway."

After a contemplative pause, Heinrich looked at his watch.

"It's almost six. If you're goin' to dinner, you'd best get ready. You can chew me up when you get back."

Eyes dancing across his face, Robin had the suspicion he knew more than he was letting on, but she wasn't going to interrogate him further in front of Kenway and the Parkins. She would let him sweat. *After the dinner, I'll hold his feet to the fire and see what else he knows. The price my mother paid wasn't just rape. It's too simple, and it's not enough.*

But I don't think it's a lie. Not totally.

She let the demon take her willingly. But it couldn't have been enough to justify striking a deal like that. Not enough to let her imprison him here in the other-house. There's more I don't know.

She stared at her hands as if they belonged to someone else. Turning them, she held them out as if to ward off a blow.

Revelation yawned before her, a chasm of secrets.

Afraid, the girl pushed it away.

5

For a child to whom every experience under the sun is new, time is a long and stately thing, passing with a gargantuan battleship slowness. An hour in a doctor's waiting room, restlessly leafing through magazines and studying the walls, becomes a hobby in itself. Every school day is a lifetime.

All this was written on Wayne Parkin's face as they made their way toward the witches' house. He carried a bottle of steak sauce in one hand and a bottle of ranch dressing in the other. Thunder mumbled to itself somewhere in the east, disconsolate, testy, as if the storm had gotten lost on the way. The iron sky roiled slowly like a dying snake, threatening rain.

The bottles felt like offerings. Robin walked alongside him, peering up at the sky. "I should've brought umbrellas."

Something about the way their shoes scuffed across the packed dirt made Robin think of a western, of outlaws and high-noon duels. "Be on your best behavior," Leon told his son. He carried the steaks in a glass casserole dish.

"Are they going to turn us into frogs?"

"No." Robin had turned the GoPro back on, but instead of wearing it herself, she'd made Wayne the designated cameraman, and he wore it on his chest with the nylon harness. The camera's red eye burned like a cigarette cherry in the darkening daylight. "Witches don't do that," she said, "that's a fairy tale. Love potions, flying on brooms, talking mirrors, that's all Disney stuff."

The good ones don't hurt you, she thought. *They make you forget so they don't get hurt.*

The hacienda seemed to grow as they approached it, beyond the aspects of perspective, as if it were swelling, lengthening, rising, and suddenly she realized how very *tall* it was, and how much of the property was bound by the adobe privacy wall. The façade towered over them at three stories (*when had it become three?* she thought), and then another six or seven feet for the bell's arch. Gothic wrought-iron spikes rimmed the top of the wall, and weeping willows on the other side of the wall obscured most of the front porch.

"It looks so out of place this far east, doesn't it?" asked Leon. "Like a Mexican fort. Bigger than I thought it was. It's less of a house and more of . . . of a compound, I guess you could say."

"It wasn't always this ominous," mused Robin. "I don't remember it looking this . . . fortresslike." As a little girl, she had played among its trellises and hidden in its vines, and made chalk drawings on the adobe walls of the hacienda. She didn't remember the spikes on top of the garden wall; in her childhood, it had been smooth enough up there that she could climb the oak tree and walk along the top of the wall, balancing with her arms straight out while Grandma Mary watched her from the living room. And when she jumped down into the gravel with a jarring *CRUNCH!,* she would look up through the front window and see Grandma Mary sitting on the sofa, applauding her dismount. Happier days.

She wondered how much of her childhood memory was implanted and erased. At this point in her life, she had given a lot of thought to what her mother had done, and eventually she came to the conclusion Annie Martine had a mind-Gift like Cutty and, to a certain degree, Weaver. But where Cutty's power involved *her* mind—telekinesis, scrying, things of that nature—Annie's gift was more like Weaver's, in that it was about influencing the minds of *others*. Erasing memories. Implanting memories.

Out of all the witches Robin had hunted and killed in the intervening years, Annie's Gift was unique. On paper, fiddling with memories didn't sound that scary or insidious, but in practice, it could be used to gaslight someone until they were utterly under your control and experienced reality in whatever fashion you saw fit. You could convince an innocent man he had committed some crime, such as murder, or if he was already a criminal, you could wipe his mind clean—nothing to confess to. No loose ends.

Or you simply drove him mad.

Flames licked inside a gas grill standing on the patio by the house, visible through a gap in the lid. Ten years before, that had been a smaller charcoal grill, the clamshell top the same candy-apple red as a new sports car. Robin had a sense-memory of Theresa pouring beer over the patties as they cooked, the Dos Equis sizzling on the coals, the smell deep and ashen and thick.

"Well, hello there!"

Speak of the devil. A heavyset woman stepped outside to greet them. Her olive skin contrasted richly against the starchy white of her festive peasant dress, which was trimmed in red and blue. Gold jewelry lay across her cleavage. "My name is Theresa," she said in a Louisiana drawl. "Theresa LaQuices. And you must be Mr. Parkin." *Mistah Paaaahkin.* "It's so nice to meet you."

"Likewise," said Leon. "This is my son, Wayne."

Theresa pressed a hand to her bosom, flashing a fistful of gaudy rings. "Oh, I know who *this* little gentleman is. Why, *I'm* the one carried him from the fairgrounds out to the road where the ambulance could get to him. We are already well acquainted, even though he don't rightly know it."

Even though Robin couldn't imagine a witch doing something so helpful, she could see the muscular Theresa toting Wayne around as if he were a bouquet of roses—Robin had found herself scooped up in those titanic arms a time or two in her own childhood. She had always been a behemoth of a woman, but the last time Robin had seen her, she was merely heavy—"Ford tough," her father Jason said about her after he first met their new neighbors, which made his wife burst out laughing—and square-shouldered. Workman's hands, thick Bilbo Baggins feet. Now Theresa's ungainly mass seemed almost pathological, a hairbreadth from "monstrous." Her fists were small and clubby like dolls' hands, but her forearms were ham hocks. Her shoulders sloped like mountainsides, and her forehead was a broad, smooth carapace.

The witch seemed invulnerable and constant, a fixture in the earth.

Gesturing toward Robin with the steak dish, Leon began, "And this is my new friend—"

"Oh, I'm well aware of who *this* young lady is." *Well awaya,* she was. "I didn't expect to see you here, I'll admit. Little Miss Martine. I ain't seen you in a dog's age. You ain't here to start no shenanigans today, is you?" Theresa put her fists on her considerable hips and peered from under her thick black eyebrows. "It won't come to nothin', mind you, but all the same, I'd really rather not have to put up with it. This ain't nothin' but a friendly Sunday dinner between neighbors."

"No." Robin shook her head, glancing at the ground. "I'm just here to eat and talk to Marilyn. I feel like we've got too much history for me to bust in guns blazing."

"A dinner truce, hunh?" The old woman squinted, assessing her, then turned and trundled across the driveway toward the house. How easily the old woman seemed to walk across the jagged gravel, as if it wasn't even there. Theresa had on a pair of slippers like nothing more than dainty satin bags on her feet, and the stones she trod on seemed no more consequential than cotton batting. "Be sure you keep it that way. I been puttin' together a mighty nice repast, and I'd hate to see it ruined by a jackass."

Jack-ayass. Leon wheezed Muttley-like laughter.

• • •

When Robin was last there, the cabinets were painted in farmhouse blues and whites, the fridge was an ancient freezer-top Frigidaire, and the floor was perpetually grimy linoleum in a brown cobblestone pattern. But now the place was all brushed steel and travertine tile, everything polished to a high gleam. The fridge was an enormous side-by-side. If she didn't know any better, she'd think she'd stepped into a showroom at a home improvement store.

Leon whistled, leaving the casserole dish on the counter. "Nice place you got here."

"Thankee much," said Theresa. She cracked the oven door open to check on something, then headed back outside to the grill and opened it. Gray charcoal glowed subtly in the evening light. "Marilyn's in the garden, if you want to visit while I knock the hooves off this beef."

Robin hesitated, taking Leon and Wayne aside. "You two drew your *algiz* like I told you to do, right?"

"Yep."

"Yeah, I guess," said Leon.

Theresa snorted, smirking as she laid the steaks over the coals with her bare hands. *Do what thou wilt,* she seemed to be thinking, *for all the good it's gonna do ya.*

The patio occupied the top of the driveway, a large area about the size of a basketball court separating the back of the house from the two-car garage. An adobe privacy wall like the one that enclosed the front garden ran clear out to one side all the way to the tree line some eighty or ninety yards out. A tall wooden gate allowed them into the back garden.

Inside the wall, they were greeted by rows and rows of trellis fences crawling with sickly ivy. Grapes withered in clusters. "A vineyard," said Leon. "Man, I could go for some wine."

Sitting at a table in the freshly mown grass were Marilyn Cutty and Karen Weaver, a large wooden pub-style table with a white linen tablecloth thrown over it. Marilyn slouched down in a chair with one elbow on the table, nursing a glass of what looked like iced tea and staring out into the pinewoods.

Seeing them together sent Robin reeling backward through the years, to afternoons spent trying to master croquet with Grandma Mary and her ancient hand-me-down mallet and balls, sharing handfuls of blueberries from the bushes by the east wall. Mornings in the cornflower-blue kitchen, making cat-head biscuits with Theresa and stealing chocolate-chip cookies out of the Premium Saltines tin in the pantry. Late nights pretending to be a mannequin while Karen pinned a dress around her tiny frame. *If you're gonna be hangin' around here like a damned beggar, I might as well put you to work*, the old woman would tell her, lifting her up and standing her on a stepladder. *Now, don't move or I'm gonna poke you.*

She ain't your grandmother, chastised Annie's twisted voice in the back of her mind. *This ain't your house.* Robin twitched as she heard a spectral echo of the meaty, drumming impact her mother's body made when it hit the wooden floor in the foyer of the Victorian. *Witches,* her lying mother had warned her about them as she died with a broken neck. Instead of wiping her mind squeaky clean as she'd always done before, Annie's final warning broke the spell, poured all those missing memories back into her, filling in all the vacant puzzle pieces.

Having her mother's memory-wipe undone, and all those clues and whispered secrets surging back in, had inadvertently driven her insane. It had taken a long time to overcome . . . and here she was again, in the thick of it.

As the misfits came *shush*ing across the close-cropped grass, Weaver stood. "Hi there!" Then she noticed Robin. *"Oooooh,* it's *you.* I thought I told you to vamoose. Y'know, I don't remember you being this stupid."

"I'm hard to vamoose. And yes, I'm plenty stupid."

Wild-haired Weaver had on a witchy-looking petticoat made out of a hundred silk scarves of as many dark colors, all tied together. It might have been ragged were it not so artfully arranged. She pushed up her sleeves. "Was the illusion not enough to run your ass outta here? I can conjure up some *real* flies, you know. Big, nasty ones that bite."

"Excuse me?" said Leon.

"I assume our self-proclaimed witch-hunter here has taken it upon herself to unload all her knowledge on you, including her gory internet videos."

"A man said in one of my mother's favorite books, 'First comes smiles, then lies. Last is gunfire.'" Robin put up her hands to demonstrate they were empty. "For the sake of transparency and trust, I think it behooves all of us to skip the polite make-believe. I'm not here to fight. Just talk."

"A palaver, eh? The hunter comes to parley?" Cutty folded her arms. "Yes. Well, the truth will out, I've always heard, so there's no reason to tell lies when we can keep it at smiles, and I think we could all do without the gunfire. You didn't bring that nasty silver dagger, did you? I'd be hard pressed to observe the rules of parley if you showed up packing the Godsdagger."

"No. It's in a safe place."

Cutty simply nodded slowly, agreeably, her eyes darting around the tabletop before meeting the girl's once again.

"I've been told what you are," said Leon. "I'm still not sure I believe it one hundred percent, but I am informed. And after what happened Friday night and yesterday morning, y'know, with the snakebite and all, I'm also not convinced violence is necessary, so consider me the dove of peace in this here scenario, yeah? I really appreciate what Miss Weaver here did for us, and I'd like to avoid bloodshed."

Her hands still raised like Madam Mim, Weaver looked back and forth between them. "Truce, then?"

"Truce," said Cutty.

"Truce," said Robin. "For today."

"For today."

The witch in the ragged petticoat lowered her hands dejectedly. Wayne looked as if he were about to jump the fence and bolt.

"I guess I knew you were going to come eventually." Weaver sighed, shaking down her sleeves. The bracelets and beads around her wrists rattled. "I'd hoped you'd 'a been smart enough not to." The three of them took a seat at the table, and Weaver sat back down with what was probably a whiskey. "For some reason, Mary has taken a liking to you and your murdering, backstabbing, coward whore of a mother, and I've tried to honor that because of our history and all. You didn't make a bad seamstress dummy, after all. But don't give me a reason to turn you inside out. 'Cause I don't give a tin shit. I'll do it."

"Your skill at diplomacy has not waned in the least, I see," said Cutty.

"Diplomacy is for cowards."

Thunder mumbled again to the east. The evening was darker than it ought to be for six o'clock, although a hard blue luminescence lingered on the western horizon. Humid air made soft halos around the candle-flames, like lamps in London fog.

"I'm surprised you guys want to eat outside," Leon said, studying the sky. "Looks like rain."

"Nah," said Weaver.

"How do you know?" He fidgeted, a coy smile on his lips that betrayed the anxious look in his eye. "Did you see it in the knuckle-bones, or tea leaves, or something?"

"Nope. It just don't rain 'round these parts unless I say it can." She smiled.

6

On the other side of the parking spaces, at the end of a row of empty slots, was an old Ford pickup truck. A camper-shell covered the bed like a turtle, the same brick red as the body. The self-declared master of hide-and-seek was looking for a place to hide, and this was the coolest possible place to hide in the entire apartment complex.

What grabbed little Delilah's attention was the bright green snake. Diamond-shaped scales uncoiled across the truck's body, from door to door. Each scale shone with its own sharp gleam, reflecting some source of light beyond the ken of the canvas. At the leading end of the dragonesque body was a great mouth full of teeth and writhing tongue, dominated by white fangs the size of bananas.

One screwhead eye gazed out at her, as big as her fist, the color of honey. Screwing it out, she discovered the gasoline receptacle underneath. The gas cap was the snake's eye! How clever.

Walking around the back she found the body stretched across

the tailgate, went behind the passenger taillight, and came out again on the passenger fender.

After that it coiled twice, and clinging tightly to the very tip was a bare-chested woman in Viking garb, her giant boobs squeezed between her outstretched arms. The barbarian Barbie gripped the last slender inch of the snake's tail as if it were a baseball bat and dug in with both heels.

It was a bit of a ratty truck to have such a gloriously cheesy picture painted on it. The girl wondered who it belonged to, and what he was like, as she reached up and put her hand on its metal belly, still warm with the day's beating. The barbarian's bulging arms, winecork nipples, and glowing lightning-god eyes stood out from the truck body around it, a paint-depth bas-relief.

"I'm coming to find *youuuu!*" Ginny called from somewhere to her distant right, shouting in a singsong voice.

Lifting the rear sash, Delilah climbed into the bed of the truck, letting it sigh back down on pneumatic hinges.

Crammed against the front of the cargo space was a fluffy black bale of pine needles. Many of the needles had slipped out and now coated the floor of the truck bed with a thin, crunchy carpet. Inside the camper shell, the air seemed sapped of oxygen—stifling hot, grainy with the smell of earth and bitter pine. The side windows were painted over with the red of the body, coloring the light from the streetlamps a boudoir crimson.

To Delilah's right as she climbed in was a burlap sack with FERTILIZER stenciled across the front, full of something large, bulbous, as big as the girl herself. Next to that was a Stihl weed eater with a well-gnawed line, encrusted with grass and reeking of gasoline. *A gardener-man,* she thought, duck-walking over to the bale of pine needles and settling down beside it. *I wonder if he plants tulips?* She loved tulips, loved the light, sweet smell of them.

"I'm going to find you," said Ginny from somewhere in front of the truck. It had been parked facing the apartment building, with the rear pointing at the dark street. Delilah could hear the little girl's new shoes clopping along the pavement as she skipped from car to car. "Ah-*ha*! . . . No, I guess not."

Delilah froze in place and slowed her breathing. Her belly rose and fell under her T-shirt and she pinched the seams of her jeans, anticipating her discovery in the hot, dark camper, studying the rough denim with her fingertips as she listened.

"Are you in here?" Ginny asked. A car door opened with a metallic crackle. A couple of heartbeats passed. "Nope." The door slammed shut, *ker-tunk!*

Sitting there in the gas-smelling dark, Delilah strained at the limit of her hearing, pine needles poking through her jeans. She slid an inch to her left as quietly as possible and pressed herself against the bristly straw bale. Ginny sounded closer. She gave a surfer-like "Whoa" and walked right up to the snake truck. "Check that out." Delilah could hear her creeping around the vehicle, taking in the entirety of the artwork. A tiny hand trailed down the side of the panel with a susurrant hiss that sounded more snake-like than Delilah wanted to admit. She shifted to get away from a pine needle poking her and rested her feet against the burlap sack.

Whatever was inside the bag was solid. Whatever it was, it wasn't fertilizer.

"Whoa," Ginny said again, this time from the passenger side of the truck. She giggled. "Look at those boobies. She looks like Thor."

Delilah could hear her breathing even over her own. Ginny was a tall, Nordic little blonde girl who never had any trouble clearing her plate at dinner and stayed stocky and moon-faced even though she was an active kid and played kickball. Delilah could see Ginny in her mind's eye, swiping a wispy lock of hair out of her big pink grinning face.

A voice called from the apartment building. "Regina! Time to come in!"

Ginny sighed. "Okay, Mama," she called back. Delilah thought about popping out to surprise her but realized she could reuse this spot next time. Why ruin it now? "Okay, Lilah! You can come out now!" shouted Ginny. "I have to go back in!"

Waiting until Ginny had left, Delilah stayed quiet. She really *was* a ninja! She had gone undetected. She got up off the floor of the bed and crouched there in the womblike red shadow, striking a kung-fu pose. "Kyah." She whispered spirit-shouts to herself. "Kyah. Eeyah." She threw a punch, and then another with the other hand, then tried to kick, but the low ceiling didn't give her enough room to maintain her center of balance, so she fell back on her butt. She caught herself with her hands, raking the inside of her forearm down the rock-chipped edge of the weed-trimmer head. "Ouch!"

Her hand landed on some angular object inside the burlap bag. It was flat on one side. She raised her arm into the dim light and saw that the trimmer hadn't broken skin, but there was a painful four-inch red welt.

Tugging back the rim of the burlap sack, Delilah saw a New Balance tennis shoe.

Time ground to a halt. Even the cicadas silenced themselves, though not all at once—dwindling to three or four, and then one buzzing razz tapered off into nothing. All thought of ninjas fled her mind. She was a seven-year-old girl again, bewildered and vulnerable and alone.

Fear didn't quite enter into it, not yet. Some lingering logic said the bag was full of old hand-me-down shoes; a load of clothes destined for Goodwill. Maybe the owner of the truck was a good-hearted man that collected old giveaways for the church or something. She pressed her fingertips against the burlap sack again and felt another shoe inside.

Good.

A big bag of shoes for the church. She relaxed and peeled the bag open a little bit more. Wrapped in a striped sock, a skinny ankle protruded from the mouth of the shoe, pale, hairless.

Delilah's mouth moved, but nothing came out.

If something had come from her mouth, it would have been "Mama, Mama, Mama," but for some reason, her voice box didn't want to work, the wind wouldn't catch the guitar strings, her throat wouldn't respond. She just kept mouthing the word over and over again. Her legs didn't want to work either. She wanted to get out of the truck, to crawl over to the sash and push it open, throw herself out of the camper shell, and run home. But she couldn't quite wrap her mind around the sight of seeing a little boy's legs poking out of a fertilizer bag in the back of a stranger's truck, and it was the confusion that kept her frozen. Instead of directing her feet to propel her outside, her child brain could only spin in place, trying to reconcile one with the other, tires in deep mud.

She touched the leg. Cold.

Dead cold.

This was incorrect, untrue, unreal. It didn't make sense. People didn't die like this. People died in hospitals at a ripe old age and their family cried over them at the funeral home, people in cheap gray suits and bifocals. They were buried in cemeteries with flowers and pretty headstones with carvings of angels and animals. *You don't walk on graves. That's rude, Miss Delilah Lee. Go 'round them.*

"Are you okay in there?" The words came out wrong. Strangled, wet. She touched her own face and realized she was crying. "Boy? Are you oh— Are you okay?"

Taking the edge of the sack opening in both hands, she pulled it up, up, up, past the boy's knees. He was wearing a pair of black gym shorts. She would have kept going, but the sack was caught on the toe of his shoe. With a terrified respect, Delilah pulled the burlap back down, covering the boy's legs, and started sobbing outright. The inside of the painted-over camper swam in red chaos, a hot-box full of blood, and she went for the back sash.

Nothing there but a round hole where the handle was supposed to be.

For the second time in as many minutes, reality ceased to color inside the lines. Delilah's hand swept back and forth across the middle of the sash, looking for the handle, but it wasn't there. The only thing marking its prior presence was the round hole in the sash frame. Inside, she could see the mechanism that operated the latch, but she couldn't figure out how to move the parts.

In the cab of the truck, someone sat up in the passenger seat.

She became moveless and silent, unwilling to give herself away, a fawn in the grass. The man fetched a heavy sigh and unlatched the cab's rear window, sliding it open. He twisted in the seat and peered inside, a silhouette crowned with a shock of fiery copper hair. She couldn't quite see his face, but his head was big. He had the affect of a pit viper, with a wide-set jaw and narrow throat.

"Hey there," said the man. His voice was dry and high, like sandpaper, like the scraping of sandstone vaults.

Delilah said nothing.

"I know you're back there, your friend woke me up looking for you."

Delilah's burning eyes refused to blink. She was afraid to take them off the wide-headed shadow in the front seat. Snot crept down her upper lip.

"What's your name?" he asked.

Nothing.

"Not talkin', huh? I can dig it," he said, emphasizing the phrase with a brief jazz-hand. "Smart. Y'know, when I was your age, I was great at hide-and-seek. Nobody could find me. I knew all the best hiding places. My friends called me Snake—'cause I could wriggle into the littlest places."

"Lilah," said the girl. She hunkered against the tailgate, shivering.

"Hmm?"

"My name is Delilah."

"Delilah," the man said pleasantly. "Pretty name. Mine's Roy. Maybe I can teach you a few things about hiding, huh? You don't want to jump in the back of a crazy-lookin' truck like this one. This is a bad place. I can show you where to hide where no one will ever, *ever* find you again." He put a zip tie between his lips and let it dangle there, as if it were a wheat-straw in a cowboy's mouth. Delilah thought it looked like a snake's tongue.

Deet-deet. The stillness was broken by an electronic alarm. Roy took a phone out of his pocket and studied it, the screen illuminating his face. His nose was pointed, his nostrils wide, his eyes thin and somehow both clever and stupid at once. As he read the message, his mean slash of a mouth formed silent words.

"Looks like I need to get back to the house. No rest for the wicked." His eyes flashed up to Delilah and he got out of the truck. The camper sash opened with a creak, allowing cool night air to pour in like fresh river-water, and the man scowled in at her. "Out of the truck, princess," said Roy, jerking a thumb over his shoulder. "Game's canceled."

Delilah clambered over the tailgate and stumbled onto the pavement.

Leaning over her, the redheaded man smiled. "Run on home. And if you tell anybody I was here, well . . . I know where you live. And I promise you, you *don't* want to play hide-and-seek with me. I know where you live." Getting back into his truck, Roy regarded her with those tiny, venomous eyes. "Stay outta strangers' cars, kid. You'll live longer."

Dinner was amazing. Kenway's steaks turned out perfectly, and to her chagrin, Robin found the witches' side dishes more than adequate: potato salad with tender little chunks of boiled egg, dusted with smoked paprika; garlic-buttered corn on the cob; bundles of asparagus spears, each wrapped in bacon and fried; scoops of bruschetta; and to cut the savory, sweet-potato casserole topped with toasted marshmallows and crushed pecans. They ate at the table in the garden, the lowering dusk kept at bay by citronella tiki-torches that smelled like grapefruit.

You know, Kenway probably can't see us inside the garden because of the wall. That felt like bad news, even though she was probably more capable of defending herself against the coven than he was. *I wonder if he's even observing. When I decided to go to dinner, I didn't fill him in on an alternate plan. No doubt Heinrich is carrying the water, though. Probably up a tree with a directional microphone, knowing him.* Her eyes scanned the dark forest, raking the pines for a glowing cigar-tip. She missed Kenway, wanted him there, should have brought him in. Needed his warm, lumbering closeness. He made her feel safe and normal, two things she hadn't experienced in a very long time. Him and his broad back, and his romance-novel hair, and his laid-back Baloo way. He made her feel like someone stood beside her against the world for a change. *Maybe that's why I like him so much,* she understood, watching the old women eat. Not that she was weak without him, but it was nice to be able to rely on someone other than yourself for a change.

"Miss Cutty," said Leon. "We were talking about how unusual your house is on the walk out here."

"Would you be surprised to know that it used to be a whore-house?"

If the man could have blushed red, he would have. "A whore-house?"

"Well, I suppose the more tactful parlance might be *brothel.* It's called the Lazenbury House, after its original builder and owner, William Lazenbury. He was a nineteenth-century coal baron from Virginia. He built it in the lawless days of Wyatt Earp and Doc Holliday. Customers came from miles around. In its heyday, that house saw its fair share of murders—gunslingers fighting over a card game, drunken brawling, jealous lovers a little too attached to the working girls."

"The murders, of course, had everyone convinced that the house was haunted," said Marilyn, sipping her tea. "But then, you get that with any old house with historical value like mine. Wanted it the moment I saw it, but I had to wait for the owner to die first."

"So, you really *are* witches?" asked Wayne.

"We are, honey," said Theresa.

"You don't *look* like witches."

Cutty smiled graciously. Robin knew enough about her to see under the mask and knew it was an act. "Pray tell, young man—what is a witch *supposed* to look like?"

Wayne's eyes danced from his father to Robin, and then he

murmured to Cutty, shrinking a little bit, "I don't know." A piece of bread touched his lips, clutched in his hands like a squirrel. He spoke into it bashfully. "Green? With all black clothes and a big floppy hat?"

"And a wart on my nose and a broom and a cauldron full of bubbling brew?"

He pushed his glasses up on his nose.

"Well, you can thank artistic license for that depiction. Pure fiction." She cut into her steak, talking as she did so. "... It's sort of like Santa Claus. You know what the real Santa Claus looks like, yes?"

"Santa Claus?" Wayne sat up, putting down the bread and pantomiming a beard. They had obviously strayed into something a ten-year-old could be enthusiastic about. "Yeah! He's all dressed up in red, and he's got rosy cheeks and a big white beard. He carries a giant sack full of toys and rides in a sleigh pulled by reindeer."

Cutty forked the bite of steak into her mouth and waved this away as if to dispel it. "A fiction, concocted by a newspaper cartoonist and perpetuated by the Coca-Cola company to sell soda. The real man looked *much* different, and didn't live at the North Pole."

"Wait, Santa Claus is real?"

"Oh, absolutely. The name 'Santa Claus' comes from *Sinterklaas,* which is the Dutch name for Saint Nicholas, also known as the bishop Nikolaos of the ancient Greek city of Myra. People left their shoes out on the stoop at night, and Nikolaos would leave coins in them." Cutty's features lightened in an open disbelief so uncharacteristic to her that Robin almost laughed in her face. "You don't believe in Santa Claus?"

"Lady, I'm a hood kid."

Leon's face twisted in disapproval. "You ain't no hood kid."

The boy shrugged his shoulders, pushing his glasses up on his nose, as if he were more chastised at being caught saying it in front of his father than possibly being wrong.

"Just because you grew up in Chicago—" Leon began, but trailed off. He looked to Cutty. "Anyway, you were saying, Santa Claus was a Greek priest?"

"Yes. He was a very generous man, and he was also one of the most powerful magicians and alchemists that ever lived. He was tall and skinny, with a long beard. Nicholas died in the year 343 and his remains were buried in Italy." Cutty swirled her tea, the ice clinking musically against the glass. She eyed Robin. "The point of my history lesson is, most things are not as others would have you believe. There is always a long story behind an old face."

"So, witches aren't the only ones that can do magic?"

Weaver stifled a burp. "Hell, no. We don't really like to call it 'magic,' by the way. That's busking, card tricks, that kind of shit."

"Witches are the most prominent manipulators of paranormal energy these days," said Cutty. "Always have been, really. Men can do it as well, like Nikolaos of Myra, but it requires artificial means. They can't do it naturally like we can. They require conduits, relics such as crystal balls, alchemy, staves. As a Christian, Nicholas used a shepherd's crook . . . which is where candy canes came from, if you can believe that.

"Whole secret societies have risen and fallen over the centuries, seeking to channel the Gift. Thaumaturgy, which is the name we use for it, is threaded into our very being. Men—wizards, warlocks, magi, magicians, whatever they choose to call themselves, can only borrow this force using crude artifacts. We are *filled* with it. Thanks be to the goddess of the afterlife, Ereshkigal, we *are* magic. All magic comes from a supernatural patron, and we are more connected to ours than any other practitioner."

Robin smiled. "You make it sound so noble."

"Is it not?"

"Not when you bleed people dry of their lives with the *nag shi*. Drain them of their happiness, their spirit—"

Cutty held up a hand. Her fingers were slender and pale, young-looking, no longer knob-knuckled. Robin realized underneath the warm, diffuse glow of the citronella candles, the old woman's face was softer, less creased than it ought to be. Younger. "You promised you weren't going to bring us any drama, littlebird."

That term of endearment brought back old, old memories. Herself as a tiny child, sitting in the Lazenbury's kitchen, eating cookies and drinking apple juice, reading the comics out of the Sunday paper or watching cartoons on the wood-cabinet Magnavox. Marilyn Cutty had a dog back then, a miniature pinscher named Penny, for the coins of copper fur over his eyes.

Littlebird. She cast a glance at Wayne. "I did."

"You're an honest soul," said Cutty. "I remember when you used to call me Grandmother. Hell, two days out of every week, you'd be up here knocking on my kitchen door, crying about your mummy and daddy fighting about this or that."

"Why didn't you get another dog when Penny died?"

Cutty stumbled. "Oh . . . well, I don't know. I suppose it just hurt too much to lose him. And besides, there was no little girl to come around and play with a dog anymore. Once you found makeup and boys and such, my little tomboy stopped visiting." She cut a spear of asparagus into several bites. "I came to visit you in the hospital after . . . after your mother, you know."

Robin blinked. "You did?"

"Oh, yes. They wouldn't let me see you, though. The shrinks told me you weren't stable enough for visitors, especially none so close to you and your mother." Cutty punctured asparagus with her fork and slipped it into her mouth. "They said it could possibly sabotage your progress."

"Maybe," said Robin. She pushed food around on her plate. "I knew it was you. Back then." Her words were grim but gentle. "Your name was the last word on my mother's lips as she died in my arms."

Leon and Wayne sat there with their forks and knives on their plates frozen mid-cut, watching this dinner theater in anxious anticipation.

"I wanted to bring you home with me, littlebird," Cutty said dismissively. "I would have raised you as my own. There would have been no . . . whatever *this* is." She made an inclusive gesture at Robin with her fork, as if pointing out her bad taste in shirts. "Blood feud, vengeance, vigilantism, I don't know."

"How?" Something burned deep in Robin's chest—not quite rage, but it was headed that way. But it didn't stop her from imagining what life would have been like if the coven had raised her. Would they have tried to make her take the oath and give her heart to Ereshkigal? "My mother never would have let it happen."

"Your mother is dead, love."

"Because of you."

Karen Weaver cleared her throat, butting in. "Your mother murdered my husband. I couldn't stand there and—and—take that lying down," the witch said indignantly. "Edgar may have been a shit, but I loved him, you know."

"So, you turned my mother into a tree?"

"Eye for an eye."

Cutty interjected, "Besides, we had to replace the *nag shi* Annie burned down." She shrugged and took a sip of her iced tea. "She brought it on herself, Robin. Annie thought she could punish her own coven and renounce her vows. Out of . . . disgust, I guess, she called it *sins,* transgressions against nature and decency, as if we had any choice. She thought of herself as a sort of whistleblower, thought she was better than us, better than her vows.

"In retrospect, she discovered she wasn't prepared to make the moral sacrifices required to live this life. It was darker, uglier than Annie expected. But that's not the way it works. Once you promise your heart to the Goddess, it's Hers forever, for good or for ill. It's like the Mafia, like Hotel California, once you're in, you don't get to leave. And you do what you can to stay alive. When you make the choice to become immortal, there are certain parts of your soul you do not get to keep."

"Killing innocent people?" Robin screwed up her face.

"You think rabbits are evil creatures? Flies? Mice? Where is your righteousness when the owl plucks the mouse from the fields? When the bear catches the fish in the river?" Cutty pointed with her fork again. "Subsistence. That's what it is. All it's ever been. You don't understand."

"You're predators, but you're not eagles. That's too noble. You're unnatural. You're rotten inside. You've been alive too long."

"Who are you to tell me when I should die? Where is your cloak, Death? Where is your scythe and hourglass?" Cutty bit her lips and stared unflinchingly at Robin. "These are laws you haven't bothered to know anything about. I'm sure you think you're knowledgeable because you've been reading Hammer's old books, but there is an old way, sacred traditions you ignore in your crusade to avenge your mother, who was not blameless. You know as well as I how she used her Gift to hide the truth from you, knocked holes in your brain every time you got close, almost turned you into a drooling idiot. She was every bit as evil as any witch Hollywood can gin up to scare mortals like these. But you haven't given any consideration to that, you murder and you murder and you think it's okay because of what you think we are. And you videotape our anguish and put it on the internet, like it's some kind of goddamned circus!"

"Forty-six people," said Weaver. "You fucking hypocrite."

Robin and Cutty faced her. "What?"

"That's how many people you've killed." Weaver jammed her steak knife into the table with a *thunk!* "The commune in Oregon, the coven in Utah, the subway church in New York, the Sand Oracle's coven . . . ."

Leon licked his lips. "I thought you said you only killed witches."

"I have," said Robin, feeling defensive. "Like nineteen. About that many—*witches!*" Again, Weaver was trying to turn the Parkins against her. Cutty was trying to talk her over to the dark side, so to speak, with her pet names and pouty, wistful, woe-is-Granny faces. A pronged attack.

Weaver's head shook slowly. "*People*. Witches *and* familiars. You little heathern, I've watched your videos."

"You think I'm a fool?" Cutty asked, her voice wry, her face disbelieving, one eye scrunched. Leon had surreptitiously turned his knife around in his fist like he was getting ready to stab somebody. "I already told you I knew you were in Medina Psychiatric. What kind of a fool would I be if I didn't keep tabs on you in some way? If I'd known Hammer was coming to fetch you from Medina, I would have killed him and took you myself. But you two were driving across the state line into Alabama by the time I got there."

Back then, she had been nothing but a confused, angry girl pumped full of meds, fried on electroshock therapy, psychoanalyzed half to death, and more than ready for the wide-open skies of Texas after spending so much time in the stark, sterilized hallways of the psych ward. All this time, she'd considered Cutty's coven passive, oblivious, sitting here in Blackfield unknowingly waiting to be killed . . . but it was now evident she was still that angry, ignorant girl. She hadn't been the cat; she'd been the mouse the whole time. Running the maze, looking for the cheese, completely in the dark.

"You were so focused on building the gallows, you didn't realize it was your own neck in the noose," Cutty said with a soft finality, her eyes sinking from Robin's face and onto her own plate. She went back to eating quietly.

"Dinner truce, y'all," said Leon. "Don't forget about that."

Robin's eyes were pinned to Cutty's face. "Why didn't you kill me? You had so many chances."

"I thought of you as my granddaughter, littlebird. That tiny girl that spent so much time lying on my floor coloring with her stinky markers . . . how could I stand to hurt you, especially after your own mother had taken so much from you? I may be heartless, but not that way."

Theresa made a droll face. "You got more willpower than me. I'd 'a done the kid in the looney bin. She's dangerous."

"Yes, well, *hyenas* have more willpower than you do, dear Reese."

Theresa huffed and dug into her food with renewed enthusiasm, as if in spite.

"At any rate, I didn't consider the daughter responsible for the mother," continued Cutty. "I still don't. Annie did what she did to us, and to you, and you had nothing to do with it. You were a guiltless bystander. I saw no reason to go after you." Her lips pursed, the corners drawn into a frown, and her next words were made hoarse by emotion. "I *loved* you, littlebird."

Pouring it on thick now, thought Robin. "That's why you let me go? You let me train to kill your kind, and you let me rampage across the countryside doing it, because you loved me?"

"Even my powers have limits."

Silence fell as the garden party ate and processed the conversation. After a while, Wayne told Theresa, "This orange stuff with the nuts is really good, ma'am."

"Thank you, *mon garçon.*"

"You're welcome."

"Sweet-potato casserole." She smirked, wiping her saucy hands on her napkin. Her face was smeared with Heinz 57. "I'll give you a piece of advice: never trust a skinny cook."

"Yes, ma'am."

"You got such good manners. I like you. Y'all all right for colored folk."

Leon choked, pounded on his chest, took a drink of tea.

• • •

"What is that spectral beast living in Annie's house?" Cutty asked out of the blue, when they had all finished eating and sat sipping the last of their tea. The crickets were in full swing, and the black forest breathed music all around them.

"A demon," answered Robin.

"A *demon.*" The witch spoke with a disbelieving curiosity.

"A cacodemon named Andras. A Discordian and an incubus. He eats witches."

None of the witches laughed, to her surprise.

"I expect Heinrich provided her the necessary texts. A meddler, that one. Probably using her to get to us, since he's a *man,* and *men* have no power over the likes of us. I'll bet he got the ritual's material from the little . . . *group* he used to be a part of."

"Group?" Robin's head bobbed back in bewilderment.

"He never told you? He was expelled from a secret society of magicians called the Dogs of Odysseus. They're conceptual descendants of the Thelemic Society founded by Aleister Crowley."

"He told me he was in a cult, and he escaped. They *expelled* him?"

"Cult?" Cutty chuckled. "Oh, no, honey, they're much more than a cult. They make the Freemasons look like the board of directors for Burger King."

Leaning over her empty plate, Karen Weaver growled, "So, *that's* why that pothead punk killed my husband? Sacrificed him to summon a 'demon'?" Her fists were clenched but did not shake. All the witches moved like teenagers, which never failed to unsettle Robin. "No one's ever brought a Discordian into the real world. This reality was sanctified against them when the Christ's blood was spilled—that was the whole point of his sacrifice." The raggedy witch sought validation in Cutty's stoic face. "Wasn't it? Or am I thinking of some show I watched on HBO again?"

"You are right, for a change," said Cutty. "In the Old Testament days, demons walked this world with impunity. The only way to seal them outside of the material plane was with a carefully ritualized self-sacrifice."

I have to admit, that makes sense, Robin considered. You didn't see much mention (if any at all) of fully materialized demons on Earth in the Bible after Jesus was crucified.

"I want to know more about these Dogs of Odysseus, Marilyn."

Something soft wrapped itself around Robin's leg. She glanced underneath the tablecloth and found a spotty gray cat rubbing himself against her ankle. She resisted the reflex to kick it in horror.

"Ask your friend Hammer about the Dogs when you see him again." Cutty smiled. "I'm sure he'd be glad to tell you all about it. Besides, I'm afraid I don't know a lot about them myself, other than they hunt witches and collect artifacts of thaumaturgy. They're quite elusive." Robin shooed the cat away and it popped up on the other side, climbing up onto the table next to Cutty. "I'm sure they're where he stole the Osdathregar you've been killing witches with. All of his reference books as well, I suppose. I wouldn't be surprised if they've been looking for him. He's quite the outlaw."

Hidden behind shreds of denim clouds, the sunset threw a warmth on the heavens like a great bonfire at the edge of the world. Kenway was probably worried about her, Robin decided, and she didn't want to be there any later at night than she could manage. Not that daylight made the witches any less dangerous, but she preferred it to the darkness.

"Before I go," she said, finishing her drink, "I want to see my mother. I think I deserve it."

"I'm impressed," said Cutty.

"At what?"

"At how civil you're being." Marilyn Cutty narrowed her eyes. "I've watched some of your videos. There is a determination to you . . . this past couple of years has made you *ferocious*. Damn near feral. Is it the memories holding you back right now, littlebird?"

What she said was "No," but honestly, Robin wasn't sure. That hate was still back there somewhere, but in the intervening time between Then and Now, it had grown cold and smooth and dark, like polished obsidian.

"You're such a bad liar," said Karen Weaver. "It's a good thing you got into killin' witches and not professional poker. You ain't killing us because you don't have the Godsdagger, and pissin' me off would be suicide. And as entertaining as suicide can be for the likes of us, it ain't a barrel of laughs for you."

"Well, come on. Who am I to begrudge a daughter a visit with her mother?" Cutty rose from her chair, unfolding herself. The cat leapt down and followed her as she walked toward the darkness at the edge of the torchlight, pulling up one of the torches as she went.

The last of the sun was enough to paint the vineyard in a muted haze of red and purple shadows. Robin followed the silhouette through the trellis rows and the citronella torch in her hand. Were it not for the sickly-sweet aroma of rotting grapes, the soft darkness would have made it hard to tell the vineyard wasn't some labyrinth of *The Shining* hedges.

Footsteps in the grass behind her. Theresa LaQuices and the Parkins had joined them. The bayou witch walked like a man, hunched over, her cannonball fists driving back and forth with each stride.

"You ain't leavin' us alone." Leon was behind her.

This entire experience must have been a shock for the man and his son, even after the past couple of days. They'd showed up for a peaceful steak dinner and ended up in the middle of a slow-motion battle of will. Robin hated to see them embroiled in it, but it had been inevitable from the moment Parkin had signed the lease on the house, regardless of how careful she could have been to exclude them.

His jaw was set in stone, his eyes a combination of fear and strength.

"I won't," she muttered to him. "Stick close, okay?"

8

Joel didn't feel like he would ever get the smell of that filthy garage out of his skin, the penny-smell of blood and the mungy stink of old engine grease. He took another shower, standing in the hot water for the better part of an hour, sipping Thunderbird out of the bottle and scrubbing until his skin was raw.

Like he'd promised Robin he would do, he had indeed slept all the rest of the morning, straight through lunch and into the afternoon. As soon as he woke up, he ate every bit of junk food in the kitchen cabinet (half a bag of Cool Ranch Doritos, three Zebra Cakes, and a strawberry Pop-Tart) and got in the shower.

Grrrrruhuhuhuhuh.

He'd taken off Kenway's combat bandage to clean his scratches, and the body wash stung as it ran down his chest. Joel winced, squeezing lather all over himself and gingerly patting his wounds with a washcloth.

(there's a demon in the room there's a demon THERE'S A DE-MON)

Blood pooled around his feet, streaks of pink. He sang Billie Holiday's "Strange Fruit" over and over, the words reedy and hesitant. Every time he stopped singing, he saw the upside-down dead man with the cut throat again, that severed larynx glistening in the workbench light.

Reaching out of the spray, Joel turned off the water, *squeak squeak squeak,* listening intently.

"Hello?" He strained to hear over dripping water.

Coulda sworn he'd heard something outside the bathroom. The clock on the bathroom wall counted down the seconds. He pulled a clean towel off of the curtain rod and draped it around his neck.

Mama's shotgun was propped up between the toilet and the vanity, a pump-action Weatherby Upland with a walnut stock. A fresh pair of underwear and pajama bottoms lay across the toilet seat. Joel whipped aside the curtain (relieved to find no one standing on the other side) and traded the wine for the shotgun. Stepping out of the bathtub, he shrugged into the briefs and pants and racked the action loudly, *CH-CHUK!,* ejecting a good shotgun shell into the toilet.

"Shit." He briefly entertained the idea of fishing the shell out, but decided against sticking his hand into toilet water.

A plastic Dr Pepper bottle full of rocks had been balanced upside-down on the doorknob. He took it down and left it on the sink. Snatching the door open, he leveled the shotgun at the hallway, his finger tensing on the trigger.

Nobody out there.

He relaxed, but only a bit.

Someone banged on the front door, making him jump. Joel padded down the hallway to the front door, looking through the peephole. A man in a black uniform stood out on the porch. Lieutenant Bowker saluted as if touching the brim of an invisible cowboy hat.

"Hambone better found my Velvet," Joel muttered under his breath, standing the shotgun behind the sofa. He opened the door.

The autumn breeze that wafted in around the officer's considerable bulk made Joel's skin crawl. "Hi there," said Bowker, saluting again. "Thought I'd stop by on the way home and check up on you. You doin' all right, buddy?"

Joel shivered uncontrollably. "Y-yeah, I'm aight."

"The hell happened to your chest?"

He glanced down as if he'd forgotten about the scratches.

"I fell."

"Christ Chex Mix, what'd you fall on, a freakin' mountain lion?" The officer watched Joel shiver and shudder. "Mind if I come in? Looks like this draft is cuttin' you in half."

"Oh, Lord, y-yeah. Come on in."

He stepped into the foyer and Joel closed the door behind him. When he turned around again, Bowker had pulled out what looked like a price-checker from a grocery store and was pointing it at him. After Joel's brain eventually settled on what it was an awkward three seconds later (a Taser), he recoiled, showing the man his palms.

"What you 'bout to taze me for?"

"I'm sorry," Bowker said, stepping forward, pressing Joel backward into the living room. "This wasn't supposed to happen. And I really hate to do this to ya. It's probably the first time we've ever really had a problem like this. Normally, he's tidy enough we can keep our hands clean."

"What you mean? Who's tidy? Man," Joel groused, "I should have stayed my ass at the Victorian. At least Granny Magic ain't gonna gun me down in my own house."

The edge of the coffee table bumped into Joel's calves. He slipped the towel from around his neck and twisted it anxiously, bunching it in his fists. Bowker had walked him far enough that the cop now stood between him and the sofa, where the shotgun was hidden. The cop's eyes wandered around the room, assessing the curtains.

They were all drawn, the venetian blinds airtight. Whatever happened to Joel would be between them and them alone. "You wasn't supposed to live." The beats of his Southern-fried accent stretched luxuriantly, like Foghorn Leghorn. "Blood for the garden, son, it's the Serpent's job to thin the herd. And it's *our* job to keep people out of his business."

"The Serpent?"

"Their man. He does what they need him to do, we keep them safe from prying eyes. In return, they let us live."

"Who is 'they'?"

"Don't be coy with me, boy. You know who I'm talkin' about."

"The witches?" Joel gaped at him. His hands sank and relaxed. The towel unfurled in front of his legs as if he were a matador in the ring with a bull. "You in cahoots with them witches killed Annie Martine? Marilyn Cutty?"

"I don't know about any 'witches,' but they run this here town. They run *everything*. They always have and always will." Bowker flicked the safety on the Taser. "And like I said, I hate to do this, but it's got to be done. No loose ends, boy. Can't have you runnin' around tellin' stories, you know."

"Cletus, you call me *boy* one mo' goddamn time and I'm gonna break your leg off and beat you with the tender end."

"I doubt it," said Bowker, firing the Taser.

At the same time, Joel held up the towel. *Toro, toro!*

Metallic confetti burst out of the Taser in a dazzling cloud of pink and yellow. The electric barbs tangled up in the terrycloth towel, *tak-tak-tak-tak*, and Joel charged forward through the weird shiny confetti, shoving with both fists. His knuckles slapped into Bowker's Second Chance vest as if he were hitting the cop with shock paddles. Bowker's feet cycled, trying to find traction, and he stumbled backward into the foyer, slipping on a rug.

Reaching behind the sofa, Joel scooped up the shotgun and pirouetted away. Bowker drew and fired his Glock into the living room in one smooth motion, shattering a window.

Darting through the living room, Joel burst through the door at the other end and came out down the hallway from Bowker. *BOOM!* A mirror hanging on the wall shattered, spraying glass all over him. He yelped and kept running all the way down to the end of the hall. *BOOM!* The glass in the back door imploded all over his hands as he wrenched it open. "Ohh! Jesus!"

The Glock barked again, flashing in the shadows. Joel shoved the storm door open and something punched him in the right thigh.

Blood spattered the screen.

Jumping off the back stoop, Joel's knee gave out and he stumbled down the back stairs, dropping the shotgun in the dewy grass. Luckily, it didn't go off. Cold air shrouded his wet body, raising goose bumps and wracking him with shivers. The backyard was only a narrow strip of grass running alongside a paved alley, and another house loomed behind a board fence. Joel staggered out into the alleyway, dragging the Weatherby by the barrel, crutching along on it, the gravel digging into his bare feet.

BOOM! Splinters exploded from the fence.

He threw up an arm to protect his face, running barefoot and half-naked into the night. Dogs barked in the distance.

"Police!" spat Bowker. *"Stop!"*

The lights came on in the house across the alley, cutting the shadows and washing away the hiding spots. Joel kept sprinting, his feet slapping on the alley's buckled asphalt.

A gate in the fence. He hauled it open and *BOOM!,* a bullet thumped into the wood slats, almost tearing it out of his hand. He forged through into darkness again, this time watched over by squares of light on either side. An air conditioner grumbled in the shadows. Joel ran full-tilt across the gravel and grass, hurdling the AC unit.

When he landed, he paused, turned, aimed at the gate he'd just ran through. As soon as Bowker pulled it open, Joel fired a shell at him.

Buckshot roared through the gap with a deafening blast. Bowker swore out loud, flinching backward into the dark. Joel racked the shotgun, ejecting the empty casing against the side of the house. He turned and ran, exploding from between two porches into the sickly blue glow of a streetlight, almost slipping in dewy grass. He ran catty-corner left, throwing himself across the hood of a car *Dukes of Hazzard*–style. *BOOM-CRASH!* The windshield behind him imploded.

He half-ran, half-crawled toward a house, the shotgun clattering across the road, the night-wind curling around his shoulders and legs. Bowker's pistol went off again, the bullet sparking off the driveway, close enough to bounce sharp little chips of tarmac off Joel's legs. Between the garage and the house was a wooden gate. He slammed into it at full speed, throwing it open.

In the last second before he turned and shut it, he could see Bowker hustling across the road in that shuffling middle-aged-cop way, mincing and huffing with his elbows up.

Behind the fence was a belowground swimming pool, where a single security light silvered the water. Frantic and bleeding, Joel sidestepped into the corner between the fence and the wall. As soon as he did, Bowker tore his way in and lumbered to a stop next to the pool.

The gate flapped open in front of Joel's hiding spot, covering him in shadow. "The hell you go?" demanded the cop, panting like a plowhorse.

Cradling the Weatherby against his cheek, Joel tried to stop breathing so hard and stay as still as possible. The alcohol in his system had all but burned off with the adrenaline, leaving him trembly but clearheaded. Warm blood trickled down his leg like a crawling spider. He was steeling himself up to close the gate and ambush Bowker when the officer turned and closed it himself.

"*Ooo!*" Joel screamed in terror, hipfiring buckshot into Bowker's chest with a blast of thunder and fire. The black uniform shirt disintegrated in a blizzard of fabric and the cop toppled backward into the pool.

Blinking away the muzzle flash, his ears ringing, Joel stood over the pool with the shotgun pressed to his shoulder, the iron sight lined up on the man splashing and gargling in the water.

Fish in a barrel.

Click. Empty. The blast he braced for never came, making him stagger. He scowled at the shotgun in surprise as if it had offended him, and flung the gate open. "Be easy, pig," he said, running back the way he'd come.

"I'm—gonna—get—" Bowker ranted with a mouth full of water, kicking and thrashing.

Running across the street, ducking back down into the shortcut between the houses, Joel saw windows shining in the dark. The impromptu gunfight had disturbed half the town. He didn't bother locking the doors when he got back to Mama's house; Bowker would kick the doors down and ruin the locks anyway. He ran into his bedroom, wriggled into the first shirt and jeans he laid hands on and a pair of boat shoes. Grabbed his cellphone, wallet, and keys.

Shotgun or wine? Shotgun or wine?

He left the Weatherby Upland lying on his bed and rescued the Thunderbird from the bathroom—no point in keeping the shotty; he didn't have time to forage the house for the rest of the shells or load them.

In the foyer, the bedazzled baseball bat stood in the urn by the front door where Kenway had left it. He snatched it up.

"Bubba, you gotta come get me," he said when Fish answered the phone. Joel shut the front door, almost stopped to lock it, thought better, jumped down the front steps, vaulting the fence with the cellphone in one hand and the wine and baseball bat in the other. The officer's police Charger was parallel-parked on the street. No keys.

"What are—" Fish started to say.

Blood seeped through Joel's jeans where the Glock had clipped him. His voice jiggled with every footfall. "I been shot. A cop came to Mama's house and tried to murder my Black ass. I'm runnin' down the hill right now."

"I'm on my way," Fish told him. "Why is—"

"Because I was supposed to *die*," Joel said breathlessly. The slope turned precipitous and he ran down the sidewalk past a row of angled town houses, moonlight showering through the mimosa trees. "I got hemmed up by a mufuckin' serial killer last night, and—"

"A *what*?"

"Dude drugged me, strung me up in a garage with a dead guy. Little boy saved me. I got out."

"The hell?" Fish was yelling. *"Why didn't you call me?"*

Joel winced at the shock in his brother's voice. "Didn't wanna bother you. You got y'own thing goin' on—"

"Didn't wanna *bother* me? Are you insane?"

"Insane—that shit is debatable." Joel glanced over his shoulder, expecting the flashing lights of Bowker's police cruiser at any moment. "Anyway, this killer is apparently on police payroll, and a boy in blue came to Mama's house to finish the job." At the end of the block, Joel cut right, running down the street. "I'm gonna hide in the park. The one down the hill where they do the farmers' market. Come get me."

"What on Earth have you got yourself into, big brother?"

"I'll tell you more when you get here. Peace be on ya." He slowed enough to slip the iPhone into his pocket and took off again, trading the Batdazzler to his free hand. As he ran, he thought about how he was going to climb a tree with the Thunderbird without breaking it.

In fact, Heinrich was not in a tree like Robin expected, but on the roof of one of the mobile homes in the rear of Chevalier Village, lying on his belly with a pair of high-tech binoculars. The night-vision optics turned the world in front of his eyes into shades of green.

"See anything?" Kenway Griffin lurked on the porch below, sitting on a rain-ruined dining room chair.

Whoever lived in the trailer either wasn't home or had moved out—no car stood vigil in the driveway; the windows were all dark. Kenway took a drag off the Camel between his fingers, squinting in the smoke. "Hey, Tombstone, it's kinda bullshit I didn't get to go eat with them. I'd really like to be by Robin's side right now, you know? And I'm the one that fixed the steaks to boot. Why didn't I get a veto on this?"

"I need you out here, Sergeant," Heinrich said quietly. "You have combat experience."

"Need me for what?"

"They're getting up from the table," said Heinrich. "Cutty walked into the vineyard. Everybody's following her."

"What?" Kenway smashed his cigarette out on the stoop.

"Now's our chance." Heinrich crawled over to the edge of the roof and let himself down into the grass, landing with a grunt. "Come on."

"Now's our chance to do what?" asked the vet.

"While Robin's got the coven distracted, we're going to go into the house and kill the Matron." Picking up a jerry can, Heinrich jogged toward the long dirt road separating the trailer park and the Lazenbury's property. Kenway followed, tossing the Camel's mashed butt into the night-wet grass and creeping after the old hunter. Across the dirt driveway, *crunch crunch crunch*. Shuffling into the grass, fingertips on cold earth, crouch-walking across the dark front yard. The jerry can swished and gurgled. The two men rested against the wall obscuring the front of the house.

"Matron? What's in the gas can, anyway?"

"Gas." The old man gave him an exasperated look. "I really don't have time for a crash course on witches right now. Imagine we're sneaking into the tower from *Game of Death* and we're here to look for Kareem Abdul-Jabbar. Except instead of doin' jeet kune do on him, we're going to douse him in unleaded and set his ass on fire."

"What the hell? From one to eleven, how high are you right now?"

"You mean to tell me you ain't seen Bruce Lee in *Game of Death*? What kind of uncultured swine *are* you, Sergeant? I'm bringing you back to my place and we're gonna siddown and have a movie marathon when this is over."

"Never figured you for a cinema buff."

"There's a lot you don't know about me," Heinrich said with a sideways glance and chuff of laughter, and crouch-ran along the wall toward the back door and the gas grill that still fumed with beefy-smelling smoke.

"I don't know if this is a good idea," said Kenway, following. "I watched Robin's video. If these women really are witches, they are no joke. I think this calls for a sustained force with a *clear* plan of attack."

"The Marines, sure. I'll get right on it, Hurt Locker." Heinrich glanced down at the glint of titanium under Kenway's jeans leg. "Or, rather, Foot Locker, I guess."

The vet sighed. "I'm beginning to understand where she gets it."

Heinrich waved it away. "We need to get into this house, if they ain't got all the doors locked up as tight as . . . ."

"A congressman's Grindr account?"

"I don't know what that is."

"Don't worry about it."

"Sounds dirty." Heinrich made a face.

"It is. Trust me, Robin would appreciate the joke."

"I'll take your word for it." Heinrich tried the back door and Kenway felt a combination of dread and relief that it was unlocked. They crept inside.

Instead of the grimy, cluttered living space he expected of a bunch of witches, they discovered a brightly lit kitchen, sparkling clean steel and travertine. Instinct kicked in and Kenway took point, leading the other man through the nearest door in that hunched-over tactical way, rolling his heels to mitigate noise. *Man, my hands feel so empty doing this without an M4,* he thought, emerging into a living room.

Some old Hanna-Barbera cartoon was on the TV—*Snagglepuss,* maybe, or *Huckleberry Hound. Bonk, bang, crash, ka-pow.* Vibrant colors made a riot of the dark living room as Kenway crept through. Bookshelf to his left. The lights were all turned off, but he could read the spines of old reference books by the glow of the blindingly bright TV—encyclopedias, wildlife bestiaries, bird books. Old novels.

"Exit, stage left," shouted Snagglepuss.

Behind the sofa, Heinrich crouched to glance at the television and survey the room. Reaching underneath his coat, he slid something out from behind his back with a hiss of sharpened metal.

Silver gleamed in the cartoon glow. Robin's weird dagger.

"Watch my back," Heinrich breathed. He pointed at his own eyes with a *V* gesture and jerked a thumb over his shoulder.

That's not how tactical hand gestures work, but whatever, dude. The veteran gave him a thumbs-up. Not for the first time, he wished he'd brought a weapon—at least the H&K 45 Compact he kept in the truck. But the old man had naysaid it. "Guns don't work on these dead-ass hoes," he'd said earlier at the Victorian house, screwing up his face and waving it away as if the mere suggestion stank. "Might as well bring a slingshot, for all the good it'll do you. Knock all the holes you want in 'em, they'll get back up and keep coming. You'll be lucky if they don't rip off one of your limbs for every bullet. You want to kill a witch, you need fire."

Gasoline sloshed in the can as Heinrich made his way around the edge of the living room to a staircase set against the far wall.

Floating iron risers led them up to the second floor. Like downstairs, the walls were painted a deep, hearty blood-red. A wrought-iron banister separated them from a fall into the living room. The landing was a wide space with two cedar bookshelves and an array of knickknacks. In the center of the landing was a long, lonely corridor where doors led to three bedrooms and most likely a bathroom.

"Lessee," Heinrich whispered. "Where you at, chick?" He pushed deeper into the long hallway, gas can in one hand, dagger in the other. "Stay here and be a lookout," he said over his shoulder. "I'm going to check these bedrooms."

With that, he opened the first door and disappeared inside. His flashlight played over the contents of the room.

From the hallway, Kenway could see Heinrich checking behind shelves, peering under the bed. It looked like the inside of a homestead lodge, with framed paintings on the walls depicting wildlife and mountain ranges, and there were bolts and scraps of cloth and half-finished seamstress projects all over the room.

This is bullshit, he mused, watching the TV downstairs play colors all over the second-floor landing ceiling. *I should be out there with Robin. She's all by herself.*

Well, she's got the Parkins with her. That Leon guy, he's got a hell of a right hook. He can take care of himself, I bet.

Come on, he's a fuckin' English teacher, man.

So? Your old Army unit had a couple teachers in it, didn't it?

True.

What was Chief Bangley, a history teacher? Social studies, whatever they call it?

Yeah, all right. All right! He rubbed his beard with both hands and rested his fists on his hips. *Man, I must be stressed out of my mind. I'm out here arguing with myself while some guy I just met is sweeping rooms in an old lady's house, looking for a witch to burn.*

"Nope," said the old man behind him.

Another door softly creaked open, the one down at the far end of the hallway, and Heinrich slipped out of sight again, fading into the dark. The second bedroom held the gray austerity of a nun's quarters but it was messy, the bedquilt and wood floor strewn with clothes and dirty dishes.

What the hell are you doing, dude? Isn't this breaking and entering? Do you really buy into this witch-hunting shit?

For real? After seeing what happened in Robin's old house, with the demon thing? The video on the MalusDomestica YouTube page? You're still having trouble processing this stuff? Are you kidding me right now?

Chills went down Kenway's spine. Heinrich emerged from the bedroom at the end of the hall and went into the third and final bedroom, the one on the left.

Probably the cleanest and most ostentatious of the three, well appointed with baroque cherry furniture and silk fleur-de-lis wallpaper in an oceanic seafoam green. The curtains were spiderwebs of white, lacy gossamer.

"Hey, Kenny."

A low, thin voice, a familiar papery rasp, coming from the dark door at the end of the hallway.

Hairs on Kenway's scalp tingled, and the sensation trickled down his arms. "Heinrich? Is that you?" His voice was barely more than a whisper. He turned to more fully confront the shadowy hallway, cartoons playing riot over his back.

"What's for breakfast?" the voice rasped again.

Definitely coming from the dark door down there. The second one, the one the old man had already searched, the one like a dirty monk's quarters.

Fingertips on his right hip, Kenway found only denim, the smooth arc of his belt. No pistol. It had been instinct to reach for it, to find the comfort of the 45's cold, angular steel.

I know that voice. Where do I know that voice from?

Creak of hardwood underfoot. His boots carried him slowly up the carpet runner, toward the deep black sliver between the door and the frame, carrying him toward some mean promise of things he should but shouldn't see. A secret. Hidden things, a broken vow, an old regret. At the threshold now. Silence beyond. His hand floated up and his fingertips pressed against the cold wood of the bedroom door. He pushed it open and confronted the void. Hinges squealed softly.

Even the darkness seemed to be solid on the other side, yielding like a black sheet. Inside the dark he could make out the ledge of a bedside, a quilt of Byzantine squares, all rendered in the monochrome of night.

Some shape underneath the quilt. Feet, perhaps.

"Hey, brother," rasped the voice, from the bed. The feet moved, the squares shifted.

"Fuck you," whispered Kenway, his voice choked and quavering. His heart thudded in his chest, a hammer beating on a kettle drum.

"I took my medicine," rasped the voice, in a shuddering, robotic way, like someone talking through a box fan. "I took my medicine already, before I laid down to sleep. I feel better."

The shape slid out of sight, and the quilt flattened.

"I feel better this way," rasped the voice.

"No."

"I'm better now," rasped the voice. "Touch me. Feel me. I'm okay now that you're here, battle buddy." A hand eased into view, sliding across the quilt. It was a man's hand, gray, waxy-looking. The fingernails were blue, the faded blue of old jeans. Despite his terror, Kenway found himself reaching out with one shaking set of fingers, trembling.

At the last moment, he flinched them into a fist. "Chris," he said. Emotion twisted his voice into a croak. "You're not here. Oh my god, you're not."

"You don't believe in ghosts?"

"Goddamn, fuck me, no, *no,* I don't." His head slowly shook back and forth of its own accord, as if he could alter reality by force of will alone. "I don't believe in ghosts. I don't. I *can't.*"

"That's a shame," rasped the buzzing voice, the buzzing of flies in a pie tin. It made Kenway think of Joe Walsh making his guitar speak with a Talk Box. "Ghosts believe in you." The gray hand darted out and grabbed his, palm cupping his knuckles. The hand was cold, not just cool

(cold, colder than 95 degrees. I remember the temperature)

it was the cold of marble, or lunchmeat

(like somebody stole him and replaced him with a ham. Right there, in that bedroom, I thought he was playing a prank on me.)

The occupant of the bed leaned forward into the light. Staff Sergeant Chris Hendry's face resolved from the shadows, and Kenway was horrified to see the black veins standing out on the man's swollen face. Tongue like a boxing glove, filling his mouth with a sea slug of purple meat, Chris's eyes cast skyward like saints in old paintings, the undersides streaked with black vessels. His skin had the white, turgid look of boiled chicken. Dried blood crusted the rims of his nostrils.

"Good morning," he buzzed.

Kenway recoiled in terror, backing out of the bedroom. His fingertips discovered the absence of his nonexistent pistol again.

"You're not real," he told the black doorway.

No answer. Motion, a shape, nothing more than a pale smear, beyond the door.

Rigored arms grasped the doorframe, and Chris's dead body pulled itself out into the hallway. The corpse emerged, slowly, silently, floating just above the hardwood floor. Chris was dressed in the clothes he'd died in, an ancient Metallica T-shirt and a pair of tighty-whities. Or, at least, that's what Kenway assumed the T-shirt had on it; the front was crusted with a spray of thick, granular vomit.

"You aren't real."

Apparently, Chris was done talking, because he had no further reply.

Cartoon colors from the television swam across his dead, bloated, emotionless face. The corpse glided toward him like an astronaut on a spacewalk, and the tips of his toes dragged along the carpet runner. Dried tears formed a powdery crust in his eyelashes. *"YOU LET ME DIE,"* Chris stated in his slow, papery, buzzing robot-voice. It had become fuzzy with distortion, like a scrambled cable signal.

The second-floor railing pressed against Kenway's back.

"YOU LET ME GET COLD," said the cadaver, hanging motionless in midair. His eyes had rolled back into his head, revealing more of the black vessels worming across his eyeballs. *"YOU DIDN'T EVEN KNOW I WAS DEAD."*

His guts all twisted up inside him, his fists clenched, Kenway sprinted for the stairs, prosthetic leg clanking down the iron risers. As he went, he thought he heard the sound of an old woman cackling, perhaps it was the TV behind him, he was running across the living room, into the kitchen, out the back door, running pell-mell down the long dirt driveway.

By the time he realized he'd left Heinrich in the Lazenbury House, he was past the mailbox. He hesitated, clomping to an ungainly stop in the middle of Underwood Road.

Go back, you coward piece of shit. Kenway turned and stared at the witches' house. His hand went to his empty hip again. Looming over him was the Parkins' Victorian house, the cupola thrust into the night sky like the devil's top hat. Heat lightning flickered silent paparazzi flashes in the red clouds. *Go back. They need you.*

"I'm sorry," he told the cooling night. "I didn't know. I had no idea you took the pills. I didn't see you do it. You never said anything."

Run, you coward. Run and hide.

"You just laid down and died. You never said anything. You never told me you were doing it. You never asked for help."

On his knees, he pressed his forehead to the cold asphalt. He wanted to pry the highway from the ground and crawl underneath it like a bedsheet. His self-admonishments were interrupted by a sound welling out of the distance, an immense, prehistoric roar from beyond the Lazenbury House like Godzilla crawling out of his grave—a deep, saurian steel mixed with the plaintive squeal of a hog, reverberating in the Georgia trees.

Tears trickled down his face as he stood.

Gunshots rang out across the night. Muffled at first, coming from inside the house. And then one final blast out on the driveway, followed by a man's scream. Crossing the road to the Parkin family's Victorian house, Kenway dug his keys out of his pocket and headed for his truck.

Yeah, there you go, run and hide.

That's all you've ever been good at, isn't it?

Rain began to fall.

Deeper and deeper into the garden, Robin felt as though they had gradually stepped out of the world and penetrated a quiet, savage wilderness where no civilized man had been in quite some time, if ever. Her imagination painted grotesque Lovecraftian coyotes lurking the trellises, tendril-eyed hounds that ate rotten grapes and anyone stupid enough to wander into their territories.

Territories, that's what it felt like. She expected to see a signpost at some point, with arrows directing her toward points unknown: WONDERLAND, 88 MILES. THIS WAY TO NARNIA. MID-WORLD, NEXT EXIT. The phrase *back forty* kept popping into her head. *Back forty. Back forty. Forty what? Miles? Leagues?* She was about to ask Marilyn how far it was to the Tennessee border when the grapevines came to an end and they emerged into a neatly mowed clearing.

Lavender made a sweet game of the evening air. Skirts of purple wildflowers unfurled to either side, lorded over by several trees drooping with dark fuchsia blossoms. Underneath the trees were pools of shadow. In the very center stood the tallest tree, an apple tree, *Malus domestica,* the reason for her being and the catalyst of her fate.

Hugging herself against a damp breeze, Robin approached the *nag shi.*

Annie's arboreal sarcophagus was tremendous, larger than any apple tree had a right to be, carrying a globe of green foliage as big as a house. The twisted trunk underneath was a stout and heavy five or six feet in diameter, stooped in burdened anguish. Bark had grown around a collection of knotholes and contour grains, and what might have been the motionless shape of a face peered out at them, a pareidolia face like the Virgin Mary on a piece of toast, smeared sideways in a half-grimace, half-smirk. Robin put her hand on the dryad's rough bark. Warmth radiated from underneath, as if the wood were a door leading to a room full of fire.

"I told you I would be back one day, Mama." She'd hoped there would be an echo of thought, a ripple of sentience like she'd received from the demon Andras, but there was only an apple tree with a faint maternal warmth. She leaned in on both hands and pressed her face to the trunk, rough against her cheek. She wanted to build a treehouse in its branches and live there always. She wondered if the plank swing was still hanging from the tree behind their old house. She would go get it and tie it up here, and swing on it every day.

"That's your mama?" asked Wayne.

Robin nodded. "She died when I was only a little older than you. Now she's resting in this tree. I think."

"You put her there?" he asked Marilyn Cutty.

The witch only stood there silently, but then said, "Yes. For killing her coven-sister's husband, and for burning the previous tree."

The boy came up and put his hand on the bark.

A swell of emotion exploded in Robin's chest at the sight of it. "She's in pain," Wayne said, the citronella flame glinting off his glasses. Cutty's long-staffed tiki-torch gave the scene a strangely cultist vibe. "Long time to be like this." He pressed his face against the tree as well. "She loved you very much."

"Yes, she did." The girl's throat burned and tears spilled down her face, threatening to turn into sobs. Between the two of them, face-to-face there in the darkness and torchlight, her voice was an intimate murmur. "She loved everybody. Everybody that was good. And even some that were bad. She tried to save her family from the coven. She made me forget things. She made me half-crazy with missing memories. She made me think I was going out of my mind. But now I understand she was protecting me. In her own screwed-up hillbilly way, she thought she was protecting me."

She turned to the old woman. "Can I talk to her? Is that possible?"

"You can certainly try." Cutty smiled. "Indeed, I read some-where that plants grow better if you talk to them. I myself have been known to come out here and have a heart-to-heart with my former protégée from time to time."

Clutching the rough bark, Robin turned her face so her ear and cheek pressed against the apple tree. "Mom?" she asked, closing her eyes, straining to hear over the cicadas. She thought she felt the first cold droplet of what the storm had been promising them all evening. "Mom, are you there? I'm back. I came back."

No answer. At least, none she thought she could decipher.

Wind whispered endlessly in Annie's leaves, swelling and ebb-ing and cackling and rushing, as if she'd summoned the rest of nature to do her talking for her. Robin balled a fist and pounded on the tree trunk, producing a dull thump. "I have something to tell you, Mama. Something I've wanted to tell you for a couple of years now." She pounded again. And again. Rearing back, she ham-mered the bark hard enough to gouge the skin on the side of her hand, and instead of that light, almost soundless *thud,* she thought she heard the hollow *bang* of a door. "I forgive you, Mama," she said, and turned, resting with her back against the tree. "You were only doing what you thought was right."

Who's there? It felt as if she were thinking in stereo—her own inner monologue on one side and a soft, almost inaudible voice on the other.

"Mom?" Silence, scary heart-stopping silence. Had she imagined it? "Are you there?"

Where am I?

"Cutty made you into a dryad, Mama. You're standing in the back garden behind the Lazenbury House. You're a *nag shi*, locked up inside an apple tree."

Oh, God.

"I'm sorry I couldn't stop them."

Baby, there was nothing you could do. I called the Owl King to protect our house from them, but turns out there was nothing he could do about familiars.

"I could have stopped Dad."

I love you, and you've got more sass than a hundred thousand Reba McEntires, but there's no chance in the world you could beat your daddy's ass, especially not if he's got a cat in him. Jason has a good seventy or eighty pounds on you.

"I could have. Somehow. If I'd known what was going on."

He picked me up over his head and threw me downstairs into the foyer like I was a bag of dirty laundry. You're a little bitty teenager and you're probably seventy-five percent pizza roll.

"Mama, I'm not a teenager. I'm old enough to drink. Daddy went to jail."

What?

"You've been here for a few years."

Oh, no.

"Yeah. Hey, but it's okay. The state took me in. They put me in Medina Psychiatric, got me on mood stabilizers. I did art therapy and watched a lot of Dr. Phil. Found out I'm pretty partial to butterscotch pudding."

Her mother's voice grew stronger as they conversed, until it sounded as if Annie Martine were sitting in the branches of the tree. Robin felt a soft, lilting laugh. *Sounds like a hoot.* A moment of silence, and then: *How did you get out? What are you doing back in Blackfield? Did you age out of the system or something?*

"Heinrich came and got me. Apparently, you knew him."

That guy. Yeah, he's all right. I met him at church. He's Moses Atterbury's son, you know, the chaplain at Walker Memorial? He's the one that gave me the invocation ritual for the Owl King. He said the only thing can scare a witch is a demon, because demons eat their magic. They're leeches.

"But not yours."

. . . No, he fed on me plenty. The Owl King fed on me for more than a decade. He was like a big ol' tick, hanging around our house, getting fat on my heart-road. Suckin' on me like the bottom of a milkshake. How do you think you were able to resist my Gift long enough to draw Norse protection runes on yourself?

Did Heinrich take care of you, by the way? I only knew him for a few months, but he seemed all right. Ain't never met a man that knew magic. I don't know why he came and got you, though. What are you to him? He don't even know you. You wasn't even born yet when I knew him.

"He can be an asshole, and he likes to keep secrets, but he taught me how to fight. Said he came and got me because he figured he owed it to you, to take me under his wing."

Good girl. The voice was fading again. *You always was good at fighting.*

"Mama, before I go, I need to know." Robin turned once more, both hands gripping her mother's bark. "What did you do?" She leaned close and whispered into the tree's jagged folds, "What price did you pay for the Owl King's help? What did you give him?"

She waited for Annie's reply, but none came.

"What did you do, Mama?"

Still nothing.

"Go home, littlebird," Cutty said quietly.

Opening her eyes, turning to face the others, Robin looked over her shoulder and said hoarsely, "What?"

"Go home," the witch repeated. "The Victorian across the street, Hammer's hidey-hole in Texas, I don't even care if you drive around in your van and do what you do to the others out there, as long as it doesn't involve this coven." Her face softened, as did her tone, and she gazed up into the tree's branches. "Annie is mine and here she'll stay. This *town* is mine. Take my advice and forget about her, and Blackfield, and me. Leave. She is paying penance for her foolishness and there is nothing here for you but heartache. And if you persist, death."

The GoPro on Wayne's chest cast a red glow on Annie's bark, firelight through a keyhole. Robin straightened and stepped back from the dryad.

"Do you remember what I asked you that last day?" asked Cutty.

"The last day you ever saw me? When me and my mom were having that fight, and I came up to your house to see you?"

"You were getting away from her, not visiting me. But yes. Remember when I offered my home to you, said you should come and live with me, and escape from your mother's delusions, until you could graduate high school?"

"Yes. Now I realize what you were doing—recruiting me."

"I wish you had taken me up on it," said Cutty. "Oh, how much easier things would have been. How wonderful and how strong you could have become. It may not be too late, you know. We are immortal. Become one of us, if you can. You will have all the time in the world to cast off that husk of immaturity and be something authentic. Something real. An heiress for the ages. Can you imagine?"

"I can imagine seeing you wish in one hand and shit in the other, and I can imagine which one fills up first."

"You were always so delightfully crude. Once we had you under our wing, we could have repaired your manners. Crafted you into a proper lady, not"—Cutty waved a dismissive hand at her—"whatever this trailer-trash road warrior is."

"I'm going to ignore that." Robin wanted to punch her, but the visual of her fist making contact with her erstwhile grandmother's face compressed her guts into a heavy wooden ball in her belly. Some random deadhead out in the Chicago projects was one thing, but this woman had sheltered and fed her for years.

"Indeed, ignorance is one of the many talents your mother passed down to you."

The wooden gut-ball splintered a little bit.

"You were trying to recruit me for your coven. You were trying to get me to give my heart to Ereshkigal so I would become indebted to you, my life-force and power would have become linked through your Matron, and you could hold dominion over me. Well, I've got news for you, chick—you know what a Matron is?"

"The oldest member of a coven. The matriarch and the love central to the survival of our people and our ways."

"No. A Matron is just the last surviving member of a dead coven. The queen bee of a dead hive. They're all failures. When you eradicate a coven except for one member, that member moves on to become the Matron of a new coven. They're all failures. You're all one long cycle of fuckups."

"I sure missed that sass," Cutty interrupted, with a sly smile. "Failing you was one of my biggest regrets."

"My mom scrambled my brains trying to keep me safe from you. What she did was wrong, but—" she started to say, but then, as quick as a camera-flash, Marilyn Cutty's face twisted into the most feral, frightening expression of rage she'd ever seen: teeth bared, nostrils flaring, brow furrowed, eyes impossibly wide. Goose bumps raced down Robin's arms.

"*You tricky little—*" snarled the witch.

The spotty gray cat had followed them out there and was sitting on Cutty's shoulder. Cutty reached up and snatched the animal down, holding it by the throat. Taking the cat's neck in both hands, she wrenched it violently in opposite directions with a sickening celery-like *crunch*.

"Holy shit," blurted Leon.

As if his brain had been unplugged, Wayne's father bonelessly sank to his knees and fell over.

Foam spittle bubbled between his lips. He writhed and thrashed on the grass like an earthworm, his eyes rolling back. Wayne ran to his father's side and tangled his fists in the man's shirt, screaming in confused horror. *He didn't put an* algiz *on himself*, thought Robin, as Marilyn Cutty flung the dead cat into the flower bed and stormed away, hitching up her skirts. *That skeptical idiot.*

"You," shouted Cutty in a frantic, staccato tone, pointing at Theresa LaQuices as she left, "kill the girl and come to the house. Hammer is there and he's trying to kill Mother with the Godsdagger."

Looks like the time for flattery and deal-making is over. Theresa turned and grinned at Robin. Her gums were jet-black, and now too were her eyes.

Throwing his son off, Leon scrambled up and hurtled into the vineyard after the witch, loping and capering, using his hands as much as his feet. The boy shouted after him and started to follow, but the frothing darkness in the spaces between the trellises cowed him and he hesitated, glancing at Robin for guidance.

"My covvy-sister Karen is good at illusions, you know," said Theresa. "And Marilyn's good at divination, manipulation. Brain stuff." She tapped her skull with a clawed finger. Theresa's breasts and thighs bulged and rolled under her peasant dress like a sack of potatoes as she paced around in front of Robin in a languid, confident way. "But do you know what *I'm* good at, girl?" Her head tilted as she said this, and at first it looked as if she were cracking her neck, but it was immediately obvious the muscles around her throat were thickening, tightening. "Alteration," she said, her voice going bell-deep, threaded with pain. "Transfiguration." Her elbows rose as if she were about to dance the funky chicken, but then her shoulders broadened, and her hands began to enlarge, and she stumbled and fell on her hands and knees. "Transformation."

Bones crackled thickly inside as if her skeleton were rearranging itself. Theresa's dress split up the back with a brittle *pop!* of white linen, revealing her shoulder blades and flabby, age-spotted flanks, and then her bra strap broke in half.

Vertebrae surfaced from the flesh behind her head, widening, standing up, becoming spines. The witch's head turned and bobby pins slipped out, her coal-black hair spilling free. Her jaw was lengthening, and she growled through a maniacal jackal grin. Her face was the gray, hairless bastard of a dozen beasts.

As the first drops of rain finally arrived, Robin fled.

11

Opening the bedroom door, Heinrich found himself face-to-face with a ghost. And then he didn't.

One second, a man floated in the hallway, in his underwear, with puke all over his shirt, his face all chalky and blown out. And then he was gone, *pop*, like a light switch. In his place was the Illusion witch.

The youngest member of the Blackfield coven ambled down the hallway with a satisfied cackle. "For a big army dude, that was easier than I thought it would be," Karen Weaver said, and she put on her shabby riverboat hat, tugging the brim low. Turning to Heinrich, she grinned, revealing black gums and mottled yellow teeth. "Now that I've gotten rid of your sidekick, let's you and me settle this like men."

"Cheap move," said the witch-hunter. Heinrich stepped out of the bedroom, fully preparing to clobber the witch with the gas can, and immediately took a haymaker to the face that staggered him against the doorframe. He slid down the wall, knocking down and breaking a picture.

The groundskeeper stood over him, the skinny ginger dude. He was lanky, but he had fists like bricks. "Wasn't you taught to knock before you waltz into somebody's shit?"

Before he could react, Ginger knelt and delivered another stunning blow to the old man's cheek. "You know breaking into somebody's house is illegal, yeah?" Punch. Lightbulbs exploded in Heinrich's brain. "I could kill you right now and there's not a jury in the world that would convict me." Shadows tried to converge on Heinrich's eyes, but he fought off unconsciousness just briefly enough to reach out and grab the ginger's sleeve. He thrust the Osdathregar into the man's forearm, lengthwise, as if he were gutting a fish.

"JESUS!" shrieked the ginger, jerking away. Fresh blood pattered on the hardwood underfoot as the blade slipped out of his arm.

Gotta get on my feet, or I'll be in a world of hurt. Heinrich rolled over onto his hands and knees. Some of his front teeth were loose. *Not that I ain't already.* Fingers of steel and leather closed on his throat and Weaver lifted him off the floor, slammed him against the wall. More pictures fell with a collective crash. Broken glass crunched under her boots. She pinned Heinrich against the tomato-red paint.

"You're stronger than you look," he gurgled.

"Spend a lot of time out in the woods," Weaver said through gritted teeth. "Back in the day, my first husband and I had a gold claim in California. We built our own cabin. You wouldn't—"

"Who gives a fuck about a cabin?" screamed the groundskeeper, clutching his arm. Crimson ran down his arm and pooled in the palm of his hand. "I'm bleedin' out, old woman!"

Irritation burned in the witch's eyes. "There, Roy, you idiot. It's fixed."

The groundskeeper inspected his arm. The dagger-wound was still filleted open in a three-inch laceration up his wrist. Blood ran in rivulets down his fingers. Whatever illusion Weaver had hexed him with seemed to make him think she'd put the Jesus voodoo on him and fixed his arm, because the expression on his face went from terror to surprise to relief.

"Oh, wow," he said, flexing his hand. "Thanks."

"Can't find good help these days," she said, and then Heinrich shanked her in the ribs with the Osdathregar.

Rip! The blade sank in all the way to the cross guard, punching through her rag-coat, the leather underneath, her shirt, and into the meat of her rotten belly. Her mouth fell open in a shocked grimace. She seized up and let go of him, backing away, hugging herself.

Back on his feet, Heinrich took the opportunity to stagger down the hallway toward the stairs. "Where d'you think you're going?" The ginger Roy had him by the coat. The witch-hunter spun on him.

A gun barrel pressed against Heinrich's forehead, cold and hard.

At the last instant, he looked away, and the gun went off next to his head with a deafening *POP*. A bullet hole appeared in the wall with a puff of sheetrock dust. Heinrich flinched in pain, grabbing his ear. The ginger tried to readjust his aim and attempt another shot, but Heinrich dropped the dagger, grabbing the gun.

This was the first step in a dance of death, "Roy" pulling the trigger—*POW*—as they did an awkward tango in the hallway, staggering around each other, Heinrich squeezing the trigger—*POW*—each trying to shoot the other with the same gun.

"Think the two of you could take this outside?" asked the witch. "I don't think Marilyn is goin' to appreciate you shootin' the place up."

"Thanks, asshole," grunted Roy. "I'm going to have to spackle and paint all this myself." Completely oblivious to the fact he was still injured, Roy was bleeding all over both of them. The pistol became more and more slippery, as if they were fighting over a bar of soap.

The pistol slid through Heinrich's wet fingers, the ginger almost fumbling it.

Lost the gun. I'm fucked.

Apparently, gaining the upper hand took Roy by surprise, because he paused mid-wrestle to glance at the pistol in his bloody fist, as if he'd forgotten how it worked, or perhaps he saw through the witch's hallucination and discovered much more blood than he expected to see.

For a few brief seconds, Heinrich found himself off guard as well. Both of them hesitated, staring at each other. *Make a move before he does.*

Do or die. Heinrich charged, Roy raised the gun.

First one to make contact was the witch-hunter, who clocked him square in the face with a right hook. Teeth against knuckles. Head snapped back. The ginger hit the floor on his ass.

Claws. The bang of bootheels. The witch, on his right.

Unarmed versus a pissed-off witch and a squirrelly Irish guy with a gun. No contest. In a growing panic, Heinrich ran for the stairs again, stumbling down them two and three at a time, nearly falling. He collided with a big plush La-Z-Boy at the bottom and darted across the living room, almost crawling.

POP! The television's screen shattered, inches from his head. He hurdled the couch. *POP!* Cotton batting geysered out of the upholstery as a bullet tore through it.

Footsteps thundering down the stairs behind him. Heinrich ran into the kitchen, kicked his way through the screen door, and ran out into the night. Rain dotted the tarmac driveway with blue polka dots. Too late, he realized he'd left the Osdathregar behind.

He was halfway down the dirt road, sprinting into darkness, when a bullet punched through his right calf.

"*UURGH!*" he cried, collapsing on his belly. Gravel bit into his knees and elbows.

Weeds to his right. The trailer park. The burning in his leg swelled until it was a red-hot iron rod in his muscle. Heinrich dragged himself toward the culvert and out of the road, already formulating plans in his head to hide among the shadows of the mobile homes, maybe crawl into the underpinning, pull out his cell, call Robin to come g—

Click.

The ginger stood at his elbow, the revolver's barrel gaping down at him. Roy pulled the trigger again. *Click.* He pressed that horrible black tunnel against Heinrich's smooth scalp, dripping warm blood on his cold skull.

Rain hushed the cicadas, hissing in the grass all around them. *Click.*

"You're lucky, you dumb piece of shit." The ginger opened the cylinder, sighed at the empty casings inside, and tipped it closed again. "You may not die tonight."

Moonlight danced on a silver blade, dripping rainwater from the tip. Weaver emerged from the shadows, wielding the abandoned Osdathregar. "Oh, trust me, dear man," she said, twirling her spoils between her fingers like a master knife-fighter, "when we're done with him, he's going to wish there'd been one more bullet in that gun." She crouched next to Heinrich as the cricket-song swelled over them from the trees, covering them in a burlap blanket of sound. "So, what the hell *was* that back there, hmm? I expected more from the ex-Dog that trained the mighty Malus Domestica." She poked him with the Osdathregar. "As a matter of fact, you fight pretty sorry. Was this your first go-round or what? Fess up, you're getting old, ain't—"

He spat blood in her face.

All over her face, from her hairline to her chin, a shotgun spray of red. Weaver didn't flinch. Didn't even close her eyes. What she did was take a handkerchief out of her pocket, un-wad it with a whip motion, and mop herself with it.

Stuffing the cloth into Heinrich's pocket, she put the tip of the dagger to his throat. "Does the little girl know she's been followin' some know-nothin' charlatan this entire time? I bet you been pullin' all that trainin' outta your ass, ain't you? Yeah, I been watchin' them videos of hers. Y'all been holed up somewhere, readin' stolen history books and doin' kung fu on each other like a couple of assholes. Hell, at this point, she's better than you've ever been. You ain't know shit, buddy. You and them Dogs you used to run with, you ain't know *shit*."

He said nothing, just lay on his back, trying not to scream or pass out from the pain in his leg.

"Why?" she asked. The witch's breath stank, a noxious skunk-and-roadkill mixture that made his head swim. "Why did you lie to her? Why did you build that girl up on horseshit and send her out to die? What was your master plan, man? Did you train her to be some kind of supernatural suicide bomber? Is that why she fights like that? What's so special about her?"

Before he could answer, a trumpeting roar the likes of which Heinrich had never heard in his life came from the vineyard behind the house. Sound filled the night with red prehistoric rage, prickled his skin with adrenaline. If he had to describe it, he thought he might go mad.

The witch glanced over her shoulder. "Sounds like your unfortunate little Girl Wonder is learning the hard way when we tell you to fuck off back to where you came from, you fuck off."

Horror drove him to kick away from the witch and try to wriggle off into the grass again, but she had him by the leg. Weaver dragged him back into the road and plunged the Osdathregar into his shoulder. Fire and ice drilled through his coat-sleeve, pierced muscle and bone, threatened to burst from his chest. He screamed, possibly the first time he'd ever screamed like that in his life, a full, shrieking wail that echoed in the valleys of the trailer park.

"You ain't goin' nowhere," she said, jerking the blade out of his body. He howled in agony and the stars in the sky tried to fade. His mind threatened to give up, to black out. "Don't pass out on me now. Sounds like the show's just startin'. You wouldn't wanna miss watchin' your little jihad come to a nasty end, would you?" She dragged him back toward the house as easily as if he were a sack of rocks.

In her other hand, the Osdathregar sang faintly as she walked, the fine, high-pitched whistle of a razor-sharp blade cutting the air. She laughed out loud, cackling. "Wait 'til Marilyn sees what the cat dragged in. No pinochle or Discovery Channel for us tonight. No, tonight, *you're* gonna be our pastime. I shore hope your schedule's clear."

12

"Go!" Robin bellowed. *"Run!"*

Wayne's eyes widened behind his torch-glared glasses, and he took off into the vineyard, following her.

Darkness and rain enclosed them. Silent heat lightning flickered across the clouds, affording her the occasional glimpse of the trellises blazing past. Wayne was running at full speed and she was pleasantly surprised to find he was not the asthmatic nerd of a thousand after-school specials, regardless of the BCGs ("Birth-Control Glasses," as they were called in the army, as Kenway might tell you).

No, that kid was *hauling ass.*

"Don't stop," she panted, clawing handfuls of air with each frantic step. Rain ran down her face, plastering her Mohawk to her scalp. "She'll kill you when she's done with me."

"My dad. What?"

"Familiar. Witch put a cat in him."

"A cat?" He glanced over his shoulder, losing a bit of ground.

"Tell you if we get out. Focus!" She jabbed a finger at the night ahead like a general. "Don't slow down!"

The ground shook, the grapevines rustled, and the night trembled with a growing rumble—the three-note gallop of the William Tell Overture: *boom-boom-boom, boom-boom-boom.* Something big was chasing them. She ran backward for a few steps, checking her six, but if there was anything back there in the dark, she couldn't see it, especially with the rain now falling in earnest and muddling her eyes with water that clung to her eyelashes.

Echoing from the vineyard to their left was a great noise of grinding and snuffling like an engine made of meat, and only after it had faded away did she understand it as beastly, inhuman laughter.

"What is—" Wayne began to ask, and the arbor trellises to Robin's left exploded as the thing that was Theresa LaQuices smashed through them.

Ivy whipped across the air and she smelled the sick syrup of mashed rotten grapes. Theresa kept going, crossing the row and crashing through the other side. *We're never going to outrun this monster.* Robin poured on a little more speed, snagging the hood on the kid's shirt. He skidded in the wet grass, with a yelp, and Robin pulled him through a gap between two of the vine lattices. She shoved him down in the grass, lying down next to him. "We can't outrun it," she told him. His breath came over her face in waves, redolent of steak. "We'll hide here, and sneak out when—"

Boom-boom-boom, CRASH! The trellis some thirty yards to the south went down in a tangle.

Whatever the witch had transformed into trampled across the grape arbor until it was halfway to merlot, and crossed several rows, smashing sidelong through the vineyard. Apparently, the coven didn't care about wine or grapes anymore, because she was giving it hell, tearing down fences left and right.

Lifting her head a bit, Robin peered up the row.

Heat lightning continued to whisper across the clouds, tracing blue sweat across the rainy shoulders of some mammoth creature, and Robin caught a flicker of pink, a glimpse of scimitars of bone jutting from the lips of a snot-slick muzzle. Theresa's black hair had become a mane of coarse wool bristles, and fat nipples jutted from a swinging belly.

Striations of cottage-cheese skin sagged down her naked ass like jagged granite. A picture of a crescent moon on her shoulder had been taffy-pulled into something like a yellow scythe-blade. She turned and scooped up air with the glistening nostrils of a boar. Theresa had become a giant amalgamation of boar and old woman, an abomination of varicose veins and stretched tattoos.

Robin swore and push-upped to her feet, pulling Wayne up with a pop of shirt-stitches and shoving him through a gap in the ivy into another row.

The three-beat gallop came at them and Theresa's tusks plowed up the trellis where they'd been hiding. The witch-hunter and the boy zigzagged across the vineyard, coursing down rows and cutting through gaps, wending and weaving back and forth. Suddenly, the trellises fell away and she found herself in an open space where a white gazebo waited in a garden. Pergolas made a cage of the arbors, grapevines hanging from their rafters in sweet, stinking curtains.

"Hide here," she gasped to Wayne, pointing him into the gazebo.

"Robin!" shouted a man's voice from the shadows.

Leaping the gazebo's banister, she ducked through a scrim of ivy and found Kenway. "The hell are you doing here?" she growled at him. "Shut up before it hear—"

He grabbed her shoulders and brushed her rain-soaked Mohawk out of her face, cupping her jaw in his big, warm hands. "Heinrich went into their house looking for the fourth witch. I ran down to my truck to get my gun, but I heard you hollering out here, so I—"

"I don't *need* saving!" Robin growled. "You shouldn't be out here!"

The trellis next to them erupted in a storm of leaves and wires and squealing hog-beast, throwing them both out from under the pergola. Robin hit the ground on her shoulders and skidded backward through the grass, her feet pedaling the sky. She rocked forward to her hands and knees.

Heat lightning flashed on an image buried in the foliage: a broad, pink-brown face the size of a car. Tiny black eyes glittered in leathery flab, and darkness fell over them again.

"You want me?" Robin bellowed. Blood ran down her neck from a cut on her temple where a wire had nicked her. *"Come get me!"*

"No!" shouted Kenway.

His voice came from somewhere to her left, on the other side of the gazebo. The razorback's enormous head swiveled in that direction, splintering one of the few posts still standing.

Inside Robin's jacket was a baby-food jar full of grain alcohol. She pulled it out and clutched it like a grenade. It wouldn't be much, but hopefully it would keep Theresa off of Kenway and Wayne long enough for her to figure out what to do. But without the Osdathregar, her options were severely limited.

"I'm over here!" She ran back into the vines and into the rain-soaked night.

Thump-thump-thump, the beast plunged through the trellis behind her and Robin hightailed it down the vineyard row, back toward the north, toward Annie's sacred grove. Theresa was so close, she could smell the boar's breath, feel the hot blast pushing at her hair. As she ran, Robin wrenched up the leg of her jeans, revealing a road flare pushed into the top of her combat boot. She pulled it out and turned to throw the jar, but Theresa was already on her. Something wet and hairy slammed into her belly and scooped her up; the world plummeted and then Robin was upside down some fifteen feet in the air, gazing at a dark maze.

Grass flew up and the horizon wheeled over her head, and the breath was driven out of her lungs as she hit the ground on her back.

Jar and flare both were knocked out of her hands, and she lay there, stunned, gasping for air. A callous moon laughed down at her through curtains of rain. Water pooled in the corners of her eyes.

This is it, she thought in fragments, *I've met my match.*

"I got you, baby," said Kenway, coming out of nowhere.

"Away," she grunted with spasming lungs. *Go away! Not your fight, stupid! This is my battle, goddammit! This is what I was born and bred for, don't you see? This is what I'm here for!*

Theresa had pulled a U-turn somewhere and came back, bearing down on them, shouldering through the vineworks. Kenway snatched up the jar, wound up like a Major League pitcher and fastballed it at the hog-witch's face.

Glass shattered across Theresa's snout, splashing her with alcohol. Robin smacked the end of the flare on the ground and it ignited with a flash, *SKSSSSSH!*, and a shower of red sparks.

She didn't have anything clever to say, so she just chucked it. The flare bounced off Theresa's monstrous face and the alcohol went up in an arc of dim blue light, sweeping up the bridge of her nose and into her hairline. The warthog shook her great face and tried to back away from the flames like a cat with a bag on its head.

Lifting her tusked snout to the sky, Theresa gave a trumpeting scream and galloped toward them.

Pop! Pop! Pop! Kenway brought his pistol up, he was firing at the flaming thing as it charged like a shrieking meat meteorite, *it's not working,* Robin thought, *nothing is working oh God,* and she crabbed away, still on her ass, but she couldn't get away in time. The meaty snout came down on top of her and drove her into the dirt, and then she was flattened against a seething, working mouth full of teeth, foul carrion breath washing over her.

Robin's hands pushed at snot-slimed lips. "Get off me!" she cried, punching the Theresa-thing in the nose.

More deafening gunshots. *Click click click.*

Wind gusted from nostrils big enough to jam her hands into, so she did. Reaching up Theresa's nose with both hands, Robin grabbed fistfuls of greasy hair and yanked it out by the roots.

"AAAAAWK!" howled the witch, recoiling in pain. It moved back enough to relieve Robin and she took a deep breath.

Kenway grasped the rims of the boar's nostrils and pushed, throwing all of his weight like a man pushing a car up a hill, trying to keep it off of her, but Theresa was too strong. She shrugged, shaking her boar-head, and he slipped loose, falling over the hoop of a tusk and stumbling by the wayside. The beast rushed at her again, opening its mouth, trying to bite her. Robin thrust out her hands. She managed to catch Theresa's nose, but her left hand skidded on mucus and slid into the boar's hot mouth.

Grinding, chopping incisors pierced Robin's forearm, tweezing the two ulna and radius bones together.

Pain unlike anything she'd ever known whipped through her system, ten thousand amps of agony along her elbow and up her arm, and she screamed in wordless horror. Hot blood squirted between those jagged yellow teeth as they rasped through the vessels in her wrist.

Theresa let go but only to gulp forward for higher purchase, biting down on Robin's upper arm, right below her shoulder.

She's eating me.

Taste buds bubbled under Robin's fingers at the back of the witch's throat.

She's eating me. SHE'S EATING ME.

Reaching toward the witch's beady black marble of an eye with her free right hand, she tried to claw at it, but it was too far away, three feet at least. She punched and punched and punched at the nose pressed against her chest, but it was like boxing a Volvo wallpapered with ham.

"Let go a' her!" snarled Kenway, and then he was working Theresa's warty cheek with both fists like Rocky Balboa, *whump-whump, whump-whump.* It simply snorted and stepped back, dragging Robin helplessly through the grass. The joint of her shoulder was a knot of torture, but it was nothing compared to her bicep. Muscle shredded and a vessel ripped open, pumping into Theresa's mouth.

When the witch laughed, she misted Robin with her own blood.

The behemoth warthog tossed its flaming head, lifting her to her feet, and the humerus bone in her upper arm broke with a hollow, singular, drumstick *SNAP!* over the fulcrum of its teeth. There was no pain at this point; her system was amped to hell and back by adrenaline, just a dull sense of *cutting, dividing.*

Again the thing that had been Theresa raised its head, rooting the girl into the air by her arm, and the skin and muscle ripped apart in fleshy strands of red and yellow curds.

Cartwheeling over two trellises, Robin landed upside down in a third as if she were a fly in a web. The arbor collapsed and she sank to the ground in a net of wire and grapevines.

As soon as she settled, she reached out to pull herself back up, but she couldn't get a grip on the wire. The instant she managed to struggle to a sitting position, her head swimming, it became abundantly clear why she couldn't grab anything.

Her left arm was completely gone.

She stared in disbelief at the ragged stump of her shoulder. Blood trickled out of the pulped gore.

There were no words she could call to mind, looking at this lie of reality, so her mind was simply a whirlpool of abstract perceptions. The remains of her left arm were something out of a horror movie, like a rubber special-effects prosthetic, leaking red-dyed Karo syrup, but it was all too real.

Blood soaked her shirt. Her stomach heaved, on the brink of vomiting. Her face felt ice-cold.

This was *real,* it was *really happening.*

Firelight flickered through the rain in front of her, and the gigantic witch-hog stepped into view. Theresa's mouth hung open, and Robin could see her arm lying inside on a yellow-purple tongue. A dagger of bone protruded from the sloppy stump. The hog tossed its head several times, swallowing the arm inch by inch like a crocodile swallows a fish, until one last gobbet of skin slipped through a gap in its teeth. Then it rumbled with self-satisfaction, thumping toward her.

Snot crept from the warthog's nostrils in cheesy strands. A few alcohol flames still licked around her eye sockets and the crown of her sweaty black mane.

Dark pulsed at the edges of Robin's eyes. She couldn't seem to catch her breath. Her body was as numb as a waxwork statue. She could hear rain falling, but she couldn't feel it on her skin. She raised her right hand to fend off the encroaching monster, though of course she had no delusions she could prevent another catastrophe.

This is it. I have officially messed up, Mom.

Wind tugged at Robin's hair, whistling into those cavernous nostrils. The behemoth overwhelmed her with bloody lips.

She reached out and grasped the rim of Theresa's snout as its mouth came open, revealing that bilious tongue and those disgusting teeth. Her own blood still stained the pebbled taste buds, still dripped from the boar's upper lip.

Restless air churned around the two of them, tousling Robin's Mohawk hair. This torrent wasn't coming from Theresa's nostrils—it came from nowhere and everywhere at once. Pins and needles swirled along her skin and deep inside, prickling up her arm in a helix of bright pain. Her right hand had fallen asleep somehow, still clutching the edge of the flabby pig-snout. No, wait, this wasn't what it felt like, it was *something else,* something strange. Alien light hummed from her fingers, tracing green radiation along her wrist, following the veins along the back of her hand toward her elbow. The bones were visible inside as murky shadows.

Something was coming out of Theresa and coursing up Robin's right arm, some kind of essence.

No, baby, a voice murmured faintly from the orchard.

The suggestion of a silhouette, half-obscured by vines and trellis. A spectral Annie Martine watched from the rows. *You ain't done. They ain't beat you. You're just takin' after your daddy now.*

The boar's flanks quivered and the beast trembled, trying to pull away, but Robin's fingers held it fast. She was a live wire, grounding the witch, but instead of electricity flowing through her, it was flowing *into* her, into Robin, draining the Stygian source where the witch's heart used to be. She could feel something withering inside of Theresa, healing over, closing up.

The libbu-harrani, *Theresa's heart-road to Ereshkigal.* The beast shook like a dog with a rope in its mouth, trying to break free, but Robin's right arm was an iron chain. *I'm sucking it out of her. I'm closing the door. She's diminishing.*

The hulking Grendel-hog was not so hulking anymore, now only as big as a horse. Heavy sheets of collagen drooped from Theresa's sides and thighs like raw dough, and her brown areolae dragged in the grass. She pulled and jerked, her cloven hooves shoveling humps of churned dirt, but to no avail.

Mom, I've lost too much blood. She looked for the spectre, but Annie was gone.

Her fingers were locked, a perfectly relentless clamp. The pergolas behind the boar were on fire, orange flames licking at a night sky, but she could feel unconsciousness lurking behind her temples.

Whatever this is, I don't know how much longer I can keep it up.

An old woman knelt on her hands and knees between the witch-hunter's legs like a midwife, as naked as the day is long, heaving and porcine and dark. The tip of Robin's thumb was still up Theresa's nose, as she still had the witch's nostril pinched in her fingers.

"My God," breathed the witch, her voice muffled. It was probably an epithet she hadn't uttered in a very, very long time.

"What—" Robin bared her teeth with effort, on the brink of passing out, going deaf from blood loss.

"*You're the demon's daughter,*" said Theresa, and then Kenway was by her side. He pressed the muzzle of the pistol to the witch's skull and pulled the trigger, barking silent fire.

As the storm raged, Robin slept.

13

Black ooze sprayed out of the entry wound, flecking his face and arms, as Kenway put a bullet into Theresa's head. Then he fired it again, for good measure. Fuck it. He pulled the trigger until the H&K's fresh magazine was empty and the slide stayed open. Shell casings littered the ground around him, and the night air hummed with the sharp smell of expended gunpowder.

Was it dead? He nudged the witch with the barrel of the pistol. His hands should have been shaking, but they weren't. His heart beat smooth and slow and hard, a steady blacksmith hammer in his neck. He didn't blink as his eyes traveled the horizon line, darting from shadow to shadow, tracking for hostiles. Something had reignited that part of him he thought gone to sleep that day in the sandbox. Kenway dropped the mag and another was in the well before the empty one hit the ground. He holstered the weapon and disengaged, and when he did, it felt like he'd dropped down out of some higher stratosphere into a vat of warm water.

And then when he turned and saw Robin sprawled out in a tangle of ivy, covered in blood, he dropped again—shot straight toward the center of the earth until he was in the deepest trench, the pressure of the ocean threatened to pulverize him, and the frigid water of panic tried to force its way into his mouth.

Her arm was ripped clean the fuck off, right below the shoulder. Blood dribbled out of the stump, a burst of crimson pulp in a sleeve of skin, and a slender shard of bone jutted out of the meat.

He immediately spun on his heel and threw up into the broken trellis. It took everything he had, every fiber of his being, every atom of his self-control, not to teleport back to Afghanistan, back into the past, to completely and utterly lose his shit and go off the rails.

"Mister!" screamed someone behind him.

He very nearly drew down on Wayne Parkin. The vet's hand actually went to his hip, his fingertips brushing the butt of his pistol.

The little boy was standing right behind him, his dark face lined with firelight from the flaming corpse in front of them. Kenway spat, clutched his knees, and spat again, the taste of bile corrosive in his mouth. "Yeah," he said, coughing, "Christ almighty, we gotta get her to the hospital." *Quit feeling sorry for yourself. This woman, this woman is changing you, changing your mind and changing your spirit and unlocking the door to your cell, she's lying there bleeding out and you feel like you "need a minute"?*

Get your ass in gear, Sergeant.

Kneeling next to her, Kenway unbuckled his belt and put it around the remains of Robin's bicep for a makeshift tourniquet, pulling it as tight as possible. Then he slipped his hands underneath her knees and back, lifting her out of the tangle of undergrowth, and he hustled toward the house. "Hey, Chicago boy," he said as they ran, his voice cracking, "you ever handled a gun?"

"You askin' me that 'cause I'm Black?" Wayne shouted at his back. "I'm a kid, man."

"Jesus, you know anything about 'em or not?"

Wayne jogged alongside him, the moon glinting on his glasses. He was plastered in mud from crawling around. "Uhh—well, I've played a lot of *Halo* and *Call of Duty*. Does that count?"

"No, damn. Damn damn damn." The hulking veteran paused to transfer Robin to his left shoulder, letting her unconscious form drape down his back. Then he drew with his right hand, moving through the dark vineyard with the pistol extended, trigger finger resting along the slide, ready to be fired in an instant. Blood soaked into his shirt. The girl was deadweight. The truck was more than five hundred meters away, at least, and he still hadn't gotten out of the garden yet. *MOVE YOUR ASS, SERGEANT,* he thought, the prosthetic ankle clanking precariously underneath him. *DO IT DO IT DO IT.*

"Is there anybody else we need to watch out for?" he gasped, wheezing, his breath billowing white.

The Lazenbury towered over the trellis rows, some quarter of a mile out. From the back, the Mexican-style house looked like a department store in the dark. *How the fuck did this vineyard get so big? It didn't look this big from the outside.*

"I don't think so," said Wayne. "The other two witches that were with us ran off to deal with that Heinrich guy. My dad went crazy and ran off with them. I don't know where he is."

The boy stopped short, shock and fear on his face.

"What?" asked Kenway, pausing only to turn, glance at him, and continue on. Robin draped over his shoulder, heavy for such a small woman. "Come on, we have to go."

"My dad is out here. Don't shoot him, please!"

"I won't." Kenway holstered the pistol and concentrated on running. The grass was wet with evening dew, which made for slippery footing, but somehow, he made it out of the vineyard, and the three of them burst from the trellis rows.

Crossing the backyard, around a table laden with dirty dishes. Rounding the side of the garage, running across the tarmac, crunching across the gravel. The powder-blue Chevy stood vigil in the darkness behind the house, and Kenway plowed into it hard, using it to stop himself with a *BANG!* in the stillness.

Pulling the door open, he pushed Robin into the passenger seat, then thrust an arm behind the seat-back and dug around for the medical kit he always kept back there. Beer can, empty rucksack, Frisbee—his hand fluttered across the smooth plastic of the emergency box. He dragged it out and opened it on the floorboard.

The tourniquet was on the bottom, under the rest of the bullshit. He opened the webbing cuff as wide as it would go and gingerly slipped it under Robin's severed shoulder, just above the belt, then started twisting the plastic rod. Cords inside the cuff drew taut until they bit into the flesh of Robin's upper arm, compressing it, choking off the blood flow. He twisted it as tightly as he dared to turn it, then used two Velcro straps to hold the rod in place.

"I got you, baby," Kenway gasped to her, out of breath.

He tossed his belt into the cab of the truck, slammed the door, and threw himself into the driver's seat.

To his credit, Wayne clambered up the rear quarter panel and flung himself into the bed of the truck without having to be directed. Kenway floored it, shredding gravel all over the garage, and rocketed down the dirt driveway.

Halfway down, someone else was coming up. Headlights bounced and wobbled along the ragged road, filling the Chevy's cab with halogen light. He squinted, blowing past into darkness, and the other car—looked like a Suburban—swerved out of the way, driving into the ditch and deep grass.

As the Chevy reached the bottom of the driveway, he checked his mirror. The Suburban turned around, the headlights sweeping across the front of the Lazenbury. "Who is *that*?" he said to himself, turning off onto Underwood Road.

Tires squealed underneath them as he gunned it onto clear asphalt, fishtailing the ancient Chevy, missing Cutty's mailbox by a hair. *Who gives a shit. We'll worry about that later. Right now, we have more urgent things to worry about.*

As he drove, his eyes kept darting over to the girl sitting next to him, who had become a gray, ash-faced phantom in the soft dashboard lights, mottled with blood and dirt, her Mohawk plastered flat against her scalp. Robin's mouth hung open, and her dark-circled eyes were thin slits through which he could see nothing but white.

She looks fuckin' dead she looks fuckin' dead was all that ran through his vibrating brain.

His mouth was as dry as a bone, his hands felt greasy. His skeleton was lightning. He blew through every stop sign and red light he came across, shooting through town like Chuck Yeager on a rocket sled. Caught air a few times. It was a miracle no cops came howling out of hiding to bust him for speeding; honestly, though, would he have stopped for them? Hell, no. Negative, Ghost Rider. They would have to chase him all the way to the hospital.

Giant words blazed neon red in the dark: EMERGENCY ROOM.

The Chevy shrieked into a fifteen-foot hockey stop in front of Blackfield Medical's ER entrance, almost slamming into a parked ambulance. The boy in the back fell with a hollow *thud.*

Pulling the parking brake so hard it nearly tore out of the floor, Kenway scrambled out of the driver's seat and the pistol fell into the floorboard with a *clunk,* forgotten. He ran around to the passenger side and opened it. Robin was slumped against the door and her limp body fell out as soon as he saw her. Kenway caught her

(god there's so much blood)

and pulled her out, dragged her into his arms again, holding her close, the tourniquet rod digging into his side,

(I got you baby I got you)

and he lifted her, ran into the ER.

Just before the automatic door slid open, he caught a glimpse of himself in the Plexiglas. His face was smeared with her blood, his beard had soaked it up like a sponge, his shirt was red with it.

People sat in rows of chairs in a waiting area, morose faces, news on TV. Swinging doors led into other rooms. Gurneys lined one wall, collapsed down like cots. An L-shaped counter spanned the back of the room, and behind it sat several women and one man, all of them dressed in green scrubs.

One of the women looked up from what she was doing, and her eyes went wide.

"Sir?" someone said to his right.

Where to go? Where to go? Where was he going? He marched into the middle of the room, arms loaded full of mangled human being, and wailed, "Help! Somebody fucking help me! *HELP!*"

Nurses and paramedics converged on him like a flock of birds. "Get her onto this gurney," they were saying, "what the hell happened," they were saying, "bring her over here," and they were barking orders at each other, medical terms Kenway might have recognized if he hadn't been jazzed out of his damned mind. He'd been cool as a cucumber right up until the moment he turned and saw Robin sprawled out in the ivy, lifeblood gushing out of her.

"Car crash," Wayne told them, breathless.

They took her from him, put an oxygen mask on her face, wheeled her through a door, and she was gone.

Of all the times, of all the places, Kenway's cellphone rang. He stood there in the middle of the emergency room, shaking like a cold Chihuahua, watching the door they'd carried Robin through, ignoring it. He realized he was crying.

"Hey, mister," said Wayne. The vet looked at him. "Your cellphone is ringing."

He took it out and checked the screen. Unknown number. He keyed the green button and put it to his ear, wandering through the waiting area. "Yeah? I don't know who this is, but can it wait?" He stifled a sob. "This is probably the worst possible time."

"Joel's been shot. I need your help."

"What? *Somebody shot Joel?*" Kenway paused. "Who is this?"

"It's his brother Fisher. I've got him at my comic shop. You're a combat medic, aren't you? You said you were. Can you help?"

"I was, yeah. Why didn't you take him to the hospital?"

A sigh on the line. "Because it was a cop that shot him. And then he shot the cop. Fuckin' blew him into a swimming pool with Mama's duck gun. We're afraid if we take him to the hospital, it's gonna get back to the cops and they're gonna try again."

"*What?* Why?"

"He says the serial killer that strung him up in the garage at Weaver's Wonderland is in cahoots with the cops—might even be a cop himself—and I guess some dude came to silence him because he made his statement to the department."

"Shit. Well. Goddamn, when it rains, it pours, don't it?" Kenway combed his fingers through his rain-soaked hair and gave a shaky sigh. "I can't really get away, man. I'm actually here at the hospital with Robin and Leon Parkin's kid. Robin got hurt, like, fuck, *real* bad. The w—" He almost said *witches,* but after what Joel had said about his brother's skeptical behavior concerning their mother's paranoia, he wasn't sure if mentioning them was wise.

"The what?" asked Fish.

"Nothing. It's nothing."

As he considered it, he noticed the aforementioned kid standing there, looking up at him with a sympathy well beyond his years. Wayne saluted awkwardly. "I've been taking care of my dad for a while now," he said. "If anyone's qualified to stay here, it's me. You go take care of Joel. He needs you."

"You sure?" He hated to leave a child by himself, even in a hospital.

"Hey," said Wayne, "if people can leave babies at hospitals, you can leave a kid that's almost a teenager. I'll be fine. You do what you need to do, okay? I been by myself before. Lots of times."

Reluctantly, Kenway told Fish, "Send your girlfriend Marissa up here to the hospital to watch Wayne and I'll come down to the comic shop."

"She works there, actually. She's a doctor, remember? She's been on shift for the last three hours."

"Hey, kid," he said to Wayne, "you got a phone?"

"Yeah." Wayne took it out of his pocket. It was an older phone, with one of the slide-out keyboards. Not quite powerful or new enough to browse the web, but enough to text.

"Be there in a minute," Kenway said to Fish, and he hung up his phone, jamming it into his pocket. "Hang out here in the ER waiting room, okay? Fish's girlfriend is gonna come out here and check on you. She works here, she's a doctor. Name's Marissa. Keep that phone on you in case."

"In case of what?"

"Shit, I don't know. In case one of us wants to find you." He took Wayne's phone and added Fisher's and his own numbers to the kid's address book.

"Okay."

"Text me, keep me in the loop."

"Okay."

Out in the ambulance parking, Kenway jumped into his truck, slammed it into gear, and roared away from the hospital.

Funny, he didn't feel quite as terrified as he had a few moments before. The panic and helplessness had burned away, leaving only a sensation of purpose. Regardless of the circumstances, it felt good to burn the candle at both ends again. People needed him again. He wasn't some asshole with a studio apartment full of shoe-gazey paintings in the middle of nowhere. He was Sergeant Griffin again. He was *necessary* again.

Hopefully, he thought as he blazed down the road into the heart of Blackfield, *Robin's still got a candle to burn.* The H&K 45 pistol lay on the floor behind his heels, slowly vibrating out of sight.

14

When Joel awoke, there was a silhouette standing in the doorway. Officer Bowker, aiming a pistol at his face.

"Jesus God!" he shrieked, scrambling backward and off the end of the futon, tumbling to the floor. A rusty sawband of hot pain raked across his thigh. "Don't shoot me! Don't—"

"Hey-hey-*hey*. Hey." Bowker turned a switch—*click click*—and a lamp filled the room with a soft glow. It wasn't the deputy at all, it was his brother Fisher, and he was holding out a cup of coffee, not a Glock. "It's all right, man! You're all right! It's me."

The walls of the cramped room were lined with bookshelves, and the shelves were full of hundreds of VHS tapes: all the best and most obscure horror and fantasy movies of the last forty or fifty years. Nestled into a space between the shelves was an old Magnavox television/VCR. A bundle of clothes lay on the end table (a shirt and a pair of jeans, both folded as meticulously as a display in a clothing store) and the bedazzled baseball bat leaned against the end of the futon.

Gauze was wrapped around his thigh in a thick band, affixed with a pair of tiny aluminum clips. Clean, but he didn't know if that was because it was fresh or because he wasn't bleeding too heavily. The stinging agony went bone-deep, as if he'd been shot with a nailgun and the nail

(AIN'T NO WAY OUT OF THERE, PIZZA-MAN)

was still in embedded in the muscle. Joel squinched his eyes until he could banish the mental flash of the Serpent shooting nails through the garage door.

(BLOOD FOR THE GARDEN)

Hangover pain ran laps around the inside of his head, the scratches on his chest were still sore, and his entire body was stiff and achy, but none of it could hope to compete with the gunshot wound in his leg. His hands shook too bad to hold a cup of coffee. "Put it over here, I'll get to it."

Fish left the coffee next to the folded clothes and sat by his brother. "How's your leg feel?" he asked, handing Joel a couple of pills.

Extra-strength Tylenol. It wasn't much, but it would have to do until he could get back to the stash at Mama's house. He dry-swallowed the Tylenol one at a time. His mouth tasted like he'd been helping himself to a litter box.

"Hurts."

"I bet. Luckily, it was just a graze. Cut a hole in the outside of your leg about the size of a quarter, but that's all. Coulda been worse. At least he didn't hit an artery or clip the bone."

Underneath the gauze was about twenty stitches. The night before was a haze of alcohol and pain, only broken up by memories of running from the police lieutenant and hiding in the park like a wino, finishing off a blood-slick bottle of Thunderbird. Fisher had picked him up on the back of his motorcycle, one of those sleek Japanese deals in cranberry red, and spirited him away. He vaguely remembered refusing to be taken to the hospital.

"Who stitched me up?"

A huge shadow stepped into the doorway with a metallic *clunk*. "Sounds like the patient is awake."

"Kenway?"

"Yeah." To his credit, the big vet had shown up with bells on. He was also about six feet tall and, fake leg or not, nearly sturdy enough to arm-wrestle a grizzly bear. Along with Fish, the veteran was plenty of muscle to hold down a struggling drunk with a wounded leg.

"How you feeling?" he asked.

"Like I been shot in the leg and like I *need* to be shot in the head," Joel said testily. God-rays of morning sunlight shifting through the doorway around Kenway's frame were sending glass shards into his brain. After his initial snap was met with silence, he added, ". . . Sorry. I'm just a little beat-up. Thank you for patchin' me up."

"Anything for my friends."

"'Beat-up' is putting it lightly," said Fish.

Stepping into the room, Kenway sat on a milk crate with a creak of plastic. He rubbed his face with both hands, visibly exhausted. Looked like shit, to be honest. Looked like he hadn't slept. "You said a *cop* shot you?"

"Yeah. Said somebody called 'the Serpent' was supposed to have finished me off. Cop said they're all workin' together. Said Marilyn Cutty owns this town." Joel tilted his head back and slumped down, pressing a palm against his eyes. Geometric shapes flashed behind his eyelids. "I'm guessin' this 'Serpent' guy is the dude I met on the internet Friday night."

"A booty call." Fish sighed. "You got to quit cattin' around like this. You gonna end up with something they don't make vaccines for."

"I got rubbers."

"Always what you say, ain't it? A raincoat ain't gonna keep you dry forever. Besides, you came within a hair of getting yourself killed by some looney-tune cracker with a knife."

"Livin' on bacon and cauliflower ain't gonna make *you* immortal, either. You can't jog your ass away from Death, he don't care how much you can deadlift." Joel picked up his coffee and cradled it under his chin. "Complex carbohydrates ain't what drove Mama crazy and pushed her into the grave, you know. They ain't gon' kill you, either."

Shaking his head, Fish walked out. A radio in the shop came on, obnoxiously loud, tuned to some local station in the middle of their drive-to-work morning chitchat. It snarled through a dozen stations before landing on classic rock. Guns N' Roses wasn't Fish's forte, but this was how his brother dealt with turbulent conversations between the two of them: blocking it out with music. Any kind, it didn't matter, as long as it was loud. *This is probably why we ain't never fixed nothing,* thought Joel. *He storms off into his bedroom and plays Kanye at top volume, and I go find something to smoke or drink.* Kenway quietly watched him drink his coffee, his hulking body hunched over with his elbows on his knees and his hands slowly wringing each other.

"You gonna give me the After-School Special too?"

Kenway briefly opened his hands in a sort of awkward, blameless shrug. "I'm just glad to see you doing okay."

"What are you doing today, anyway? We didn't pull you away from hangin' out with that little witch-hunter with the perky ass, did we?"

"She's in the hospital."

Joel twitched in surprise. "What happened?"

"She went and had dinner with the witches. They tried to make dinner out of her. One of 'em turned into a giant hog and bit her goddamn arm off." Kenway rubbed the back of his neck, staring at the floor with that thousand-yard stare.

"Like, what the *fuck*?"

"Yeah."

"She gonna make it?"

The vet shrugged. "I don't know. I hope so. I called a couple hours ago. The doctors seem hopeful. She's stable. She lost a lot of blood, and I did what I could. I drove her myself."

"Jesus Christ." Joel sipped his coffee. Black, only sweet enough to take the bitter edge off. Hot enough to fog up his eyeballs. Oily. Vaguely salty. He sighed. "He put butter in my damn coffee."

"Gross."

"Yeah." Joel stared at the cup, grinding his incisors together. "The cop came to my house. He knows where I live. I can't go back there to lock up. They're gonna leave my doors wide-ass open and I ain't gonna have nothin' left . . . if I can ever even go back."

"I'm sure it'll be okay. I don't imagine the cops would leave your front door unlocked."

"I didn't imagine they'd show up out of the blue and try to shoot me, either." Setting his coffee aside, Joel wallowed his butt out to the edge of the futon and braced himself on the armrest, trying to stand up. He hissed as the imaginary nail in his leg drove a little deeper.

"Take it easy," said Kenway. "I don't want to have to take somebody else to the hospital this weekend."

"Take it easy and give it hard, that's how I roll."

He put the clothes on, starting with the shirt. The jeans were a little harder. Every inch of denim drove the rusty nail in his thigh a centimeter deeper. "Damn. He said this hole in my leg was the size of a quarter. The French Quarter, maybe." He blew through pursed lips and opened the door at the end of the couch, limping through. On the other side was a narrow stairway leading up to Fisher's apartment over the comic shop. He put his good foot on the first riser and steeled himself for the climb.

Taking a deep breath, he picked up his right foot and put it on the second riser. His thigh flexed, pulling at his stitches, grinding the denim against the bandage. Sharp, hot pain swelled in the muscle as if there were a lit cigarette trapped under the gauze.

Twelve steps to go. "God help me."

Halfway up, he had developed a system; he leaned to his left, bracing himself against the banister screwed to the wall, and lifted himself with his left leg, holding his right out stiff to the side. Instead of stepping up with it, he humped it up on the left. By the time he had reached the top, his left thigh was on fire and sweat was running down his temples. He stood at the top of the stairs to survey Fish's apartment.

Superhero posters hung at tasteful intervals—*Avengers, Hulk,* and *Spider-Man* movie promotionals, artsy minimalist pieces, and comic-book panels so big the individual colors pointillized into sprays of primary-color dots and bold fronds of sharp white lettering. *BOOM! BANG! POW!*

A large flatscreen television stood on a low-slung entertainment center with a small collection of video-game consoles. No sofa. Nowhere to sit, really, except for a beanbag chair right in front of the TV. The only other piece of furniture in the room was a tread-mill on the opposite side of the room, but it faced the wall, running up under a computer desk with a MacBook on it. It was a standing desk; the woodgrain surface came up to Joel's chest, standing on a sturdy telescoping frame.

He hadn't been up there since his brother had bought the place, he realized with shame. Really ought to visit more often, and not under duress like this.

The kitchen was a spartan nook on the other side of a Formica breakfast bar, everything done up in 1960s greens and whites. A window above the sink overlooked Broad Avenue, the daylight shooting razorblades into his eyes. He went to the fridge, drank straight out of a carton of orange juice to wash the taste of sleep out of his mouth, then went into the bathroom to piss.

Something darted into the bathroom while he was standing in

front of the toilet. Fisher's cat, Selina, meowed, curling around his ankle.

"What up, cat."

He flushed, washed his hands, took another few swigs from the orange juice in the fridge, and flopped down in the beanbag chair to rest. A long, groaning sigh rolled out of him and he wiggled himself deeper into the Styrofoam peanuts.

A remote control lay on the floor next to the beanbag. He aimed it at the TV and pressed the Power button, but the TV didn't come on. Instead, the treadmill behind him growled to life and slowly climbed to jogging speed.

Perplexed, he got up and searched the desk. A control panel that looked like something from a Houston space terminal was mounted to the back of the desktop. He stopped the treadmill.

Selina jumped up onto the entertainment center as he limped over to the TV and turned it on with the power button. The eight o' clock morning news filled the screen with the pitted high-def face of an anchorman, and the cat sat in front of it, stretching luxuriously and throwing out one leg so she could sit and run her tongue down her haunch.

"Well." Joel scowled. "I didn't wanna see the screen anyway."

A shiver passed through the cat, some weird shudder rolling up her back. Selina hunkered down, her eyes darting around the room as if she'd heard a mouse behind the baseboards, but she didn't get down and start hunting. Then she stiffened, sitting pretty as if she'd suddenly remembered where she was, and proceeded to glare daggers at Joel's face. The anchorman talked into the cat's back, her tail curling back and forth under his nose. "Sources say that the driver was not intoxicated, but a police investigation is still ongoing in this case. We'll return to this to give you details as they emerge."

Joel sat back down in the beanbag and stared right back at the cat. "The hell *you* looking at?"

Selina meowed.

"Get down. Boo. Giddown. Hiss."

The cat scowled at him, if such a thing was possible.

Since the cat had decided to park her hairy ass in front of the TV, Joel occupied himself by looking at the buttons on the tread-mill remote. There were a hell of a lot of buttons for a machine that did precisely one thing. It was almost as intricate as the TV remote, with buttons for speed and incline, as well as a tiny LCD screen with a line graph for peaks and valleys and a menu for running different types of cardio sessions. *I'll have to come back up here and see if Fish'll let me use his treadmill. It'd be cheaper than the gym, that's for sure.* He turned the treadmill back on and revved it up as high as it would go. The sheet of texturized rubber scrolled across the plat-form with a high, whining burr. *Damn. You fall on that and it's all over for yo ass.* He pressed the Power button, which stopped the belt.

Selina padded into the kitchen and leapt up onto the counter. She found a light switch on the wall by the microwave and pawed at it.

"Eww, hey, get down," Joel called from the living room. He hated when cats got on kitchen counters. They kicked around in their litter boxes, shoveling up sand and shit with their paws, and the thought of preparing food on Fish's counters where the cat was walking around with her shitty feet sent a chill down Joel's spine.

"What you doin', cat?"

She managed to flip the light switch and the sink growled loudly. She'd activated the garbage disposal. Joel stretched to look over the bar, struggled up out of the beanbag chair and stood up.

Just in time to see the cat slink under the faucet and shove her own face into the sink drain.

GGRRRRRRROOOOOWWNT!

Blood sprayed up out of the sink, spattering a fine mist across the kitchen ceiling.

A shock of amazed adrenaline whipped through Joel's body.

The grinder inside the garbage disposal bogged down like a

truck in deep mud, snarling low as it chewed Selina's skull into pulp. The cat went apeshit, flailing around, spinning, beating herself against the inside of the basin, making that scribbly-fussy Donald Duck quacking sound.

Snapping out of his startled trance, Joel ran into the kitchen nook (almost slipping on blood) and turned off the disposal.

He stood there in a stunned silence, his hands laced on top of his head.

Eventually, he found the power of speech again. "What the actual fuck. Jesus Christ, what the hell just happened," and then the logical conclusion was "Fish is going to *kill* me."

Joel pushed the treadmill remote into his pocket and picked up Selina's limp, headless body by the tail. He scanned the nook, looking for the garbage. It was in a tall cabinet in the corner. He put the dead cat in the bin. Then he felt terrible putting the cat in the garbage, but it was making a hell of a mess, so he dug a fresh bag out of a bag under the sink and put the cat in that.

"Why did you do that, cat?" Joel asked the garbage bag in an accusing, astonished hiss, shaking it. "Why did you *do* that?"

Clenching and unclenching his fists, he stood at the sink shaking in excited fright, his eyes alternating between the window in front of him and the sink full of blood. He ran the water and used the sprayer hose to knock most of it down into the drain, but there were clumps of hair and . . . *gristle* stuck in the toothed rubber gasket that kept silverware out of the grinder.

Silverware, but not cats.

A drop of blood fell off the ceiling and tapped the counter. Joel hobbled into the bathroom to vomit. It was a good puke, a projectile gush hard enough to make his thigh throb. Day-Glo green and stank of Thunderbird and orange juice. *Blue and yellow make green Ziploc seal.* He spat and flushed the toilet, lingering over the bowl, hunched forward with his hands on his knees. *Why in the name of God did I just see a house cat commit suicide?* He took a dirty towel out of the hamper and wiped the blood off his head and shaking hands with it. A crazy idea came out of left field: *she coulda come to me, I would've talked her down, come on, cat, you got so much to live for,* and he barked out crazed, disbelieving laughter.

Bloody footprints led into the bathroom, ground into the carpet and plastered on the linoleum.

"Ah, damn." Joel wet the towel and lowered himself onto his hands and knees with a grunt of pain, using the towel to scrub at the red prints. "Jesus. Jesus, I don't know what I done, but I need you to give me a break now. I'mma need you to gimme the wheel back and let me drive for a minute."

When the toilet finally finished refilling itself with a noisy sigh, Joel heard voices through the vent under the sink. The radio in the shop had stopped.

Fish. "No, I haven't seen him all day."

Light glimmering on the ceiling caught his attention and his head tilted back. Joel sat on his haunches, shooting straight up like a meerkat.

"Are you sure?"

The frenetic blue flashers of a police car were strobing through the bathroom window. He got up and stood on the edge of the bathtub, looking through the casement window behind the shower, his heart thumping. For three insane seconds, he was convinced the law had come to arrest him for killing Fish's cat, and then the reality of the night before came crashing down around him.

A Blackfield City Police cruiser was parked in the diagonal slot-parking in front of the comic shop.

Bowker had found him.

"Yeah, not a peep." Fish's voice wafted up from the heat register. "I talked to him last night on the phone . . . sounded like he'd been drinking. He's probably still passed out at his mama's house. What did he do?"

Joel very nearly pissed his pants. He briefly thought about going back to scrubbing the blood off the floor, but decided to close the door and hide in the bathroom. He threw the bloody towel in the hamper and pressed his back against the wall. "You got to be kidding me," he murmured to himself, eyeballing the ceiling for guidance. "How did this Rosco P. Coltrane–lookin' motherfucker find me?"

"We been to his house," said the other voice. It was familiar, but it didn't sound like Bowker. *Where have I heard that voice before?* "He ain't there, sir. This is the next logical place to look."

How did they know he and Fish were brothers? *I mean, there's the fact we both got the same last name, but come on, lots of people have the same last name.* It was quite a jump of logic, even for Joel's paranoid state of mind. *Maybe they talked to Miguel. That's it. Oh, I gotta have a talk with him . . . if I get out of here in one piece.*

"I hate to have to tell ya, but you're wasting your time. He and me, we're kinda on the outs these days. You know . . . family stuff. He hasn't been here in months. Are you going to answer my question? What did my brother do?"

The police officer grunted. "Family stuff. Yeah, I can understand that. Well, last night, your brother assaulted a police officer. Put a load of buckshot in his vest, almost killed him. *Tried* to kill him."

Kenway. "That doesn't sound like the Joel I know."

"Maybe you don't know your brother as well as you think you do." The officer paused for a beat and said, ". . . So, what are *you* doing here? According to the hours of business up there on the door, it don't look like the shop's open yet. But here *you* are."

"I come down here to hang out every weekend and most evenings," said Kenway. "It gets awful quiet at my place when it's nobody but me."

"Today's Sunday. You don't go to church?"

"I'm not really a churchgoing man, Mr. Euchiss."

Euchiss . . . Euchiss . . . Joel tried to place the name. It wasn't one he'd heard before. "That's a surprise, down here in the South," said the cop. "You don't believe in God?"

"Honestly, that is a can of worms I'd rather not open this early in the morning."

"So, what d'you do?"

"I'm a sign-maker and a painter."

"Ah . . . . Well! You there, you must be the proprietor of this fine establishment. D'you mind if I take a look around?"

"Don't you need a search warrant for that?" asked Fisher.

"Not if I have probable cause. Do I *have* probable cause?"

Fish hesitated a little too long. ". . . No."

"Your lips are saying *no*, but your eyes are saying *yes*." Euchiss started toward the back of the comic shop. "Other officers may not appreciate pushback, but you know what? I *like* a challenge. Victory is so much sweeter if you've had to fight for it."

"Adapt and overcome," said Fish, repeating his life mantra.

"I like that. Mind if I borrow it?"

"Go right ahead."

"This shouldn't take long. I'm sure I don't need an escort. You two can hang out here. I'll be right back."

"I'm pretty sure you need a warrant," said Kenway.

"I'm pretty sure you need to shut your mouth."

A half-minute later, Euchiss's voice came from the bottom of the stairs. Before his arduous climb, Joel had forgotten to close the stairwell door. *Dammit.* "Looks like somebody's been sitting in here, sippin' on a cup of coffee. There's a blanket in here too. Whoever it was, they was sleepin' on the futon."

"Somebody ate my porridge," said the baby bear.

Fish said, "The heat works best in that little back room, so I like to sit in there with my blanket and watch the news when I get up."

"I hope you don't mind if I don't take your word on that, Mr. Ellis." Euchiss chuckled. The thumping of shoes on the stairs told Joel the cop was coming up. He got back down on his hands and knees and looked under the door as a head and shoulders rose up from behind the banister.

What he saw trailed fingers of ice down his spine. That same shock of red hair . . . that narrow, corded neck and arrowhead jawline . . . those beady black eyes.

It was B1GR3D. Red was a cop.

15

Ain't no way out of there, pizza-man. "Oh lord, oh heavenly God," Joel whispered under his breath, his face pressed against the blood-smeared tiles. His heart was going Mach 3. He could feel it in his neck and hands. "You got to be shitting me."

(call me the Serpent)

Euchiss paused at the top of the stairs. "What in *all* the hell happened up here?"

(that's what the papers back in New York used to call me)

"What?" called Fish.

"Is this *your* mess, Mr. Ellis?"

"Mess? What are you talking about?"

The cop stepped cautiously into the kitchen nook. "There's blood and hair all over the kitchen, man! It looks like somebody tried to mulch a raccoon in the garbage disposal."

Fish charged into the apartment, thundering up the stairs and into the living room.

"What the hell?"

"That's what *I'm* sayin', Mr. Ellis. You might want to work on your taxidermy skills if you're gonna—"

Euchiss went silent. Joel's heart thumped hard like the 1812 Overture, throbbing in his temples. Cautiously, the cop crossed the room, and Joel heard the soft plastic slurp of vinyl against gunmetal. *The footprints on the carpet. The footprints leading into the bathroom. He saw them.* "I know you're in there, buddy," said the cop. Standing directly across from the bathroom door. "You might as well come on out. There ain't nowhere for you to go."

"Joel!" squawked Fish. He was shouting, raw-voiced, on the verge of tears. *"Why you kill my cat? The hell is wrong with you?"*

Reluctant at first to let Red/Euchiss hear his voice, Joel hesitated, his hands floating up alongside his face out of pure instinct. "—*I didn't*, I didn't do that! The cat did it! I was sittin' in the beanbag, watchin' TV when—"

"You tryna tell me Selina turned the garbage disposal on all by herself? And stuck her own head in it?"

"Y-yeah!"

"Do you understand how fucking crazy that sounds?"

"Yeah." Joel's throat burned with fear and guilt. Everything seemed unreal, glossy and false, like the bathroom's tiles were going to break off and go spinning into a black void, leaving him adrift in a cosmos of lies.

"You need to come on out of there," said Euchiss. "Don't make me open that door myself. You ain't gonna like it when I do."

On his hands and knees again, Joel peeked under the door. The stitches in his leg pulled painfully, the agony blunted by the Tylenol. Directly in front of the bathroom was the treadmill, some six or seven feet away. Euchiss had stepped up onto it—to provide better footing than the carpet, to give Joel room to come out of the bathroom, to give himself distance to fire his pistol, Joel didn't know . . . but it gave him an idea. He took the treadmill remote out of his pocket and got up on one knee, grasping the doorknob.

Aiming the remote under the door, he screwed up his nerve and pressed the Start button.

Zerp! The treadmill belt, already turned up as high as it would go, whipped the cop's feet out from under him. Joel flung open the bathroom door to see Euchiss's head smack against the edge of the desk.

Bursting out of the bathroom, Joel leapt the treadmill, vaulted the banister and landed halfway down the stairs, popping a couple of stitches. Hellfire raced up his leg, but he ignored it, jumping again straight down to the bottom and darting through the open door. Juked to the right to get out of the videotape room. Sprinted across the comic shop toward daylight.

Lieutenant Bowker turned around in surprise, reaching up to pinch the cigarette in his mouth.

Joel froze, his heart dropping into his stomach.

"Good morning!" the officer said cheerfully, throwing down the Marlboro butt and shoving him in one fluid motion, bouncing his head off the doorframe. Lightning flashed behind Joel's eyes and then he was facedown on the sidewalk, rough grit sandpapering his naked chest. "Nice to see you again, boy." Bowker wrenched his arms up behind his back, zip-tying his wrists together. The officer turned him on his side and allowed him to get his feet underneath him. "You thought you was gonna get away?"

Sunshine cut the brisk October air like a hot knife, turning the cement into a griddle. The pain in his thigh was extravagant, bright as a cattle-brand, and it eclipsed the world.

Looking up and down the street, Joel saw a few people on the sidewalk stop to rubberneck. Of course, they were all white. "Go ahead and look, assholes," he said under his breath. "Look at me in these cuffs. You like it, don't you?" Salt tainted his mouth and he licked at it, found blood from a busted lip. Twisting, he tried to stomp Bowker's knee, but the cop threw his ass out like a cabaret dancer, scooting out of range.

"Help!" Joel shouted into the morning stillness, trying to wrest his arm away. "They're gonna kill me! *Help me!*"

"Ain't nobody gonna kill you, y'idiot," growled Bowker, hauling the back door of the police cruiser open and bundling Joel inside. To his relief, the lieutenant didn't bang his head on the roof on the way in.

"Help!" Joel shrieked, and Bowker slammed the door in his face.

He was on his side. He wallowed and kicked to a sitting position and pressed his forehead to the window so he could see Fisher and Kenway come out of the comic shop, the tall veteran supporting, almost dragging Euchiss. Next to Kenway, the policeman looked like a little boy. Euchiss sat down on the exterior windowsill, hunched over and cradling his head in the bowl of his hands.

Cool wind breathed through the mesh partition in the cop car. The front windows were rolled down, so Joel could hear what they were saying. "Opie! What the hell happened to *you*?" asked Bowker, hovering over the other cop.

Euchiss looked up, squinting into the sun. "I fell."

"You fell," sneered the lieutenant.

Euchiss gave him a glare that could melt steel. Joel was abruptly all too aware of who wore the pants in this partnership, even though the physically imposing Bowker technically outranked the red-headed patrolman. "Assaulting and evading a police officer," said Lieutenant Bowker, turning his attention to Fisher. "Your brother's got his plate full, ain't he? Would you like to explain why you were hiding him?"

Instead of taking the bait, Fish leaned into the passenger-side window of the cruiser. "I don't know what happened to my cat, but I'm gonna follow you to the police station and bail you out. You can explain on the way home."

"Ain't no bailin' me out. They ain't gonna put me in jail," Joel said, pleading with his eyes. "They're gonna take me somewhere and put a bullet in my head." He thrust his knee up for emphasis, wincing at the stab of pain. "They already tried to shoot me once. They're gonna—"

A look of irritation dawning on his face, Bowker pulled another zip-tie out of his patrol belt and came up behind Fish.

"Hey, no! *No!*" cried Joel.

Fisher started to turn, but the lieutenant had snatched one wrist and twisted him back around, pressing him against the side of the car. "You're fit as a fiddle, huh?" the cop asked, zip-tying his wrists together.

"Whoa, the hell are you doing, dude?" asked Kenway. "Fisher ain't done anything. Hold up."

"What are you doing?" asked Fisher. "Let me go—"

"Arresting you for harboring a fugitive and resisting arrest." Joel leaned back as Bowker opened the door and crammed Fisher inside, piling them on top of each other. He wriggled backward, trying to get out from under his brother.

"When I get out of these cuffs," said Fisher, "I'm going to kick your ass. And *then* I'm calling my fucking lawyer."

Joel pressed himself against the opposite door; Fisher looked feral, like he wanted to rear back in the seat and kick him to death. The situation was almost funny, if it weren't so dire—reminding him of sultry summer evenings in their parent's car as children, Mama and Daddy in the front seat, Joel and Fisher in the back. *Stop touching your brother! Don't make me turn this car around!* His head tilted back and he licked dry lips. "My leg is killin' me. Look, man, I didn't kill your cat. I swear to God it turned the garbage disposal on by itself. I don't know why, but it did." He looked up and nodded toward Euchiss sitting on the windowsill holding his head. "And that guy," he said, in a confidential mutter, "is the serial killer I got away from. The one Bowker called 'the Serpent.'"

Fish stared. "*That* guy? But he's—"

"Yeah, a cop. Like I told you, they're all in it together. They're workin' for those witch-bitches out in Slade township. The ones that lived across the street from the Martines. Maybe Mama wasn't so crazy after all." Joel shifted in the seat, inching his fingers up to the waistband of the jeans he was wearing. He pulled it down, revealing the right cheek of his ass and the scar on his skin. "I'll be damned. It all makes sense now."

"What does?"

Bowker's cellphone rang, cutting into their conversation with the theme to *Bonanza*. "Y'ello."

Glancing pointedly down at the ass-cheek he was displaying, Joel said, "Look. The brands Mama burned into our asses when we were kids. They were 'protective runes' like what that Robin girl's got tattooed on her chest." A four-lobed Y about an inch long had been scarred into the flesh of his right buttock. An *algiz*. The middle lobe of the rune was longer than the other two, making it look like a rooster's footprint. "Robin Martine called it Al-Jazeera."

"The Arabic news network?" Fish winced in confusion. "What have *they* got to do with this? That woman's daughter is in town? You been talkin' to her?"

"Yeah. I don't know, maybe your cat committin' suicide was those witches tryin' to do something to me, and this thing on my ass saved me. Maybe I was supposed to kill myself and Selina got it instead."

Fish pursed his lips, giving him a wry look.

Hanging up the phone, Bowker told Euchiss, "Change of plans." The redheaded scarecrow got up and put on a pair of sunglasses. "Boss called and gave us a job to do. Come on. We got to go down to the pound and take some cats out to the drainage. For some reason, all of a sudden, Cutty wants us to nix every cat they have."

"What about these two?"

"We got bigger chickens to pluck. They can help us."

"Chickens?" Kenway asked, face darkening. "No, I want to talk to you two. You guys are making a mistake."

Ignoring him, the pear-shaped lieutenant lumbered around the back of the cruiser and got into the driver's seat, and Euchiss plopped down on the passenger side.

"What about that guy?" asked Euchiss, jerking a thumb at the veteran as he put on his seat belt. Joel glanced out the back window and saw Kenway standing in front of the comic shop, a keyring full of keys in one hand, looking confused and increasingly furious.

"We'll take care of him later. We ain't got the room in the car for his big ass, anyhow. And to be perfectly frank, I don't relish the idea of trying to put cuffs on that big blond bastard. I get the feeling he could skull-fuck both of us at the same time with his hands in his pockets." Bowker put the car in gear and backed out into traffic. "He'll be all right until we get back, he thinks we're goin' to the station. When we get done with this, we'll grab somethin' quick to eat and come back here, have a word with him."

"What if he comes to the station?"

"Well, then, we won't be there, will we, dumbass?"

Euchiss turned and glared at Joel through the partition screen. Joel stared back, wary. "I bet you thought that was funny, huh? Runnin' that treadmill with me standing on it?" Euchiss asked, venom in his voice. "I think I mighta got a concussion."

"What, you expect me to be sorry about it? You had me chained up in a garage. You were gonna cut my throat."

Euchiss pointed a jittery finger at him. His lips stuck together as he spoke. "Blood for the garden, asshole. Forget cutting your throat—I'm gonna string you right back up and cut your head clean off with a hacksaw like one'em raghead terrorists. Won't *that* be—"

"Hey, enough of that head-cuttin' shit," warned Bowker, back-handing him across the chest and jamming a finger at his face. "We ain't no damn Taliban."

Discomfited, Euchiss turned around and folded his arms, sitting back like a little boy throwing a tantrum.

The lieutenant shook his head. "You can pitch a fit if you want, son—I don't give a rat's ass who y'know. But I got lines, and you steppin' on 'em. My mama raised me to be a God-fearin' man, not no heathen savage."

"God-fearin' men don't do what you do," said Joel.

"Did I ask you for your opinion?" Bowker snarled over his shoulder. "I ought to shoot you right now for what you did last night with that scattergun. But we got things we got to go take care of, and you can lend a hand. You've been *voluntold*."

Restaurants and gas stations scrolled past the windows in a parade of colorful logos. They drove west along Broad and south onto Main, cutting through the heart of the downtown commercial district. Lunchtime traffic surrounded them in a scrimmage of lights and steel.

Fisher pressed them. "Where we going?"

No answer.

• • •

The police Charger slithered through downtown Blackfield, passing the university and its thirteen-story library, leaving the surface streets for more and more obscure neighborhoods. Bowker's convoluted path cut through subdivisions Joel had been to a number of times, mostly to buy weed.

Dealers and sex workers milled up and down the sidewalk in front of run-down tract houses with boarded windows, and weeds sprouted from the walls of abandoned, broken-eyed factories. Convenience stores with iron bars on the windows. Grimy, slat-sided cottages on overgrown lawns strewn with dirty toys. A googly-eyed old woman in a nightgown stood at the roadside with an oxygen tank, screaming gibberish at passing motorists.

Exposed hips of granite jutted from hillsides. The lieutenant finally slowed and pulled into a side street that wound into a wooded area, and the houses became fewer until there were none at all, only dead brown trees reaching for the sky and leaf-litter on rolling hills.

Just when Joel thought they were leaving the city altogether, the car grumbled into a gravel parking lot. A metal sign zip-tied to a chain-link fence told him they had arrived at Blackfield Animal Shelter. The only other vehicle was an unmarked box truck. Bowker pulled in, over to the side, and the two cops got out, letting themselves into a large brick building. Euchiss came back and opened the cruiser's trunk, taking out a hunting rifle. Joel wasn't sure what caliber, but it had a bolt action and a scope. He took out a box of cartridges, slammed the trunk shut, and disappeared into the shelter.

Once they were gone, silence fell over the car, broken up by indecipherable garbage honking out of the police-band radio. Fisher's eyes were full of fear and confusion. "What are we doin' at the animal shelter? Didn't they say something about cats?"

"Beats me. I don't even wanna know."

"What were you saying about protective runes and witches and Robin Martine?"

His forehead pressed against the window at an angle, Joel tried to see through the windows of the shelter's main building. Inside the fence enclosure was a labyrinth of chain link: smaller pens for individual dogs. From where he sat, he could see dozens of large-breed canines: Rottweilers, German shepherds, a small army of pit bulls.

"Well, according to what Robin Martine told me, the witches' magic is guided by words and symbols." Joel went on to explain to his little brother what Robin had told him and Kenway in the truck after leaving the hospital. "The symbol branded on our hips is the same one tattooed on Robin's chest. It protects you from their magic, like bug spray protects you from mosquitoes, I guess. Hell, I don't know. But I think it has something to do with your cat committing suicide."

Fish gave him a death glare.

"No, I'm serious. According to her, the witches can sacrifice cats and send their souls into people, creating zombie slaves. And the symbols on our asses kept us from getting enslaved."

"Supposing I believe this bullshit," said Fish. "If that's true, and some witch made my cat sacrifice herself, where did—" He bit off the end of the sentence, as if he'd tasted something sour, his face twisting briefly in anguish, "Where *did* Selina's soul go?"

Joel had no answer.

The two of them sat in frustrated, anxious silence.

After what felt like half an hour, Bowker and Euchiss finally came out. The lieutenant went to the far side of the building, opening a large swing-gate in the fence. Euchiss carried the hunting rifle out to the box truck and reversed it into the enclosure, disappearing around the building.

Bowker came toward the cruiser, pulling his pistol.

As he walked, he pulled the slide, loaded a magazine, and let the slide drop forward, *ch-clack!* Joel's heart jumped into his mouth, but the cop stood next to the car, staring out into the woods and rubbing his goatee.

A few minutes later, the self-styled Serpent strode out of the enclosure and Bowker opened Fisher's door, while Euchiss opened Joel's. "Get out," growled the killer, pulling him up by his armpit. Joel staggered, the gravel bruising the soles of his bare feet. "You try anything and my buddy blows your brains out." He dug in his pocket and came up with a utility knife, whipping it open. Joel flinched, but Euchiss held him fast, cutting the zip-tie cuffs.

Then he twisted Joel around by the shoulder and shoved him toward the animal shelter. "Walk."

Joel rubbed his wrists. "What are we doing?"

"Did I say talk?" Euchiss cut Fish's cuffs, then pulled out his Taser and loaded a fresh cartridge. "We're going to perform a little manual labor. Miss Cutty wants us to load a bunch of cages onto this truck and carry 'em out to the quarry."

The four of them went into the chain link enclosure and around the back of the building, down a gravel path to where the box truck had been backed up to an open door.

As they approached, Joel could hear the yowling of cats from inside the shelter. Inside, they were met with a pitiful sight. Maybe two hundred wire kennels were stacked in a spacious concrete room, six to a column, small, more like raccoon-traps than kennels. The raunchy smell of cat feces made an eye-watering murk of the air, and an army of tiny paws reached through the gleaming bars like prisoners of war in a medieval dungeon.

"Jesus," said Fish.

"Start loading these cages onto the truck," said Euchiss.

"What are you gonna do with 'em?"

"That's for me to know and you to find out." The redheaded killer urged him on with the Taser. "Zap zap. Get to work."

The polished cement floor was ice-cold and marble-smooth under Joel's bare feet. He went to the nearest stack of kennels—this one only three cages high—and laced his fingers into the bars, lifting it up. The fluffy cat inside reached out and pinned his hand with a paw, pleading in a smoky voice. "*Yowwwww.*"

Joel glanced at Bowker. The lieutenant tucked the corners of his mouth back in a mean, imperative smile. *Go on, now, do what you're told.*

16

A couple of hours later (without his cell Joel couldn't tell, as though constant access to his iPhone had damaged his perception of time), the two brothers pushed the final kennel into place.

Surprisingly, all but three of the cages fit in the back of the truck. Euchiss took two of them and put them in the cab up front. Bowker urged Joel and Fisher into the cargo hold with the cats and pulled the rolldown shut on them.

The air stank of cat piss, and the space they were confined to was only the last couple of feet of the compartment, a gap two feet wide, nine feet tall, and seven feet across. Joel sat down and listened to the officer put a padlock through the handle, which was a feat in itself, because the darkness was a near-unbearable chaos of agonized groaning and keening. He leaned back against the wall and rubbed his face in exasperation and fear. The cats were too loud to talk to Fisher, so he closed his eyes and tried to think.

Prayers seemed trite and useless. Joel thought of himself

nominally as a Christian, but he hadn't been to church since he was a teenager and was always at a loss for words when someone asked him to say grace over dinner. It was no different today as he rode blind and disoriented back into the hustle and bustle of urban Blackfield, but the irony was not lost on him that if he'd gone to church that morning (it being Sunday), he probably wouldn't be in this mess. Who thinks to look for a fugitive in church?

Once he'd exhausted his reserve of plans and mental preparations—daydreaming about leaping out at Euchiss when he opened the back of the truck, usually getting shot or Tasered for his troubles—he played around with the visual of Fisher's cat killing itself, turning the scene over and over in his mind like a Rubik's Cube. The way the cat had hunkered down and stared at Joel. The fixed gaze of a predator watching for movement, sizing up a target.

Where did the soul go?

The truck drove a shorter route than the one they'd taken in the police cruiser, but more circuitous. He counted at least seven stops, four of which were at traffic lights (this was determined by the fact the driver only made a cursory effort to stop at stop-signs). The animals never stopped yowling. If anything, it only got worse, increasing whenever the truck paused and the engine quieted.

The Tylenol was wearing off, and his leg radiated heat through the bandage, throbbing and aching.

He had actually dozed off when the truck's horn blared. An engine somewhere off to their port side revved, rising in volume, and then, *WHAM!*, an incredible force slammed into them, throwing Joel onto his hands and knees at Fisher's feet.

Someone had sideswiped them. The tires barked a squealing tremolo, *EEEEE-E-E-E-E!* Wire kennels toppled over in a riot of metal and screaming animals. The offending vehicle crashed into them again, partially caving in the wall and knocking down cages. Lasers of daylight streamed in through pinholes bashed into the side of the cargo compartment. Joel scrambled toward Fisher, and the man dragged his brother into his lap, clutching his head in powerful arms.

For a few seconds, Fish's cologne overpowered the cat-stink. *If I live through this, I'll never bitch about him doing keto again. I'll do whatever he wants.*

Bowker managed to keep the truck more or less on the straight and narrow, but some sort of structure collided with the right side and scraped endlessly down the fender like rolling thunder, drumming at regular intervals, a giant metal heart, *boom-boom, boom-boom.*

A guardrail.

As soon as Joel placed the sound, a tremendous noise—a great shuddering *BOOM* like the world tearing in half—told him the truck had broken through, and the entire cargo compartment capsized to the right. Joel and Fisher and a hundred and forty-two cats slammed into the starboard wall and free-floated for about two and a half seconds.

Instead of crashing into water like he'd anticipated, the truck pile-drove itself into solid ground.

Forward momentum threw every cage into the front of the compartment and tore the brothers away from each other. Joel cartwheeled backward into the pile of kennels, bounced, and fell on top of Fisher. The ceiling sheared open with a furious, ear-destroying roar.

And then, silence.

• • •

Blood dripped on the back of his head, an insistent *tap, tap, tap.* Joel opened his eyes to find himself lying on top of his brother, his face pressed against Fisher's chest, listening to a chorus of tuneless, defeated howling. He was pinned under a tangle of cages. Dead, dying, and injured house cats lay in slumped piles of hair all around him, suspended in a labyrinth of bent wires.

Fish groaned. "What happened?"

"We crashed."

A familiar chemical smell tainted the air, overpowering the cat urine. Gasoline. Diesel? "We gotta get out of here," said Fish, and he tried to stir.

Sharp pain needled Joel's left shoulder. "Oww. *Quit moving.*"

Fish relaxed. Joel tried to push himself up, but the cages were too heavy. A cat's paw groped at his face.

Adrenaline ripped through his core, his heart flaring, and he tried to push again. This time, the cage against his back snapped, and a wire bar twanged like a broken guitar string, scratching his side.

"Hold on!" someone shouted from up the bank, feet thumping through dry leaves. "I'm comin'! Hold on!"

Gazing through a galaxy of aluminum wires, Joel saw the back door was smashed open, and through it he could see the bridge they'd fallen from, and the guardrail they'd smashed through.

A smashed-up Chevy was parked on the shoulder. Kenway Griffin ran sideways down the slope in an awkward loping gallop on his prosthetic leg. The big veteran took hold of the roof where it'd been peeled away and hauled on it, tearing it open further.

"Hey," he called over the howling of the cats, spotting Joel through the twisted bars. "I'll get you guys out. Hold on." He worked his way down the side, wrenching it down as if it were the lid of a tin of sardines, filling the box with sunlight. Reaching into the cargo compartment, he started grabbing at kennels and dragging them out onto the bank. "I need to retire from my goddamn retirement." The cats inside the kennels complained, but right now, his first priority was freeing Joel and Fish.

Fisher coughed in Joel's ear. "You all right?"

"Yeah." Joel winced. "Got a wire jabbin' me in my back and I got one foot in Hell, but otherwise, I'm aight. You?"

"You had your tetanus shot, right?"

"No, but it looks like I'm gonna need one."

"How did you find us?" Fish asked Kenway. "Was that you made the cop crash?"

"Followed you guys all the way to Glen Addie, but I lost you at a red light." Pulling on a cage, Kenway lifted it over his head and flung it into the weeds. The cat inside was already dead, flopping around limp and shapeless. "I was driving around the 1800 block, thinking of checking the animal shelter—since it was the only thing out there that made any sense—when I saw those two cops and followed 'em."

The next cage was stuck fast and the cat inside, a black short-hair with white patches, yowled pitifully. Kenway pulled until it let go with a *twang* and he gently set it aside. "I don't know why I rammed the truck," he said, grabbing another one. "It seemed like the thing to do. Those guys are shady as hell and I figured you were in the back."

"It's a good thing you did," said Joel.

"Figured they were gonna try to finish the job they started last night. Take you somewhere and kill you. Guess it seemed safer to run the truck off the road and pull you out than try to stop 'em and get myself shot like they shot you."

"I'm glad you believed me."

"It's hard to disbelieve a gunshot wound to the leg."

Fisher coughed again. "Come on, man, hurry up. We need to get out of here." The smell of diesel fuel was growing stronger. "Those two cops. Are they out? Are they out there?"

"I ain't seen 'em," said Kenway. "Looks like they're still in the front."

Bracing himself against the wall of the compartment, Joel did a push-up and found the load on his back was considerably lighter, affording him a few inches of wiggle-room. "Almost there," said Kenway. He laced his fingers through another kennel and paused.

"What is it?"

The veteran was staring into space, hunched over with his shoulders squeezed into the roof opening, frozen as if listening intently.

"Why'd you stop?"

"Nnnrrrrrrrr." Kenway growled, a weird nasal growl like an impression of an airplane. Choking and snuffling, he shrank away from the opening, disappearing.

Daylight poured through in his absence.

Joel met Fisher's eyes and the two of them struggled with the cages. Enough of them had been taken out, they had room to push the rest out of the way. Fish reached up over his head, shoving the last couple of kennels toward the gap. Dragging himself underneath them, he pulled his body through the hole and out into the grass.

Orange light flickered from the back of the compartment. Through the chaos of wires, Joel could see a fire guttering somewhere deep in the pile of kennels. The diesel had leaked into the cargo hold and something had set it ablaze. The smoke was foul, thick and pungent. He shoved at the cages, crawling forward, and Fisher pulled them out from the other side, throwing them away.

Finally, he was free. Joel dragged his legs out and lay exhausted in the churned-up dirt. The truck had come to rest on its right side at the bottom of a slope, next to a river. Above them was a vast white sky, mottled by charcoal clouds.

"*Rrrrooowwwwwrrrrll,*" said Kenway.

The vet was doubled over in a crazy Spider-Man pose on his hands and feet, crawling along the riverbank and staring at them.

"The hell are you doing?" asked Fisher.

Suddenly, Kenway lunged at him, slamming him against the back of the cargo box. Fish bounced off the aluminum sheet and the two men went down with Kenway on top, hissing and growling like a man insane. The vet's hipster man-bun had come undone and his hair was a wild blond Tarzan mane. He tried to bite Fish and the smaller man pushed at him, fending him off with a bloody forearm.

One of the cages lay next to Joel, bars twisted in every direction, the cat gone. He grabbed a bar and bent it until it broke free, then scrambled over to Kenway and stabbed it through his shirt, feeling skin give way.

"ROOOOWL!"

Flinching and screaming, the veteran rolled off of Fish and spidered backward. One of his shoes pried free of his prosthetic, stuck in gluey mud, the sock still inside, revealing a foot that looked like a car part. Joel stared, kneeling in a three-point stance, the wire jutting from his fingers like a knife fighter. That feeling of unreality came back.

His brother snatched up a rock and threw it—*"Bitch-ass bitch!"*

TOCK! Kenway blinked as the rock hit him in the forehead. He fell over and writhed like a crushed bug, holding his eyes, his heels grinding furrows in the dirt.

In the fight, Fisher had been pushed backward on the ground, and his pants were shucked down off his hips, revealing one butt cheek. Joel caught a glimpse of the *algiz* brand on his ass. *The cat sacrifice,* he thought. *The witches were trying to send Selina into me and turn me into a maniac, but it bounced off of my* algiz, *then off of Fisher's* algiz, *and went into Kenway downstairs.*

"Hold the man down," he told Fish, scooping his hand through the mud.

"What?"

"Just do it!"

Fish clambered up and clapped his hands to Kenway's biceps, pinning him down. Kenway snarled at the sky and twisted back and forth trying to free himself, a livid purple bruise rising over his right eyebrow.

Grinding up mud in his hands, Joel ripped the vet's shirt open. A tan, hairy belly glowed underneath. Joel painted Robin's *algiz* on him with the mud, and then Kenway overpowered them, throwing Fish aside. Joel crawled away, using the side of the box truck to climb to his feet.

Flames crackled inside the cargo compartment, and when Joel looked inside, he saw the beginnings of a roaring bonfire. He swore out loud and pulled out a cage with a howling cat inside, and another and another.

God, there are so many, he thought, pitching the kennels into the weeds like a baggage-handler.

"What's *wrong* with him?" shouted Fisher.

Thick spittle-foam collected between Kenway's lips as he convulsed violently and thrashed his arms and legs like a man electrocuted. His eyes rolled back in his head. Struck by indecision and driven by the smell of burning cat-hair, Joel couldn't figure out what to do—help Kenway? Save the cats? Yell at Fish to help him get the cages out of the fire?

The dilemma was rendered moot when Kenway opened his mouth and the face of a cat pressed itself out between his teeth, eyes squinting, fur matted.

"What the shit?" wheezed Fish. *"Selina?"*

The vet's face had become a livid lavender. He grabbed his neck with both hands as if he was trying to pull off his own head and rolled over on his hands and knees. He convulsed again—this time slowly, methodically, his stomach tensing the way a dog sicks. His whole torso inchwormed back to front, his shoulders bunched up to his ears. Selina's head protruded from his mouth like a big hairy tongue.

Reaching up with one hand, Kenway took hold of the cat's neck with an A-OK gesture and pulled.

The cat let out a strangled duck-squawk.

Standing half-naked in the mud under a cooling overcast sky, black smoke billowing past, Joel lost his handle on real life. Somehow, the threads of reality had unraveled to the point his mind refused to put two and two together anymore, and all of a sudden, he forgot what his hands were for. The only thing he could do was watch helplessly as Kenway struggled with the cat, gagging and choking.

"Stop screaming and go check on those two cops," said Fisher, shoving him in the other direction. He had been screaming? Joel shook his head and a pang of dizziness almost sprawled him in the weeds. "I said *go!*" His brother went back into the cargo compartment and pitched a kennel outside.

Smoke billowed out. A few seconds later, he emerged, barking hard wet coughs. He didn't go back in.

Staggering through the mud, Joel went around to the driver's side of the truck and was confused to see a wall of black, dirty machinery. Then he remembered the truck had fallen over on its side; the door was now on top. He climbed the underside of the cab and pulled himself up and over the running board.

Through the window he could see the two men inside. Euchiss was unconscious behind a deflated airbag, slumped against the passenger side door with blood trickling down the side of his face, but Bowker was dead. *Extremely* dead. The steering column had been driven backward, but the Second Chance vest he'd been wearing had prevented it from impaling him. Instead, it had caused the armor plates to squish his torso like a sandwich, breaking his ribs and pinning him against the seat. His eyes and throat bulged like a toad and his face was grape-purple, pink viscera flowering from his mouth. A starburst of blood flowered across the windshield in front of him.

Luckily, the window-glass was smashed out. Joel reached into the cab and plucked the Glock out of Bowker's hip holster, jamming it into the back of his jeans.

Movement on the other side caught his attention. Euchiss's eyes were open, and he was staring straight at Joel.

Without a word, the cop pointed his Glock up at him.

Joel recoiled from the window and jumped down into the mud, heading back to the rear of the cargo compartment.

When he got there, Kenway was lying in the undergrowth where he'd fallen, cradling a blood-wet cat in his arms like a new mother and looking thoroughly wrung-out. "Uuuunngggh," the big man grunted hoarsely, and closed his eyes, exhausted.

By now, the fire was licking up out of the hole in the roof. Cats screamed inside in a great siren-chorus of panic and agony, consumed by the flames. Fish was on his knees in the mud, his eyes red and streaming down his face, though Joel couldn't tell if it was because of the smoke or because of the cats.

"I can't save them," Fish sobbed. "I can't get in."

"We got to go," said Joel.

Fish got up, still weeping. Kenway lay in Roman repose, his head lolling back, his eyes closed. The newly reborn Selina wriggled out of his arms and shook herself, fleeing madly into the treeline. Fish watched the cat escape with dazed eyes, as if he couldn't quite process it.

Kenway opened his eyes. "My throat. Killing me."

"Come on," said Joel, grabbing his hands. "We got to go. Get up. We got to go. Redhead still alive, and he armed."

The brothers helped the vet up off the ground and they headed up the slope toward the highway. Kenway's pickup truck waited for them at the gap in the guardrail, the right quarter panel smashed where he'd driven it into the box truck.

A sluggish, raspy voice echoed off the trees. *Where you goin'?*

They all looked up. A blood-soaked Euchiss had climbed over his partner and was now standing up in the sidelong driver window as if it were a tank hatch. He pulled the rifle out of the cab hand-over-hand and cycled the bolt, *chik-a-chik!*

Joel reached behind his back and came up with Bowker's pistol, pointing it at the Serpent. It went off as soon as he tugged the trigger, firing with a paper-bag *POP!*, and the bullet kicked sparks off the side of the box truck. Euchiss slithered down into the window for cover.

Reaching the roadside first, Joel went around to the driver's side of Kenway's truck. The highway was a lonely country two-lane out in the middle of nowhere, stretching toward the horizon in both directions. Soldier pines made an impenetrable wall on either side of the highway under a sky like stirred milk. There were no power lines or poles, which made the road look naked, unfinished.

The Chevy's door was open and the keys were still in it, but the front passenger corner of the truck was smashed in and smoke snaked out from under the hood. Joel twisted the keys and the engine grunted laboriously.

The windshield spiderwebbed with a delicate smash, raining glass all over the dash, and Joel dove out onto the highway. Lying on his belly, it occurred to him Euchiss could still see him underneath the truck, but when he peered through the gap, he saw that the shoulder of the road and the remains of the guardrail concealed him well enough.

Fisher and Kenway came bounding around the back of the truck and hunkered down behind the Chevy's bed. "Wouldn't start?" croaked the vet, wincing.

"No."

"Now what?" asked Fish.

Kenway's fingers curled over the bed wall and he peered over the edge. A bolt from the blue exploded on the other side, whispering across the forest, and a rifle round pinged off the truck cab. He ducked and moved toward the front of the truck, and that's where he paused in surprise.

To Joel's bewilderment, he laughed.

"I been lookin' for you, Betsy. Come here, baby." He reached into the open driver's door and grabbed something from under the seat—the handgun he'd dropped at the hospital.

"Oh, y'all in for it now," said Joel, elated. He elbowed his brother. "Soldier boy done got his peacemaker."

"You have a pistol too, idiot," said Fish.

Joel looked down at Bowker's pistol.

"Yeah, but he's actually *good* with his."

Ejecting the magazine, Kenway checked the rounds inside and slapped it back into the weapon. Then he stood, braced his forearms on the Chevy's sidewall, and calmly started unloading on the man in the box truck at a measured, purposeful pace. *Pop. Pop. Pop. Pop.* The pistol's muzzle nodded to a smooth rhythm, never off level. Shell casings popped out of the ejection port, tinkling to the asphalt at their feet.

Eight rounds into the volley of gunfire, the slide locked back. Kenway turned the pistol to the side in confusion. "Shit, jam—"

Thunder broke across the sky, echoing off the trees.

A bullet fanned the vet's hair back in a mist of blood.

Both brothers swore out loud as Kenway toppled over backward and slapped against the asphalt.

Crimson dripped from a wound at the crown of his forehead.

"No!" shrieked Fisher. *"No!"*

Joel looked away, squeezing his eyes shut and covering his face, trying to collect himself.

Staring into the abyss behind his eyelids, listening to Fish curse over the dead man, he knew they had no other recourse but to run or be shot. He could hit a man point-blank with a shotgun, but with a pistol and a handful of bullets, Joel knew he had no chance against a trained cop's scoped hunting rifle and what was undoubtedly a whole box of rounds.

He tangled a hand in Fisher's shirt and pulled him to his feet. "Let's get out of here."

17

At least the fire had taken care of the cats, which was what they'd come out there to get rid of, anyway.

When Euchiss finally managed to get out of the overturned truck, he twisted his ankle jumping down. He sat on the tailgate of the big blond guy's Chevy for a few minutes, massaging his ankle and waiting for someone to happen by with a vehicle he could commandeer, but the road to the quarry was a long and lonely one. Nobody came out this way except for the pulpwood trucks going to the clear-cut out on the ridge, and that had dried up a year before.

No more traffic.

They had only been six miles from the quarry when the big blond guy with the beard ran them off the road.

He kicked the man's corpse for good measure before he left.

Tall pine trees crowded around him, and the ground was a carpet of rusty red needles. Four-fifths of a box of 6.5mm rustled softly in his pocket.

Two hours into the pursuit, the pain drained out of his ankle and it'd become stiff and swollen. Euchiss paused to examine it and found a port-wine bruise the size of a baseball across the outside of his heel. Sprained. Damn.

He took his phone out and woke it up. No signal. His police LMR was also out of the picture—too far away from town for the walkie. He fussed quietly to himself, swearing in his New England accent. In his other hand was a scoped Nosler M48 Patriot rifle, carried underhand like a briefcase. *Oh, well. Cutty would be pissed I messed up. Better I get this tied off by myself, ASAP. Solo mission it is.*

He wriggled back into his shoe and picked his way over a brook. On the other side was the decades-old remains of a barbed-wire fence, and several yards to the south was a NO TRESPASSING sign. *We've been curving in a northeasterly direction,* he thought, slinking through the rusty wires like a wrestler getting into a ring. *Must be getting close to the mines.*

The aforementioned quarry Bowker had been heading to lay at the far end of a network of mine shafts snaking through the belly of Red Hill Mountain. The locals called it the Mushroom Mines because the damp conditions inside the cave caused white fungus to grow on the wooden tables and scaffolding. The air inside was soupy with spores. He wasn't sure if it was poisonous, but he and Bowker never took any chances and usually went in with gas masks.

Shit, he thought, pausing. *You dumbass.* He'd forgotten his mask in the truck.

Crossing increasingly steep and stony terrain, they were in the foothills of Red Hill Mountain now. Up ahead, the trees thinned out, and Euchiss found himself on a bare shelf of limestone overlooking a large gorge some two or three hundred yards across—the sort of gap that would have warranted a bridge were it more traveled. Briars and heather choked the bottom, but the sides were steep and clear.

The Ellis boys were scrambling up the opposite bank, picking their way through the boulders and briars. They were almost to the top, no more than a stone's throw from the tree line. Euchiss threw himself down and shouldered the rifle, a frisson of glee coursing through his body. A quick adjustment to get an optimal angle, cocking one knee up, and he thrust the gun forward, resting his elbows on the cliff and looking through the scope. In the sharp magnification, he could have reached out and plucked the two men off the valley wall with his fingers.

Etched into the upper receiver was a single word: MAGA. Euchiss licked his lips and steadied himself, the crosshair settling over the Mandingo with the buzz cut. Breathe in, breathe out, relax. He tugged the trigger back until the firing pin hammered the cartridge. The sharp, hollow *CRACK!* surprised him and sent a pulse of pleasure through his testicles.

Dirt spewed up inches to the right of Fisher Ellis's head. He looked over his shoulder, scanning the gorge wall.

"I'm up here, you dumb cuck." Euchiss cycled the Nosler's bolt, ejected the empty casing, and chambered a fresh round. Something went off with a *pop* like an M-80 and a bullet whirred into the trees behind him. He peered through the scope and remembered the faggot with the shaved head had stolen Bowker's Glock. Joel fired several more rounds, all but one whizzing into the trees behind Euchiss. "You can't hit me from there with that. Who are *you* foolin'?"

He took aim on Joel, who seemed to realize the futility of shooting back and threw the empty pistol into the gorge. As Euchiss was getting ready to pull the rifle's trigger, his trousers vibrated and a jangly melody came from his pocket.

Being this high up, he must have gotten a signal. He dug out his phone and grunted in irritation at a text message.

WHERE U AT? CUTTY WANTS UPDATE

Euchiss sighed and looked through the scope. Joel had made it to the tree line, and his brother was almost over the gorge bank.

Euchiss put the crosshairs on his back, center mass, and fired another round. That warm ache hummed in his balls again at the sound of the blast. This one plugged Fisher in the upper left arm, blowing a chunk of meat all over his brother.

By the time he'd cycled the empty casing out and sighted on them again, the fag had pulled him out of the ravine and they were running into the trees. The pine trunks flickered across their fading bodies like a picket fence.

Euchiss snatched up his phone and typed a text.

HAD ACCIDNT ON WAY 2 QUARRY. LT DEAD. CHASING 2 GUYS @ RED HILL ON FOOT. COME GET ME. TAKE E ACC ROAD, BRING GUN. ILL B AT MINES IN ABT 45 MIN

The reply was immediate:

ON MY WAY

18

Kenway Griffin opened his eyes and rolled over onto his hands and knees, disgorging that morning's Burger King breakfast on the asphalt. The puke burned like magma in his stretched and abraded throat.

Blood dribbled on the puddle of vomit. He touched his hairline. Electric pain shot across his scalp.

Dragging himself to his feet, he staggered across the highway and examined his head in the wing mirror of his truck. His hair was sopping wet and his whole face was coated in streams of crimson. As far as he could tell, the rifle bullet had skipped off the crown of his skull, cutting his scalp open and knocking him unconscious. *Dad always said I was hardheaded.* His eyeballs throbbed in dull agony. He climbed into his Chevy and tried to will the nausea away, tried to summon the cool, collected warrior that had bubbled up back in the vineyard, but the Chevy wouldn't stop spinning. Several minutes passed before he realized the wind-shield was shot out.

The truck full of kennels was now a roaring bonfire, black smoke rising in a column to the white sky. Cats yowled helplessly from their cages out in the grass, safe but abandoned.

The cat.

What the hell happened with the cat? He remembered reach-ing into the cargo compartment of the overturned truck, and then nothing until a few minutes later, on his hands and knees in the mud, choking. He'd vomited then too, but it wasn't food, it was *hair.* A huge wad of hair that scratched his gullet coming out.

Felt like strep throat, needles in his esophagus. Kenway swal-lowed with a wince. The hair had claws. He remembered holding a cat in his arms. Had he saved the cat from the fire? He couldn't be sure. It had been wet; he knew that much. Maybe it'd fallen in the river? He casually leaned over and vomited again, this time nothing coming up but sour bile.

Sweat ran down his face, cutting streaks in the blood. Did he have a concussion? He didn't think so, but it was possible.

Hey, man, you all right?

Fuck, dude, his fuckin' leg is gone.

Somebody help me start a saline—how are we gonna fix the medic without the medic?

God, he felt drunk. He grabbed a wad of Arby's napkins out of the door pocket and mopped at the blood on his face with trem-bling hands, scraping it out of his eyelids and the creases beside his nose as if he were removing makeup. All he could manage to do was smear it around. *Lucky, so goddamn lucky,* he thought, wad-ding the napkins up and tossing them into the floorboard. Two near-death experiences in his life. If he made it out of here, he was going to have to go skydiving or swimming with dolphins or ride a bull named Fu Manchu or something.

Found his leg, Lieutenant. Non-viable.

Where did they get popped?

TCP 6. *There was a mo-bile IED coming in from the south, and Griffin stopped because of the fucking kids. There were kids in the road, in front of the vehicle.*

Fuck 'em, he should have kept driving. He knows better.

He closed the door, his head tilting back in exhaustion as the Chevy slowly rotated in place. Saliva pooled in his mouth. Not for the first time, he wished he had the first-aid kit in there, the one usually in the glove compartment. He'd used it on somebody recently, but he couldn't remember who, or where he'd left it.

Smoke no longer roiled from under the hood. *Might as well give it a try while I'm in here.* He took the ignition in one bear-paw hand and twisted it. The engine gave a sick grunt but refused to turn over. He tried it again. Still nothing. He sat back and rested. Thought about puking again, but he didn't have anything left. Rolled down the window and spat.

In the side mirror he caught a glimpse of a vehicle coming down the road. He squished himself down,

(VBIED IT'S ANOTHER CAR BOMB FUCK GO GO GO)

his knees pressed against the dash, his balls at six o'clock on the steering wheel. A few moments later, the driver drew even with the Chevy and slowed, rubbernecking at the crash.

When there was no explosion, Kenway relaxed. *You're not over there anymore. Get your head out of your ass.*

Whoever it was put it in Park and let the engine idle. Kenway thought about getting out, asking for help, but something about it seemed wrong—why would they simply sit there silently instead of getting out to go look for survivors?

Drowsiness crept in around the edges and he clenched his fists, trying to will himself awake. His hands shook. His skull felt like it'd been cracked down the middle like a walnut.

Keep it together.

The slam of a car door.

Someone walked around to the Chevy. Kenway kept his eyes closed, held his breath, and pretended to be dead, which was easy, as he already had the disguise down, with the gash running along the part in his bloody hair.

"Nice shootin', Tex," said a hoarse voice right next to the open window. The man coughed and walked away. Kenway opened his eyes to see who it was.

The redheaded cop, Euchiss. *How long was I out?* Euchiss had changed his clothes and took a shower, evidently, judging by the lack of blood. One of his wrists was swaddled in a bandage.

Euchiss got back into his vehicle, pulling away. Kenway peered over the windowsill, catching a glimpse of a red Ford pickup and what appeared to be an airbrush painting of a Valkyrie with big boobs, catching a giant snake by the tail. He watched through the arch of the steering wheel as the pickup dwindled down the lonely highway.

Staring in disbelief, he recognized the artwork as the giant snake he'd painted on commission ages before.

Grrrrowl, chugga-chugga-chug. He tried the key again. *Grrrrowl, chugga-chugga-chug.* He coughed, spat blood out the window, and turned up the radio. Lynyrd Skynyrd told him to be a simple kind of man.

19

After a couple hours of running on the treacherous forest floor, Joel's feet felt like hamburger, but he had nothing on Fisher. Blood ran down his elbow from the gunshot wound in his shoulder. His face had gone from a dark brown to a sort of charcoal-purple, and his lips were almost lipstick violet.

They emerged from the woods into a gravel clearing furrowed with dry tire ruts. To the far right was a collection of unfinished buildings, all naked studs and black-felt roof. Building supplies lay rotting in the elements. A stone bluff loomed over the clearing, topped with a crown of longleaf pine, and an enormous cave led into the depths of the bluff.

At first, he wanted to hide in the unfinished building, but he realized it would only be a matter of time before Euchiss found them there. "Come on," he urged Fish, mincing across the sharp gravel. "We'll hide in the cave."

Inside, smooth cave-dirt burned his aching feet with cold.

Anemic white sunlight filtered in through a dozen holes in the wall, revealing enormous rooms with flat, cracked ceilings. Graffiti spray-painted on the jagged stone declared long-dead relationships and cryptic war-cries. *BRAVERY IS NOT THE ABSENCE OF FEAR. ED BRIGHAM WAS HERE (AND SO WAS ARDY) 1976. FRODO LIVES!*

"I dunno," said Fish.

Thunder broke outside, and a bullet whip-cracked against the lip of the cave, flicking chips of rock.

They ducked and ran deeper into the mine.

The main shaft drove straight into the heart of the mountain, side tunnels branching off at constant intervals into side rooms. The air was thick and close, wet, musty. Moisture speckled Joel's face. It didn't take long to lose nearly all light, stranding them in a void of darkness traced only by the distant star of the cave opening behind them. He could cover it with one hand.

Euchiss stepped into the void's only sun, a tiny silhouette. He slipped a flashlight out of his patrol belt and turned it on, shadows capering at his feet. "I know you're in here," he called, his voice a flat, raspy echo. "There ain't no other end to this mine. You're trapped. Might as well give up now."

Go to Hell. Joel stepped out of the light into a side room and into total darkness. Fish followed, clutching his shoulder.

"You go to the other side," Fish whispered.

"Why?"

"Get a rock or something. Hide in the dark. I'm gonna come out with my hands up and distract him. You come up behind him, hit him with the rock."

"That's a crap plan. He's going to shoot you."

"Do you have a better one?"

He didn't. Joel crossed the river of light again and into the dark, shuffling around, his hands fluttering across the floor. No rocks—at least none of sufficient size—but there was a metal bucket with a rope attached to the handle, a heavy coal pail. The rope was spongy and wet but intact. He carried the bucket to the edge of the shadow and held it aloft like a flail.

As he waited for the cop to get close, something occurred to him. What if Euchiss happened to point the flashlight this way before he could spot Fish? What if he shot Fish on sight? His lungs itched. He needed to cough; every breath he took seemed more and more congested until he was shuddering.

Blue-white light swarmed across the floor as the flashlight came closer. Euchiss's Oxfords scuffed across the hard-packed dirt. *Come on, come on.* Joel extended his arm back, bracing for action, getting ready to swing the bucket at the cop's face. Euchiss came around the corner into view, his Maglite a cone of hard white. He'd slung the rifle over his shoulder by a strap and drawn his service Glock.

No! The flashlight was wobbling in Joel's direction! The circle of light swept back and forth and brushed his toes.

"Hey, fucker," said Euchiss almost casually, and flashed him in the eyes. Joel flexed, started to step forward, but Fisher coughed. The beam of light swung in the other direction and revealed Fish standing in front of a long wooden table, his hands up, squinting. "*There* you—" Euchiss began to say, the pistol in his hand following the flashlight.

Joel lunged blind, swinging from the side with a right cross. The bucket cut an arc through the air and missed completely.

Euchiss flinched and snorted laughter, but Joel followed through, swinging the bucket around his head, and hit him on the second go-round. The bucket whipped the redheaded killer square across the face, burying him in a cloud of black soot and knocking him flat on his back.

BANG! The Glock flashed, and the flashlight's beam danced across the ceiling. The bucket hit the floor and left Joel holding a rotten rope.

"*Run!*" shouted Fish.

He considered grabbing the light, but the pistol made him think twice. He ran after his brother's fading footsteps and they fled headlong into the silk shadows of the cave.

• • •

The constant fear of stepping off into a vertical drop made Joel reluctant to run full-speed. He was completely and totally blind in the depths of the mine shaft, and had no idea what he was running toward. Fish, on the other hand, seemed to have no such reservations, and Joel could only track him by the sound of his sneakers clapping against the sooty stone ahead. As he ran, he kept his right arm extended, trailing his fingertips across the rough surface of the wall.

Behind them, Euchiss was swearing at the top of his lungs, cycling through a thesaurus of every curse he could come up with, and threatening every conceivable form of torture. *"You broke my goddamn nose! I'm gonna rip your dick off and feed it to birds!"*

Deeper and deeper they went, the air thickening to a warm soup. Joel didn't have any kind of cloth to cover his nose and mouth with, so he settled for breathing through his teeth and spitting every so often.

After twenty minutes of running, he slowed to a jog. The cop's shouting had dwindled away, leaving them in a bone-chilling silence. His mouth tasted like he'd been eating cheese and his jeans were wet where his stitches had come loose.

"Wait up, Mr. Goodbody!" he pleaded with the invisible Fish.

"I ain't waitin' up for shit. Come on."

"You need to slow down before you run off in a hole. I ain't carrying your no-carb ass out of here with two broke legs."

"He's done shot me once, I ain't about to sit still and give him another try. This ain't Chuck E. Cheese, Joel, this motherfucker ain't here to win tickets." He pronounced it *Johl* instead of *Jo-elle*, which he only did when he was pissed off. Joel figured it was his version of calling him by all three of his names. "Now how about you shut up before he hears us?"

"We ain't exactly church mice."

"Well, you ain't helpin'!"

The tunnel extended on and on, some three or four hundred yards, he guessed, or maybe a quarter-mile. Or ten miles. Who knew?

Ten or twenty minutes later, his sight returned and the darkness became a faint, dreamlike hint of gray rock as light bounced in from some distant opening. A colorless square loomed ahead of them, only a shade lighter than the black around it.

Rough surfaces led them into a tunnel that ran perpendicular to the first one, and as Fish stepped into reflected daylight, Joel understood they'd reached a branching path. The right-hand shaft led toward the source of the sunlight. He came out into the intersection and squinted at a point of fierce white.

Wind whispered and the sound of the cicadas drifted down to his ears. Fish took off running and a gun thundered behind them. A bullet ricocheted off the cave wall in front of Joel with a flower of sparks.

"I see you down there!" shouted Euchiss.

The brothers burst out into fresh air and found themselves in an enormous rock quarry occupied by a handful of dilapidated wooden structures—a tall coal elevator and several small cabins. Beyond the buildings was a large pond full of rust-orange water, milky and placid.

To his surprised horror, Fish stopped and put up his hands.

"The hell you doin'?" Joel asked in shock.

"You'd be smart to join in, buddy," said a man standing next to a red pickup truck, pointing a revolver at them.

He wasn't *dressed* like Euchiss—he had on a pair of Wranglers, snakeskin boots, and a blue chambray shirt—but he had Euchiss's *head*; he had the man's beady eyes and skinny throat and Irish-red hair. Gauze had been wrapped around one forearm.

Exhausted confusion hit Joel so hard, it was like a physical blow to the skull. *Did he teleport in front of us? Is this witchcraft?*

"I'd like you to meet somebody," said a voice from the darkness behind them. Cop-Euchiss came out of the cave with his rifle tucked under his arm like an English fox hunter, pale cave-dirt smeared all over his black uniform shirt and trousers. His nose was a splat of blood in the middle of his sooty gray face. Cop-Euchiss smiled, joining his arm-bandaged Marlboro Man doppelgänger by the truck. "This is my brother, Roy," said the cop, clapping his brother on the shoulder. "Say hi, Roy."

"Hi, Roy," said Roy.

"Folks call me Opie on account of my hair, but my name is Owen," said Cop-Euchiss.

Twins.

"This here's who you were talkin' about when you were jabberin' about the Serpent in the car earlier," said Owen, spitting blood on the ground. "I take it our dearly departed Lieutenant Bowker said something when he came out to your house yesterday."

Roy smiled.

Twin Serpents.

"It's okay," said Roy, "people have been confusing us for each other since we were kids. It's nice to see you again, by the way, pizza-man."

"*You're* Big Red?"

"The one and only."

"I should shoot you right now for breakin' my nose." Owen lowered the rifle in a sharp, disengaging way and leaned it against the side of the snake truck. "But before we kill you, I want to show you something." He opened the snake-truck's camper shell and pulled out a steel pole as tall as himself, and then another, and screwed them together. On the end of the two-piece pike was an L-shaped hook. "These were made to catch snakes," he said, putting on a pair of rubber gloves. "But sometimes, we use them to dredge the drainage if we ever need to." He cut across behind his brother and sauntered toward the pond, snorting loudly as he went, as if building a loogie. He spat blood again. "Come on."

Roy urged the brothers along with his own rifle.

A boardwalk led from the base of one of the cabins and ran down the hill, becoming a narrow dock. Owen led them down the dock onto the rust-orange water, the polehook thumping along like a walking stick.

Monster-movie fog hovered around them, and the water was cloudy with some blotchy substance that resembled vomit. "Them women we work for, Cutty and them, they must think we're stupid or something. They like to be secret-squirrel about it, but we know they get up to weird shit. Devil-worshippin' and black magic and whatnot." Owen spat blood in the water. "They do what they do and we do what we do, and they do it when we ain't there. Fine with me, I don't want to see it. Roy here works for 'em part-time, so I don't go up there much. I'm okay with that. They freak me out."

At the end of the pier were two cinder blocks, and on top of them was a plank with two beer cans and a bottle. Somebody's shooting range. Owen turned the polehook over and dipped it into the water. "This little pond didn't always look like this," he said, lowering it hand over hand. "Shaft flooded when the miners hit a big vein of iron sulfite and pyrite back in the day." Owen manipulated the pole like a gondolier. "Mines below the water table usually flood if you don't pump 'em out regular, but this baby is fed by a gee-oh-thermic source. That's a hot spring." He flashed them a smug grin over his shoulder. "You don't want to swim in this shit, though. From what I've been told, the iron sulfite dissolves in the water to create sulfuric acid. The county clerk calls it 'acid mine drainage.' That's why it smells like farts." He gestured around the pond, coughing once, softly. "As you've probably guessed by now, sulfuric acid makes this little spot a fantastic place to get rid of things. Everything you throw in here drifts toward the shaft in the middle and disappears into the mines underneath, never to be seen again. It can't be dredged by divers because of the acid and the heat, and it can't be drained because of the spring. Nobody can touch it. It's *perfect*."

The water stank in a caustic, chalky way, burning Joel's eyes with the smell of rotten eggs. He coughed.

"Still want me to whip you?" asked Roy.

Joel glared at him, pointing at the rifle. "If you let me stick that gun up your ass."

"Kinky." Roy laughed. "So, how was that steak?"

"I've had better."

"Sorry, it must have been the carfentanil I injected into it after I cooked it. How the hell did you get out of that garage? That roll-up was still locked when I got the door open. I didn't see a damn thing back there in the dark."

"Magic, cowboy. I'm a witch too, you know?"

Roy's smirk was a suspicious one. Joel coughed, breathing through his mouth again. The rotten-egg sulfur smell was getting to be too much.

What came out of the water wasn't a cat kennel full of bones like Joel expected, but something that looked like a piece of tinsel. They stepped aside so Owen could lay the pole down on the dock, and he picked up the metal with his glove.

"It's a retainer," he said, holding it up.

"Neither of them two Jehovah's Witness boys last month had braces," said Roy. "Must have been the girl from Thursday." He coughed. "I don't remember her having dental work, though." He coughed again, into his sleeve, and Owen tossed the retainer back into the water.

"This is where you assholes were takin' the cats?" Fisher's fists tightened, his biceps flexing. He was covered in sweat, and he was so pale from pain, he'd gone the gray-purple of a California Raisin.

"Yup." Owen made an inclusive gesture, waving his gloved hand. He seemed to relish talking about the pond, like a proud fisherman demonstrating his secret spot. "We been dumping cats in here for ages. Shelter fills up four or five times a year. Only reason there were so many in there today was"—*cough, cough*—"we been up north with the girls all summer. I'd say there's probably a good two or three thousand dead cats down there, if not more."

"Jesus Christ," said Joel. "Why?'

"Hell if I know. The girls want us to kill as many cats as possible. No skin off my teeth. I think it's fun."

Joel stiffened. "They're making cat-people zombies."

"*Zombies?*" asked Roy. "The hell you talkin' about?"

"Don't worry about it." He fought the urge to kick one of them into the grotesque water. *I wonder how fast it burns. I wonder if they'd scream.* "Why are you showin' us this? Why the science lesson?"

"Because I want you to go down knowin' ain't nobody ever gonna find you," said Owen. "Nobody will *ever* go lookin' for two soy-boy niggers, especially not at the bottom of a eighty-foot sulfur spring. You're going into the acid and you're gonna be down there until the Second Coming." He smiled. His teeth were red with blood. "*That's* for the treadmill."

"Man, let's do 'em and get out of here, I'm chokin' to damn death," said Roy, slinging the rifle over his back and drawing his revolver.

"Sounds like a plan. My nose is killin' me anyway. I got to get to the hospital or somethin'." Owen stepped on each of his gloves, pulling them off, and pulled his Glock out of his service holster.

Joel's heart surged. "*Wait—*"

Pointing the pistol, Owen shot Fish in the face.

Red brain-matter billowed across the air in a fine spray and the whip-crack of the shot whispered through the trees.

Breathless and surprised, Joel watched Fish topple over

(he would dream of this very moment, forever and ever amen, on the eternal DVR of his mind, backward, forward, and in slow motion)

and crash into the rust-colored water, flat on his back.

The two redheads turned away as the splash flecked their skin and clothes with acid-water. Joel squinted against the droplets, letting them dot his naked chest, arms, face.

The acid should have hurt, he assumed, but he couldn't feel anything because he'd gone numb from the inside out. His heart tumbled into the pit of his stomach; his legs gave way and he fell on his hands and knees, staring down at the shadow that had once been his brother. Joel slumped forward, his forehead on his fists, his fists on the dock. All those times they'd fought, it would all now go unresolved. All those years they'd drifted apart, Joel taking care of their demented mother while Fisher steered clear of the blast radius, afraid and stricken at seeing her deteriorate; they'd never get to fix that.

It was gone, forever and ever.

Desolation shattered his thoughts. All he could do was stare bleakly. The wound in his leg had burst its stitches as he'd knelt, but it was a thousand miles away. His lungs were squeezed empty and he couldn't fill them again, like the hand of God was around his chest. His eyes swam with dangling tears, turning the planks under his hands into a dark kaleidoscope.

Looking up from the water, he saw a huge black dog.

Joel's blood turned to ice water. The dog stood on the opposite bank, watching intently, a whip-thin hellhound that seemed to shimmer as if it were a reflection set free from the acid lake. The Euchiss brothers didn't appear to notice the emaciated animal, and if they did, they didn't see fit to mention it.

"I figured I'd do him first, in front of you," Owen said, coughing politely. He spat into the water. "That was for the bucket."

"Cruel, brother." Roy pulled the revolver's hammer back. The grumble of an engine reverberated from somewhere far away, sounding for all the world like a bumblebee in a tin can. "Sometimes, I think you got a mean streak in you."

Anger unlike he had ever known in his life filled Joel's heart and head and guts and fists. He turned his head and growled venomously at the muzzle of the magnum. He wanted to beat the living shit out of both of them, he wanted to pound them with his fists until his arms broke, until his body gave out, until the stars rolled up like sackcloth and the sun went dark. *"I'm going to fucking kill you,"* he said through his teeth. His face throbbed with rage.

Roy smirked. "Little late for gettin' pissy, don't you—"

A voice echoed from the cave at the top of the slope. Freddie Mercury howled, *"Who waaaants to liiiiive foreverrrrr?"*

"The hell is that?" asked Owen, looking up.

A blue pickup truck barreled out of the mine shaft, bearing down on them with one headlight.

Blood streaming down his forehead, Kenway Griffin stared through the Chevy's smashed windshield. His face was a crazed mask of rage, teeth and eyes gleaming in his blood-caked face.

Even as the truck swerved toward the pond and the boardwalk, Owen fired three shots from the Glock. *POP, POP-POP.* The first bullet sank into the smashed quarter-panel; the second and third punched through the hood and knocked the rear window out. Kenway slammed up onto the dock, his engine squealing, and drove toward them. The boards crackled and popped under the weight of two tons of metal, threatening to collapse, leaning forward.

Three things happened simultaneously:

1. Roy flung himself into the water,
2. Joel threw himself flat on his back,
3. and Owen fired one last panicked shot into the Chevy's crooked grin, screaming *"Police!"* as if that would work.

The Chevy slammed into Owen, the murderer's body clattering against the grille like a bag of bowling balls, and its undercarriage roared over Joel's face with barely an inch of clearance. He rolled over onto his belly to watch the truck drive off the end of the dock into the acid pond with an incredible splash.

In a daze of adrenaline and fumes, he stood up and his eyes wandered giddily around the scene. The truck must have carried

Owen away, because he wasn't anywhere in sight. Roy thrashed around in the red water to his right, screaming incoherently, his blue shirt turning black. Joel stumbled down to where the home-made shooting range used to stand. The Chevy's ass end stuck up out of the water like the Titanic, air bubbles gurgling out from under the body.

"Aaugh!" shouted Kenway as he ripped the frames and broken glass out of the cab's rear window, wedging himself into the gap. "Jesus! *Jesus Christ!* What is up with this water?"

"It's acid! Get out of there!"

The tailgate was a few feet away, and the bed only had a few inches of water in it toward the front. Joel stretched out and stepped on the bumper, one foot on the dock and one foot on the Georgia license plate. "Climb back here, man, come on, I'll get you out."

Kenway hauled himself through the back window and out, flop-ping like a newborn rhino into six inches of acid runoff. "Oh, ahh, shit," he hissed, scrambling onto his hands and knees. Soupy water gushed through the gap between the bed and the frame, soaking his shirt and pants in foul rusty patches. Taking the vet's hands, Joel pulled backward with every bit of strength he could muster, and Kenway clambered up and over the tailgate, throwing his weight over onto the dock. He sat up and gave Joel a hand back across, and the two of them sat there coughing, watching the truck sink into the pond. Queen's operatic howling slowly became a gargling chant until the radio shorted out with a crackle.

Ripping off his ruined shirt, Kenway threw it in. His back and belly were mottled with patches of pink, raw skin. The mud *algiz* in the middle of his chest looked like half-assed war paint. "God, oh God," Joel wept, shuffling back and forth on his hands and knees at the side of the dock, but Fisher had already submerged, fading away into the corrosive depths. "Where *is* he? I can't see my brother no more, Jesus, he's dead, fuckin' *dead,* he's dead."

"Where is he?" asked Kenway. "Did he fall in?"

"They shot him. That son of a bitch shot him in the head. God help me, I saw his brains. He fell in and now he's gone."

CLACK! The entire wooden platform shuddered and shifted, one of the boards coming loose and falling in. Kenway helped Joel to his feet. "Let's get off this thing"—*cough*—"and away from this water before we end up in there too."

They hobbled up to the rocky shore and rested, coughing, trying to catch their breath. Roy Euchiss lay motionless at the edge of the water. Most of his hair had burned off, leaving him as straggly-bald as a baby, and his clothes were waterlogged tatters, everything stained vomit-brown. Blisters were forming across the back of the man's neck and around his eye sockets, big pillowy blisters that were butter-yellow and translucent, like Dial soap. He was covered in angry red welts and it looked like he was sweating droplets of blood. But what struck Joel, and startled him so badly, was that Roy's ears and nose and fingers had turned as gray as ash.

The rotten dock finally collapsed, crashing into the water with a flat noise and a harsh clatter of nails and bits of wood. Concrete pylons jutted up from underneath it, as pitted as golf balls, and stained red. Joel scanned the other side of the acid lake, but he didn't see the strange black dog anymore. Maybe it had been some kind of trauma mirage or something. *That's a thing, right? Sure.*

"I need to get back to the hospital," said Kenway.

The veteran's blood-slimed face and the pink patches across his skin had begun to turn an angry red, and his jeans were smoking and had become like threadbare linen, fine and screenlike. His scalp was split in the middle, and it looked like he was having a hard time keeping his eyes open.

Joel said, "Okay."

Climbing into Roy's snake-truck, he sat in the driver's seat and listened to his heart continue to break. He thought about the sight of his brother toppling backward into the water. The passenger door opened and closed. Kenway sat sprawled on the passenger side, his head back and his mouth tilted open like a man already dead.

The keys were still in the ignition. Turning the engine over, Joel grabbed the windshield-wiper lever in a fist and wrenched it down, almost breaking it off. "Oh, hell, this ain't my Velvet." He grabbed the gearshift jutting up out of the center console, then paused and swore again. "I can't drive a stick."

"I think I might have a concussion," said Kenway. His voice thrummed at the lowest register, a vocal fry muttering from the back of his throat. "You better fake it, buddy."

20

Rain tappled restlessly on the hospital window. From time to time, the wind would rake a gust of water against the glass.

Even though Robin felt like a mashed insect, the hospital bed and duvet were astonishingly comfortable. The mattress felt like something she could sink into, warm and deep. Her legs were more or less pain-free except for a dull ache in her right knee, but she was sensitive, and the rough linen felt pleasurably like burlap.

A bandaged blond head was buried in a pair of folded arms, nestled into the duvet.

She reached over and stroked his shoulder, and her abdomen howled in tormented chorus with the stump of her left arm.

Kenway sat up slowly. "You're awake."

"I'm awake."

"How do you feel?"

"You know how they say hot dogs are made out of ground-up lips, foreheads, and assholes?"

"Yeah?"

"I feel like a hot dog."

Kenway smiled in exhausted sympathy.

"What the hell happened to you?" she asked, focusing on the bandage around his head. One of his eyes was ringed in a purple bruise. "Hell of a shiner."

"It's been a rough weekend. After I shot a witch and drove you to the hospital, I got in a gunfight and caught a graze across the top of my skull. When I woke up from that, I drove my truck into a lake made of acid." He leaned in close. "I think I killed two, maybe three cops," he whispered. "Also, I think someone hit me with a rock."

Robin stared at him, mouth open. "I leave you alone for ten fuckin' minutes."

"They were dirty," he said, glancing at the window. "The cops, I mean. And they were trying to kill me and Joel, so I guess it's self-defense? I don't think anybody knows about it yet. I'm honestly not sure what to do. We drove away in the killer's truck. Which I regret, because it's a piece of shit. I really traded down."

"I was right. We're all kinds of fucked-up."

"We're fighters," he said, shaking his head. "Like I told you the other day. We're in the shit. This is us. We're ghosts. We went to Narnia. This stuff doesn't happen to normal people. We're extraordinary."

"Extraterrestrial, maybe." She sighed. "Well, it wouldn't be the first time I've had to keep my mouth shut about a dead dirty cop."

"They killed Joel's brother Fish."

"Fuck!" she spat. Her heart sank. Robin sat back, her head flouncing into the pillow, and stared at the wall. *Fuck fuck fuck.* Too much bad news to take at once, especially after the night in the vineyard. The angry burn in her abs faded. "Take me out to the pasture and shoot me. I'm no good to you anymore. I'm glue." Her stomach gave a gnarly growl. "I'm also starving."

"I'll get you something." He laboriously stood up, leaning on his chair, and dug in his pocket for change. A lap tray on a floor-stand stood next to the bed, and there was a cafeteria tray on it, covered with a lid. She didn't have to open it to know the food inside would be cold. "I'll have to get you something from the vending machine. It's too late for dinner. Is that okay?"

"That's fine. What time is it?" She thought. "What *day* is it?"

"Monday night, about nine."

"I slept all Sunday night and all Monday?" She frowned and glanced at the ceiling. "Where's Wayne? Did he make it out okay?"

"He's fine. Rode in the back of the truck while I drove you here myself. I didn't trust the ambulance to get here in time, and to be honest, I didn't think about it much because after I saw what condition you were in, I was in autopilot. You were bleeding like—well, like a stuck pig."

"What about his dad?"

"I haven't seen him. Wayne came to the hospital with me last night. He hasn't been to school—he's afraid to go home. He couldn't sleep in these chairs, so he's in the waiting room down the hall."

"Leon will be fine. There's no reason to kill him, so the witches will let him stick around. We can un-familiar him with an *algiz*."

"Good. I've been worried about that. So has Wayne."

"What about Heinrich? Have you seen him?"

Kenway shook his head. "Not since he went into their hacienda. I think he walked into an ass-whooping. I helped him get inside, but then . . ." He trailed off. "I saw something that scared me."

"What did you see?"

"A ghost. I think. A very personal ghost."

"An illusion, probably. Weaver didn't go into the vineyard with me, so she must have stayed behind. Probably ambushed you with a hallucination and drove you out of the house to get you out of the picture." She sighed. Whatever mess Heinrich had gotten himself into, he deserved it. "This is *his* fault. If he hadn't gone in there like that, Marilyn would have let us walk out of there and I'd still—" Robin looked down at where her left arm had been. Thick bandaging and gauze. Not even a stump. Everything was gone right up to the shoulder. Peeling back the adhesive gauze and padding, she could see it out of the corner of her eye: a swollen hump, bristling with hairy black stitches, stained with orange Betadine. A hot bomb of loss and dismay dropped into her chest, and tears sprang to her eyes. She pressed the padding back down, less out of a desire to protect it than to hide it.

"What happened?"

"The bone was too damaged," he told her. "Lot of splinters. They had to take everything up to the joint."

It couldn't be helped; she cried, big wet pitiful boo-hoo sobs, saltwater streaming down her face. Kenway came over and bent to kiss her forehead, which only broke her heart even worse. "What am I going to do?" she asked. "What kind of a witch-hunter am I going to be with one hand?"

Kenway bit back a sad smile. "I do okay with one leg."

Shame burned her face.

"I don't know how I'm going to keep doing this with one hand," she said. "This is all I know. It's all I've ever done. I can't even open jars now."

"We'll figure something out." His smile became earnest and she reached up to feel his face, combing her slender fingers through his gingery beard. "I can be your cameraman," he said, his mustache brushing the pad of her thumb. "We'll figure out the rest as we go." Giving her hand one last squeeze, he left the room. Robin stared at the dark television.

Rain clattered softly against the windowpane.

Her cellphone lay on the bedside table. She picked it up and logged into Facebook, Twitter, and then YouTube, and finally her Gmail account. All of them were full of posts, emails, and comments from strangers emotionally invested in her video series:

Where are you?

What's going on?

Are you okay?

You haven't posted any new videos. What's happening?

Did you kill the witches?

It was true she marketed and produced the video series as if it were a fictional affair: scripted, staged, cinematic. Where the public-facing front of her "business" was concerned, it was common knowledge the videos were fake. Seriously, witches that turn into monsters and people possessed by cats don't exist, right?

Right about now, I wish they didn't.

But the people that watched her videos treated them as if they were real. They commented on each upload with words of encouragement and asked after her well-being, remarked on how attractive she was (even though she didn't believe that, not for a second), begged her for a chance to fight alongside her. Ex-military, male and female both, asked to join her personal crusade, sometimes dozens a week. A national spectrum of neckbeards and Don Juans alike professed their love for her. Cops offered their protection on the downlow and insinuated they'd turn a blind eye to the legal vagaries of her adventures, while female true-crime fans—adherents of TV shows like *Cold Case Files* and podcasts like *My Favorite Murder*—posted selfies of red apples with combat knives stuck into them—because of her exploits hunting down wife-beaters and child-molesters, she had become their patron saint of vigilante feminism, a real-life Punisher.

Searching the nooks and crannies of her mind, she couldn't think of anything to tell them. Seemed like all those millions of people following her shenanigans thus far deserved a well-thought-out, optimistic, detailed answer, and right now she didn't know if she had one in her.

Besides, it was damn hard to type with one hand.

She tested the speech-to-text function on her phone, but the pain meds had slurred her speech and the results were less than satisfactory.

"The rain in Spain falls mainly on the plain."

The brain in Spain follows mainly on the plane, it typed.

"The rain in Spain falls mainly on the plain."

The rain in Spain hauls manly only praying.

"Come on, you asshole. I know how to speak English."

Come on your asshole, uno how do speakeasy?

Kenway came back a little while later with cheese crackers, candy bars, chips, M&Ms. It looked like he'd bought half the machine. She teared up again at the sight of it all.

"Okay, okay," he said, piling red bags into her lap, "you can have the Cheez-Its."

Her sobs broke up into pained chuckles.

Since it was October, several cable channels showed marathons of horror movies. They sat up all night, eating vending-machine snacks, drinking vending-machine coffee, and watching masked maniacs slay their way through half a thousand promiscuous teenagers.

At some point, Robin slithered out of the bed feeling gross and wiped herself down with a wet paper towel, but she had to do it with the lights off, going through her ablutions by the night-light over the sink. Every time she caught a glimpse of that stitch-haired vacancy on her left side, it was everything she could do not to burst into tears again. The effort it took to avoid this, and the constant pain and itching, felt as if it were slowly driving her mad.

Crawling back into bed, she fixated on the TV screen so she didn't have to see the expression of pity and sympathy on Kenway's face. Every time she noticed his hurt puppy-dog look, she wanted to throw Cheez-Its at him, throw the TV remote at him, anything to make him stop. She was still somewhat upset by his decision to jump into the fight in her defense last night. *You could have gotten killed.* She stared at his big dumb face. *If anyone's going to be killed doing this, it's me. Not you. You're not a ghost or an alien. I'm the one that took on this life. Not you. You're not the fucked-up one, I am.*

He noticed her watching him and his face softened into a tired-eyed smile. Robin looked away, locked on to the TV screen again.

The longer the movies droned on, the heavier her eyes got. She finally fell asleep again about the time dawn-light turned the window shades blue.

21

She woke up again around lunchtime. Kenway showed up with a plate of sushi and two blueberry parfaits from the hospital cafeteria, and revealed he'd retrieved her camera and MacBook, along with her utility van.

"You've been a busy beaver," Robin asked.

"Yeah. I don't know how we're going to get Leon back, though, without you and Heinrich. I don't know shit about witches, or how much use I'm gonna be with this gash on my head. It's a concussion but I've been released from observation. They said to take it easy for a few weeks, but I have the feeling you're not done."

"As soon as I'm back on my feet, I'm going up there myself to end this." She flexed her hand. "Theresa told me something right before you put a bullet in her head: Andras—the demon—he's my father."

"Do you believe her?"

"I don't have any reason not to. Makes sense, given the time frame. My vision of her summoning Andras must have taken place before I was born, not after." *That means if Heinrich knew when the summoning ritual took place,* she thought, *he lied about what the demon means to me. He knew the price my mother had to pay.*

It was me.

I was the price.

"Is that how you made the transformation go away? Was that you?"

"Yeah. Demons eat their magic. I don't know how or why."

Kenway talked with a mouthful of California roll. For hospital sushi, it was pretty damn good. "So, you think you're gonna go back up there and do it again? Suck the magic out of them like you did Theresa?"

"If I can."

He stared at her, his eyes searching her face. "So, what does this mean? You're half-demon?" She shrugged. It was a novel concept for her, too. "I thought you said witches couldn't *have* children."

The nub of her left shoulder itched like ants were crawling around in it. She was about due for her pain meds again. She rubbed the padding gently as she spoke, careful not to pull the stitches. "I didn't think so."

"I wish Heinrich was here," he said, staring at the window. "We could ask him. Maybe he knows."

Robin scowled at the TV, clenching her remaining fist. "If Heinrich was here, I'd punch him in the goddamn nose for lying to me. And for ruining my life."

• • •

After lunch, she transferred all the footage from the camera to her laptop, and spent the afternoon editing and uploading it, while watching more horror movies with Kenway. They made it through *Sleepaway Camp* (which lost a lot of its nostalgic effect with all the censoring) and *Day of the Dead* before Kenway got up and put on his jacket.

"I'm gonna go pick up Wayne and bring him up here," he said, jingling keys. "He's at school."

She surrendered a dim smile. "Thank you for taking care of him. Thank you for *everything*, really. You don't have to, but you are, and that's really good of you. You know? You don't even know these people. Hell, *I* barely do. I only know them because they're living in my old house."

"What else am I going to do? Besides, I like doin' things for people like this. I like having a purpose. Sitting around my apartment feeling sorry for myself and for Chris Hendry, painting depressing pictures—what kind of life is that?"

Feeling sorry for myself. Robin nodded. "Yeah, okay. Well, be careful out there. It's been raining."

He saluted, letting himself out.

She sat in the bed, editing footage until her bladder was about to burst. She'd been to the bathroom once that morning already, as soon as she got up, and twice last night—a laborious, pain-wracked trek on cold tile—but the coffee she'd had with lunch was going right through her. Leaving the MacBook on the duvet, she swung her legs down onto the floor, slipped her feet into a pair of gift-shop slippers, and shuffled into the bathroom.

The itching in her shoulder was getting worse. She massaged the bandage, which wrapped around her boobs like a binder and held a thick wad of absorbent material against the surgery area. "Damn, I'm glad I can afford insurance," she told the cold, desolate bathroom, releasing a stream of urine into the toilet.

When she came out, a man sat in Kenway's chair: a handsome, clean-shaven fellow in a neat suit of rich navy blue.

Everything else about him was pale: his wolfish alabaster face, his limpid seawater eyes, his bone-blond hair. His angular stick-figure frame—along with the creepy black cane in his hand—made him look like a European fashion model. He had affixed an enamel pin to the lapel of his jacket, and there was something about it so familiar, it actually made Robin's skin flash cold, but she couldn't quite place it.

Then she understood. It was the same pin she'd seen on Heinrich's nightstand—the green-and-gold dog head in profile, surrounded by laurels and a banner inscribed with unreadable symbols. Around the dog's neck was a longbow.

Her heart beat a little faster.

"Hello," she said, surprised. "Can I help you?"

"You don't know me, but I know you." He smiled tightly. "My name is Anders Gendreau. We've been watching you, Ms. Martine. You're one of the most prolific witch-hunters that's ever operated in the United States."

"There are others?"

"Only my people, currently, and maybe a few others. And Heinrich. I don't suppose he ever told you about the group he used to be a part of." He spoke eloquently, with a hint of an accent she couldn't quite place, and a saccharine, gentlemanly manner that made him seem like a character from a Tim Burton movie.

"He said he escaped from a cult," she replied. "Marilyn Cutty said something about it last night, right before she ordered her coven-mate to tear my arm off. Which, you know, wouldn't have happened if you'd been there to help me. *Where the hell* have you guys *been* all this time?"

The corner of Gendreau's right eye twitched. "If you'll sit and listen, I'll explain everything."

"How about you explain my foot in your skinny ass?"

He cleared his throat, looking bemused. Robin sat on the bed in a huff.

"Heinrich Hammer, whose real name is Hank Atterberry, was once a member of our organization, the Dogs of Odysseus. We're a society of practicing magicians, and proudly count a number of famous, influential individuals among our members."

"Hank Atterberry?" said Robin, stiffening. "No wonder he changed his name. Sounds like he should be some retired guy living in a shitty little house in Tennessee, yelling at the raccoons that keep getting into his garbage."

Gendreau chuckled.

"So," Robin continued, "The 'Dogs of Odysseus,' huh? Quaint. Your basic secret world-governing cult, right? You're the Illuminati, aren't you?"

"Not so much. We're more like . . . the Avengers. The superhero Avengers, not the old British Avengers Steed and Peel."

"There's a British Avengers?"

"Before your time, I suppose. Before mine as well."

She snorted grimly.

"Too precious?" smirked Gendreau. "The UN of magic, then."

"A tribunal."

"Nothing so barbaric." He produced a folded piece of paper from his jacket pocket and handed it to her. She found a black-and-white sketch of the Osdathregar, in high resolution. On second thought, it was—what do they call them? Lithographs? Woodcuts? One of those, something you'd see in a history book. "I'm here because you and he have something that belongs to us. Well, a lot of things, mostly books, a small fortune in historical documents, but this is the main thing I'd like to address."

Sitting here in this hospital bed, staring at this drawing, Robin felt as if she had drifted out of the shallow end of the pool and into a deep darkness.

"We've been trying to find his hideout for several years now, and searching for you for about a year, ever since you started posting videos of your exploits to YouTube." Gendreau's grin displayed the toothy canines of a meat-eating man. "You're a hard woman to track down, living on the road like that. We knew where you'd been, thanks to your videos, on about a week delay, but we never knew where you were heading." The toothy grin faded. "But that's no matter now, is it? Here you sit in front of me, and here I sit, and this is the end of the line."

"How did you finally find me?"

"Your videos indicated you were in Blackfield. From there it was a simple matter of going to your childhood home in Slade Township. But when I got there last night, you were being evacuated." Gendreau sat back and leveled the black cane across his knees. "I decided it wasn't in either of our best interests to interrupt your trip to the hospital."

"Why didn't you try to contact me through my YouTube channel? Or my Facebook? Or my Twitter?"

Gendreau glanced at the TV, sighed, and said to her, "We've emailed you several times this year, to no avail. I figured Heinrich had poisoned you against us."

"I have a particularly aggressive spam filter. Also, I get like a thousand new emails every day through the business address on my YouTube channel, and half of them are crazy-ass bullshit from people that really should be taking their medication. So, if I got one email in a hundred thousand emails talking nonsense about dog magicians, and those other ninety-nine thousand, nine hundred and ninety-nine emails are all talking about third eyes, Sasquatch, reptilian politicians, and blonde Nordic angels from deep space, please excuse me if I didn't take it quite as seriously as I should have."

The shaft of his cane was made out of a twisting dark shape that seemed organic but not very wooden at all. The head was a pearl the approximate size of a billiard ball.

He smiled. "Admiring my cane?"

"It's different."

"It's made out of the penis of an Indian bull." He raised it until it pointed straight up in the air, and Robin couldn't help but draw the obvious parallel. "Which makes it an apt magical conduit. The pearl contains a heartstone, a *libbu-harrani* drawn from the breast of a witch. The pearl was formed around it, in the mouth of a giant clam."

"That's gross as hell. Why would you choose to carry that around?"

"I didn't. It was simply the artifact I resonated the most with, out of the dozens of charmed items in the Dogs' lockup. Believe me, if I didn't have to carry a huge dehydrated phallus around like some kind of magical Ed Gein, I wouldn't. I'd much rather have a pocket watch, or a lighter like Rook, or a pair of scissors like Elena. But this grotesque thing was the only object in Francis Gendreau's collection with curative properties."

"Who are Rook and Elena? Are they magicians too?"

"Yes, they are friends of mine. We are all students and collaborators in the Dogs of—"

"—Odysseus, yes."

"Indeed."

Wonder if I could close Gendreau's heart-road if I touch the cane. She probably could. But in this state, the man would make short work of her if she tried. She considered asking him for a demonstration of his magical abilities, but in a place like a city hospital, unleashing arcane power had the possibility of drawing unwanted attention.

Better safe than sorry. She folded the paper and gave it back. "I assume you're here for the Osdathregar."

"Down to brass tacks, I see. Yes, at some point in our professional relationship—and by *our* I mean *me and you,* and by *at some point* I mean to say *within the next couple of days*—I'm here to retrieve the dagger."

"I don't have it."

"That much is obvious. I assume Heinrich has it, wherever he's hiding."

A pack of cheese crackers lay on the bedside table; she picked it up and tore it open with her teeth, taking out one of the crackers and cramming it into her gob, talking with her mouth full. "He's not hiding, as far as I know. He's still with the witches. He could be dead, for all I know, and good riddance. Lying bastard." It felt good to have new hate for someone inside of her, a freshly stoked fire in her chest. The cold, desultory determination she'd felt for Marilyn had dwindled over the last five years to a dull ache. But now she had a new face to want to punch. It was a driving, satisfying need that gave her an edge. She didn't trust this weird magician guy as far as she could throw him—and today, that was about half as far as she could have thrown him yesterday—but if he could line her up for another shot at both the coven and Heinrich, then she would play along and see what he had to offer. *If his deal turns out to be rotten,* she thought, studying his face, *au revoir, toodle-oo, auf wiedersehen. Hit the road, Jack.*

"That's too bad." Gendreau stood the cane on the floor. "Marilyn Cutty's coven is now in possession of the Osdathregar. It may very well be beyond our grasp now."

"*You* can't go get it?"

The magician's sleek, vulpine smile reappeared, but this time, it was tinged with regret. "Cutty is quite powerful, even by herself, never mind the fact she's got two coven-mates and a Matron. With the Osdathregar, the danger would only be moderately lessened. Assaulting her property without the dagger would be like attacking the White House with a salad fork."

"What if I told you I killed her middling coven-mate last night with my bare hands?"

"I'd call you a liar. Not only that but a *damn* liar."

She corrected herself. "Well, with *this* hand." She held up her right fist. "As you can see, I seem to have misplaced my other one."

The magician wheezed a chuckle. "So you have. At any rate, beside the fact you can only kill a witch by pinning her down with the Osdathregar and burning her to ashes, the youngest member of her coven has almost a century on you."

"Theresa LaQuices transformed into a huge boar-monster and attacked me and the people I was with, and bit off my arm. Before I passed out, I grabbed the hog's nose like this," Robin said, and pinched the rim of her nostril, "and somehow, I managed to draw the power out of her and close the *libbu-harrani* inside her. I didn't let go until she was back to human again, and then my friend Ken-way blew her brains out."

"Bullets don't work on them—" began Gendreau.

"This time, it did." Robin bit the other cracker-half and chewed, making a mess all over the sheet. "I think closing the heart-road turned her human again for a few minutes."

Gendreau openly boggled at her. "The ritual Heinrich gave to your mother all those years ago," he said, his words coming out in a breathless murmur, "your mother was . . . *taken* by Andras, wasn't she? He's an incubus, isn't he?"

"No. She gave herself willingly." Robin's lips were numb with epiphany, and so was her hand. "And I'm the offspring of that en-counter. I was the price for the demon's protection. I was the deal she made. A child for protection."

"The demon got her with child somehow. *You're* that child. And you've got that, that *way,* that *talent* of devouring their power, don't you?" The man shifted uneasily, his eyes wide and staring. "So, *that's* why Heinrich gave the ritual to your mother. He wasn't try-ing to bring Andras into the material world, he knew he couldn't do that. By God, he was trying to bring *you* into it."

Anger flared in Robin's chest. "He *engineered* my entire exis-tence?" she demanded. "Why? Why would he do that?" Absent-mindedly, she reached up to rub at the padding over her stitches again, trying to quell the constant itching that had flowered there since last night. The pain underneath was monumental (especially here on the back end of a dose of Percocet), but it was nothing com-pared to the phantom-limb itching.

"To buy his way back into the Dogs." Gendreau leaned forward. "We assumed he was trying to replicate what got him drummed out to begin with: trying to summon a demon and use it against the witches." He cleared his throat politely, pointedly, *ahem.* "We have rules about trying to conjure demons, as you can imagine. Fully summoning a demon into the material plane for that specific purpose would be like wiping all of Europe off the face of the planet with nuclear bombs just to get rid of Italy. Besides, no one's gotten a demon through the Sanctification since it went up. Not only is it against our law, it's functionally impossible."

"But he figured out how to use a demon to craft a secret weapon that would make it through the barrier." Robin gave a shallow, petulant sigh. "Me. Annie was his Trojan horse, his drug mule, to get *me* into the material plane."

"Exactly. He knew the—"

"No." She glared at him. Robin knew what he was about to say, and she knew better. She knew *Heinrich* better. "He *hoped.* He didn't know for sure. My mother was his guinea pig. The demon could have killed her, and he would have found someone else to manipulate."

Gendreau went quiet. He swallowed, smoothing his tie down his chest. As she watched him fidget (so unlike her first impression of him), she realized he was anxious. Afraid of her?

He had a right to be.

And if he double-crossed her, or turned out to be a flake and his flowery exposition fell apart, she would give him a good reason to be afraid.

"You are . . . a cambion," he said, finally, with a grim, revelatory wonder.

"What's that?"

"It's a very old word for a being half-human and half-demon." He cleared his throat and leaned forward, his head sinking and his eyes closing as if reaching back in time. Then he looked up at the ceiling, and at Robin. "Enfans des demons. *Cambion* is a word for the term *changeling,* first published in the 1818 *Dictionnaire Infernal,* and stems from the Celtic root *kamb,* meaning *crooked.*"

Crooked? Robin frowned. As if she didn't have it bad enough this week. As if she weren't crooked enough already, with her candy-van and her gory videos.

Time passed while she stared at her duvet and Gendreau sat

there, quietly, doing nothing but staring at her. She supposed the magician was allowing her to absorb and internalize what he'd told her. The academic, self-satisfied expression on his face—like some haughty tenured professor that's gotten his idiot students to work through some moderately difficult equation—made her want to clock him in the chin. But something told her the Dogs of Odysseus's imperative against demons might extend to her, and that needed to be addressed.

She sighed. "So, now what?"

"The ball is now in your court, cambion. Go after Cutty yourself, and retrieve the dagger."

"I meant 'now what' with *you*. You said your people have a thing against summoning demons. I thought secret occultist societies were into that kind of thing. For that matter, why *do* you hunt witches, anyway? Aren't you guys and witches like this?" she asked, twining her index and middle fingers together.

Gendreau shook his head. "The Dogs of Odysseus have come a long way since Aleister Crowley's death. His Thelemic Society splintered into a dozen disparate factions, some following the path of White, some following the paths of Black and Red magic. The Dogs are one of White and light. We were once a dark collective called the Aster Argos after Crowley's Castle of the Silver Star, until my grandfather Francis Gendreau ascended to a leadership position in 1964 and moved the headquarters to Michigan. The Aster Argos became a White organization called the Dogs of Odysseus and dedicated itself to the dissolution and eradication of Black magic like Ereshkigal's witches, as well as the collection, cataloguing, and destruction or storage of Black magic artifacts."

Something told her his occult Avengers gang wasn't as virtuous as he made it out to be, but she didn't interrupt. She was enjoying the history lesson, regardless of how little she trusted him. If it was a fiction, it was an engaging one. But why would he lie about the group's provenance? Who would bother constructing such an elaborate history? No, the betrayal would come down the line.

When it would hurt the most, like Heinrich. They would string her along just long enough to get what they wanted, then throw her to the wolves.

Still. She was stuck, in the hospital. For now. So, history lesson it must be. She would burn that bridge when she came to it.

"Why dogs, though?"

"In Homer's epic poem *The Odyssey*, the main character has a dog named Argos, a greyhound. Aster Argos means *dog star*. While Odysseus was gone on his twenty-year adventure, Argos stayed behind, protecting his master's property from the men that schemed to take his wife and home." Gendreau's eyes came down to the pin on his lapel. He held it closer so she could see the details of the dog and bow. "We are the guard dogs that serve to protect the world of mankind from those who would call dark energies to claim or destroy it. That's what the symbols around the perimeter mean, by the way—our motto is *Loyalty is Strength*."

Folding the cellophane over the rest of the cheese crackers, Robin put them back on the bedside table. "So, what does all this mean for me?" she asked, picking crumbs off the duvet and folding them up into the napkin from lunch.

"What does all this mean for you as far as being part demon, you mean."

She nodded, not looking up.

Gendreau sighed. "I expect I'll need to consult with the others and see what they say." He studied her at length. "As for what *I* think: if it were entirely up to me, as soon as the Osdathregar is back in our hands, I would leave you alone and let you go back to what you were doing. You seem to be getting on pretty well to me. *Damn* well, honestly. In hindsight, I suspect it's because of your demon heritage. You've probably been sipping at their essences without knowing it these past few years, growing stronger with every kill, the demon side of you unconsciously nibbling at their heart-roads. It's probably why you're sitting up and cracking jokes two days after your arm was bitten off by a monster." The corner of his mouth rose in a half-smile. "Didn't that seem strange to you?"

After the last few days, it was hard to pick out what was the strangest, and sitting up watching the *Halloween* series on AMC the day after amputation surgery seemed like the least strange of all.

Robin stared at the MacBook sitting open in front of her, trying to process all this new information. She'd been keeping her mind busy with video editing all afternoon, but now there was no way to block it out of her head. The pieces of the last two years—hell, her entire *life*—were coming together and creating a great jagged-edged puzzle picture.

So, this is who I am, she thought.

A liberating revelation, to be sure, to finally find her identity buried at the bottom of the Goodwill pile of life. She had never been sick that she could recall. She was none the worse for wear from the smoking. Come to think of it, she'd weathered injuries that would have incapacitated lesser people—dislocations, beatings, cuts, bites. She was covered in scars that should have landed her in a grave years before.

She rubbed the padding on her shoulder again. It felt like she had ants under her skin, which did not bode well under these circumstances. She hoped Karen Weaver wasn't screwing with her in some long-distance bid to drive her out of town.

"I'll do my best to convince the Dogs to leave you alone," said Gendreau. "It may help to introduce you to them, and allow them to see how—*ahem*—relatively harmless you are. You're no rampaging monster, I can see that as plain as the nose on my face."

The sleek magician got up from the chair and went to the door. Before he pulled it open, he turned and tucked one hand behind his back.

"When—"

"You know, I don't think I like the idea of my fate being up to a bunch of know-it-all cultists I've never met." She scowled at him.

"How do I know I can trust you? One of your 'Dogs' has already royally screwed me over. How do I know you're not going to do it too?"

"How do I know I can trust *you*?"

"Because I got a trophy from YouTube for getting a million subscribers. They don't hand those things out to every Tom, Dick, and Harry, you know. You have to earn YouTube's trust."

The magician laughed. "Would it make you feel better to know they give us licenses, and we have to qualify with our artifacts and prove we can safely use them before we are allowed to carry them?"

"It would make me feel better if I didn't have to prove my integrity to a man that looks like the Prince of the Elven Realms and smells like a spice rack."

The magician did not laugh. "Maybe it would make you feel better that we know how many crimes you've committed in the course of your self-imposed duties, and yet we chose to send a lone emissary to speak to you directly instead of simply informing the FBI about your activities, showing them documentation of said activities, providing them with the relevant arrest warrants, and then telling them where you are."

"You haven't done that because you need me."

"Indeed. You are the first cambion born in two thousand years, and my grandfather wants to study you for our research. And you haven't stabbed me and subsequently jumped out the window because you need the Dogs to help defeat the Blackfield coven. So, evidently, we need each other. I propose a compromise."

"I don't need shit."

"Other than help shifting gears in your stick-shift utility van, tying your shoes, and buttoning your fly."

"That's a low blow." Robin winced.

"You are not the only one here capable of antagony, Malus Domestica." Turning back to the door, Gendreau added, "As I was about to say, my sarcastic new friend, when you're ready to go after Cutty, come get me. I have something that may help you. I'm staying at the Lake Craddock cabins down by the interstate." He smiled and hitched the pizzle cane into the air, to Robin's disgust. "The little café at the top of the mountain has the *best* view."

After he left, she sneered at the door. "I'll shift *your* gears, asshole," she said, and then took out her phone to look up the definition of the word *antagony*.

22

After Gendreau left, Robin put on a pair of sweatpants and went to the cafeteria for something to drink, wishing the hospital served whiskey. Sitting at a table in the back was Joel Ellis. The pizza chef was fully dressed in a sweater and jeans, though his skin was livid with tiny cuts and scrapes. The do-rag on his head matched his undershirt.

"Hey, man," she said, sitting down at his table.

"What are *you* doing here—" he started to say, and then he sat up in shock. "What the hell happened to your arm?"

Robin glanced at the padding. "Oh, this?"

"Yeah, *this*, chick. Y'dadgum *arm* is gone." He got up and sat closer, on her left side.

She rubbed the cotton again. *If only my arm was still there so I could scratch the damn thing.* "Sounds like we've both got a story to tell." She took a deep drink of her soda to wet her whistle. "I guess I'll start, since you seem to be so up in arms about my . . . arm."

She told him about going back into the Darkhouse and receiving the demon's vision, right on up to the doomed dinner party and the Hogwitch biting her arm off.

"Sweet baby Jesus," said Joel. "You're that thing's *daughter*?" He pulled out a labeled sandwich baggie with yellow pills in it and swallowed one with his drink. "Sorry." He belched. "I'm not high enough for this shit." This declaration segued into *his* story about getting jumped at his house by Bowker, getting shot in the leg, the truck crash, the cat fire, Fisher's execution, and the Queen ambush at the sulfite drainage pond in the quarry.

Damn, she thought. *Bunch of dead cats.*

The witches are planning a siege.

"I'm so sorry about your brother." Robin's remaining hand clasped Joel's.

His eyes sank to their combined hands and he stared at their knuckles. When he'd given the moment room to settle, and he could talk without choking up, Joel told her about yesterday. "The county cops came to talk to us after we told the nurses how we got hurt . . . I guess the hospital called the law. I rode out to the Mushroom Mines with a couple officers to show 'em the cat truck and Bowker's body, and told them what happened up at the quarry. I let 'em know it was self-defense, told 'em about Fish. They're investigatin' everything, I guess. We're not being charged with anything—nothin' *yet*, anyway—but neither one of us can leave town until it's finished. They said something about dredging the pond, but with all that acid, I don't think it's possible.

"Anyway, it turns out Bowker and Euchiss were the only two cops on the take. None of the others knew anything about it. Or at least none of them admitted anything." Joel took his hand back and studied it grimly. "They didn't believe me when I told 'em who was behind everything, though. For all I know, they're all in on it, and they let Foghorn Leghorn and Chickenhawk eat shit and washed their hands of the incident." Joel darkened. "The cops may come and talk to you."

"That's fine." She opened her Styrofoam cup and crunched some ice. "So, they said they'd been dumping stray cats in that drainage pond for years?"

"Euchiss said there was two or three thousand down there."

Robin studied the people around them—nurses, doctors, patients. She wondered how many of them were carrying around a secret cat. *God, that sounds crazy as hell,* she thought, not for the first time realizing the things she had to talk about, and the things she had to deal with, were just as crazy as anything Mike/Mark from Medina Psychiatric had to tell her. *Ten thousand shillings in a potato sack.* "They've been familiarizing the city. With that many cats, they've probably got their claws into a third of Blackfield's population."

A man in a white lab coat standing in line for hamburgers stared at her. Even from here, she could see his honey-colored eyes and the vertical slits of his pupils.

Maybe not so crazy after all.

"My mama burned these into me and my brother when we were little." Joel showed Robin the *algiz* branded into his hip. "Must have been what kept me and Fish from being taken over." He leaned an elbow on the table, supporting his head with a hand. He looked exhausted. "So, what happened with Fish's cat?"

"Must have been Cutty." Robin stole one of his French fries. "She took over the cat and tried to familiarize one of you with it kamikaze-style. I've seen it before. It didn't work, though, because you had the *algiz* on you. But if it didn't go into you and it didn't go into your brother, where did it go? Who else was around?"

"Your boo Kenway."

"*Kenway?*" she asked, eyes widening. "Really? He didn't say anything about it to me."

"I don't think he knew. I don't know if he blocked it out or what."

"There you are," said the big veteran, sitting down. Wayne Parkin was with him, wearing a bookbag. The boy stared down at the table and ate a granola bar in tiny, disconsolate bites.

"Speak of the devil." Robin reached over and squeezed his shoulder. "Don't worry, dude," she told him, staring into his eyes. "We are absolutely going to save your dad." Speaking to the whole table, she announced, "Tonight. I'm going to go up there and end this. Tonight."

Kenway frowned. "Are you sure you're up to that?"

Their eyes were all locked on her. A feeling of angry misery passed briefly over her, followed by a sensation of anxious responsibility. It was surprising to realize she actually sort of liked it, this feeling of purpose, and of being held to a task. It shouldn't have been. She had grown accustomed to being relied on by the subscribers to her YouTube channel.

But this was different. These people, they were *real*, physical, close enough to touch, and they had real stakes in the game she was going up to bat in. Robin took a deep breath and sighed through her nose, feeling burdened.

"I'm goin' with you." Joel tapped the table as if he were putting down a poker hand. Cool resolve materialized in his eyes, a steely effect Robin wouldn't have thought him capable of. Pride swelled in her chest. "They killed my brother. I'll be damned if I'm gonna let 'em get away with it without puttin' in *my* two cents' worth."

"You know I'm goin' too." Kenway folded his arms, his elbows on the table. "Being your cameraman sidekick, and all."

The ball was really rolling now. Robin regarded them all with respect and anxiety and only hoped she could keep them all alive to the end. "I'm used to working alone," she said, giving them the Batman spiel. "I can't protect you all."

Shit, I can't believe I forgot to mark Kenway.

"Speaking of protecting, I am such an asshole," she said, grabbing Wayne's backpack and digging a black marker out of it. She pulled up Kenway's shirt and drew an *algiz* rune on his chest. "With everything going on, I totally forgot to put one of these on you back at the house on Underwood the other night. That thing with the cat is totally my fault."

"We can protect ourselves—I think we've proven *that* to be true." Joel sat back and folded his arms. "*I* ain't afraid to smack a muhfuckin demon with the phone. Ring-*ring!*"

"Maybe," said Robin, drawing another *algiz,* and then one on each of Wayne's hands for good measure. "But these help."

• • •

"You said you quit taking your antipsychotic medication over the weekend," Kenway said when they got back to the hospital room. "How long have you been taking that stuff? What did you say it was?"

"Abilify." Robin climbed into the bed and sat on the duvet. The TV was still on, and it was still turned to a horror movie, this one being *Psycho.* Anthony Perkins's black-and-white face filled the screen as they talked.

"What does it do?"

Wayne sat in the chair next to the bed, rummaging through his bookbag, which looked quite full. *Kids these days have a lot of homework,* Robin thought, watching him. He still seemed despondent, always watching the floor with a frown, and she couldn't help but feel for him. *He's still broken up over his dad missing. Man, I have got to pull through for this kid.*

"Umm . . ." She rubbed her face in thought. "It's a dopamine agonist."

Kenway shrugged in confusion. "Mickey Mouse–style, please."

"Okay: dopamine is the pleasure chemical. Your body releases it when you do pleasurable things, like cocaine, sex, when you get chills from listening to orchestral music. An agonist makes you more receptive. It's used to treat low-dopamine conditions."

"You really know a lot about this stuff," said Kenway.

Robin shrugged. "A couple of years living with taking them every day, you eventually learn a few things about them."

He paced back and forth between the bed and the TV. "Since we found out you don't actually *have* schizophrenia—the voices and hallucinations have been Andras trying to draw you here, back to your childhood home—then I imagine the Abilify's been, what, double-dipping your dopamine? If that's even possible?"

"I guess it has. Maybe? I don't know." She laughed. "I guess that makes me double-dopey, dude."

Putting his weight on one foot, Kenway leaned his elbows on the footboard. He did that from time to time, presumably to give his prosthetic foot a rest. He looked like he needed a break too. Beat all to hell, with bags under his eyes. "So, maybe it's what's been suppressing your demon side all this time. Maybe having a high load of dopamine in your system keeps a lid on that side of you."

Another tingle of itchiness. Robin rubbed the dressing again, wincing at the deep ache. "When you lost your leg—" She hesitated. "Did it itch all the damn time like this does?"

"Yeah," said Kenway, tugging at his jeans leg so the prosthetic foot glistened in the sunbeam coming through the window. "It still does, sometimes. I can tell you a trick they taught me at the VA for dealing with that kind of thing if you want."

"Please. It's driving me nuts."

"What I do is, if my phantom foot itches, I take a hand-mirror and put it next to my foot so the reflection of my good foot overlaps my fake foot, so it looks like I still have two real feet. And then I scratch the real foot."

Robin angled her head so she could see her shoulder out of the corner of her eye. "Where would I put the mirror? Between my boobs?"

"Uhh. Good point, I guess."

Someone knocked at the door and a doctor let herself in, checking her watch. "Good afternoon, folks," she said quietly. Despite the authoritarian white labcoat and clipboard, the visitor's shock of dark hair and youthful face made her look like a teenager.

To their surprise, it was Fisher's girlfriend, Marissa Baker. Robin was glad to see her eyes were normal and not the gimlet screwheads of a familiar, but her face was drawn and dark. "I'm Dr.—oh. Hi."

"Hi," said Robin.

"You're . . . Joel Ellis's friend, right? Robin? I remember you from Game Night." Marissa noticed the other people in the room. "Hi, Kenny. It's good to see you."

"Hey," said Kenway. He stepped in for a hug, which Marissa stiffly accepted. "Are you doing okay? Hey, why are you *here*? I mean—"

"Please." Marissa warded away any further questions with a hand. "This is how I deal with things. I work. If I go home, I will be by myself, with nothing but my thoughts, and that won't be good for anybody, least of all me." The room paused, everybody awkwardly assessing each other. Marissa stared at Robin's chart as if it had been written in some other language, then looked up at them. "Ms. Baker will have a hard time later. Right now, Dr. Baker has shit to do." She glanced at Wayne. "Sorry—*stuff* to do."

The boy shrugged.

"I'm going to take a look at you right quick." Her very human eyes rose from the clipboard and widened, magnified by her glasses. "Wow, you're already up and moving around?"

"I come from hearty Irish stock," said Robin, closing her MacBook.

"Evidently. Your paperwork says you were . . . in a car accident?"

"Yep."

"Jesus." Marissa hung the clipboard on the end of the bed. "How fast were you driving?"

"Not fast enough, apparently."

She shot Robin a look of grim concern and glanced down at the scars running up the witch-hunter's wrist. "It pains me to ask and I know you probably don't want to hear it, but . . . you're not having suicidal ideations, are you?"

"Not these days." Robin sucked her upper lip, noticing her noticing the scars. "So sue me, I took it really hard when they stopped making 3D Doritos."

"Gonna have to take your gown off for me to examine you." Marissa stuck her hands in her coat pockets, eyeing Kenway and Wayne. "Are you all right with your friends being in here for that?"

Wallowing around in his chair, Wayne faced the wall. "I can turn around like this." He opened the textbook he'd been reading again. "Is that okay?"

"That's fine," said Robin.

She met Kenway's eyes and he stood there obliviously for a second. "Oh, right." He turned to face the TV and watched an Arby's commercial.

While Robin shrugged out of her hospital gown, Marissa's brow went up in recognition as she glanced over her glasses at Wayne. Digging in her pocket, she took out a pair of purple nitrile gloves, wriggling her hands into them, *snap, snap*. "I thought you looked familiar. I didn't expect to see you back so soon, Mr. Parkin. How's the leg? I trust you've been staying away from the snakes this weekend."

"It's a lot better," Wayne said over his shoulder, pushing his glasses up with his knuckles. "Thank you. No, no more snakes."

"You aren't into country cures too, are you?" Marissa went to work peeling off the adhesive gauze and removing the dressing. Orange Betadine and dried brown blood made a pit in the center of the absorbent padding. "It's been one hell of a weekend," she was saying in her clipped Midwest cadence. "I'm starting to wonder if my medical license is becoming obsolete. First, some lady brings in a kid with a snakebite she's put a witch-doctor poultice on and he's walking around that night and even sneaking out of the hospital. I mean, really? And now I've got a girl that lost her arm in a high-speed car accident and she's up two days later, joking about oh . . . *What the hell is that!*"

An iceberg dropped into the pit of Robin's stomach.

Even though her chest was still on stage, Wayne and Kenway immediately turned to look. Marissa had completely removed the dressing, revealing the angry, gnarled flap of skin where the wound had been sealed over in a huge U of whiskery stitches and glinting steel staples.

A black tendril four or five inches long was tonguing its way out of the surgery scar, reaching out like a time-lapse video of a tree-sprout germinating from an acorn.

"Unnnh!" grunted Kenway. "What the hell."

Wayne stared. "Whoa."

The tendril writhed and explored like an earthworm seeking moisture, groping around Robin's armpit.

On closer inspection, it was the red-black of red wine or a dry kidney bean. The worm-thing didn't stink—didn't even have a smell outside the fact her armpit was right there—but the sight of it was enough to turn her stomach. Robin covered her eyes and faced away like a little girl getting a vaccine, but she could still feel it licking insidiously at her ribs and the swell of her left breast, the faint tickles of a ghost-finger.

She stared in terror at the insides of her eyelids, shaking. "What in the world *is* that? Why is it *inside* me?"

"Hell, *I* don't know!" Marissa's voice broke.

Panic set in and then she couldn't seem to get enough air, there wasn't enough oxygen in the room no matter how hard she gasped for it. "For the love of God, get it *out* of me. Get it out get it out get it *out.*"

Marissa licked her lips in thought and her head darted this way and that, searching the room. "Dammit," she said, patting herself down. "I don't have anything to grab it with."

"Use your fingers!" cried Kenway.

"Yes, well, all right, then," said the doctor, and she put her left hand on Robin's ribs, gingerly taking hold of the tendril with her right in a sort of pen-grip, as if she were going to sign her name on the surgery scar. It snaked back and forth, curling around her finger, and she tucked her face into the pit of her own shoulder to gather herself.

"So help me God," Marissa said with a muffled cough, and pulled the tendril.

Even under the Percocet, it hurt like it was stapled to her very heart. Robin shouted into the quiet hospital room as tears flooded her eyes. "*RRHHAAAAAAAAHHHH!!*"

The doctor let go and stepped back with her hands up in surrender, shaking like she'd been shot at. "Wait right here," she said, ripping off her gloves as she strode at the door—*at,* not *to;* she pretty much walked *at* the door in her haste to get out. "I'll be back in two shakes." She snatched the door open and stepped outside, pulling it shut.

"Come on." Robin slid out of the bed and crammed her feet into her combat boots, digging through the overnight bag Kenway had packed from the clothes in her van. She wriggled into a T-shirt and jeans and zipped the bag shut, picking it up. "We need to get out of here."

"What? Why?" asked Kenway.

"Because I don't know what this thing in my shoulder is, but I feel like they're not going to be able to get it out without really hurting me." Robin went to the door and pulled it open a crack, pressing one eye to the gap even though she didn't know who she expected, if anyone at all. "Also . . . I think it's got something to do with Andras, and I really don't want hhh—I don't want doctors messing around with it."

Good God. Skin crawled down her spine. She'd almost said *human doctors.*

Other than a few nurses bustling up and down the hall and a man sitting in a wheelchair at the end, there was no one on the wing. She looked back at the man who had followed her this far and told him with her eyes she needed him to go a little farther. Kenway's face tumbled through concern and confusion, settling on grim acceptance. He put all of Wayne's stuff back in his bookbag and grabbed the baggie of pain meds off the nightstand.

"Okay," he said, shoving the pills into his pocket, "let's go, lady."

The nonchalant scurry down the hall and past the nurses' station was a lot less intense than Robin anticipated, though she couldn't have told you who she thought would show up to stop them. Riding four floors down in the elevator was an exercise in restraint, because the tendril was nosing around inside the sleeve of her T-shirt like a cat lost in a bedsheet. Looking at it made her want to throw up. Wayne happened to see it out of the corner of his eye and he sidled away against the wall, folding his arms.

"Did that really hurt as much as that scream made it sound?" asked Kenway. "Is it attached to something?"

"I think so. Felt like it."

The elevator door clunked open and the three of them hustled through the lobby. "Ma'am?" said a woman sitting behind the help desk. She called again, a little more insistently this time. "Ma'am?" Robin pushed the front door open.

To her surprise, the sun made her sneeze, and with the Percocet in her system, it jarred her like a blow to the head, and she had to steady herself against one of the protective pylons in front of the crosswalk. As soon as she gained her bearings, she took off running into the crowded parking lot, her combat boots clopping across the tarmac. She forgot Kenway said he'd driven his land-yacht of a pickup into the acid lake, so she half-expected to see it in the parking lot, but her Conlin Plumbing van was parked out there instead.

The top of scrawny Wayne's head appeared from the labyrinth of cars, and then Kenway came jogging awkwardly along on his fake leg like a bicycle with square wheels. He unlocked the doors and the three of them piled in. "Are we going to save my dad now?" asked Wayne from his perch in the back of the van.

Robin's heart plunged a bit at the excited hope in his voice. "Not yet, bud. I gotta see a man about something first."

He bit back a frown. "Where we going?"

"To the cabins up by Lake Craddock," Robin said, pulling on her seat belt. The gruesome worm-thing sticking out of her stitches was seven or eight inches now, long enough to curl lasciviously around the vinyl strap. "I know somebody that can help us save your dad . . . and who might know what the hell *this* thing is."

23

The old white van coursed down the highway into the hills north of Blackfield, passing through the township of Slade, or at least the primordial wilderness people referred to by that name. Other than the turnoff for Underwood Road (which gave her a shiver as it whipped past the van) and a few other roads, there was little else out this way for almost ten miles other than a few abandoned shack-houses and the Slade Volunteer Fire Department. Everything else was pine trees, as far as the eye could see.

On the way out of town, she'd noticed men and women standing stock-still in parking lots, like scarecrows over fields of steel and paint, turning to watch them pass with glittering feline eyes of jade and venomous honey. Meerkat strangers frozen in storefront windows and gas stations with pump nozzles and shopping bags in their hands. Cutty was watching them through Blackfield's eyes. Robin didn't say anything. She didn't want to upset Wayne.

Soon, they came into a little valley with a neatly mowed rest stop and a visitors' center, presided over by a stately four-lane interstate running west to east. Traffic *shush*ed overhead at breakneck speeds as Kenway slipped underneath the overpass.

Beyond the overpass was a tiny hamlet consisting of a Texaco gas station that had seen better decades and a convenience store, lit up like an airport. Down the road behind the store was a clean Subway sandwich shop that seemed embarrassed by its own cozy grandeur in the middle of all this hillbilly austerity. On a better day, Robin would have wanted to swing by and grab a sandwich, but they'd left her appetite back at the hospital.

At the end of the highway, an access road climbed a slope choked with pine trees, where LAKE CRADDOCK had been tool-burned into a wooden sign over the road. Kenway started up this road, rumbling up the hill toward the log cabin.

A sign next to the cabin announced it as the rental office-slash-tackle shop. They didn't bother stopping, heading deeper into the pines.

Eventually, they hooked to the right and followed a ledge along the south side of the mountain, rising higher and higher until the distant buildings of Blackfield became specks of gray and light twinkling in a landscape of green fur. Gravel driveways branched away from them now and again, leading to quaint little hunter-lodges. The road bent back on itself at the edge of a several-hundred-foot drop and continued to climb until they finally broke into a clearing at the top.

Here, the trees thinned out and the road became a large parking lot. At the other side of six rows of empty slots was a sprawling Brady Bunch split-level with splintery gray walls. A sign out front called it TOP O' THE MOUNTAIN CAFÉ & INN. Kenway parked at the sidewalk and they marched up the hill toward the restaurant, climbing three flights of crosstie steps in a broad zigzag. To the north, the mountain crumbled away into a treeless granite headland, revealing a sparkling seagull-gray lake and a distant horizon of naked trees.

At the top, the big vet paused and leaned against the aluminum handrail, sucking in a great big breath of air that had rolled in off the lake and brushed up the mountain. Lowering himself onto one of the crosstie steps, Kenway leaned back on his elbows. The bandage around his head was a phosphorescently clean white. "I need to sit down for a minute, okay? Gettin' dizzy."

In this dim white end-of-the-world sun, she saw a much older man hiding behind that long blond surfer-hair and copper beard. His neck had an almost reptilian texture, leathered by a desert sun in a savage world thousands of miles away from there, and his forehead was creased with lines. His eyes were closed, and in any other circumstance, Robin supposed his grim face would have been serene. The wind teased his cottony scruff and would have played with his hair if not for the bandage around his head.

For a moment, she could see the old man he would be one day. "When this is over," she told him quietly, "we'll get a boat and go out there for a while. You and me. We can relax out there."

He seemed to wake up from a grim daydream, his eyelids rolling slowly open. His eyes focused on her. "Sounds nice." He got up, dusting his ass. "Okay, I'm good."

Wayne pulled the front door open and let them in.

The Top O' The Mountain Café was quiet for lunchtime. Deathly quiet, in fact, and there wasn't an employee in sight. This made sense, it being a Tuesday in the off-season. The three of them slipped through a shadowy foyer, passing racks of tourism pamphlets and a cash register, down a short corridor past restroom and kitchen doors, and into a cavernous great hall. To the right was an open dining area with a dozen white-draped tables, chairs neatly turned on top of them. The walls were floor-to-ceiling plate windows, affording a beautiful view of a dismal October lake to the north and miles of woodland to the south, the white sky hemmed by the jagged jawline of Blackfield.

Tucked into a dark recess to their left was a rustic bar. Anders Gendreau leaned behind it like an old-timey soda jerk dressed way above his station, peering at them from underneath a rack of glass goblets. "It's about time you got here, cambion," he said, tossing a bar towel over his shoulder. Against the dark blue suit, it almost resembled a sort of holy vestment. "I can only drink so much gin before I'm useless."

He poured Robin and Kenway each a finger of bourbon, then poured Wayne something that looked like gin or vodka out of a bottle with an orange on the label.

She frowned. *Cambion. Crooked.* "Please don't call me that."

"What? Cambion?"

"Yeah."

The magician nodded deferentially. "If you like."

Wayne sniffed the drink, sipped it, and coughed. "Man. I don't know how my dad goes crazy for this stuff. Tastes like straight gasoline."

"Don't worry, little man. One day you'll develop a taste for the finer things." Gendreau looked over his shoulder at the choir of multicolored bottles. Against the mirrored back wall, the collection seemed infinite, and in the reflection, their doppelgängers stared back with haunted eyes. "You won't find any of those finer things here at the Hayseed Café," he chuckled, "but you mark my words. Every good man knows the virtue of a smooth libation."

"I'll take your word for it, mister."

"So, what are we doing here?" asked Kenway, wincing appreciatively at the taste of the liquor.

"This is Anders Gendreau," said Robin. "He's from an organization called the Dogs of Odysseus. Anders, these are my friends Kenway Griffin and Wayne Parkin." She indicated them with the bourbon glass as she introduced them. "Wayne is the owner of the ring that opened a way into where the demon's trapped."

"Pleased to make your acquaintance." Gendreau held out a hand. Wayne shook it. "I bet it would enchant you to know we are magicians."

"Magicians. Of course there are magicians." Sitting on a stool,

Kenway poured himself another finger of bourbon and threw it back. Distantly, Robin wondered if he should be drinking liquor with a head injury. "Witches, demons, giant pig-monsters, and rings that open doors to Hell—why didn't I think there would be magicians?" He put down the shot glass with a *clunk* and eyed the witch-hunter. "Next you're gonna be telling me Bigfoot exists."

"I plead the Fifth," said Gendreau.

"Hey, can you do magic like a Dungeons and Dragons wizard?" asked Kenway. "Like, if you need to fart in a Starbucks and you don't want to leave your stuff alone, can you cast Silence on yourself so nobody can hear you rip one?"

The magician choked on his drink and wiped his mouth. "No. Actually, knowing my luck I would accidentally cast Zone of Truth." He blew a raspberry noise. *"Yes, that was me!"*

Kenway guffawed into his bourbon glass.

By that point, Robin's Percocet was wearing off again and the pain had returned in earnest, but there were three distinct sources of agony now: the papercut screaming of the stitched-and-stapled scar itself, a deep, knotty kinking she supposed must have been the muscles or ligaments that were once attached to her triceps, and then there was an ache in her rib reminiscent of the side stitches you get when you're running.

"I have an issue, Mr. Wizard." Robin grabbed the left hem of her shirt and hiked it over her shoulder. This revealed her left breast, but at this point she didn't care. It also uncovered the writhing foot-long earthworm-thing hanging out of the nadir of the U-shaped surgery scar.

"I'm not a wizard, but—" Gendreau flinched. *"What the hell!"*

"You don't know what it is?"

The bloodworm, as Robin had come to think of it, had grown longer on the way over there (or perhaps more of it had emerged, and perhaps there was a whole *coil* of the thing inside her chest, and that horrible thought made Robin want to pitch herself through the closest window), but it seemed to have calmed, and now dangled from the stitches, the end twitching every so often in the come-hither motion of a cat's tail.

"*Great Odin's codpiece,* no, I do not!" exclaimed the magician, coming around the bar to get a closer look, a disgusted grimace spreading across his vulpine face.

Wan sunlight picked out a blue vein wandering across the cream-white dome of her left breast, and her skin prickled at the visual of that repulsive subtle tendril sliding through the warrens of her arteries. "I feel as though I should know," he said, hitching up his cane in that jaunty way again. "It seems supernatural in nature."

"You think?"

Faint indignation flashed in his glacial eyes and he narrowed on the tendril again. This close to his face, she noticed how intense his eyes were: gas flames in porcelain. The magician reached for it, hesitated, then drew up his courage and took the worm in his bare hand. His fingernails were clipped to a microscopic uniformity and reflected the windowlight as if carved from soapstone.

It curled around his knuckles.

"Hurt me when the doctor pulled on it," she told him. "I think it's connected to something." She swallowed terror and added, "Something inside."

Heat radiated from Gendreau's hands, as if her hip was too close to a stovetop, and she angled her head to see it was the pearly head of his cane. He held the simmering orb close to the tendril and let his eyes slip closed. He rubbed the tendril between his thumb and forefinger, rolling it softly, squeezing it, and then he released it and stood straight.

"What are you doing?"

"Testing it," he murmured. The cane-tip rested on the floor by his foot. "It's not a separate creature," he said with an authoritative finality. Robin studied his haughty, borderline-impassive face.

"What do you mean? You mean it's become *part* of me now?"

"No, I mean it hasn't become 'part of anything.' It *is* you." Gendreau's thumb worried at the smooth surface of the cane's iridescent white head. "There's only one life, one individual source of vitality occupying the space you're standing in—other than your intestinal flora and mitochondria and all the bacteria on your skin and the Demodex on your face, of course—and that is *you*. There's nothing else. That . . . *spaghetti noodle* . . . is your flesh and blood."

"What does that mean?" Kenway stooped with his hands on his knees, his eyes wide and brow severe. "Is—is she growing a squidleg to replace her missing arm? Can demons even *do* that? Grow back limbs?"

"Do I look like a demon expert?" Gendreau's face twisted as if he had a lemon wedge in his mouth. "At any rate, if she were going to grow something, I must say, what a horrendous thing to substitute a perfectly good arm with."

Robin scowled. "You're not helping."

His face softened. "Ahh. Well, who knows, really. You absorbed Theresa LaQuices' heart-road at the point of her death, yes?"

She nodded knowingly but said nothing, urging him on with her pointed silence.

Gendreau spread his hands as if it were obvious. "Her particular Gift is the talent of transfiguration, alteration—if I were a betting man, I'd say when you absorbed the witch's *libbu-harrani*, you also inherited her Gift. In this case, you've inherited the ability to reconfigure yourself. It looks like your unconscious mind is trying to grow something to replace the arm Theresa took."

Robin rubbed her face with the hand that wasn't an octopus tentacle. "Jesus freakin' Christ. Could my unconscious mind come up with something that doesn't look like carp bait?"

"Oh, hello," Gendreau interrupted. "What's this?"

She glanced at his face, then at the object of his focus: her shoulder. "What?" Her eyes ached as she stretched her neck to look.

"There are *two* now."

Wayne adjusted his glasses, gazing through the bottom, his nose wrinkling like an old man reading the newspaper. "There's another one coming out next to the first one."

"Oh, God, give me my meds," Robin pleaded, jamming her fingers into her jeans pocket and fishing out the baggie of Percocet. The sharp pain of the U-scar was getting worse, dulling into a coarse, grinding torment, fibrous and blunt, like chewing popsicle sticks. A headache bloomed at the base of her skull. Going over to the bar, she grabbed the club soda tap, hauled the sprayer hose out, and put a Percocet in her mouth. She thought it over and gave herself another dose, then sprayed them down her throat with club soda.

"Errruuhuhuh." She shuddered at the bitter taste.

A chilling thought passed over her: the sound she'd produced reminded her of the dragon-gargle Andras made when he exhaled.

(crooked cambion)

Robin pushed it out of her mind and let the soda hose reel back into its socket.

"Are you—" Kenway started to say.

"No, I'm really not okay," she observed with a gentle scoff. "I am *miles* from okay."

"Perhaps you should take it easy for a couple of days and let nature take its course," said Gendreau. "Cutty's group is weakened by the loss of its eastern corner, and it will take some time to find and recruit a fresh member. In the meantime, I can prepare myself."

"No. It's got to go down today." Robin tugged her T-shirt back down. The tendril snaked back and forth under the fabric. "They've got Wayne's father. I've got to get him out of there. And the longer we wait, the more pod people they'll be able to make, and the more prepared Cutty, Weaver and their Matron will be when we actually come. We're wasting time."

"All right." Gendreau stared at her, his face gradually darkening. "All right. We'll have to make do with what we've got. But we're going to have to storm the hacienda like the damned Blitzkrieg, yeah?" He breezed past her, carrying his cane by the literal shaft. "We can't give 'em any time to react."

The magician led them outside to the narrow patio that served as the front porch. Feathery flakes of snow sparrowed down from the washrag sky, melting on the cement. Wayne stopped short. "Whoa, it's snowing!"

"Weird," said Kenway. "Isn't it a little early in the year for snow?"

Robin held up a hand to catch snowflakes. "It's a little early in the *decade* for it. It hardly *ever* snows here."

Gendreau shrugged with a knowing smile.

Instead of taking the zigzag of stairs back down to the parking lot, he cut left and went down a sloping sidewalk leading along the restaurant's north side. An access road curled around the back of the building for deliveries. Gendreau crossed this and made his way to a balcony erected at the edge of the lakeview bluff.

Coin-op binoculars punctuated the balcony's parapet. Two people stood at the edge, watching the wind kick skirls of sunlight across the water's surface hundreds of feet below. Sitting at their feet was an enormous dog, a skinny black beast with interminably long legs. Down feathers of ice danced around them like a scene out of a snow globe. "Friends, Romans, countrymen," said Gendreau as they approached.

"Do you think *Deliverance* is based on true events?" the woman asked him, turning away from the lake. Elvira's spooky face stared out from the front of her T-shirt, and her arms were livid with tattoo sleeves of skeletons and curlicues.

"God, I hope not," said Gendreau. "Friends, these are my colleagues Sara Amundson and Lucas Tiedeman."

"I'm using these binoculars to look for sexually ravenous troglodytes, but all I can find are birds." Sara's lipstick was bloodred, her fingernails were as black as murder, and her hair was silver-white, shot through with streaks of pink. Jutting from the prow of her skull was a spiraling bone point about seven inches long.

Robin liked her immediately.

The man standing next to her was dressed like an FBI spook, in a black suit and tie. Even though the sky was a pool of dirty cotton, his eyes were inscrutable behind a pair of shades. What Robin could see of his face was young and handsome, with a princely profile. *Too* young, maybe—she could see him getting carded a lot.

While they were talking, Wayne knelt to address the skinny black dog. Reaching out to pet it, he was startled when his hand passed into the dog as if he were reaching into a hole.

Wayne jumped to his feet. "What the heck?"

"Once upon a time," said Sara, "people believed the first person buried in a new graveyard would have to linger there as a ghost and protect it from the Devil. They served as a sort of guardian spirit, who would defend the churchyard from thieves and vandals, and lead the newly deceased into the afterlife. Well, they didn't want to get stuck here on Earth after they died, so whenever they started a new graveyard, the first thing they buried in it would be a dog. And forever afterward, that dog would manifest on the property as a 'church-grim.'"

Protect it from the Devil. Robin looked into the strange dog's eyes and saw only black pits, holes in the sable fur of his face. He lay down, ignoring her. He was faintly see-through, like meat sliced too thin. *I guess I don't qualify as the Devil, then.* "So, he's a ghost?" she asked as a certain sort of relief came over her.

"He is. He was buried in an old French graveyard in the Upper Peninsula of Michigan, back in the seventeenth century and the days of fur-trading and the Hudson's Bay Company. When we found him, he had no gravestone and no name. So we named him Gévaudan, after the Beast of Gévaudan, of course, being French. He followed us home and he's been running around with us ever since. Gev was a greyhound in life."

"Wait, so ghosts are real?" asked Kenway.

"Sure," said Gendreau.

They stared at each other awkwardly for a full ten seconds while Kenway waited for him to elaborate, which he did not do.

"All right," said Kenway. He sipped from the glass of bourbon he was still holding.

"This is the assault team I've assembled to help us storm Cutty's stronghold," the magician said, changing the subject. "Each one has in his or her possession a *libbu-harrani*, a heart-road artifact imbued with a Gift, confiscated from a defeated witch. Mr. Tiedeman here has the unusual talent of 'channeling.' I'm sure you're familiar with this, Miss Martine," he offered. "Amelia Burke could do it."

"Yeah." Robin asided to Kenway and Wayne, "Channeling is the ability to shift and focus energy." She had fought and killed Amelia Burke in a condemned mall in Iowa. The witch had rail-gunned a baseball right through the engine block of her utility van. "I've done a little research on it, and from what I can understand, the energy is derived from the adenosine-triphosphate of the body's mitochondria." Also known as ATP, the cell energy produced by ancient foreign organelles living inside the cells of the majority of living beings.

Molecular biology, started in high school and continued in Heinrich's training. Robin had spent dark, lonely nights during that monastic first year locked up in his Texas compound, learning about her new enemies and studying the techniques that would help her exact the vengeance she thought she needed.

But apparently like everything else Heinrich told her, his theory on channeling was bullshit too. "If only it were that simple," said Gendreau. "That would make for a temporarily accelerated metabolism every time the individual used his or her Gift—but that isn't the case." The magician's pale hand clapped on Lucas's shoulder. "We've done our own research, since we can capture and contain the witches' heart-roads and we can observe their properties at our leisure. No, we believe the Gift of channeling stores and redirects bosons."

"Bosons?" Robin was at a loss.

"Bosons are what give matter its mass," said Wayne. "People call it the God Particle because it's part of the glue that holds the universe together."

"*Yes!*" Gendreau pointed at him, *you win the kewpie doll,* a grin breaking across his face. "What a clever little boy you are. Yes, that is why channeled objects exhibit disproportionately concussive force. We only managed to come up with this theory after years of experimentation with CERN's Large Hadron Collider."

Wayne blinked. "*That's* what the LHC is for? You guys are researching *magic*?"

"We were given access to their results in exchange for funding. The LHC was constructed for legitimate scientific research, but during the construction, our leadership was made to understand its potential in the world of supernatural sciences, and we've . . . diverted funds in their direction. It's a mutually beneficial arrangement." Turning, Gendreau marched out several paces away from Lucas and the edge of the parapet, doing an about-face with a swirl of jacket. Sara moved away as well. "Now, if you'll all take a few steps back, Mr. Tiedeman here can demonstrate the power of channeling."

Kneeling, Lucas picked through the dead leaves until he found something suitable, which turned out to be an acorn, new and green at the tip. He held it up to them as if it were a card trick—*if the audience will please examine the ace of spades and ensure it has not been altered in any way*—and made an OK with his fingers, the acorn pincered between his thumb and forefinger. This, Lucas held for five, ten, fifteen long seconds, his arm beginning to tremble like a weightlifter at the end of his reps. Robin thought he was trying to squeeze it to pieces, but then he spun on his heel and whipped his hand toward one of the coin-op binoculars mounted on the parapet, his tie flapping.

His hand opened up like a pantomimed pistol, his index finger pointed out—*bang bang, my baby shot me down*—and the acorn razored across the air into the teardrop-shaped machine, embedding itself, *ptank!,* in the steel housing. Both eyepieces exploded with sharp crystalline snaps and the whole machine came loose from its pedestal, plummeting over the side.

Sara looked up from the gorge even as the binoculars continued to tumble down the mountain, cartwheeling along the rocks through a glitter of quarters. "I can't say I approve of unsolicited vandalism, but . . . impressive as always, gunslinger."

"Lady Amundson, on the other hand," the magician said, gesturing to her with his pearl-headed cane, "possesses the Gift of illusions and conjurations, much like Karen Weaver. She is the one responsible for this anomalous weather."

"I normally make people hallucinate monsters, but I figured making you see a physical manifestation of your worst phobia might've made a bad first impression." Sara emphasized each point with a sinuous gesture. Illusory snow danced around her hands, transforming into monarch butterflies, which then burst into flames and burned into flakes of ash. "Bedbug monsters, rainbow LSD monsters, monsters made out of tax paperwork, ugh, all kinds of monsters. Kinda my thing."

Lucas Tiedeman grinned, straightening his necktie. "Welcome to the A-Team."

Polishing off his bourbon, Kenway tossed the ice off the cliff and sighed into the empty glass. "Either I need a lot more of this or I've already had way too much."

24

The magicians were staying in one of the larger lodges down the hill, a rustic frontier shack full of fragrant cedar furniture, dizzying quilts, and mounted deer heads. Robin and Wayne helped them load their belongings into their vehicle while the head-bandaged Kenway took a bathroom break. "We've still got the cabin for the week," Gendreau told her as they crammed luggage into the back of a Chevy Suburban. "But if we don't survive Cutty's wrath, it wouldn't do at all to leave our things here where the normals can find them."

Robin elbowed Wayne. "I'm so glad they don't call us Muggles. That would be too much." The boy grinned, the white windows flashing on his glasses. "We're gonna go get your dad, okay?"

He traded the grin for a sad but confident smile.

Sara Amundson joined the two of them as Lucas and Gendreau hauled the last couple of bags. Robin eyed the horn sticking out of the part in her hair. "What's with the, uhh . . ." She made an A-OK with her hand, pretending to loop an imaginary unicorn horn on her own head.

"It's a wig," said Sara, tugging the horn. Her entire head of hair lifted up to reveal fiery red underneath. She readjusted the pink-white wig, twisting it back down onto her skull. "Last Halloween, I went as what I like to call a 'Murdercorn' and everybody liked it so much, I thought I would do it again this year."

"Don't let her lie to you." Lucas shut the back of the Suburban. "She's been wearing it ever since."

Sara lowered her head and jabbed him in the arm with the horn. He backed away, making the sign of the cross with his fingers. "The Murdercorn is murderous."

The seven of them piled into the SUV. Gendreau drove, Lucas sat up front in the passenger seat, Robin sat in the back with Sara and Wayne, and Kenway in the cargo area with the luggage. Gev the ghost-dog had disappeared; Wayne seemed confused and disappointed until Sara told him that was just how Gev was. He would show up later, usually when they least expected it. "He comes and goes. He's like a cat."

"A cat only minimally tethered to this plane of reality," said Lucas.

The minute she was nestled in, Robin felt old and salty by association. She reflected on the past couple of years and the battles and hardships she'd had to endure alone at the hands of America's witches, and she couldn't help but feel like the one hardass in a car full of untested rookies. Suddenly, the Suburban had the silly yet claustrophobic feel of a clown car. *They're not taking this seriously enough, including Gendreau,* she thought, looking around at them. Sara gave her a pinched, disaffected smile that didn't touch her eyes. *It's a field trip for them. Willy Wonka, a woman in a unicorn wig, a beanpole dog, and a Quentin Tarantino character.*

I've got half a mind to tell them to stay in the cabin and let me handle Cutty.

This is my fight, anyway.

A sensation of impending doom came over her, as if she'd

bought a ticket on the *Titanic*. Pain throbbed in her shoulder. She caught a glimpse of herself in the rearview mirror and marveled at how sallow her face looked. Her eyes were dark pits in her face, glassy in the watery daylight.

Down the mountain they drove, winding back and forth through the switchback and the hairpin curves running across the south slope. The woozy snaking of the top-heavy vehicle turned Robin's medication-and-booze-marinated guts into a churning lava lamp. When he got to the bottom and passed the cabin office, Gendreau paused at the frontage. The Subway's sign glowed yellow in the failing afternoon light. "Last chance," he said, peering through the windshield. "Anybody for a last meal?"

Lucas grunted. "Your confidence inspires me."

"Let's get this over with," grouched Robin. Every movement of the Suburban made her want to throw up. The feeling of her worm-arm-thing curling and flexing gently by her side wasn't helping.

They crossed the road and headed under the interstate toward Blackfield. Robin peeled back her shirt to uncover the red-black tendril, and Wayne subtly cowered away from it. The sight of him leaning against the window dug deep and left a splinter of embarrassment inside.

"Oh, my God," said Sara. "What the hell is *that*?"

"According to Gendreau, it's my new arm." Robin picked it up the same way he had, the coil of sausage-flesh draped over her palm like fine jewelry. Not only had it grown another several inches while they were getting ready to leave, but now it was as thick as a finger. "Evidently, I absorbed Theresa's gift for transfiguration when I closed her heart-road, and it's causing . . . *something* to grow in its place." She hoped it wouldn't turn out to be a tendril forever. A six-foot squid tentacle would definitely strain things between her and Kenway for sure.

"There's *two more of 'em*," said Wayne.

Sara leaned forward to see better. "Jeez, they're braiding together."

Out of the corner of her eye, Robin thought the entwining tendrils resembled a sort of ponytail made out of Slim Jim jerky. Nausea turned her stomach into a cement mixer, and sour saliva leaked into her mouth.

"Stop the car," she almost shouted, unbuckling her seat belt.

As soon as Gendreau pulled to the side of the highway, Robin wrenched the side door open. She went to her knees on the shoulder of the highway and gargled hot vomit into the dry brown grass, audienced by a wall of pines and a sun-faded soda can. The tentacle under her shirt coiled and flexed.

Exhaustion settled over her and she rested, trying to catch her breath, wheezing through a rawhide throat. Someone got out and before she knew it—or could say otherwise—Kenway was crouching beside her. "You don't have enough hair to hold out of the way when you puke," he said, the dull glint of his prosthetic leg peeking out from under his jeans, "but I can at least be there to help you get back up."

Tears tumbled down her face (when had she started to cry?) and she spat again and started to wipe her slimy mouth on the collar of her T-shirt—a thing people do when they're not used to being in the polite company of civilized humanity—but Kenway was there with a wadded-up napkin. She wiped her face down with all the ceremony of scrubbing bugs off a car fender.

"Other than Heinrich—and I'm not even sure about him—the last person I can remember ever giving half a shit about me died years ago. Mom was all I ever had. Even in high school." The wind plucked and pushed at the wadded-up paper in her hand. "I don't know what to do with you. You're like . . . a riddle, man. A mystery I need to solve. What do you even *see* in me?"

"All those YouTube subscribers," said Kenway. "What—four, five million people? I've never even *met* five million people. There aren't even that many people living in this town. And you walk around thinking you're alone in this life." He shook his head.

A breathy, sarcastic laugh. "This life is so jacked up, Kenway."

She looked up at him. "Demons. Witches. Magicians. Ghost dogs. Are you sure you want to be a part of it?"

"*Am* I a part of it?"

"I'd like you to be."

His beard separated, revealing a grin as warm as sunshine. "Yeah. I think I'd like that very much."

Robin chuckled and combed a hand through her unruly Mohawk. The ID bracelet the hospital had put around her wrist scuffed across her forehead. She'd forgotten about it. Biting the paper until it broke, she held it into the wind, watching it twitch and dance. Her fingers let it fall and the hoop curled into the afternoon, rolling along the roadside like a tumbleweed.

"I forgot to thank you for coming to my rescue back there in the vineyard." She squinted into the wind, regarding Kenway's face. "I didn't need it—"

"Obviously."

"—Obviously, but nobody else has ever helped me before."

Empathy written on their faces, the misfit magicians (how much that sounded like some dirty-Southern-rock band from the eighties, don't hand me no lies and keep your hands to yourself) watched this interlude from the car. "You've got lots of help now." Kenway reached out with his big hands and framed her jaw, wiping the tears off her cheeks with hard leather thumbs. "Whether you need it or not."

• • •

Underwood Road. The road sign waggled in the breeze like the palsy of an old man, at the edge of a road-shoulder stubbly with juts of broken hickory, a weathervane pointing in uncivilized directions. The Suburban was still parked by the side of the road where she'd gotten out to blow chunks. Robin leaned against the car with the door open, her forehead on her arm and her arm on the frame, trying to let the fresh air settle her stomach.

"You okay?" asked Wayne. He had taken off his glasses and was buffing the lenses with his shirt.

"Yeah, it was . . . the Percocet, the bourbon, being cooped up in the car, *this* thing—" She shrugged the shoulder with the blood-worm hanging out of it. "Got to be a little much for me. Needed some fresh air."

"Are you *sure* you want to do this today?" Kenway was beside her. He followed the line of her eyes to the road sign and put his hand on her back. The tendril curled as he did so and she felt him tense up, but he didn't snatch his hand away. God, but she loved him for that. She really did.

For sure, she was having second thoughts; her mother had been locked inside that tree for half a decade now, and a few days wouldn't make much of a difference.

But—

"—They've got Leon," she said. "I can't leave him there."

Gratitude loosened Wayne's features. She could tell he wanted to say something like *My dad's tough, he would understand if you wanted to psych yourself up before you jump into Hell,* but the relief, and the eagerness to rescue his father, kept him from opening his mouth. She hoisted herself into the seat and pulled the belt across her lap. "Let's go. Make hay while the sun shines. Strike while the iron's hot."

Kenway lingered in the door, assessing her.

Finally, he slithered into the back of the Suburban and she pulled the door shut, *clunk.* Gendreau put on his blinker, waited for a Camaro to go *shush*ing past, and pulled back out onto the highway, crossing the median and turning into Underwood Road.

The magician drove like a car commercial. His pale, slender fingers handled the steering wheel in a delicate, businesslike way, a conductor-motorist that poured the Suburban down Underwood's sinuous length. Georgia's ever-present trees enclosed them with wet, skeletal trunks still stained a raw strawberry-blond by the weekend's rains.

NO TRESPASSING. The sign was still nailed to a tree, speckled with bullet holes.

It occurred to Robin the South had a lot of these signs distrib-
uted throughout the wilderness as if the great landgrabs of the co-
lonial days had never truly ended, the countryside still scissored
into a patchwork of a thousand hidden estates. She saw fewer of
these signs up north, almost none in New England except for the
wilderness of Maine and swaths of upstate New York. The commune in Oregon had them but only because the hunters that used
to own the property had put them up; the witches didn't need
them, didn't *want* them because they *liked* it when trespassers
showed up uninvited.

Welcome, sir, have a seat, have a beer, welcome to Hotel California.

The things she'd seen crisscrossing the country, following Heinrich's leads, following Heinrich's orders . . . the human finger-bones
hanging from porch eaves in gruesome wind chimes, the skull-
bowls spackled with burnt blood, the decaying figures sitting in
iron gibbets—so much like mummies, shriveled paper skin glued
to thin rods of bone, hands clawed around their knobby knees,
stiff lips stretched across yellowed skulls—the cries of children
locked in cellars, their child minds scrambled by the Gift of illusion. Yes, it worked both ways, you know, the crones can make you
see things, and they can make you *not* see things as well.

But those horrible sights were still buried down there, deep be-
neath the surface, memory-sharks that only breached and flashed
their cuttlebone teeth in the dead of night. Those children she'd
saved, all grown up one day, will sit straight up in the bed next to
their wife or husband as the last foaming tide of a nightmare ebbs
into the darkness of sleep. Nightmares of things they saw as children but have forgotten as adults, their childhoods stolen by smiling hags with chips of ice in their eyes, hobgoblins who would have
eaten them—or, worse, stolen their hearts for an ageless corpse-
queen—if not for a punk-rock witch-hunter and the gleaming silver dagger in her hand.

She was still lost in thought when Gendreau stopped at a stop
sign.

Another highway crossed in front of them, running perpendicular to Underwood Road. As soon as Robin's eyes drifted north, she knew it ran all the way out to Miguel's Pizzeria in the mountains. They had met the road on the other end of her childhood home, the "shortcut" Kenway had driven when he had first taken her back to her skeezy candy van to lie in the dark and cold, miserably horny and staring at the ceiling.

"Did we pass it?" Maybe she wasn't paying attention—she had been pretty deep in her own head there for a few minutes.

Confused, everyone turned to look. Robin's sallow face reflected in Lucas's black tactical shades. "I think?" asked the magician. "I guess we did? I don't even remember going through the neighborhood and seeing the trailer park on the left."

Gendreau said over his shoulder, "Shall I turn around and go back? Or are we on the wrong road?"

"It's the right road," said Lucas. "Underwood." He reached under the front seat and brought out a folder, opening it. "That's what the file says. I mean, we were here the other night, it's not like we're lost."

"It's the right road." Robin scanned the road behind them. "But something's wrong."

The Suburban dipped into the oncoming lane, doing a U-turn back onto Underwood, and Gendreau piloted them into the woods again. This time, Robin clutched the headrest in front of her, her head on a swivel as she watched the road for landmarks.

Power poles kept a steady cadence on the right side of the car, and the familiarity of almost twenty years tinged every leaf and sign they passed. The familiar swoop and sway of the road's subtle waveform settled over them once more, but this time, Gendreau slowed until they were at a funereal pace, the asphalt grumbling under their tires, trees parallaxing past at walking speed.

"Wait a minute," said Robin.

She stared through the left-hand windows of the Suburban, where a power pole loomed by the road's shoulder.

Kenway shifted. "What is it?"

"The power lines are on the left side now." Robin looked through the left window, then over Kenway's shoulder through the rear window. "They cross the road at the Lazenbury. I know because the line comes down Underwood on the side of the road my old house is on, then the lines cross the street to the transformer in front of the Lazenbury, where lines go up to the hacienda and over to the trailer park, and from there, the lines stay on that side until it gets to the highway going up to the pizzeria."

Making a three-point turn, Gendreau maneuvered the Suburban east again, putting the lines on their right.

A few minutes later, Lucas said, "Now the lines are on the other side."

"Karen Weaver is hiding the house." Sara Amundson peered up at an angle through her gray window. The tint layered a sullen darkness over the world outside. "I know it. She has cropped that *whole quarter-mile* out of the road. Like cutting the middle out of a string and tying the ends back together."

Gendreau put the Suburban in reverse and they whined backward—slow at first, and then faster, until they were racing backward toward the west, the engine whining with an inhaling burr like an electric track-car.

"Stop," said Sara. "Let me out."

They drew up short, catty-cornered in the eastbound lane. Robin threw open the back door and got out, followed by Kenway and then Sara. The illusionist clawed the Murdercorn wig off her head and tossed it into the backseat, letting the wind comb fingers through her brilliant red hair.

"Look. You can see it there." Sara pointed east, at the south side of the road.

A splintery power-pole towered over them sixty feet away, topped with gray beehive electricity components. Rubber-coated wires emerged from the couplings, protruding into the air some twenty or thirty feet, where they *faded away*, as if God had stooped down with a giant Pink Pig drafting eraser and rubbed it out of existence.

"What the hell?" asked Kenway, shading his eyes against the drab white sky. "What is this, the Bermuda Triangle?"

Taken as a whole, the arrangement over their heads seemed to refract like a pencil inserted into a glass of water. There was no visible difference in the unending army of trees all around them, but when you paid attention to the power cables, you could see where Weaver had excised the Lazenbury and everything around it. The power line coalesced into being on the north side of the road and hooked into the couplings at the top of another power-pole.

"Can you nullify it?" Gendreau's cane rapped on the road twice as he walked, and then he directed the tip at the strange refraction. "Or reverse it?"

Taking a piece of chalk out of her pocket, Sara drew an increasingly complicated series of sigils and symbols on the asphalt: concentric circles, words in some flowing, inscrutable script, geometric diagrams, intersecting lines. The more she drew, the more her face darkened with irritation, until the chalk snapped in half and she looked up at them from where she knelt. "I can't even find the edges. Except for that weird lensing with the power lines, it's almost seamless. It's like trying to open a fire exit from the outside, except there's not even a door. It's a blank wall that I know has a door on the other side of it."

A desolate satisfaction came over Robin. "Now d'you see how powerful they are?" she asked, trying not to sound smug.

"I was *always* aware." Indignity soured Gendreau's aristocratic face. "I've seen this sort of thing before, Miss Martine . . . but not this well done. The others, they've—you could get your fingers under the illusion, to so speak, and pry it up like a rock so you can find the worms underneath. But this . . . I can't find where in the fabric of space and time the illusion begins and ends. It's completely flush with reality."

A bird came sailing across the trees, a big black crow. As it drew near the place where the cable refracted out of view, she almost expected it to disappear, slipping into oblivion as soon as it crossed that invisible boundary and possibly reappearing a few minutes later, but it passed by without so much as a flicker.

As she stared, the visual image of the bird vanishing pushed an idea into her head. She rounded on Gendreau. "Can you *un*-conjure something?"

"I've never heard of it before, but yes, I suppose you could. I mean, you can *conjure* things—"

"—So why can't you *un*-conjure them? *Banish* them?"

"That would explain why the illusion is so finely grained." Gendreau stared at the smearing end of the powerline, rubbing the corners of his mouth. "Yes . . . yes, perhaps what she's done is, instead of . . . yes . . . ." The bull-pizzle cane came to rest on the pavement and he tucked a hand into the breast of his suit blazer. ". . . It's not an illusion at all, is it? Weaver has un-conjured the area around the house. She's pinched a pouch out of the fabric of reality and sewn the gap shut, isolated it, like a pocket hidden in the lining of a jacket." He stood there staring blankly at the sky, his mind idling high and out of gear. "There's no gap to find because there isn't one."

Sara folded her arms. "Riddle me this: how do you get into a house with no door?"

"You make one," Wayne suggested from the Suburban.

Goose bumps of excitement tingled across Robin's scalp. "Yes! Your ring!" She strode straight to him as he was climbing out of the car and clutched the boy against her chest in a one-armed hug. "Your ring! We can use it to get into the isolation!"

He grinned, tugging the ball-chain necklace out of his shirt, revealing his mother Haruko's ring. Gendreau and Sara came over, and the thin magician stooped to level his face with Wayne's, his hands on his knees.

"Is this it?" he asked. "The ring that opens magic doors?"

It sounded about as silly as it possibly could, coming from this character, but there wasn't really any way of getting around it. Life is stranger than fiction, as they say. Wayne explained how it worked. "And from inside the dark, scary version of my house, all the doors lead to other places in town."

"Like a hub," said Robin. "The only problem is, the demon is in that Darkhouse, trapped, waiting for prey to come into his cage. And I'd bet magic isn't *all* he's willing to eat."

• • •

A few minutes later, they were back in town. As soon as the Suburban slipped over a hill and they were greeted by the first thrust of civilization, Gendreau pulled into a Sonic Drive-In to grab something to drink while they planned their next move. Robin ordered a Sprite to help calm her stomach and sat back, sipping the soda, relaxing as the coolness funneled down her chest into her belly, unlocking a tight band of anxiety around her lungs.

Her heart rumbled feverishly inside the birdcage of her chest, throbbing down her arm and into her feet. Gendreau started the Suburban and backed out of the Sonic stall, pulling into traffic. She didn't know where he was going, and he didn't seem to either; he seemed to be driving aimlessly through Blackfield, stalling for time.

"You're bleeding," said Sara.

Robin opened her eyes and examined her shirt. A slick of red ran from the top of her shoulder all the way down her side, and when she peeled back her shirttail, she saw it was spreading into the waist of her jeans. The nausea returned, but it was tempered by the chill of the soda.

A hand appeared from the front seat, clutching a fistful of napkins: Lucas, his eyes still unknowable behind those black sunglasses.

She took them and pressed the wad against the surgery scar, dabbing at the blood, gasping at the fresh pain that erupted underneath.

The tendril-braid thrashed under her shirt, painting red hoops and commas across her belly.

"Sorry about the mess I'm making in your car, Andy," she told Gendreau, hissing through her teeth.

"It's a rental," he said quietly, without turning around.

Silence fell over the car as Robin hiked up her shirt and dabbed at the blood seeping out around the thing in her shoulder. It was as big around as a garden hose now, pushing the staples out and loosening the stitches, stretching the wound open. The flap of skin that had been inside the U-scar was now a shriveled epaulet lying on top of the tendrils. There were five of them now, closely intertwined into a hard but yielding cable. Felt like warm, wet rubber.

Lucas's hand appeared again, this time holding a spool of Scotch tape.

Robin accepted, confused. "What's this for?"

He handed her another cache of napkins. "Tape it over the, umm—" He traced a circle on his own shoulder with his fingertips, *wax on, wax off*.

Robin tucked her shirt under her chin to keep it out of the way and sat there for a baffled moment trying to figure out how she was going to dress her shoulder with one hand.

"Here, I'll help you," said Sara, reaching for the tape and napkin.

"Thank you."

Sara pressed the napkins to her amputation. "Here, hold this down."

She held the napkins in place, glancing back at the woman. Sara Amundson could have been an Old Hollywood lounge singer, buxom and pretty, her red hair an Aphrodite tumble. She must have read Robin's eyes because she said dryly, "It's okay. I've seen worse. So, what are you thinking for our plan of attack?" she asked, trying to distract her patient.

Robin thought about it, sipping her drink. "Wayne, how did you get into the Darkhouse the first time? Are there specific ways or methods you have to get there from here? You said you got there from your room at the hospital."

"Yeah," Wayne said through a mouthful of hamburger. A speck of lettuce stuck to the corner of his mouth. He knuckled it in. "But you can't go back there, 'cause Marissa and the hospital security's gonna want to keep you, ain't they?"

"Yes, I can't go back there. Not right now."

"Well, me and that Joe-elle guy came out through a painting in Kenway's apartment." He chewed the hamburger up and swallowed. "Maybe we can go in the same way."

An old man selling homegrown produce out of a raggedy-ass *Sanford and Son* pickup stood up from his lawn chair to watch them pass. His hands gnarled into stiff claws, a slow, angry grimace forming on his face. His eyes were not his own; they were hollow cat's-eye marbles, full of the cold coin-light of tapetum lucidum.

"Hi-ho, Silver, away," Gendreau sang, heading back north.

"Keep going straight." Kenway gave the blond magician directions to his art shop in the historical district. He startled Robin with a reassuring hand on her good shoulder. "When you get to the Bojangles, keep to the right and turn on Broad. My place is a couple blocks down. It'll say GRIFFIN'S ARTS AND SIGNS on the window with a big red gryphon."

Robin's face flushed and she flashed a smile back at him. He didn't withdraw his hand right away. His eyes were deeply warm and locked on her face, darting from eye to eye to nose to mouth.

You make me hope I survive this, she thought.

The magicians' vehicle approached the four-lane intersection of Broad and Main, and Gendreau maneuvered them into the right-hand lane, the turn signal metronoming. His gas-flame eyes burned at them in the rearview mirror.

A trumpeting horn shook the Suburban.

Brilliant headlights turned the inside of the vehicle into a blinding lightbox. Robin spun to see where it was coming from and found herself face-to-face with the front end of a garbage truck.

The driver door opened and a man leaned out, or at least she thought it was a man; he was as bald as a bedpost and his skin was an angry, welted red.

Teeth glistened in the pit of his withered mouth. His ears were black holes, and deranged eyes stared from deep in his knothole eye sockets.

To Robin, he was the angel of Pestilence.

Joel Ellis marched mindlessly down the sidewalk through Black-field, his hood up and his hands jammed into his pockets. The sky threatened rain, and part of him hoped it would come again. It suited him today.

It had been a pretty good thumper last night, and something about torrential downpours made him feel safe, made him feel buffered against the slings and arrows of the world. Caveman remnants nestled in the nooks of his brain told him creatures afraid of getting soaked didn't go out in the rain to hunt, didn't brave the elements; if he stayed in his cave with his fire and his spear, he would be okay. Nobody goes out in the rain. Nobody will get you while it's raining.

Mama's house had a tin roof (and did he ever love the sound of rain hitting those warbling red sheets), but that's not where he was headed this evening. He was headed for the comic shop. It was close enough to the hospital to walk to, and when he got there, he could decide where to go from there. All that mattered now was finding shelter, and it had nothing to do with rain. If he decided to go back to Mama's house (never *his* house, always *Mama's* house, even though she hadn't lived there in years), he'd take the bus or something. Or borrow Fish's bicycle.

His brother had given him a key to the shop. *In case you ever wanna get out of that dark, musty house, you know.*

As he walked, Joel studied the key in his hand. It had a Captain America cover on it—the back end was coated in rubber like a car key, blue-and-white-striped, with a red circle and a white star inside. It was a commercial key for a commercial lock, and it felt like an alien artifact in his hand, a lightsaber, Excalibur, a tool meant for someone vastly more important than himself.

As he was crossing the Martin Dupree Bridge over the river, traffic hissing and crashing obliviously behind his back, Joel found himself racked by sobs and unable to see where he was going. He clutched the guardrail of the bridge and stared through a quivering screen of tears at the dark quicksilver some thirty or forty feet below. Heartache coiled hotly around his chest, twisting the breath out of him until black spots, cigarette burns on a film reel, bloomed in his eyes. Wind blustering up the channel boxed him with wet, cold fists. Another part, darker and less vestigial, shoved in meanly next to the caveman neurons in his brain, told him to jump. Rationality told him the fall wouldn't kill him. The water wouldn't even hurt him at this height. He'd just be going for an impromptu swim.

Though, if there were rocks hiding under the surface, he'd probably break his legs.

"Goddammit," Joel told the river in a pinched growl, wishing he could rip the guardrail out of the cement with his bare hands. There was something *missing* now, wasn't there? An out, a back door—under it all, there had been an emergency exit, and now that it wasn't there anymore, he recognized it for what it was: Fisher had always been his golden parachute, he knew, for when living in the house their mother had died in would become less of an inability to move on and more of a masochism, maybe a self-flagellation. Punishment for not being able to repair the woman that had raised them. He knew in the back of his mind he would one day tell the difference and step back, and Fish would be there waiting to help him back up.

What happened ain't your fault, big brother, Fish had said one day.

Serendipitously, they had run into each other at Kroger. Joel was so drunk he was sweating, and Fish was trying to talk him into staying at the shop and sleeping it off. *You couldn't stop her and you couldn't fix her, and it ain't even your place to. Sometimes, people lose their minds and all you can do is watch it happen and make it easier on 'em and move on.*

Fuck you. Joel had stumbled away, getting the last word (as he always did, as he always had to). *You didn't even try.* He turned around there, in front of the registers, yelling at his brother in front of God and everybody. *You didn't even try to fix her. You ran off and left me to pick up the pieces!*

"Why didn't he shoot *me* first?" Dry birdshit ground under his thumb like flour. "Why didn't that asshole shoot the one that *didn't* have everything in the world goin' for him? Why not *me*?"

He lingered there until he'd collected himself, and went back to walking, watching his feet eat up the sidewalk.

What was he going to do with the comic shop? He didn't have any idea how to run it. All he knew was making pizza and drankin' and color-coordinating his clothes. Maybe he could sell it. *No, you idiot, you can't sell it. That's all you got left of him.* Then what? He could move into the loft apartment, maybe. No. Wouldn't work. Mama's house was paid for, and Fish was still leasing. Unless he could turn a profit on a store that hadn't seen black ink since the first six months it'd been open, he'd be out on his ass. He couldn't even count on his meager savings. That money'd be gone in a flash if he had to throw it at a commercial property.

Didn't that kid with the magic ring say something about Fish giving him a part-time job at the shop? That was one nerdy-ass kid. Maybe he could get ahold of him and bend his ear. What was his name? Wayne Newton? No, that's that white dude in Las Vegas. Wayne Parker? Parkin?

"Unh!" he grunted, knocked out of his thoughts as a woman shoved past.

White. Mid-thirties. Had on a red wool peacoat and black leggings, gold hoops in her ears, Ugg moonboots. Her crinkly dark hair streamered out behind her as she ran. "Watch where you goin'!" Joel called after her, dimly aware she was dressed way too nice to be running down the sidewalk.

Another hand slammed into his back and he caught himself over the guardrail. A man in a Members Only jacket sprinted by and Joel surged after him in a rage, snagging his coat. *"Who do you—"* he started to say, and then the man rounded on him. Instead of the angry warning Joel expected to come out of his mouth, it was the ridiculous, grimacing puff-adder hiss of a movie-of-the-week vampire.

The man's eyes were the split jade of a cat's. "What the *fuck*." Joel recoiled, baffled, putting up his dukes.

Members Only turned and ran. Another woman came along behind him as well, and that's when Joel scanned the parking lots and sidewalks around him and realized while he'd been walking with his head down, watching his feet eat up the sidewalk, the world had come alive with running people. In every direction, men, women, and children sprinted north at top speed, some of them loping along like chimpanzees. They were heading the same direction he'd been walking: Broad Avenue.

With an expression of deepest confusion still on his face, Joel jammed the Captain America shop key into his pocket and started jogging in that direction. Whatever was going down, it couldn't be good, and he wanted to get behind a locked door ASAP.

26

The disfigured man shouted something—*screamed*, actually, the shrill, mad whoop of a baboon—but she couldn't understand him over the Suburban's radio. Then he drew a rifle out of the cab of the garbage truck and settled it into the valley between the open door and the doorpost, hunkering down, staring through the iron sights at her.

"Look out!" shrieked Robin.

Thunder cracked down the street and a hole appeared in the Suburban's windshield, turning it into brilliant lace. Scrambling for the handle, Kenway opened the cargo door and was about to get out when Gendreau threw the Suburban into reverse and gunned the engine. The sudden lurch threw him on the floor and the door crashed shut, narrowly missing his feet.

"Piss and potatoes," Gendreau swore breathlessly, turning to look over his shoulder, the wheel shaking in his hand.

Another whip-crack, and the passenger-side window collapsed, showering them in sea-glass diamonds. Through it, Robin could see the blistered mutant with the rifle again, watching them attempt to flee. The street reeled out from under their tires with a juddering scream as Gendreau jerked the wheel and did a flawless J-turn, whirling out in reverse until the car's nose was facing the other way.

"Good moves," said Lucas, his foot on the dash.

Unfortunately, the car that had been behind them was still going at surface-street speeds. They were so close, Robin could see the panicked expression on the driver's face. The magician veered around them into the correct lane and the man with the rifle fired again.

What felt like a bomb went off under the car—no, the rifle bullet had struck their rear driver tire and exploded it. Vulcanized rubber flapped rhythmically against the wheel well like some insane war drum, *TUMP-TUMP-TUMP*, and the Suburban lurched up onto the sidewalk and into a fire hydrant, knocking it down, filling the cabin with cold spray. It continued on, smashing into a brick wall.

Weirdest thing—just before the impact, she saw Sara hit Gendreau's seat . . . and the woman's face seemed to *glitch*. For a second, it was like the shock wave had dislodged a digital mask, her features contorting.

And then Robin's face smashed into Lucas's headrest.

Silence.

Blood, paint-thick on her fingers. Her nose leaked a bib of blood down her chin. Robin shimmied around, trying to get away from the seat belt, and the tendril-braid-thing under her shirt squirmed angrily, the tape around her dressing pulling loose. Gendreau stirred like the Scarecrow from Oz coming to life, his mental gears winding up, glass falling out of his platinum china-doll hair. Then they all were, Sara and Kenway and Lucas, coming out of their individual daze, docile turtles from shells.

"What the *frick*!" snarled Sara, in stunned outrage.

"Sending your defensive driving teacher a Christmas card," said Lucas. He fought the airbag in his lap, trying to get out from under it.

Then: a strange, rising wail outside the car, distant, a faraway siren. But it was high, too high, nonsensical, small and multiformed like a fleet of tiny police cars. Their tiny tin wheels crackled along the sidewalk as they rushed to her aid from some tiny police station, their roller-coaster howl shrilling into the evening. *No,* Robin thought, as Wayne found his glasses and put them on. The left lens was knocked out, giving him one goofy magnified eye. *I've heard that before.* Those tin wheels were the faint clatter of shoe soles on asphalt.

Familiars.

The city of Blackfield was coming for them.

"We've got to get out of here," she told them all, panic overcharging her system. Loose glass rattled, settling like Pachinko pieces through broken gaps as they undid their seat belts. "We have to *go.*"

Tumbling out of the car, Kenway slammed the door shut in Robin's face. She undid her seat belt and tried to open the door, but something pinned it shut. A newspaper box. "The city is full of cat-people, and they're coming," she grunted. "They're on their way here to tear us limb from limb. Cutty's playing her ace card. It's a cat-bomb. The entire town just went *Night of the Living Feline.*"

As soon as she said this, a shadow passed over the oceanic shimmer of the busted windshield and an arm exploded through the passenger-side window, grabbing Lucas by the jacket collar and hauling him out the window, safety glass crashing down his shoulders. Through the ragged gap Robin could see people shuffling back and forth in a dark parody of a mosh pit, crazed faces and clawing hands.

More arms reached in for Gendreau, and he jabbed at them with his cane. "Back! *Back, damn you all!*"

The rear tailgate door flew open, and Kenway tangled his fist in Robin's T-shirt, fumbling for purchase on her armpit, trying to pull her through the cargo area. Out in the failing daylight, Robin rested against the Suburban's rear bumper, a busted taillight throwing hot red across her face. Cold water blasted out of a hole in the sidewalk.

All three of them bled from the glass; Kenway's shirt had a ragged punk-rock slash over one shoulder, and glass glittered in Sara's cardinal-red hair. She was on her hands and knees, blood streaming down her face, looking around in a daze.

"Get off me!" Lucas shouted on the other side.

Robin staggered around the car to help him, but someone tackled her against the Suburban's rear fender—a big woman in a brown spring parka, a shopping bag still looped around one elbow. The woman hissed madly, trying to claw her throat open, and Kenway wrenched her away, throwing her to the asphalt.

Robin's demon tendril was going crazy, writhing, pushing out her shirt at an angle. She jerked her bloody shirttail up to her shoulder to uncover it and discovered a grotesque braid of fibers in the rough shape of an arm, bent at the middle in a macabre imitation of a human elbow. Fine red peach-fuzz grew from the backhand side of this new appendage. Bristling from the end were five dark roots as smooth and steely as meat hooks. She willed them to flex like fingers and they did, crimping and creasing in all the right places.

This was her inheritance from the shaggy, monstrous stranger that had attacked her mother, she understood now, suddenly faced with the new normal, this inner darkness, this insidious evidence of her mother's pact made physical.

Forced to confront it, Robin couldn't look away. She hated it but was fascinated by it at the same time. She made a fist and slammed it against the Suburban's body.

It left a sharp dent. "Well, I'll be damned."

The intersection seemed frozen in time, idling cars littered all over the road, their doors thrown open, exhaust guttering from their tailpipes. The traffic light turned red for cars going nowhere.

A clamorous gang of familiared people had gathered around them. Dozens of brainwashed people inched closer, green and yellow cat-eyes shining at her, their fingers bent into rigid claws, their stupid, blunt human teeth bared in distorted grins.

"Come on!" Robin told them. *"Come get me."*

One of them peeled off and ran at her with a choked snarl, and her sinuous new arm lifted him by the throat and flung him back. Another one, a tall woman with a stupid expression and a Carhartt jacket, ran at her and Robin rounded on the woman, slapping her across the face hard enough to cartwheel her into the crowd.

Incensed, they ran at her as one, a surging mass of people.

Behind the teeming crowd, the dark shape of the garbage truck loomed, a glass-eyed green monolith. Kenway was wrestling with two people now, both of them trying to bite his face. The pestilence-mutant fired the rifle again, and one of the familiars, a tall, thick redneck in Wranglers, jerked as if he'd been goosed. A hole blew open in his neck and sprayed Kenway with red gristle. The veteran shouted and threw the man aside, shoved someone else away.

"We gotta go!" Robin shouted to Sara over the roar of the fire hydrant.

One of the familiars shoved his way through the crowd, and at first, Robin couldn't believe what she was seeing—Joel Ellis? How could he be a pod person if he had an *algiz*?—but then Joel shouted, "Y'all follow me! Come on!" and took off running east up Broad.

The gunman sat down to reload. Time to move.

"Follow that guy!" Robin shoved Sara and Kenway after Joel, and turned back to the crowd to catch an elbow to the face. A man in a puffy jacket lifted her and slammed her against the Suburban, and lunged at her throat with his teeth. She shrugged, scrunching her shoulders, and his bristly mustachioed face wedged against her cheek as he howled nonsense cat-noises in her ear.

Levitating off of her, he suddenly floated away as if repelled by a broad force. Lucas Tiedeman had snatched him up by his neck and the waist of his jeans.

He flung the snarling man into the crowd as if he were nothing but a suitcase and turned back to Robin, pointing after the others. "Run, I got this." His spook suit was sopping wet and he was deathly pale—milk-white, even, his skin almost translucent like fine marble. He had channeled the man's mass into *himself*, making his own body heavier, his skin more resistant, and his blood was having trouble pumping through it. Lucas was a Greek statue, clothed in black.

Regret burned inside her chest. "This wasn't how it was supposed to—"

"We knew the risks when we signed up for this field trip. *Go!*" Lucas lumbered into the fray, fists and feet bouncing off of his stony body, familiars hanging from his arms. *"DISTRACTION!"*

A hand snatched at her T-shirt, at her arm. "Let him work." Gendreau, his eyes severe, his hair a nest of milkweed fluff. Deep gouges ran across his eyebrow, blood dripping into his white button-down. "Come on, let's go."

Reluctantly leaving Lucas to the fight, she fled with Gendreau and Sara down a city street choked with running people. If she'd seen photographs of it, Robin would have been hard-pressed to tell if the photos were of a European football riot or some podunk town in Georgia. Wild-eyed civilians poured from the restaurants and shops lining the historical district, funneling out of doorways and storming into the road.

Some of them galloped sideways in a simian fashion, pawing across the pavement on their hands; most of them ran like velociraptors, their shoulders bunched up by their ears and their hands bent under into obsequious pianists' hands, banging imaginary Steinways. It looked like a production assistant in the video for Michael Jackson's "Thriller" had been passing out doses of LSD. Kenway led the escape with his fists, forging through the seething crowd toward some point. Robin fought the men and women off with the half-assed Krav Maga and movie kung fu Heinrich had taught her. Augmented by the demon arm, she was a force of nature, throwing leaping haymakers and hammering knees and elbows into chests and faces.

A frantic bark echoed off the buildings flanking Broad Avenue.

The throng of familiars parted and a big black dog came loping out of nowhere, mouth full of green napalm, ghostly fire streaming from his eyes like the Hound of the Baskervilles. Familiars scattered in every direction, braying and hollering. Even Robin stopped short until she realized who she was looking at. The cavalry had showed up to draw the crowd off of them. Gev the church-grim.

Stumbling onto the sidewalk, Joel Ellis stared at the flaming ghost-dog. Surrender flashed across his face as if he were thinking, *Hell, that ain't the craziest thing I've seen, and it's only gonna get worse.*

"We'll hide in the comic shop," Joel told them, his arms up. Something colorful flashed in his hand. "I got the key!"

The terrifying phantasm-dog ambled along behind them, snarling and challenging the familiars as they got close. A meticulously painted Spider-Man and Batman appeared ahead of them, the comic shop's window mural flickering into view through the mob. Joel ran for the front door and jammed the key home, his hands shaking. "What y'all crazy-ass white people done got me into now?" demanded Joel, the lock disengaging with a double-barreled *clank.* "I got people acting like cats, garbage-men shooting at me, and now we got freaking demon dogs in the middle of town?"

"It's all in your head, my friend," Gendreau told him as they all ran past into the darkened shop.

"Of *course* it is." Joel tossed a hand and rolled his eyes. "It's all in your head, Joel, it ain't real, Joel, now put on this pretty white jacket and take your medicine, Joel. Lord give me strength."

As soon as they were inside, he pushed the door shut on its hydraulic hinge and locked it again. Robin counted them . . . Kenway, Gendreau, Sara, Joel, and herself. Her heart lunged painfully. *"Where's Wayne?"* she shrieked, surprising herself. *"Where's—"*

"I'm back here!" a voice called from the darkness.

Such intense relief settled over her, she could have collapsed. Robin fumbled past her friends and into the depths of the comic shop, where Wayne stepped out of the shadows. He'd found a Batman cowl somewhere and was shrugging into it.

She snatched it off his head, eliciting an indignant yelp of pain, and squeezed him against her chest. "I thought we left you out there, kiddo."

"Nope." He rubbed his ear. "I'm right here."

Standing by the window, they watched Gévaudan distract and fend off the crowd, trotting back and forth, barking ferociously at them. Joel studied the church-grim with a strange mixture of hope and alarm on his face, eyes wide, eyebrows furrowed and high.

"You okay?" Robin asked him.

He slowly surfaced from his reverie, his eyes cutting over to her. "Yeah, I think I seen a ghost, is all."

As the familiars tested the spectral canine, dancing in to bat at its noncorporeal body and leap back, Gev faded with all the ceremony of turning off a television. The sudden disappearance left the cat-people stupefied, and they boggled at the space where it'd been with vacuous screwhead eyes.

"Get away from the window before they see us," warned Gendreau.

Heeding his advice, they retreated deeper into the shop, gathering in the clear space at the back where Fisher had once held Movie Night. Someone tripped over a chair with a clatter. Kenway's face was a smear in the darkness, the windowlight sparkling in his eyes. "Where'd that kid in the Blues Brothers suit go?"

"Lucas?" Gendreau sat in a chair, wheezing. "He'll be all right, I think."

"Why didn't *you* magic those people?" Kenway asked. "You look like you could more than handle yourself." He caught his breath, his face drawn into the grimace of a side stitch. "You look like the third member of Siegfried and Roy went off and started a menswear line."

"What witty commentary, coming from the lead vocalist of a Nickelback cover band. Where is thine sling and shield, warrior?"

Kenway snorted derisively.

The atmosphere in the dark room chilled as everybody paused, and for a long, pregnant moment, Robin thought Kenway was going to take a swing at the magician. Then he chuckled, shaking his head, breaking the tension.

"I didn't participate in the combat," said Gendreau, "because I am not, ahh, versed in combative magic."

Sara sat down to rest as well. "Anders is a sensitive. He's our . . . supernatural GPS. He's how we found you Sunday night, and he's how we knew which hospital they took you to. He's not a battle-mage."

"I am also a superlative alchemist, and I am quite useful at curative properties—removing poisons and illnesses, knitting small wounds, that sort of thing." The slender magician sat back and tugged at his jacket, straightening it. "I was made an official *curandero* in Chile six years ago and some call me Don Gendreau, the Healer of Caddo Parish."

"*Some* as in, like, twelve people," rasped Sara.

She had found a roll of paper towels with the party supplies on a table in the corner and was mopping at the now-tacky blood on her forehead. Gendreau got up and went to her, his hands gravitating to her face. "Here, love, let me take a look." He *tsk-tsk*ed, combing through her hair. His delicate hands probed a gash at her hairline, his fingers sweeping and flourishing. His fingertips traced delicate sigils on her skull. "You poor dear; banged your head pretty badly, didn't you?"

"Oh, stop petting me and fix it, please."

"Okay, enough banter. We need to figure out what we're going to do now," said Robin. "I don't think we'll survive another round with the Thundercats out there."

At least a hundred people shambled back and forth in the street, picking fights with each other and sniffing the air. Many of them had taken off their clothes, and three of them rutted madly in the middle of the street. "Man, I've never seen this many familiars in one place before. Most I've ever seen was at that casino in Nevada." One of the familiars peered through the gap created by Spider-Man's thighs and his retinas flashed white-green in the black silhouette of his head. They hunkered instinctively, watching over the edge of a shelf. "Darkness can't save you."

"Where is your sign shop, Kenway?" asked Wayne. "Maybe we can make a break for it."

The big veteran thought about it, rubbing his nose with his forearm. His hands came to rest naturally on his hips. "Umm." He pointed one way and then the other, turned around, then jerked a thumb over his shoulder. "About a half-block that way. On the other side of the street."

"Isn't the canal behind us?"

Kenway nodded. "No, it's behind my shop. But I think I might know where you're goin' with this. There's a storm drain in the alley behind *this* shop. I know because I've been back there to throw out garbage. It probably runs past the drainage grate in my garage and empties in the canal out back. You figure we could use it to sneak over there?"

"Yeah." Wayne got up and went through the door in the back, shouldering past the movie screen hanging from the ceiling.

Joel followed him. "Hold up. Make sure there ain't no fire alarm."

The adrenaline in Robin's system faded, her shoulder singing hallelujah. She sat down in a booth and pulled her shirt back down, ferreting her new left arm out of the sleeve. Blood still leaked freely from the surgery scar, and now all of the stitches had been broken, the staples pried loose and jutting out haphazardly, so they caught on the fabric.

"When you finish with Sara," she asked, "will you do something about my shoulder? It's killing me."

"Almost done."

In the gray light seeping through from the front of the shop, she could study the arm's fibrous surface, a thick plait of hard but yielding cables, like a tight gauntlet of tire-rubber, pliant yet hard. Taking her demon hand in her human hand, the silky copper hairs brushing her palm, Robin was overcome by a chilly awe.

Does he know? Does Andras know who I am? What I am? The next question was *Will he recognize me?* but she realized she didn't care.

Or perhaps she did; she wanted the demon that took advantage of her mother's fear to see her face and know her as she killed him. Compelling, irrepressible anger billowed up inside of her and Robin wanted to smash things; she wanted to destroy and pulverize. *That thing is going to die for what it did to my mother and what it's done to me. For the life it's forced me into.*

"Wow," said Kenway, leaning on the booth table. "So, your arm grew back. Pretty damn sweet, yeah?"

Robin nodded, forcing a smile.

When he spoke again, she could tell his smile had drained away and left him cool, his voice low. "I know it's weird. And it's hard to deal with. I don't know what to tell you." His own hand curled around hers and it registered she could feel it with the Andras-arm, she could *feel* things with it, and compared to the hard demon-skin, his fingers were as soft and warm and fragile as a very old man's. Instinctively, Robin shrank away. She didn't want her strange demon hand to touch him.

"If my leg grew back, I wouldn't care *what* it looked like," he said. "You know? I'd be happy just to have it back."

A sick thought occurred to her. *Is he jealous this happened, that it grew back?* Was there a part of him that felt . . . felt a kinship, or a satisfaction when he'd found out she'd lost her arm to Theresa? Robin brushed it aside. *Of course not. What kind of a person would he be to think that way?*

Her fears were vanquished handily when he leaned over and kissed her on the forehead.

"I like you anyway, the way you are," he said, and kissed her on the forehead again. "Hell, I think it looks badass—you're, like, a superhero now," and then he kissed her on the mouth and pleasure rippled through her chest, her heart thumping.

Robin reached up with her human hand and clung to him, mashing their lips together, and kissed him back. His beard clouded against her face.

"Thank you," she said, finally.

Her cheeks were wet. She scraped them dry with the demon-hand and winced at the hard crag of her thumb.

"For what?"

She didn't know what to say, so she kissed him again.

27

The bedazzled baseball bat glittered like a disco ball, flinging arrows of light all over Fisher's videotape room. He'd found it where his brother had left it Sunday morning, propped against the futon, along with the half-cup of cold coffee he'd never finished. Joel stared at the coffee, thinking about Fish and the strange black hellhound. *That dog. That was the dog I'd seen at the acid lake, just after—after Fisher—*

For the millionth time, the pistol in Owen Euchiss's hand barked fire into Fisher's face and Joel watched his brother's body capsize languidly into water the color of bile. Joel had closed his eyes but he didn't flinch, weak acid spattering his face and chest.

Movie posters were tacked to the walls here. They had a theme. Black heroines. Pam Grier in *Foxy Brown*. Rosario Dawson as "Claire" in *Daredevil*. Letitia Wright as "Shuri" in *Black Panther*. Grace Jones as "Zula" in *Conan the Destroyer*. And last but not least, Gloria Lynne Henry as "Rocky" in the horror epic *Phantasm*. Joel focused on them, trying to stave off another anxiety attack over the lingering image of his brother's final moments. The two of them had loved these women, in different ways—Fisher was in love with them, while Joel idolized them, Zula and Rocky in particular. Something about Grace Jones's feral, unflinching beauty and watching Gloria knock the Tall Man's spheres out of the air with her nunchaku gave ten-year-old Joel a thrill. Those fade haircuts were the icing on the cake.

"Mister."

He snapped out of it. Wayne was a collection of shapes in the darkness. "Do you have a key for this back door?" asked the boy.

The movie room—Fisher's personal home theater, at least as theatrical as a futon in a closet and a thirty-year-old TV and VCR could be—had three doors: the one leading back to the shop, the one on the right leading to the stairway to Fisher's loft apartment, and one on the left at the end of a short hallway. That one went out back to the alleyway.

"I don't know." He fished the shop key out of his pocket.

They stood there in the shadows, regarding each other.

"I'm sorry aboutcher brother, mister Joe-elle." Wayne's glasses reflected the light from the shop in a bulging square of white. The eye revealed by the missing lens was warm and full of concern. "He was cool. A real nice guy."

Joel sighed, glancing up at the posters. Rocky posed with her nunchucks with the rest of *Phantasm*'s characters, artfully arranged around her.

"He taught me something cool."

Joel smiled wanly. "Oh, yeah? What did he teach you, little man?"

"Adapt and overcome."

"Ah, he gave you the Hulk monologue," said Joel. "I heard that one a few times. He was real into the big green guy, wasn't he?"

"Yeah."

Choosing action over more thought, Joel led Wayne down the little hallway to the fire exit. The more he did, the less he could think, and the less he thought, the less he could watch those brains spray on the Movie Night screen of his mind.

Feeling around the surface of the door, he found another commercial deadbolt. He unlocked it and pushed the door open. Silver daylight rushed down the inside. Beyond, a narrow alleyway ran to vanishing points in both directions. Boxes were piled in one corner by a steel utility door leading into the water heater closet, and two recycling bins leaned against the far wall. A chain-link fence framed the area on both sides. Joel was peering into the storm drain when a dark figure came out of nowhere, crashing into the fence and scaring the hell out of him. He flinched, raising the Batdazzler.

Blood ran down the man's temples in heavy blotches and made glossy sealskin of his black suit. His shirt was ripped open.

"It's Lucas," said Wayne, opening the gate to let him in.

The magician staggered into the enclosure, arming blood and sweat from his forehead with a trembling hand. His once-impeccable suit hung from him in black-and-white tatters. "God*damn*, I thought that was the end of me." He leaned against the wall. "Everybody make it okay?"

"Yeah."

Lucas thumped his chest with pride. "Then my glorious sacrifice was not in vain."

They brought him into the comic shop, where Sara gave him a hug and Gendreau shook his hand. "Good work back there, soldier," said the self-proclaimed curandero. "How did you get away from the mob?"

"Well, I lasted about ten seconds and then they had me on my back, kickin' and scratchin' the shit outta me." Lucas collapsed into the booth, where he fished a cigarette out of his shirt pocket

I COME WITH KNIVES · 273

and shakily stuck it in his mouth, patted himself down for a lighter, didn't find one. "But then I heard a roar—I guess Sara did something?—and then everybody ran away. I don't know where the burnt-looking guy with the rifle went, he ran off while I was gettin' worked over."

"Excellent. We're all in one piece. Now, we've got things to do," said Robin, getting up and heading for the back door. "We don't have time to sit around chitchatting."

"Slow down." Kenway stopped her by the movie screen, his shadow sharp on the giant white-silver sheet. His hand lightly cupped her elbow. "Take a minute. You just got out of the hospital and lived through a car accident *and* a mob. I thought you wanted Gandalf over here to take a look at your shoulder."

She hesitated, her face grim.

His look of concern became one of reproach.

Sighing, she came back and unfolded one of the Movie Night chairs, plopping down into it. Gendreau took off his jacket and pushed up his shirt-sleeves. His shirt was tailored, but without the Willy Wonka blazer, his sleeves belled at the elbows and narrowed at the cuffs. With his platinum-blond hair, Arctic eyes, and Nordic face, it made him look a bit like a cover model for a romance novel, or a character in an Anne Rice vampire movie. "All right," he said, as he pulled up Robin's shirt. "This may hurt a bit at first—I'm going to pull the rest of these staples out, because I can't quite achieve the effect I need with them in the way. And then I'll need to press the wound together manually."

"Whatever you need to do, doc," Robin said noncommittally. She took off the helmet and let her head tilt back. "I took another couple of pain pills a minute ago. I figured I might as well, since I threw up."

A hard, workmanlike sort of temper had come over her since Joel had seen her last. *This must be her Go Mode,* he decided. *This was what it looked like when the going got tough and Robin*

274 · S. A. HUNT

Martine shifted into Four-Wheel Drive. That, or the pain is making her surly.

"You're pushing yourself too hard," said Kenway.

She pointed at him. "You have no idea what I've been through—"

"I know what running yourself into the ground looks like," Kenway said, grimly. "I didn't get my Purple Heart flipping burgers at McDonald's. Let the medic help. You can't keep fighting if there's nothing left of you."

"I'm sorry." Robin winced as Gendreau picked the bent staples out of her. Her eyes were rimmed in red. "I didn't mean it that way. I'm saying . . . I've pushed myself harder than this."

She stretched the neck of her shirt open and pointed at a scar on the left side of her chest, high, directly under her collarbone. "This came from a girl in Connecticut last spring. She stabbed me with a pair of kitchen shears. Missed my heart by two inches." She pointed to the tiny pink commas peppered up her arms and the blade of her jawline. The pea-sized pit by her ear. "Scratches. From Neva Chandler and others. God, those bitches always scratch. Bite marks from a dog Heinrich used to train me." She hiked up her left jeans leg and pointed at her shin, even though it was too dark to really see. "Got whacked with a shovel in Florida, ended up with a minor fracture. I've broken three toes and two fingers." She waggled the fingers of her right hand. "I'd show you one of those broken fingers, but Theresa took it. Along with the rest of my arm."

The more scars she explained, the angrier and more harried she seemed to get. Ferociously unbuckling her belt, she ripped her fly open, shucking her jeans to her knees with one hand, flashing panties. Her voice took on a choked, raw quality. "I got burnt all over my legs tryin' to light up this witch in St. Louis—" Her thighs rippled with pink, gnarly patches of long-healed burns. "I been doin' this for a long time now. I can *handle myself,* goddammit. So don't patronize me, okay?"

"I need you to quit moving," Gendreau said blandly.

Irritation clouded her face. Her eyes briefly danced between the curandero's, and then she pulled her jeans back up.

"We're all a little stressed right now," he continued. "So, let's utilize this all-too-brief moment of solitude and take a fucking break. Can you do that?"

• • •

The noise of the crowd outside gradually diminished to an occasional shout. Joel thought he heard police sirens, but it was so far away, it could have been more cat-yowling from the familiars.

Kenway stood at the edge of the generous Movie Night space, leaning against a rackful of action figures, his ankles crossed so his prosthetic leg lay on top.

"I love you," he said, after a while.

"No, you don't," said Robin.

He thought about it a minute and said, "Yep. Maybe I do."

She shook her head. Her voice was still rusty. "Look at me. Look at this thing I have for an arm now. You just *think* you do. Why would anybody love me?" The demon-hand flexed with a stony rasp. "Look at it. It's a piece of *him*. My stupid mom made a deal with him and now I have to carry a goddamn piece of him. I belong in Hell with the rest of the devils." Her front incisors met in a disgusted grimace as she balled a demonic fist. She growled through her teeth, "What even *is* this?"

Gendreau had no answer. Neither did anyone else. Sara pretended to be absorbed in picking her fingernails, while Lucas read a comic book. Kenway stared at the floor as if chastised, his brow dark.

"It's *you*, is what it is." Joel got up and knelt by her.

Robin looked down at him and he felt a thin ripple of fear. There was a terrible, angry thing in her eyes, a sweaty sort of madness come to the surface, and suddenly it was as if he were a knight supplicating to a medieval lord drunk on both power and liquor. The baseball bat even completed the analogy, because as he took a knee in front of her, the business end of it rested on the floor and leaned against his knee like a sword. The fake diamonds glued to the wood even mirrored the faint light as a blade might.

He thought to hold her human hand, but had the idea to take the strange dark hand; he held it and was struck by how alien it was, like a sculpture of a human hand made of driftwood and sooted in a fire—a human hand but larger, the fingers hooking in blunt claws. Fleecy red hair grew all down the back of it in a singular finlike shag and ended in a final punctuating tuft over her knuckles. Up close, he could see veins of dark green tracing between her jagged knuckles.

It was the most foreign, outlandish thing he'd ever seen.

"*I* love you too, girl," Joel said, gazing up at her half-mad face. "We're almost brother and sister, you and me. We grew up together, remember?"

She said nothing, but the corner of her mouth twitched and her eyes lost a bit of that fearsomeness.

"You really think of me as a sister?"

"Y—Yeah, I do." He still wore his silk do-rag. He took it off and bunched it in a ball in his fist against his chest.

"I never had a brother before."

Joel smiled. He had put on eyeshadow and eyeliner that morning before he'd gone back to the hospital, and even though it was dark and he was slick with sweat, he knew he still looked good. "You do now."

"It's okay," she said, a bit dreamily. "I'm sorry the meds made me forget you. It's been a long time, Joel."

"You the same Robin I grew up with, aight?" He put his other hand on top of the dark hand, and it was as if he clasped the horny, splintered base of a broken branch jutting out of a tree. He wondered if the hand hurt, as dry and hard as it felt. "You're that same little girl me and my brother ate breakfast with in that big ol' house. You remember what I said at Miguel's?"

"Ain't nothin' in this world good bacon can't make better." Robin's eyes focused on his.

"That's right. Same little girl me and him played with in your big ol' backyard. We used to take turns swingin' on that swing back there, you and your mosquito. What was his name?"

"Mr. Nosy." A faint smile. "I still have him. He's in my van."

"He must be old as hell now."

"Falling apart. I've had him fixed so many times, I can't even remember." The smile spread a bit more. "I love that stupid mosquito so much." A fresh tear re-wet the track on her face. "I remember playing dress-up with you and Fish in my room in the cupola. You used to love puttin' on my mom's old dresses and pearls. I remember."

Joel stroked the strange hand. "You're still here. You're that same little girl with that same stuffed mosquito. Only you grown up now, and there's a *little* different but not much. I've changed too—there's been a few dirty things in my system and my lungs are prolly as black as my outsides by now—but under it all, I'm still that little boy in your mama's old dresses and high-heel shoes too big for my feet."

All the hardness had drained from Robin's face, though her tone was still a bit lost, as though she were speaking from the far side of another world. But with each word, she seemed to get a better handle on herself.

"Yeah. We're still the same," she said, her eyes warming. "Okay."

He let go of her demon-hand and she balled her fist again. The sound of it flexing was simultaneously like the creak of oiled leather and the thin, fibrous crackle of wicker.

"This ain't *him*," Joel told her, taking her woody fingers in his. "It ain't. This is *you*, girl. It's just a little more badass than the rest of you."

She nodded and wiped her cheeks with the back of her human right hand.

"You can't go through this life and not pick up a little shit here and there. We are all the sum of our lives, hon . . . and we all gotta carry a piece of crazy to the end." Joel got up off the floor, using the Batdazzler as a cane. The bullet-graze across his thigh had been re-closed at the hospital, and now it hurt only when he bent his knee. Of course, the pain meds they'd given him were helping. "Yeah, you got a *big* piece. But I'mma help you carry it, aight?"

She nodded again, and a hardness came back to her, but it wasn't the Crazy-Eyed-Lord-on-His-Throne, Off-With-Your-Head look again; it was a positive and steely resolve. The *lost*-ness was gone. Joel sensed he had dragged his childhood friend back from the edge of some dark, destructive promontory.

"I love you, yeah?" His tone said this was not optional. "And this boy over here"—Joel pointed at Kenway with the end of the bat— "he love you too. Dig on *that*."

Robin wiped her face again. "I can dig it. Yeah."

Clank, clank, clank.

The sound of someone knocking on the front door echoed back to them. Everyone seemed to shift into a combat stance. Kenway turned and peered through a gap between the shelves. "Who the hell . . ."

"I thought I heard a police siren earlier," said Sara. "Maybe the cops are trying to disperse the familiars. Hell, maybe the familiars have even come back to their senses."

"No. I don't think—"

A man stood on the other side of the glass, his hands cupped around his eyes so he could see through into the shadows.

The rifle-toting mutant. Roy Euchiss.

"Hey, anybody in there?" called the ruined man, wispy strands of hair haloing from his acid-burned head. "I know you're in there." He gave a ragged cough. "I saw somebody moving. You open yet? You got this month's *Batman*? I'm a fan, you know." He raised the rifle, shouldering it. "Don't get up. I have a key."

The first shot thundered in the comic shop like a judge's gavel.

A hole appeared in the Plexiglas door. "Shit, we got to get out of here," said Lucas, and the magicians ran for the back door, cutting through the movie room. Kenway grabbed Robin's hand and led her away, but at the last second, she pulled herself free and turned to look.

"What are you doing? Come on!"

Placing his bedazzled bat on the sales counter, Joel took hold of his sleeve, ripping it free of his sweater. "Y'all go on out the back. This the man killed my brother." He tore the other sleeve off, revealing his biceps, still muscular from days carrying stone pavers and bags of fertilizer in the summer heat. With his sweaty fade and naked muscles, he looked every bit like the women on his brother's movie posters. Rocky and Zula would be proud. He picked up the bat and flourished it. "This shit ends here."

BOOM! Roy fired another bullet through the glass and started kicking the door, rattling it in the frame. A cardboard standee of Iron Man fell over with a *clap*.

"You sure?"

"I got this, baby."

Leaning through the doorway, Kenway held out a fist to the pizza-man. "Beast mode, man."

Joel fist-bumped it. "Beast mode."

"Speaking of beasts," said Sara Amundson, as the others fled out the back, "I'll stay here and give you a hand, if that's okay. I'll make a monster."

Joel shrugged. "If you—"

CRASH! The front door imploded. At the same time, Sara vanished.

Glittering grit crunched under his boot soles as Roy Euchiss stooped underneath the mullion barring the middle of the door, passing through the gap. The rich, buttery stink of gunpowder mixed with the feeble vanilla funk of old comic books.

Up close, Roy was horrendous. His ears had deteriorated, leaving ragged stumps of raw skin, edged in black. Two gaping Lon

Chaney *Phantom of the Opera* nostrils marked where his nose had melted, and one of his eyes was a milky cataract. The skin all over him was like the world's worst sunburn. He racked the bolt on his rifle. An empty brass casing flipped out and tinkled across the glass sales counter.

"Where the fuck are you, ya brother-killin' porch monkey son of a bitch!" he bellowed with a wrathful shiver.

"Y'all killed my brother first—" Joel yelled, anger stripping him of self-control, and he knew it was a mistake as soon as *brother* passed through his lips. Roy's head jerked in his direction and he shouldered the rifle, firing. A box exploded above Joel's head, peppering him with bits of plastic and paper. Racking the bolt, Roy stormed down to where Joel had been hiding, looked up, saw him crouch-running around the other end, and fired at him.

BOOM! A *Walking Dead* coffee mug shattered.

Joel scrambled across the aisles of toys and games. The rifle coughed fire again, and a hole appeared in a *Monopoly* box behind him. He crawled as quietly as he could, trying to put as much space between him and that gun as possible.

His shoulder bumped into a knee and he found himself looking up into the telescoping jaws of an alien. Joel almost screamed until he realized it was Fisher's replica Xenomorph statue.

"Attention!" bawled an amplified voice outside. *"This is the police! You are ordered to disperse!"*

The cops? Joel crept behind the Alien statue. Had the cops come to put the hurt on the mob out there? The crowd became chaotic, screaming and angry. Footsteps raced past the broken front door. Familiars snarled ferally.

"Get your asses outta here!" continued the bullhorn warning. *"Right—"*

It was cut off by the hollow slap of gunfire.

"You might as well stop running," warned Roy, turning and striding back the way he came, following the sound of Joel scuffling against the carpet. He racked the bolt, loading a fresh round.

Boxes throughout the comic shop blew open in shreds of card-stock, one or two at first, like the first kernels of popcorn in the bag. Roy stopped to look around in confused surprise. They were all cracking open in a percussive symphony, *POP-POP-POP!* Action figures tumbled to the floor in a rain of plastic arms and legs.

"What kind of trick is *this* shit?" Euchiss asked the shadows. "Let me guess, here's the twist: you're some kind of Negro hoo-doo magician descended from Haitians or Jamaicans or somethin', right? Ain't that how these things always go? I watch movies when I ain't cuttin' throats, you know. I ain't *completely* uncivilized yet. I love a good movie. Especially when there's plenty of chaos to go around." He giggled madly. "The more crazy, the better."

Something brushed Joel's ankle. A tiny plastic superhero scuttled under a shelf. Another miniature man slid past, and another. The floor was an ant-like armada of action figures, all tumbling and rolling toward the other end of the sales floor.

Roy opened his bolt, checked it, slammed it home again. "Well, listen here, Afrocadabra: you ain't got *nothin'* on Miss Cutty, I can tell you. She got more magic in her pinkie finger than in *all* your queer little body."

"You'll never win, Red Skull," said a tiny voice.

As if by instinct, Roy spun and fired at it. *BOOM!*

Captain America flipped ass over teakettle into the shadows. "I am vengeance!" said another voice, behind him. "I am the night!" Others chimed in, growing into a cacophony of chirping battle cries:

"This is where it ends, Skeletor!"

"Thundercats, Thundercats, Thundercats, *hooooo!*"

"Transformers! More than meets the eye!"

Soon, the voice-chip recordings of dozens, *hundreds* of action figures swelled into a singular angry robot chorus, a dissonant and anticipating pitchfork mob. Vibrations welled in the floor, radiating from some ponderous epicenter in the middle of the shop, a rumble that rose and opened into a slow roar.

Rising from between the racks was a great mound of jack-shapes, a head and shoulders and then a towering many-colored gestalt, five feet, six feet, seven feet tall, a Grendel made of action figures. It lurched down the aisle toward Roy on two swimmy elephant feet as if it were wading in deep mud, light glistening on shins and biceps. Sightless electric eyes winked all over, red and green laser-dots flashing and flickering like Christmas lights. The synthetic bravado of battery-operated ray-guns and lightsabers hissed and whizzed from deep inside: *pew pew pew! Bzzzz-bkow! Boom! Bling-bling-bling!* The dwindling electronic *eeeeewwwww BKSSHH* of a blockbuster bomb. Roy made a face, wincing almost in embarrassment. "Is this supposta *scare* me, pizza-man?"

Joel stepped from behind a shelf and swung the Batdazzler up into the rifle, shattering every finger-bone in Roy's left hand.

Fake diamonds broke loose, glittering across the carpet. The Serpent's right hand impulsively pulled the trigger, *POW!*, tearing through boxes of toys, and he screamed in pain and rage. Raising the sparkling baseball bat, Joel brought it down in the middle of the gunman's forehead with an impact that jolted his forearms, numbing his hands. Roy backpedaled, collapsing against a shelf, and the whole thing toppled over in a spill of sleeved comics.

Before he could get up, Joel lunged in and hammered him across the chest. Ribs gave way underneath with a muffled, delicate *crunch*.

"UUNGH!" Roy corkscrewed out of the way and *BANG!* like a drum, Joel knocked a splintery hole in the back of the wooden shelf. Diamonds pattered across the wood. Roy spun off onto the floor, hugging the rifle, and as soon as he fell on his back, he came up with it, the barrel pointed at the pizza-man. The Batdazzler raised, Joel paused in terror at the sight of that gaping black barrel.

Hot madness roiled up inside of him, becoming a strained, kamikaze sort of bravery. "*Shoot me, son!*" Joel bellowed at the supine killer. "*Shoot me, you burnt-up Wonderbread motherfucker!*"

Roy pulled the trigger. *Click.*

"Shit!" he hissed, and racked the bolt.

Joel clubbed the rifle out of the way, striding across the back of the fallen shelf, and stomped his chest as if he were killing a particularly foul insect. Bones flexed protestingly under Joel's foot.

"URRRFUNNNNCK!" Roy spat, saliva misting. He rolled over, abandoning the rifle, and beetled away across the carpet, drooling.

"You look like somebody peeled a hot dog," Joel snapped.

Having knocked so many of the diamonds off, the Batdazzler was little more than your average baseball bat. Joel stepped down from the overturned shelf and walked almost pleasantly alongside the belly-crawling serial killer. He twirled the bat in a jaunty, careless way, but his face was the essence of grim, hard-bitten rage.

"This for all 'em cats you burnt," said Joel, and whipped the bat hard across the killer's spine.

Vertebrae snapped with a soft crackle. The Serpent screamed into the darkness of the comic shop. He turned over and put up his hands, trembling, his eyes wide and pleading. Only his upper body did so, his waist helixing, his legs sprawled uselessly where he'd left them. Joel nosed the bat sharply back and forth, knocking his hands out of the way.

"*No!*" Roy screamed. "*Please!*"

"This for my brother," Joel grunted. The bat slammed into Roy's face on the diagonal, caving it in with a thick, wet *sputch* and cutting him off mid-scream.

The business end stayed in the ruins of Roy Euchiss's face. One eyeball bulged from underneath the wood, staring at the floor. Joel stood up slowly, warily, as if he were afraid the floor were about to fall in.

"Adapt and overcome," he told the corpse.

28

The witch-hunter led them through the grate behind the shop into a storm drain. Only about waist height, the drain was filthy, strewn with old trash and dried mud; it was all she could do to keep from dry-heaving. Kenway struggled along behind her, his prosthetic leg scraping on the concrete. Gendreau, Lucas, and Wayne duck-walked, the curandero's jacket rolled up under his arm so it wouldn't get wet.

Sixty or seventy feet in, the ceiling opened up to the ink-blue clouds of the afternoon sky, and through a grate extending the width of Broad Avenue they could see the familiars shambling around above. Shoes clomped across the steel as the crowd capered back and forth, shrieking and fighting each other.

"I forget," said Lucas, bringing up the rear, "how long does the feral stage last after a dormant familiar is activated?"

"Several hours," grunted Gendreau. "Depends on the witch. But Cutty? Who knows?" A little girl on her hands and knees over the grille searched the darkness for them, her fingers laced through the steel slats. Her eyes were softly luminous moon-dimes.

"*Attention!*" echoed an augmented voice above. "*This is the police! You are ordered to disperse!*"

Lucas blinked. "Police? Do they think it's a riot?"

"*Get your asses outta here! Right—*" The amplified voice was interrupted by the high *crack* of a grenade launcher, followed by chemical hissing and the *rakka-tak* of nonlethal rounds and the chest-thumping *boom* of beanbag shotguns.

Tear gas wafted down through the grille with a pungent reek, making Robin's eyes water. "It's happened before. There was a pretty bad incident with familiars in California last year. The governor claimed it was a riot over that court case. You know, the minority shooting where the cop got off?"

"Christ," said Sara. "Which one?"

Familiars ran past, their shoes clattering across the grille.

"That was you?" asked Gendreau. "The Dogs of Odysseus suspected it had been familiars."

"Yeah. I was trying to burn Adeline Stidman and she had the whole damn neighborhood after me. Chased me into a college campus, had the campus police involved. Biggest fuckup ever. Anyway, I guess when people don't have any other explanation, people make shit up to fill in the blanks, you know?"

Gendreau chuffed humorlessly. "Connect the dots."

"Here we go," said Kenway.

Robin had been so focused on moving, she hadn't noticed they'd crossed both lanes of Broad, gone under the opposite sidewalk, and were underneath his sign shop. A grille showered the drain floor with warm yellow light.

Black engine grease made the floor into a disgusting skating rink. The two of them positioned themselves under it.

"Super gross," said Wayne.

"Sorry," he said. "This is where I park cars for vinyl wraps. They have a bad habit of leaking fluids." Kenway gripped the drain grille with both hands and braced himself, pushing. "Damn." He stood up, bent over at the waist, and raised himself until his shoulders and the back of his head were against the metal, and he pushed with his legs. After only a few seconds, he was straining so hard, he was vibrating. "Unnngh, *damn.* It won't move. It's glued in by all the muck. It might even be bolted down."

Robin pressed her human hand to his chest, gently shooing him out of the way. "Here, let me try."

"I don't know how—" he started to say.

She cleared her throat. "Trust me."

Taking his place, Robin looked up through the grate. She could see the ceiling of the garage. Kneeling on one knee, she reared back with the demon hand and struck the grille with her open palm as hard as she could. Her freakish left hand, twice the size of her right hand and as hard as a tree stump, clanged noisily against the steel.

Dry grease rained down onto them and Robin shielded her face, scraping her lips with her shirt. She'd expected it to hurt to some degree, even though it was tough, but there was nothing. Only the reverberations of the impact traveling up to her shoulder.

It was sort of liberating, to be honest—what else could she do with this? How sturdy *was* this thing? The fibers were each almost as big around as her original arm; they had stretched out the U-shaped scar like a yawning mouth, the edges strained and ripping until the hole had been five, six inches across. Skin pulled taut over the scabrous blackwood bone that was now her new arm. The self-proclaimed curandero had worked his strange shamanic healing magic on her (she still hated calling it magic, and now she felt this was because the word *cheapened* something she'd come to know and fear as a powerful force), and without the bent staples embedded in it, the surgery wound had scarred over.

Now the pain had abated to a constant arthritic ache. Whatever Gendreau did had blended her skin with the demon-skin; the cells combined in a jagged, organic fashion, interlocking and growing together, like splinters embedded painlessly in her flesh. It was as if she'd been born this way, and in light of Joel's pep talk, she supposed she had been.

She slammed the demon-hand against the grille again, producing a slap-bass *thrum* of steel. More foul dirt crumbled onto them.

Kenway spat and coughed. "Man, that is heinous."

"Can we hurry this up, please?" complained Gendreau from the darkness behind them. "My knees are killing me."

Robin steeled herself and took a deep breath of cold, foul air, then whacked her demon-hand against the grille, *CLANG,* and again, *CLANG,* and again, again, again, *CLANG CLANG CLANG.* Each strike was accompanied by a grunt of effort.

Finally, the grille came loose, scraping and shifting upward. "There, I loosened it for you."

Kenway stood up in the drain, shoving the metal free. "Hardy-har," he said, and let it fall to the side, the hinge chiseling up more of the loamy grease-dirt. He lifted himself out and then gave Robin a hand up, and the two of them helped Wayne, Gendreau, and Lucas out.

The pitter-patter of little feet made Robin look into the pit. The phantom greyhound Gévaudan whimpered, only visible by his glowing eyes. "Sometimes the abyss looks back." The church-grim gave a great big shake, jitterbugging across the drain floor, and disappeared. He reappeared in the garage and trotted silently up to Kenway's apartment, flowing up the stairs like black smoke.

As he did, Joel watched intently.

"What's up with you and the ghost-dog?" asked Robin.

"He was at the mine pond when those two white boys shot my brother. Standing on the other side, watching."

She wasn't sure what to say to that.

Luckily, Gendreau saved her from putting her foot in her mouth. "That is a church-grim. They patrol graveyards, protecting the church from vandals and thieves, and they accompany departed souls to the afterlife." He smiled as warmly as he could manage. "If the grim was there when your brother was murdered, it most likely escorted him safely to a better place—wherever that might be."

Joel stood there, absorbing this, as Kenway led the magicians up the stairs. After a moment, a tear trickled down his cheek and he knuckled his eyes clear. A confused smile touched his lips.

"Sounds like a real good boy, then," he said, and followed Robin up the stairs.

• • •

All Kenway's works of art hung on the wall over the fridge and cabinets, intricately arranged so each made room for the other and left little of the wall itself uncovered. Robin noticed the darker, more introspective paintings were down at the ends, framing the brighter, lusher ones in the middle, which made the presentation feel like a mosaic of a sun in outer space, as if viewed through a mail slot.

"Very nice work, I must say, Mr. Griffin." Gendreau spooled off some paper towels to wipe at the grease on his plush-looking jeans, even though his shirt was a black finger-painting. "Do you ever sell any?"

"I've had some offers."

Wayne put his ring to his eye, looking up at them. Then he let it dangle from its chain and climbed up onto the kitchen counter, pushing aside a bag of chips, and very carefully slid up onto the top of the fridge. He put the ring to his eye again and pressed on a tall portrait depicting a horse's white foreleg, each muscle and vein rendered in exquisite, almost nightmarish detail.

The canvas billowed a little bit like sailcloth but otherwise didn't move. No dice. Wayne turned on his butt, kicking a fridge magnet off onto the floor, and splayed his hand on the surface of a painting of a shirtless woman as viewed from the back. Like the horse leg, this one was also in bright, washed-out colors and sharp photographic detail.

With a faint *click,* the painting swung inward on darkness. They all paused to regard it in awed, stony silence. Gendreau pontificated with his arms wide. "I've seen a lot of things in my time, but this is remarkable, simply remarkable: an interdimensional crawlspace."

"I'm gonna go in first," Robin told them, lifting herself up onto the island in the middle. She crouched next to the stove. "If that thing is waiting to amb—"

A huge orangutan arm slithered out of the hole in the wall, covered in matted red hair. It was so big it was unreal, a Halloween-spider decoration, with long, knuckly fingers and too many of them.

Gendreau shrieked like a horror-film ingénue.

The cacodemon's hand folded around Wayne's throat and pulled him against the wall with a *thump,* the bicep flexing, dragging him inside the hole. It happened so quickly, and had taken Robin so much by surprise, that at first she found her body unwilling to move. But as the boy slid through into that deep velvet darkness, he shouted her name.

"ROBIIIN!"

That was enough to animate her. Reaching up with both hands, she grabbed his ankle, and for a brief instant, they were playing tug-of-war with him, and then his foot slid out of his sneaker.

Wayne slipped into the dark.

"No!" She dropped the shoe and scrambled on top of the fridge, thrusting her left arm into the hole before Andras could close it.

The painting slapped shut on her wrist and bounced open again.

Before she could second-guess herself or the others could follow, Robin grabbed the edges of the crawlspace and hauled herself through into the upstairs bathroom of 1168 Underwood Road.

• • •

She vaulted the sink headfirst and hit the opposite wall, punching a hole in dusty sheetrock. The medicine cabinet clicked shut and the mirror shattered, shards of silvered glass crashing into the sink.

"*Robiiiiin!*" screamed Wayne from deeper in the house.

As she made her way down the hall, pinballing back and forth with her hands out, her eyes became used to the dark and a fungal, formless subterranean light gave shape to the furniture.

At the end of the hall stood the demon, Wayne under his arm like a football.

Goddamn, but that thing was *huge.* No wonder the children had been so afraid of it. A thrill of terror racked her system. It was all head and lanky frame, an enormous black-green chimpanzee with jagged dinosaur legs and a giant mascot head. Before he slipped over the banister, he flicked those Edison-bulb eyes with their throbbing sea-green filaments back at her. Robin gave chase, hurling herself onto the demon's broad back. It was like leaping onto a wicker sofa with a rug thrown over it, with the same dirty-woody smell of neglect and musty filth. Andras's skin actually *creaked.* She sank the fingers of her black left hand into his hairy-splintery flesh and found he was, indeed, hollow on the inside. He was a wicker sculpture made of a hundred thousand cords all wound together.

Unlife jostled and rustled inside, as if his heart were a trapped bird. Andras shrugged his free arm, twisting back and forth with a sound like breaking branches, and the scissor-blades of her fingers drew loose. Robin whipped free of him and tumbled to the floor in the foyer. The demon tossed Wayne down and stalked toward her. The boy collapsed next to the baseboards; his glasses fell off and skittered across the hardwood.

(welcome home)

The words flickered in Robin's head like a pilot light, a secret match-flame, less words than abstract concept-shapes, Rorschach blots. She would not give this violating devil the dignity of an answer. Robin flourished the strange left hand and ran at him, fury compounding inside of her. She meant to sink those claws into him again and tear him into pieces and see what was inside.

(the ring thank you for opening the door once again)

he said, flinging one hand across his chest in a capeless parody
of Bela Lugosi's Dracula,

(i will finally be free)

the demon told her, and as Robin came at him, he backhanded
her. That long insectoid arm batted her out of the way, a beam of
hard bone piling against her right side. She hit the wall with an
OOF and crashed through a curio arranged with dusty pictures,
sprawling on top of jagged things. Robin's heart thundered in her
chest and she was flushed with an incredible heat, almost embar-
rassing in its fury. "This is all *your* fault." The knot in her throat
burned. "*You* are why I'm here, and why I am the way I am, and
why my mother is dead." *Cambion. Crooked woman, half-monster.*
She wanted to cry, to sob in defiance and rage at this monstrous
creature, this avatar of corrosive lust, but she refused to give him
the satisfaction.

Andras grinned with a rack of teeth like jags of broken wood.
She plunged the hand he had given her into his belly, breaking skin
too hard for her human hand to damage, and pulled it open like
Christmas wrapping.

Fluttering sensations moved up her arm and touched her face.
She opened her eyes and pure disgusted fear shot a cold iron bolt
through her core.

Spiders.

He was full of spiders,

more fucking *spiders*,

THOUSANDS OF THEM,

crawling out of the empty darkness inside his body and up her
arm, a legion of bristling marbles marching toward her face.

Each one was a nightmare unto itself, she sensed, an embodi-
ment of some base desire, a walking prejudice or an evil thought; in
the three seconds that passed as they scuttled out of hiding, Robin
caught intrusive thoughts—flashes of murder, physical violation,
undiluted hatred or lust. Andras picked her up by the scruff of her
neck as if she were a kitten. He held her against the wall.

(you are me)

he said, and she could hear the grin in his mind-voice

(you are me and i am you)

and to her shock and terrified surprise, the swarthy skin of her draconic left arm began to *spread,* leeching across her collarbone and under her clothes, filling her in with its wicked hardness. Sinister, gleaming edges shredded the fabric of her shirt and hoodie, revealing the demon inside.

Black widows poured out of him and enveloped her from left to right, carrying a payload of licorice-smelling ink, engulfing her breast until it was a round bulb of wicked thatch. Her soft pink-brown nipple transformed into a rusty bolt head. Spiders crawled into her mouth. Andras was infecting her with darkness, infesting her, corrupting her, *changing* her.

Rays sifted through pig-iron twine. Blades of gold shimmered across the ceiling. She looked down and saw her heart behind her chest; she could actually *see* it like the sun in a picnic basket, a pulsar burning and blazing inside of her with a warm amber light. *My God, is that me? Is that mine?* she thought, her lips stiffening, her eyes burning, her hair turning to crimson straw. Her tongue hardened into a pitted black blade.

A framed photo hung on the other side of the hallway. Her own reflection swam in the cloudy glass. Her face blackened and warped, her eyes bulged and shined from deep within, dirty green foglamps. Her pupils were sharp electric pinpricks.

(I AM YOU AND YOU ARE ME)

Andras laughed, the sound of a whetstone coughing down the length of a sword blade.

—*Cambion, crooked cambion*—

"No!" she cried. Her voice was a watery scrape. She inhaled and the breath shook dirty cords in her chest. *Grrrahuhuh.* "NO!" she cried again, and hammered Andras with an iron fist.

The demon's sternum cracked and he let go of her, stumbling away, clutching his chest like he'd had a heart attack.

"I am *not* you!"

Both of her hands were spun from smoky iron thread and dry vine, and hair the color of merlot grew down her wrists in woolly shags like the sleeves of a wizard robe. "You can claim me all you want," Robin snarled up at the owl-headed wicker man. The words were oily and metallic, syllables chiseled from oak and steel. She pounded a fist against her chest, "But you'll never get that last five percent. I am *not* you! *My heart is my own!*"

Fear, real fear, and bewilderment guttered in the demon's dull lamp eyes. She ran at him and plunged both fists through the mesh of his chest, ripping him open.

Piles of spiders spilled out in a whispering rush, recluses and orb weavers, tarantulas and fat, scuttling wolf spiders. Wayne shrieked somewhere, but Robin did not falter or relent. Clutching the demon's bear-trap lips, she gripped the rim of his lower jaw and tore his face in half. Inside his head was the biggest spider of all. Eight finger-bones as long as umbrella ribs unfolded from the ruins of his wicker skull. Onyx eyes glistened at her from a clump of bone the yellow of unbrushed teeth. Gripped by disgust, Robin hauled it out of its shattered shell, wrestling it over to the nearest window.

The massive yellow crab-spider tried to bite her face, lunging between her arms with clicking-grinding mandibles.

(LET ME GO, LITTLE ONE)

Revulsion shot home like a dead bolt. He had recognized her for what she was. Andras knew she was his daughter.

A term of endearment from this monster?

Intolerable. She jammed one of her spun-iron elbows against the window and the glass shattered, shards sucking violently away into the deepest darkness Robin had ever seen.

On the other side of the frame was nothing. Not a space with nothing in it; there wasn't even a space. Just a lightless vacuum. And yet . . . a silvery malevolence breathed back there, an invisible entity she could only feel as a pulsing idiot wrath.

Faintly, distantly: the tuneless trilling of flutes.

Thrusting the bone-spider through the broken window, Robin shoved it out into the void. Andras disappeared, its flailing legs swallowed up and away.

Satisfied the creature was gone, she inhaled—*grrrrahuhuhuh*—and roared into the nothing, *"Fuuuuck! Yooouuu!"* It felt impotent, a wretched scream into an unfeeling abyss, but it had a certain gratification.

29

Red rust stains dragoned down the porcelain under the faucet. Dirty tiles marched across the walls in broken, snaggle-toothed rows. Robin found Wayne in the upstairs bathroom, lying in the clawfoot bathtub.

The medicine cabinet door was still shattered. Wayne had pulled it open, trying to find the way back, but behind it was nothing but glass shelves arrayed with ancient orange prescription bottles. She could see all this because her heart continued to shine through the fibers of her chest, illuminating the house around her.

"No!" shouted the boy, curled into the fetal position in the tub. "Please don't kill me!" He turned and threw something at her. "Just take it! Please don't hurt me!"

Crooked, she thought sadly. She picked up whatever he'd thrown and found his remaining shoe. "I'm not going to hurt you," she said. Her voice seethed, deep and hot like a Ferrari engine.

The boy only shivered harder.

"We've got work to do." She knelt by the tub. "Look at me, Wayne." Robin handed him his eyeglasses. He took them and slid them over his terrified eyes. She held out his shoe as well, the laces dangling.

"Oh, my God," Wayne said, one lens still broken out. Blood trickled from a cut in his hair. "Is that you? You really *are* a demon."

"Only ninety-five percent." She tapped her chest, where the shining evidence of that last five percent rested. A loud but muted kickdrum thumped in time with her nuclear heart, sending subtle ripples across the room. *Lub-dub. Lub-dub. Lub-dub.*

"I can't get the crawlspace open." Wayne pointed at the broken mirror. He spoke in the petulant, tired tone of a boy that can't get to sleep.

She stood at the sink, her dark fingers curling around the basin's edge.

"I can fix this, I think."

She picked up a shard of glass and slipped it into the door of the medicine cabinet. Then she took another and slid it into place next to the first. It should have taken her a long time, but the mirror was dirty and had broken in large glimmering daggers held together by filth, having shattered outward from a point in the center.

Placing the final shard, Robin pressed her fingertip to the starburst of silver cracks and concentrated.

While Gendreau had been healing her surgery scar in the back of Fisher Ellis's comic shop, she had been subtly tapping the *libbu-harrani* heart-road buried in the pearl at the end of his cane, drawing off some of his curative power for herself. She couldn't get much of it, as the source of the energy was buried deep inside a thousand nacreous layers of calcium carbonate, but it was enough for this. Sliding the pad of her demonic finger across the refractive edges, Robin traced each crack out to the frame of the mirror. Each time she did so, it faded, the glass smooth and unmarked underneath, as if she were erasing them.

"There we go," she said, thumbing the final crack away, revealing a clear, whole sheet of glass. She stepped back to admire her hand-iwork.

Taking his mother's ring out of his shirt collar, Wayne lifted it so he could look through it and focus its magic, and opened the cabinet door. The stark glow of the fluorescent lights in Kenway's kitchen sifted through. To Robin, the light fell brisk and sharp, hostile, like the chill of a winter door left open. She diminished into the shadows, stepping away until nothing was visible but her luminous eyes and the pulsar-heart still throbbing in her chest.

"Go," she told Wayne.

"No."

"Go." Robin took his shoulder. "Go to Kenway's apartment and wait there for me."

"I want to go with you," said Wayne, backing away from the dimensional window. "I want to save my dad. I want to help you."

She sighed, making that disturbing underwater-engine noise again. Her voice was an impossibly deep rumble. "You can help me one last way before you go back. You can help me find the door into the Lazenbury."

"Okay."

"Robin?" called someone from the other side of the mirror-hole. Sara Amundson. "Wayne? Are you . . . you okay in there?"

Kenway, his voice shaking: "Is that you?"

"Tell them not to be afraid of me."

Wayne climbed into the sink and leaned through the portrait-mirror hole. He glanced back at her. "You can't go out there any-more, can you?"

"It's . . . cold out there. Cold like . . . fire." Counterintuitive, but she knew deep inside if she went through that hole and tested the Sanctification that kept Andras locked out, she would burn in that superfreeze, as if the thermometer had gone all the way past zero and come back around to the top.

He turned back to the kitchen. "She can't come through the window," Wayne told them. "But she—"

"Is she okay?" asked Joel.

Kenway sat on top of the fridge, looking through the hole. "Babe? You there? Are you okay?"

"I'm fine," Robin told him, even though she wasn't, not really. In her present condition, she felt no pain; she felt godlike, perhaps, indestructible, aware only of the press of the floor against the soles of her feet and the constant draft of supernatural cold. He stared at her. The sensation of invincibility melted away under his warm eyes, leaving her feeling naked and vulnerable.

"I'm coming in," he said, climbing into the hole.

Wayne scrambled out of the way and Kenway clambered over the sink, lowering himself to the bathroom floor.

He stood in front of her, abject wonder and terror in his eyes. "Is that really you?" he asked, reaching for her. At first, she wanted to move away, or maybe push his hand back, but she let him touch her, rake his fingertips softly down the coiling slope of her chest and feel the rough wasp-nest swell of her left breast. The starshine of her heart filtered through his fingers.

His hand found its way up to her cheek and stayed there. She closed her luminescent eyes and pressed against the cooling cup of his palm.

"You're still beautiful to me," Kenway said. "If not even more than before."

A rusty laugh bubbled up out of her. "You think a demon is prettier than me?"

"Uhh . . . ." His hand twitched.

". . . I'm kidding."

"Your skin kinda reminds me of a Shredded Mini-Wheat."

"You're really pressing your luck there, dude."

The others were coming through now. Sara climbed through first, and then Lucas, who helped Gendreau down from the step of the sink. "Simply remarkable," the curandero said again, eyes wandering the decrepit bathroom.

Getting as close to the hole as she could tolerate, Robin looked out at the pizza-man. Joel sat on the fridge with his elbow in the dimensional hole, as pretty as you please. It could have been the driver-side windowsill of his Black Velvet.

"Are you staying here, then?"

He gawped openly at her. "I'm afraid, sister."

"It's okay to be afraid. But I'll protect you, baby. That's what a big sister does."

"I've lost a lot this week. The way my life is, when things go, a lot of things go. I'm scared. This is the closest I ever been to losing everything. But I do kinda want to see the end of this. Even if it's just so's I can go to bed at night and know in my heart it's over. You know?"

"Just a little bit more to go, if you can take it."

The moment lingered between them for a second. "You say you gonna protect me if I come with you?" Joel asked, getting up onto his knees. He was clutching the Batdazzler, which must have seen a good bit of action, because it was sleeved in vivid red blood and most of the bedazzle gems had been knocked off. "You gonna pinkie-swear me that shit, sister?"

She linked fingers with him. "I pinkie-swear. I'm sorry I wasn't there to protect you and Fish. I'm sorry I wasn't there to protect your mother from her fear. But I'm here now and making up for lost time."

"All right," he said, and he climbed through into Hell.

• • •

After trying every door in the house—including the back door, which led into the go-kart garage in Weaver's Wonderland, where they found Joel's car and the body of missing police officer Michael DePalatis—the one they needed turned out to be the front door, and Robin couldn't overlook the irony. Apparently, the front entrance of both 1168 and its Hell-annexed alter ego were linked in some deep way.

No rush of wintery cold came in when Wayne opened it, even

though she could plainly see the front porch of her childhood home outside. It was nighttime out there, but she wasn't sure if that was because it was getting close to six or because it was *always* night in this strange new aberration of a time zone.

"I don't feel the Sanctification out there," Robin told them.

"Perhaps it doesn't apply to a piece of reality when someone has tied it off like a balloon animal," said Gendreau.

With a brief pause, she put her hand outside. There was a bad moment where she felt the creep of ice—as if there were a holy residue—but then it passed. "It's safe." She stepped out onto the porch and they followed her.

Someone sitting in the swing down at the end loosed a shriek worthy of a Sioux warrior and vaulted the railing into the bushes.

"Pete?" called Wayne, squinting into the darkness. "Amanda?"

"Batman? Is that you?"

"Yeah, it's me." Wayne walked down to the swing where Amanda, her brothers, and little Katie Fryhover cowered in the dark. Evan and Kasey Johnson stood in front of their sister, wielding a golf club and a skillet, and shields devised from garbage can lids.

"Hey, hambone, was that you I heard scream?" asked Joel.

Pete hugged himself bashfully. "No."

Unfamiliar constellations hung low in the night sky like electric bulbs screwed into the clouds. The trailer park's mobile homes were pale, dark-eyed hulks run aground on a black shore. There were no lights. The de-conjuration must have interrupted the electricity in the power lines.

"Looks like when Weaver tied off the neighborhood," said Kenway, "she took Chevalier Village and 1168 with it."

Evan Johnson coughed, wiping his face with his sleeve. "It's been dark out for like two days straight. The power went out, and all of a sudden, the sun went away at like three in the afternoon yesterday."

"Ever since," said his brother, "we can't get out. The night makes a wall."

"The night makes a wall," echoed little Katie.

"Me and Evan tried to get out." Kasey pointed west with his golf club, down the road. "But it's like the air gets *hard*."

Evan giggled in spite of himself.

"It's like we're in a giant aquarium, you know?" said Amanda, standing up. Katie Fryhover clung to her leg with the desperation of a castaway on a life preserver. "We don't know what's going on. Our parents don't either."

"It's the witches," Wayne told them. "They did this. And we're here to fix it."

Pete came swishing through the grass, dusting off his shorts, and climbed the front steps. When he saw Robin, he stopped short, his hand on the banister. The other hand held the strength-test hammer.

"It's okay," she told him. "It's me, Robin, the crazy chick with the camera."

"What the hell *happened* to you?" he asked in the bravely rude way that is the kingdom of children.

"I did the drugs. All of them."

Lucas Tiedeman burst out laughing.

"We came over here to Wayne's cause it's the farthest away from the witches' house," said Amanda. "It seemed safe. Well, the safest place, anyway. The witches never come over here. I think they're afraid of it." Her eyes wandered out to the trailer park. "My dad seems like he is, too. He won't leave the house."

"He's been drinking since the sun went away," said Evan. "He sits in the dark and drinks and stares out the window."

"Maw-Maw sleepin'." Katie Fryhover peeked at Robin and hid her face again.

Kasey Johnson's makeshift weapon sank until the end rested on the porch. "None of 'em will go outside," he said, his tone flat and demoralized. "Not even our neighbors, like Mr. Weisser and Mrs. Schumacher. They won't even answer the door when we knock."

"I think you should take your friends to the hole back to my apartment," said Kenway, his hand resting on Wayne's shoulder.

"Make yourself at home. There's some stuff in the fridge if you get hungry. I don't know how long this is going to take."

"Okay." Wayne waved the other children into the house. "Come on, guys."

They followed him willingly enough, but Pete stopped at the front door and turned back to Kenway. "Hey, mister?" he said, hefting the carnival mallet. "Take this with you." He offered the mallet to the tall Nordic vet. Kenway's big mitt closed over the wooden handle and he lifted it over his head like a barbarian straight out of a Boris Vallejo painting.

"Mjolnir," Wayne said in awe from the foyer.

Kenway flourished it. The big hammerhead made a swooshing noise through the air. "Thanks, kid."

"Kick 'em in the ass, man," said Pete.

"Oh, I almost forgot—" Taking off the GoPro harness, Wayne handed it off to Robin. "Here's your camera, ma'am." He smiled and pushed his broken glasses up on his nose. "Thank you for lettin' me be your cameraman for a little while."

"Thank *you.*"

She adjusted the straps and put it on Kenway.

"And now your watch begins, Mr. Cameraman." The GoPro's evil red on-air light burned in the dark, a solemn, watchful eye.

With a soft and concluding *click,* the front door eased shut behind them, leaving the magicians, the veteran, the pizza-man, and the demon-girl alone on the front porch.

Sprawling in front of them was a twilight zone of shadows, interrupted only by the sight of the pale mobile homes marching darkly into the distance, a cemetery for giants. The night was windless and heavy, a smothering summer twilight three months too late.

No crickets sang. The silence was absolute.

• • •

Above them, the sky remained a chintzy model-town facsimile of the real thing, the stars almost low enough to reach up and touch.

With no wind and no nightlife, the trees around them were a silent wall of black paranoia, beat back only by the crunching of their heels. The road leading to the Lazenbury was a dark and lonely one, winding forever through suboceanic darkness. Robin's glowing heart illuminated the path around them but did nothing to assuage the feeling of being watched.

"Is that who I think it is?" asked Sara.

A wooden crucifix stood by the road.

Nine feet tall, confronting them like a warning. Heinrich Hammer was pinned to it with long roofing-nail spikes through his wrists and wire around his elbows.

In the green-yellow light of Robin's pulsar heart, the blood running in blotchy ribbons down his chin and chest was a glassy obsidian. He'd been worked over good; his legs were obviously broken by the crazy bandy way they angled, and his chest was a litany of gills, a dozen fleshy pink stab wounds. The witches had stripped him of everything except for his slacks, but his black duster caped from the back of the cross like Christ's tomb shroud, the sleeves tossed over his shoulders as though he were being embraced by the Grim Reaper himself.

As they approached, Robin was surprised to see his eyes crack open.

He coughed weakly. "Hi, folks."

"Evening, asshole," said Robin.

Heinrich spat blood into the weeds. He stared at her with one glassy, jaundiced eye. The other was swollen shut. "See you found your daddy. I bet you got some questions, huh—" His gentle prodding was cut off by a wet, productive cough.

"Is this why you trained me to kill?" she asked.

"Yeah."

"You weren't helping a bereaved girl find closure. You were sharpening a sword. *Your* sword." Robin got up close, close enough to smell the sweet, coppery smell of blood, and . . . something else, something both ammoniac and sugary. "Your golden ticket back into the Dogs of Odysseus." Ah, he'd pissed himself. That's what it was.

"You tried to break one of our cardinal rules, Mr. Atterberry," said Gendreau, taking off his jacket and stepping closer to raise a hand. "Bringing a demon through the Sanctification. Did you think we'd let you back in if you actually managed to *break* it?" Ectoplasmic energy skirled up and out of the curandero's slender arm, a throbbing cloud of motes the color of red Christmas lights, as if the sparks of a campfire whirled around Gendreau's hand.

"I thought I could tame the demon," said Heinrich. "Filter it, *extrude it,* through the girl."

"*Extrude?*" Robin made a face. "You make me sound like goddamn espresso. I'm not the best part of waking up, you fake-ass-kung-fu Obi-Wan shitdick. Why don't you hurry up and die before I turn that crucifix around and jam it up your ass?"

"You thought you could *smuggle* my girl here," said Joel. "Fuck was you thinkin'?"

Heinrich sighed. "I messed up. I did; I freely admit it. I made an ambitious mistake. But hey, look at it this way—you didn't turn out so bad, did you? Right?" A fat tear cut through the blood on his face. "My God, look at you, Robin—*cough*—you're—"

"A monster."

"—beautiful! You're *beyond* extraordinary." He chuckled, and the chuckles turned into full-fledged (if exhausted) laughter.

"What's so funny?"

The crucified man shook his head slowly, dejectedly, and his grin drooped into a desolate grimace. She thought he'd started laughing again, but the convulsions turned out to be silent sobs. Drool slipped down his chin in a spider-silk strand. "You have no idea what Cutty is up to in there," he told them. "Their Matron. They were hiding her upstairs, in the attic. After they caught me, they took me up to see her."

"Yeah?" Gendreau twitched. "Who is it?"

"She *claims* to be Morgan le Fay."

"The sorceress fairy-queen from Arthurian legend?"

Sara folded her arms. "You are so full of crap. Impossible. Morgan le Fay wasn't even real. Those were stories."

"Hey, don't shoot the messenger," said Heinrich, and he coughed hard, spitting into the weeds.

"Even if that *is* le Fay up there, she'd have to be *hundreds* of years old."

"Almost two thousand years old," said Gendreau. "According to Arthurian legend, Arthur Pendragon defended Britain against Saxon invaders in 510, 520 AD. He *was* real, if embellished. If Morgan was real, she was contemporary to that time." He stared at the dirt under their feet in thought, drawing curative runes with the tip of his cane. "She first appeared in an 1170 book by Chrétien de Troyes. I can't remember the name, though. Oh, no, wait, it wasn't de Troyes, it was *The Life of Merlin* by Geoffrey of Monmouth."

"You can remember all that," asked Sara, "but you can't remember your order between the radio and the window at freakin' Burger King?"

Lights were still on in the Lazenbury, hollow orange eyes in the black. Robin searched the windows for silhouettes. "If their Matron is really Morgan, she's . . ."

"Old as hell?" asked Lucas.

"To put it bluntly," interjected Gendreau. "And more powerful than any witch alive." The unspoken insinuation was obvious to Robin. *We may have bitten off more than we can chew.* She hoped she was the secret weapon Heinrich had intended her to be.

"Fuck that noise," said Joel, leaning on his baseball bat. "If you're trying to make me wish I'd stayed behind, it's working."

"I didn't see much of her." The old witch-hunter flexed one arm as if getting comfortable and jerked in sudden sharp pain, crying out, his legs twitching and curling like back-broken snakes. His cries were desperate, pitiful, and nothing at all like the commanding, brooding presence he'd been back in Texas. Fresh blood dribbled from the nails through his wrists. "They're tryin' to bring Ereshkigal back. They been trying for a long time. It's why Annie's apples are so fat. They been savin' 'em up for the resurrection." Heinrich hung his head. "I was too big for my britches. We *all* was. Cutty and her Matron have been here since the inception of Blackfield itself." He grunted and cried out in pain again. "I'm sorry I dragged you into this, baby girl."

"If you'll open your eyes again, you'll see I'm neither baby nor girl. Or even human."

Heinrich studied her with drowsy eyes.

"Get out of here," he said. "While you still can." He coughed, spattering Robin's wire-coil chest with blood. "However you got here, use it to get back, and stay away. This some Plan 9 top-level Pentagram Pentagon black magic. They gonna jump up and down on you 'til you die."

"Can't leave until this is done." She pointed at the mission house. "My mother is in that *nag shi.* I'm not going to abandon her again. I can't have her back, but I can set her free."

Even in his state, Heinrich still managed to give her that under-the-eyebrows *you better do what I say, girl* look. She knew it well; she'd seen it enough over the last few years.

"That don't work on me anymore."

When he couldn't elicit a change in her, the old man turned to Gendreau. "What's the verdict, Doc?"

"Hypothetically, with more time, I could pull you back from the brink." The curandero shook a handkerchief out of his pocket and wiped his bloody hand on it. "But you'll die before I can make much of a difference. To be honest, I'm surprised you've lasted this long."

"The human body is a miracle thing, Doc," said Heinrich with a scoff. "It can take a good whooping before it gives up. And I ain't never gave up." He coughed and choked, grimaced, spat to the side. "Before you go, will you take me out a Hawaiian and light it for me? They're in my coat pocket behind me."

Robin dug around, found the box and the Zippo. Tapping out

a cigar, she paused to drag it under her nose, savoring the rich coconut smell.

"'S'good shit, baby," said Heinrich.

She stuck the cigar in his mouth, and if she'd told you she didn't
do it to shut him up, she would have been by all rights a liar. He
walked it in with his lips. She flicked open the lighter, ignited it,
and lit the cigar with it. He took a deep draw and a cloud of smoke
billowed out of his face, and he winced, his hands flexing against
the nails and fence-wire.

"I can't fuckin' reach it."

She dropped the lighter in his shirt pocket and patted it neatly
in place. "You'll figure it out."

As she did so, a pendant tumbled out of the collar of his shirt—a
cameo, an oval containing a carving of a woman's face in profile.
He used to tell her it was his mother, back when Robin was fresh
out of the looney bin and still dumb as beans.

It felt warm. Felt strange with potential.

"So, are we cutting him down, or what?" asked Kenway.

The moment caught in their throats as the band of impromptu
witch-hunters stood around the cross, watching Robin's unearthly
face. Finally, she told them, "No. If he's tied down, he can't find
some fresh new way to betray me before he meets his maker." She
pointed to her own face. "He's responsible for this. I don't want to
see what else he's got up his sleeve."

"We're just going to let him die up there?" asked Sara.

"You play shitty games, you win shitty prizes. He brought this
on himself. He almost got me *and* Wayne *and* Kenway killed, going into the Lazenbury behind my back. He pissed off Cutty while
we were in the orchard and got Wayne's father familiarized. Not to
mention Lucky Luke back in Texas. He's a conniving old man that
only thinks of himself and tricks children into fighting his battles
for him. This time, he wasn't fast enough or clever enough to dodge
the consequences of his actions."

"I went into that house myself to keep you safe," growled Heinrich.

"I was trying to keep you out of the fight, even if that meant an ass-beating for me."

"So, a last-minute change of heart?" She stepped close, jabbing a modern-art finger in his face. The wellspring of light in her chest throbbed with fury, glittering in the blood on his chest. "Do you have any idea how full of shit you are? Do you know when to quit? Do you ever? You turned me into a monster. You don't give a rat's ass about me past the fact I represent a weapon to you. You act like you're proud of me, but you're not proud of who I've become as a person. You're not proud of how I've thrived in spite of what you've put me through. You're only proud of me in the same way a dictator is proud of his best general." She rapped on her arm and brandished her claws. "You care about this. You're proud of this." She knocked on her chest where her heart shone through. "Not about this. This means nothing to you, always has."

He had no reply.

"So, no," Robin said, walking away, turning her back on him. "We're not cutting him down."

Heinrich grinned, squinting in the smoke, the Hawaiian caught in his teeth. "You a cold-ass cambion, Robin Martine. Colder than a well-digger's ass. After I saved you. After I gave you purpose. I gave you a home. I gave you the tools you needed to avenge your mother. I carved you from one of my own ribs. I am a good man, and you know it. I was good to you."

She stopped walking, pausing mid-stride, and stood there, willing herself not to march back to the crucifix and beat the man the rest of the way into death. Her fists were tight, but her hands still shook. She turned to the others to speak. "A bad man that did one good thing in a whole sea of bad shit doesn't make him a hundred percent good. Bank robbers don't get to go free because they spent the stolen money on their kid's Christmas before they were arrested."

"You don't believe a man can change?"

"All men believe they are good men, but good men are only

good because they consistently do good things for good reasons.
You don't get to draw a line in the sand and say, 'Everything I do
past this line is good.' That's not for you to decide. You are a thief
of historical artifacts, a con man, a cultist, a kidnapper, and a murderer. I didn't thrive because of you. I thrived *in spite* of you. You
set up this game from the get-go and forced me to play it. You don't
get to crow about how you helped me win it."

He took another draw on the cigar, and blew it from the corner
of his mouth with a pained wince.

"Rock on, then, baby, rock on, then."

30

The dirt road seemed interminable, a ribbon of dust and gravel snaking into the false night. As they came closer to the Lazenbury, they got quiet, abandoning conversation, assumedly trying to preserve some element of surprise. Robin had put on Gendreau's jacket, buttoning it closed to mitigate the shine of her heart inside her chest. She looked back at the others. Gendreau's face was the picture of dark focus, but Lucas, Joel, and Sara were scared as hell. She knew why Joel was scared, but why the two magicians?

"How many have you killed?" she asked them.

Lucas spoke to the ground. "Three."

"What about you, Sara?"

Sara didn't speak at first. Eventually she said, "My Gift isn't meant for combat."

"So . . . none."

Irritation simmered in the back of Robin's mind, but what Gendreau said next fizzled it. "She's not here for fighting," mumbled the curandero. "She's the most talented conjurer and illusionist in the order outside of my father. Sara is here to dispel Weaver's illusions for us."

"Ah."

Lazenbury House hulked at them from the darkness like a ghost ship. Faintly to the north, past the end of the driveway, were the rollups of the garage. Except . . . the longer she looked at it, the less it resembled a garage and the more it appeared to be a stable. The doors shimmered and wavered, and she could see Cutty's green Chevy Nova resting on a layer of scattered straw and rushes. And then it was a horse, a chestnut quarter horse, tail swishing against the night.

Fists clenched at her sides, Sara leaned forward as if pressing her forehead against some invisible surface, immense concentration on her face.

The Lazenbury itself came alive with raucous noise and movement. Playful fey laughter of young women, tinkling piano music, shuffling boots, the heady *thunk* of glass mugs on hardwood tables. Windows that had been clear and modern, double-paned to retain heat, became warped and cloudy leaded glass.

Through them Robin could see shapes moving back and forth, as if there were some kind of party going on inside. An electric wall-sconce next to the exterior-opening kitchen door jiggered like a film reel and suddenly it was a gas lantern, dull and hissing with a sick green-orange light. The door itself transformed, melting with LSD fluidity from an aluminum screen door into a heavy wooden one with a head-sized password hatch cut in the middle. Iron pencil bars were bolted over the hole.

Lucas asided to Gendreau, "Why didn't you *tell* me you were taking me to a whorehouse?"

"Because it hasn't been a whorehouse for almost a century." The curandero tapped Sara. "This is, I'm assuming, an illusion. Can you dispel it?"

"I'm trying. It's really stapled down." The illusionist raked her fingers through her flame-red hair, tousling it, and her hands went back to her temples. "I'll keep working on it."

"You do that," said Robin, opening the kitchen door, releasing a burst of fragrant steam and a wave of incredible heat. "I'm going in."

"Not by yourself, you ain't." Lucas followed her.

Gendreau grumped. "Oh, hell. Wait for me."

Lit only by gas lamps on the walls to either side, the hot kitchen was a bustle of movement. Three Black women and a Black man in greasy white smocks shuffled in a coordinated dance between two bubbling stock pots, a brick oven full of Halloween-orange light, and the gruesome cadaver of a wild boar

(stab it with their steely knives)

suspended on a spit over glowing coals. Both left haunches, the flank, and half the face were gone, leaving clinical cross sections open to the heat of the air. An empty skull, a crabbish cluster of teeth, pallid stripes of rib-bone. Robin looked away, queasy.

A preoccupied, dreamlike ignorance hung over the scene like Scrooge being shown his own memories by the Spirit of Christmas Past, and the cookies took no notice of their new visitors—or if they did, paid them no mind. "Aww, hell naw," said Joel. "They got the brother and the sisters back here roasting the pig and washing the dishes and shit. This is some real-talk bullshit. There better not be a colored man behind the bar."

"Well, it *is* a turn-of-the-century cathouse," said Robin. "Come on, let's keep going. I don't want to be here any longer than absolutely necessary." She pushed through a swinging door and went into the saloon.

Filthy workmen in chambray shirts and dungarees played cards, told jokes, and drank at five round tables in what should have been Marilyn Cutty's living room. Cigarette smoke hovered around an iron chandelier arrayed with hurricane lamps. Women in bustiers and striped hose leaned against an upstairs railing. Below, a bar ran across the room on their left, staffed by a ginger in arm-garters and a villainous mustache. At the far end was a player piano, where someone in a ratty hide coat and hat sat on a stool, tickling ivories.

The barman poured liquid honey into a glass and pushed it toward a grungy hobo in a Stetson and a leather duster.

Kenway stared. "Did we wander into the holodeck from *Star Trek,* or what?"

"This is quite possibly the most realistic illusion I've ever seen." Gendreau's face was grim. "Hell, I'm not one hundred percent sure it's not a conjuration . . . or even, God help me, a temporal anomaly."

"It's not a time-warp," said Sara, snapping her fingers in front of a man's face. He sifted through his poker cards, oblivious to her attempts to distract him.

"Time-warp?" Joel held himself. "It better the hell *not* be."

"Do they know we're here?" Robin asked. "Do Weaver and Cutty know we're here?"

The piano stopped abruptly, mid-melody.

Eyes burned at them from every direction as the miners and cowboys looked up from their liquor and card games and fixed on Robin and the Dogs of Odysseus. The pianist wheeled about on her stool and clutched her bony knees, standing up. "Yes, we're quite aware you're here." Karen Weaver's dark-rimmed eyes blazed underneath the floppy brim of her hat, a loose hat cord under her chin. She looked like an elderly Annie Oakley in her tweed vest and leather coat. One hand softly closed the piano's key cover and rested there. Weaver's other hand went to the hat cord and worried at it. "How did you get into my poke?"

"Your poke?"

"My tesseract," Weaver said sharply, impatiently, as if talking to an idiot. "My tesseract, *my tesseract!* You know what that *is,* yes?"

"Tesseract! A simple-enough astrophysics concept," said Joel Ellis, from behind the group of magicians. "The folding of space to make a distance shorter. Folding point A to point C to eliminate point B, bringing two spatially distinct locations into closer dimensional proximity to drastically reduce travel time. Also known as a hypercube."

Everyone in the saloon turned to look at him.

"What? Y'all think I don't know about some of this extra-ass shit? I read fantasy too. Muhfuckin *Wrinkle in Time*. You ain't Fisher Ellis's brother all your life without pickin' up some science. Aight?"

Nobody said anything.

"Y'all wrong for that." He shook his head. "Hey, y'all do y'all thing. Look." He pointed. "It's a witch."

Weaver stepped away from the piano, her age-spotted hands clutched over her heart—or at least where her heart should have been—and she retreated to touch it again as if the keys could lend her some degree of protection, or comfort. "Well, of course, of course. The colored boy has the right of it. But ay; what happens to point B, then? Ah, you're standing in it, you are, you are. This is the land between: my . . . poke." The witch continued to stare at Robin. "Who are *you*? . . . *What* are you?"

"Annie's daughter." Robin took off the plush navy jacket and handed it back to Gendreau, revealing the lighthouse pulse of her heart. "It turns out the ritual my mother used Edgar for—"

"Killed!" screeched Weaver. *"My husband, killed!"*

"—*killed* Edgar for wasn't entirely wasted. She *did* manage to summon a demon. But it was an incubus. She made a deal with the demon to bear his child in exchange for his protection."

"A half-breed, then." Weaver's face soured. "Got the blood of a demon in you. Should have expected as much. Always was a mystery to us how your mother could have given birth to you after her sacrifice to the Goddess . . . We always assumed she'd been with child since before. Children carried through the ritual usually come out stillborn . . . ."

"The demon made her human again, long enough for her to hold up her end of the bargain."

"And got her with child, didn't he?" The witch remained by the piano. "Oh, but you're such a deadly beautiful snake, aren't you? A regular prize. A changeling, I think. You know, I've never seen a demon before. Marilyn says they're dangerous; they *eat* magic, you know, they feed on the energies out there—" She swept a pensive hand at the ceiling, as if the afterlife rested just outside.

All the desperados' eyes tracked Robin as she took a step across the saloon. "But when we're here among the living," she said, "we prefer to suckle on the heart-roads of witches."

Weaver recoiled, shaking.

She shouted, "Don't you take another step, you snide hobgoblin, you worthless cur-dog! You stay away from me, you hear? I *told* you not to come here. But you didn't listen. You *never* listened." The witch bit back a grimace, flashing her buckish front teeth. "Always knocking on the door, *let me in, Gramma, let me in,* little whelp screwing up my seamstress work." She pinched at the air to emphasize. "I thought maybe if I left a few of my needles in the carpet, you'd stay out of my sewing room, maybe a few pricks in your pink little feet and you'd stay the hell *out,* but nope! I'd get up to go piss, and when I came back, you'd be right back in there again, pulling out my pins and knocking my dummy over! And Marilyn didn't care, oh, *no,* she'd laugh and laugh, and tell me, *She's just a little girl, Karen, you had a little girl once, you know they're a handful,* and yes, I had a little girl once, but did she have to rub it in?"

Robin took another step.

The witch pointed at her. "Go back where you came from, goddamn you!" she said in a rapid, poisonous hiss, "I'm not going to tell you again!"

"Enough of this—" Robin lunged at her, clutching Weaver's jacket.

It came away in her hands as if the witch had slipped right out of it. When she looked up, she saw the witch had evaporated, leaving Robin holding empty clothes . . . if she'd ever really been there at all. She turned to say something, and saw *all* the cowboys now had Weaver's face.

Two, three dozen Karen Weaver clones played cards at the tables. The man drinking at the bar was Weaver. The ginger behind the bar was Weaver, mustache and all. Even the cathouse ladies upstairs were Weaver, her eight mushy old hippie tits wobbling in their bust-cups like tapioca pudding.

"Time to take you all out to the woodshed and give yuns a whoopin," said one of the gambling Weavers, tossing back a glass of whiskey.

The Weaver bartender rolled up her sleeves, flourishing handfuls of gleaming black claws. "Yessssss," she snarled, her face lengthening, her mouth drooping open. Wolfish teeth dripped saliva on the bar.

Weaver-doubles all over the saloon rose from their chairs, stripping off their hats, faces and fingers stretching, becoming swarthy and hideous. Their eyes deepened, darkened, red marbles glittering in black pits. Kenway let the carnival hammer drop into his other hand and rolled his neck with a sick crackle.

"Nope," said Joel, shaking his head. He lifted the bat, pointing it at the nearest witch. "We ain't about to do this."

"Ah, well, you see—" Gendreau started to say.

The saloon exploded into movement as every witch in sight descended on the magicians like a murder of screeching ravens.

"—*Piss and potatoes!*"

Snatching up a deck of poker cards, Lucas started whipping them overhand into the crowd. One of the witches fell away, a Jack of Diamonds sticking out of her chest, and collapsed on the floor, melting into smoke.

Thwock! thwock! thwack! Kenway's hammer echoed off the high plaster ceiling, swinging in great overhead arcs. The vet staggered from one encounter to another, smacking their foreheads in a frenzied game of Whac-A-Mole. Witch-skulls whiplashed, bouncing off Kenway's bloody mallet head. "Little Bunny Foo-Foo!" he sang with maniacal glee, "a-runnin' through the forest! Pickin' up the field mice and boppin' 'em on the head!"

Witches all around them jittered and hiccupped like video glitches as the illusionist Sara made obscure symbols in the air with her fingers, trying to dispel the imagery. Gendreau defended her with his pizzle cane, twirling and striking with some clever sort of martial art. The fist-sized pearl at the end made for an outstanding bludgeon.

Robin waded into the melee, attempting to grab a Weaver and suck the juice out of her, but it was like herding cats—the clones would flinch or duck, fending her off with chairs and bar stools, juking out of the way. The two she managed to lay hands on vanished into pungent smoke.

"One of them's got to be the real witch!" she told the magicians, "grab one and hold her and let me—"

Something hard slammed into her shoulder, almost knocking her down. Kenway winced, lifting the carnival hammer. "Woop, sorry!"

"Watch where you're swingin' that thing!"

"Yes, ma'am!" He turned and smashed it through a chair and into a clone's head, evaporating her. Then he missed a swing at another one and upended a table with it, scattering beer, broken glass, and nineteenth-century dollar coins. A witch leapt on his back and sank her yellow fangs into his shoulder. *"Aaaaah!"* he shouted, twisting and writhing, trying to get her off him, colliding with tables and people alike.

Gripping her by the hair of the head, Robin wrenched her from Kenway's back and marched her over to the bar, where she slammed the old woman face-first into the polished counter, breaking her nose with a thick *bang.* Simultaneously, the nose of every Weaver clone in the room exploded with black goo as her real face propagated throughout her illusionary army.

This one didn't disappear.

"Got you now, chick," said Robin, and grasped her by the throat. Oily blood streamed out of Weaver's nose, dripping from her hellacious gargoyle teeth. Concentrating, Robin pushed her consciousness into the witch as a sort of ethereal mental pseudo-pod, and found the heart-road deep inside. Then she withdrew, pulling the energy with it like a fishhook. It came thin and watery into the center of her being, and a dank, salty taste welled in her mouth.

The light of her heart flashed brightly through her chest, casting disco-ball flares around the room. Weaver gasped. The skin of her face became sallow and shrank taut, every curve and socket suddenly reliefed in sharp detail.

"*Nooo!*" cawed the witch, wresting herself out of Robin's grip. The other shadow-Weavers converged on Robin as the real one shrank away, and she found herself battling a flock of shrieking harpies. They shoved her down on the floor and raked and wrenched at her with their claws. "*I'll kill you, you wretched, hell-spawned little heifer!*" screamed one of them, wedging her nails under Robin's skin and tearing it away in a tangle of wires. Another one scrabbled at her ear, ripping it. "*You and your mother took my Edgar away! I'll swallow your soul!*"

"Not if I swallow yours first." Robin punched her with a wire-coil fist, shattering the witch's teeth.

The head of Kenway's mallet came down on a clone's head, snapping her neck. Weaver's double collapsed like a house of cards, mushrooming across the floor in a carpet of smoke. Lucas hauled one away and threw her down on the floor, stomping her face; she, too, went *poof.*

The big veteran growled, hooking the handle of the mallet under a witch's chin. The two of them were locked in a staggering dance, the big veteran strangling her with the hammer. Robin watched out of the corner of her eye as the witch in Kenway's arms finally gave up, going limp—

—*and turned into Sara Amundson.*

He let go with a stifled scream, and Sara's slack body crumpled at his feet. The hammer fell out of Kenway's shocked hand. As she went down, her face twisted and distorted, losing its shape, becoming something rudimentary and scarred. Her eyebrows disappeared, the bridge of her nose flattened, and her nostrils became two Voldemort slits in a melted face.

"Oh, God!" screamed Lucas, shoving a path through the witches. Gendreau stood paralyzed with horror and confusion at the edge of the room, watching this tragedy play out.

"Watch out!" screamed Robin.

But the other Sara behind him was already stepping forward, transforming back into Weaver. The witch hooked an arm around the curandero's neck.

At the last instant, he spotted the blade and squeezed his eyes closed. That was probably the worst part—he saw it coming. The knife in her hand flashed, and she zipped open his throat as easy as you please. A sheet of arterial blood poured into the collar of Gendreau's effete white shirt, staining it a rich watercolor red.

Weaver shoved him and he stumbled over a broken chair, faceplanting onto the dusty boards.

The witch cackled, flaunting the knife.

Black blood made an inky bib down her face and chest. "You thought you were gonna beat the greatest illusionist that ever lived, did you? You thought you could see through my tricks, eh? Well, Ole Miss Tricksy got the best of *you*, didn't—"

"*Eerraaahh!*" roared Lucas, hurling the remainder of his poker cards.

A dazzle of cards whirred across the saloon, passing through an open gauntlet formed by the crowd of clones, and tore through the true Weaver like a volley of fléchettes fired from a rail gun. Cards struck and lodged in the wall behind her. A card protruded from the divot between the witch's eye and nose.

Taking advantage of the distraction, Joel launched himself forward and swatted the witch across the skull with the baseball bat. The battle must have weakened the Louisville Slugger, because it exploded with an echoing *CRACK*, sending shards of wood in every direction.

Every shadow-clone in sight disappeared as one, extinguishing en masse, and the saloon itself flickered like a bad television signal. Weaver slumped onto her knees, *thump-thump,* and fell over.

One second, there were overturned tables and poker chips and smashed pint glasses all over the floor. Reality seemed to crossfade, and suddenly they were standing in Marilyn Cutty's living room; the flatscreen TV had been knocked over and smashed, the chairs were against the walls, and the sofa had been shoved into the entertainment center, but otherwise, they were back in the twenty-first century.

"Somebody help, goddammit!"

Lucas sat on the floor, with Gendreau dragged up into his lap. The curandero was holding his own neck, trying to magic it back together, blood squirting through his glowing fingers.

"Must—" He choked, blood gurgling out of his mouth. "I can't—" His face was a drawn gray and his eyes were huge and terrified. "—Whug."

He can't concentrate, thought Robin. *He's lost his mind with terror.*

"Don't speak." She took his cane and clutched the cue-ball pearl, gazing into its smooth, iridescent white surface as if it were a crystal ball. She pushed her mind against the pearl and felt the heart-road inside. Muffled, weak, a whisper through a pillow, the thoughts of a chick in an egg. She could take it, take it all, but it would require time. Twenty, thirty minutes, at least.

Time she didn't have. She whacked the pearl against the floor.

"What are you doing?" asked Lucas.

CRACK! She banged it against the hardwood again. "I'm trying to get at the heart-road inside," she told him. "I can use it to fix him"—*CRACK!*—"but I can't get it out fast enough with this hard matter around it."

"That's the conduit," said Lucas. "The conductive material."

"For him, maybe. He's attuned to this thing. I'm not."

"Wait." Kenway stepped in, raising the carnival hammer. Robin snatched her hand away and he brought the massive chunk of wood down on the pearl, exploding it into three heavy chunks with a puff of white dust.

Embedded in the largest piece was a tooth.

Bewildered panic beat wild, terrified wings against the inside of her skull. She picked it up, and indeed, it was a human tooth: a pristine white molar.

"Shit gets weirder and weirder with you, sister," said Joel, leaning over her. "You know that?"

"Come on!" shouted Lucas.

"Yeah, okay." Squeezing the tooth in her fist, Robin tapped the paranormal energy inside, reeling it out like fishing line.

Visions from the eighteenth century clouded her mind, attached to the power pouring from the tooth. Images of a petticoated woman tied to a maypole; men in buckled shoes. She ignored them and put her other hand on Gendreau's throat

(*Lucretia Melcher: we of the town of Philadelphia—*)

and directed the ectoplasm from the heart-road up her left arm and down her right and into Gendreau. The pulsar in her chest became

(*—hereby sentence you to be burned at the stake—*)

a stuttering supernova strobe, turning her arms into sizzling Tesla coils. The bleeding stopped as Gendreau's cells mingled, reattaching to each other, intertwining his severed carotid and jugular.

(*—for the crime of being a witch.*)

Bandy red muscles that had been split reached for each other and braided. The ragged smile stretching across his skin pursed together and resealed from ear to ear like the lips of a Ziploc bag. She felt for a pulse in his neck and found a bare sliver of movement, a fleeting squirm under the skin. The relief overwhelmed her and she sat back with a near-delirious moan.

"Oh, my God," said Lucas, looking over her shoulder. "You did it!"

"Did what?" asked Sara.

Kenway hauled the woozy illusionist up to a sitting position. She coughed and gasped for air, holding her throat, pain written on her features. The melted, scarred look had disappeared, her face having returned to the way it'd looked all day—beautiful, with deep green eyeshadow and rich red lips.

"What happened?" Sara croaked.

"Uhh . . ." Kenway glanced at them. "The witch tricked me, and I choked you out on accident."

Sara coughed again, wincing, glancing daggers of ice at the poor man. Then her eyes fell on the blood-soaked curandero in Lucas's lap. "Oh! *Ohhhh! Doc!*" She struggled to her knees and hovered over Gendreau. "Is he gonna be okay? Is he *alive?*"

"He's still alive, but . . . I don't know." Robin fixated on the tooth in her palm. "I don't know."

• • •

Karen Weaver dragged herself across the living room floor through a steak-sauce puddle of her own rotten blood. Dozens of Bicycle playing cards bristled from the wall above. The queen of hearts was buried in Weaver's face up to the number, leaving only a tab of paper showing, as if her brain had been bookmarked.

She'd been shot full of holes by thirty-eight of them, six of them lodged in her ribs and spine. She was half-carrion, her supernaturally altered cells half a century old, rejuvenated by the life-force stored in Annie Martine's apples . . . but a severed spinal cord is a severed spinal cord, and Karen no longer had the use of her legs.

Robin stood over her.

The witch rolled over and put up her shaking hands. The eye on the card side of her face was lax and dead, unmoving. "I'm b-beat, you wuh-wearisome harlot." Her mouth pooled with black. "Leave me buh-be."

Kneeling, Robin took hold of the lapels of Weaver's riotous rag-coat, lifting her. "*You* may be done," she said, her voice without fire or ice, "but *I'm* not." Her mind dived for that dark power again. This time, she found a thread of warmth and recognized it as stolen life-force, the give-a-shit from what Heinrich would have called Annie's *flora de vida*. She drew them both out, the heart-road and the life-force, and internalized them. Weaver's face emptied, a jaundiced canvas pulling tight across her skull. The witch's nose caved in like a spoiled jack-o'-lantern and her eyes retreated, shriveling. Her lips thinned, shrinking back to reveal horsey yellow teeth, giving her the silently screaming face of a peat-bog corpse.

"I'll be waiting for you," the witch wheezed in an arid whisper, "in Hell," and she died for the second time.

• • •

Marilyn Cutty's clairvoyance proved to be to her advantage, as neither she nor her Matron were anywhere to be found in the Lazenbury. Robin explored the house, moving purposefully from room to room like a SWAT cop. The second floor was occupied by the witches' three spacious and palatial bedrooms, each one containing a four-poster bed and resplendent with each woman's tastes—for Weaver, a room straight out of the Ponderosa. For Theresa, the austere room of a nun, piled high with moldy dishes, half-eaten food. For Cutty, a frilly Victorian nest of paisleys and silks.

In the last bedroom, a hatch and ladder led up to the attic. She pulled the hatch down and climbed into darkness, her shining heart cutting the soft shade. The attic was enormous, running the length and width of the house. Dusty furniture and assorted bric-a-brac made a dark, cluttered labyrinth; this she trickled carefully through, constantly on the lookout for an ambush.

Half-hidden behind an armoire was a simple door. She pushed it aside and behind it was a small room with a bed, a television, and a window overlooking the vineyard grove. A chair sat abandoned in the middle of the room, arrayed with cushions and a warm blanket.

Heading back downstairs, Robin wondered if the Matron really *was* the Morgan le Fay from the Arthurian legends. A hot pang of shame drilled through her when she thought of the talk she would have to have with Wayne. Leon Parkin was nowhere in the house either. What would the boy say? What would he *do?* What would *she* have to do?

Of course, she would have to hunt down Cutty and her Matron wherever they went. That was a given . . . this blood feud didn't stop just because Robin eliminated her coven. The two of them had probably jumped ship to settle down somewhere else, God knew where. But that was their way, wasn't it? The witches were most often nomadic. They roamed like rats from town to town, country to country, looking for a place to chew a hole and make a nest. But some of them put down roots, and that's where Robin found them.

Wayne would undoubtedly want to go with Robin to find Cutty.

Could she allow that?

Did she have a choice?

He couldn't stay here by himself. He needed to have a real life, a *normal* life, go to school and live in a house, not in the back of a van, running from maniacs and starting fires.

On the way through the living room, she checked on Gendreau. The blood-soaked curandero was breathing shallowly, his eyes open just enough to see her. They closed and his face pinched in pain.

The kitchen was abandoned and dark, no boar, no oblivious chefs. She fetched a glass of water from the tap and took it to Gendreau. It felt a bit strange to see real people get really hurt—and almost *die*—and realize how long it takes for fully human people to get over their injuries.

Now I know why I've always been so strong, she mused to herself, looking at her strange wire-and-vine hands.

"Come to the order's compound in Michigan. Come meet Frank." Gendreau winced, whispering. The slash across his throat was now a jagged pink lightning bolt. "We'll figure out how to help you."

"Help me, or kill me?" She folded her arms. "Or do experiments on me?"

"Can't promise the alchemists won't want a urine sample." Wincing again, he swallowed. His voice was now full of ragged vocal fry, so much so he almost sounded like a robot. "But we're not the Pentagon. Nobody will be dissecting you, promise."

Sara combed his hair out of his face, petting his head. "Shut up, man. Rest yourself."

"So, now what?" asked Lucas.

"Cutty's flown the coop with the Matron. Took Wayne's dad with her, too."

"She left her dryad here?"

"No way Cutty could have dug up Annie by herself in two days, much less transport a tree half the size of the Christmas pine in Rockefeller Center. Guess she considers herself and her Matron more important than the *nag shi* tree." Robin sighed. "She can always make another one, after all."

"True. Man, that kid's gonna be bummed his dad wasn't here."

"No Osdathregar?" asked Sara.

"No. They took it with them, unfortunately."

"Then our only weapon is out of our reach. It's up to you now, I suppose."

A few minutes passed as Robin considered her options and let them comfort Gendreau.

"Kenway," she said, finally.

"Hmm?"

"Will you come with me into the vineyard?" She studied his face, looking up at the gauze still around his forehead, stained with old brown blood. "I don't want to go by myself. I want you with me." Her hand rested on Lucas's shoulder. "You guys stay here and take care of Doc."

Kenway got up out of the chair he'd been sitting in, with the hammer across his knees. Now he stood and wordlessly slung it over his shoulder.

"You too, brother," she told Joel.

To his credit, the pizza-man wordlessly stood and came with her. On the way through the kitchen, he grabbed a carving knife out of the block on the counter island to replace his broken bat.

• • •

Night rested in the vineyard clotted and cold, a tangle of shadows rustling with dying grapevines. Robin's heart sifted through the trellises in soft tines of gold.

Kenway and Joel walked silently alongside her, flint in their eyes.

The veteran's furrowed brow and downcast face almost made him seem as if he were a pouty little boy, and suddenly she wanted to be far from this grave place, somewhere warm and far away from the world where she could be alone with him. He noticed her watching and smiled, though his eyes were still hard.

Without Weaver around to alter the lay of the land back there, the vineyard turned out to be a lot smaller. The first time she'd been through it felt like they'd walked for miles, passing out of the world and into the leagues of some alien wilderness of vines and fences. Now it only took them a moment to reach the end of the property, and even the landscaping seemed smaller than she remembered it: four scant patches of purple flowers and stunted trees barely twice as tall as the fence, all of it scattered with lavender flagging in the wind.

Energy washed up on the shore of her mind, cold echoes of Weaver's power. Robin could feel it ebbing slowly. She cast her eyes skyward at the stars, which had begun to flicker and fluctuate, like some kind of malfunctioning 3-D, zooming in and out in frenetic stutters and flashes. The Georgia pines around them undulated in mad waves like an oscilloscope, bolts of green electricity laddering upward between the trees.

Only had a few minutes until the poke straightened itself out, and her demon body would be destroyed by the Sanctification.

"Damn," she said, as they entered the grove at the end of the path. "We need to hurry this up before the de-conjuration collapses. Won't be good for me when we rejoin reality. The real world doesn't like demons."

The *nag shi*, the dryad, the Malus Domestica, her mother Annie Martine stood in the center of the clearing. All the apples were gone. The tree had been picked clean. That, at least, Cutty had been able to undertake in the last two days.

Solace and irritation passed through her. To Robin, the apples represented the witches' repulsive influence, and to see her mother rid of them was like seeing a loved one come out of rehab, free of heroin and ready to live again. But she knew when she faced Cutty, the witch would have devoured as many of the life-giving fruit as possible, making what would have already been a hard fight into a true bloodbath.

"I'm back, Mom," she said quietly, as the forest quivered and the sky crawled. "Marilyn is gone." Wind sighed in the tree's leaves, a sound Robin would swear until the day she died carried a certain relief. She placed her hands on Annie's rugged hips and closed her eyes. Her mind relaxed and flowed downhill through the slopes of her arms, into the apple tree.

Behind her eyelids, darkness, silence.

She had the feeling that she was standing at the bottom of a dry well; she could even smell the dank, fossilized memory of water.

Mom?

Lustering softly in the narrow space, a spirit turned to regard her with lambent eyes. Guarded exhaustion came from the other mind in lieu of words, like the nonsense murmur of someone waking from a deep sleep after a long day.

It's me. Robin smiled. *I'm here. I came back. I beat them and I'm here to get you out.* The warmest light she'd ever felt poured from the presence as Annie recognized her.

Love, it was love and sorrow and regret, and a vacant space in Robin's center filled up with such overwhelming affection that at first, she could no longer speak, paralyzed with secondhand adoration, as if she could see herself from the outside. *It's okay,* she thought, *it's okay,* because she knew the regret came from her mother. *You didn't know what would happen when you summoned the demon, but it's okay, everything turned out okay for me.*

Not only was love filling her up, she realized, it was Annie herself, her mother was moving toward her, *into* her, this consumed woman who had spent years trapped in this spiritual sweatshop spinning straw into gold, spinning the town's prosperity into lifegiving apples. Robin enveloped the spirit as it stepped into her and suffused her with elation. She took the last fragment of her mother into her arms and held her until the dry well that had been her cell inside the tree was empty and cold.

"Oh," breathed Kenway at her side.

She opened her eyes and took her hands away from the apple tree's now-cold bark, dimly aware that she'd been crying, *sobbing,* tears spilling down her face.

Her hands were soft and human again.

Both of them. She studied her left arm with astonishment and found it whole and functional. *New,* even—the scars that littered her arms were gone without a trace. Taking her mother from the *nag shi* had imparted some measure of humanity to her once again, as if accepting Annie's very human spirit had imbued her with that which she had lost.

Knees buckling, Robin sat on her ankles like a penitent in the dewy grass, holding herself, lost in a happiness so stunning and so savage, it was almost grief.

Slipping his arms under her, Kenway lifted her, staggered up onto his titanium foot, and carried her out of the vineyard. Joel stayed behind, watching the apple tree grow dark and gray, and he had an idea. He reached into his pocket and came up with his lighter, a cheapo gas station Bic, and his last two cigarettes. He cupped the cigarette with his hand and lit it, taking a deep draw to get the cherry going. Placing the lighter at the base of the tree like an offering, Joel stomped on it until the plastic cracked and the fuel inside leaked out. He kneeled, touched the cigarette to the puddle of lighter fluid, and it went up in a *blorp!* of blue flame.

"Checkmate," he said, and stepped back.

As the tesseract twitched and faded around him, and the reality of the neighborhood returned to normal, Joel smoked and watched the tree burn. He found a little concrete bench by the garden and sat on it, smoking and resting, until the fire climbed the trunk, and the branches held out bouquets of flame, and tickets of gray ash drifted into the sky.

31

They wanted to hold Fisher's funeral at his comic shop—seemed like the most natural place, since his body couldn't be recovered from the acid pond, eliminating the need for a viewing at Lane Funeral Home—but when they realized how many people were coming, it became obvious there wouldn't be anywhere near enough room in the tiny shop to hold a crowd of that size, even if they took out the booth tables in the back, the comics racks, the action-figure racks, and the point-of-sale counter. To say nothing of the fact the shop was an active crime scene because of the dead serial killer.

So, about a hundred people clustered here in Rocktown, high above Miguel's Pizza, in the mountains east of Slade Township. Mourners stood in deep corridor crevices and on top of rocks, and stone shelves, and boulders, wet leaves making a soft carpet under their feet. Framed portraits of Fish himself had been arrayed on the rocks leading up to the promontory, along with some of the pop-culture artifacts from his shop—a *Lord of the Rings* helmet, Thor's Mjolnir hammer, Jason Voorhees' hockey mask.

Glittering with sweat, Joel stood between Robin and Fisher's girlfriend Marissa on the cliff edge.

Turned out, Fisher Ellis had been quite the avid rock climber, and Rocktown had been one of his favorite places. Joel had chosen to climb up the rock face from the pizzeria, believing that ascending the hard way was the best and most honest ritual to honor the memory of their dearly departed friend and brother. Some of the attendees had also climbed up. The older and more infirm (as well as the terminally lazy, like Robin) had driven up on the exit road on the back side of the mountain.

The pizza-man had required lots of help and tutelage, and it had taken him all morning, but he made it, and you could see the pride and accomplishment written all over his face.

To their credit, the magicians showed up as well. The healer Anders Gendreau and the illusionist Sara Amundson were dressed nicely, although for Gendreau, with his black corduroy jacket and snug-fitting black slacks, that meant his everyday garb. With her fiery red hair, Sara was radiant in a black sundress and sensible black flats (in Rocktown, heels were asking for a broken ankle). The channeler Lucas was all geared up and sweaty in street clothes; he and Joel had made the climb together.

At some point, Robin found herself walking alongside Sara in a deep, shadowy crevice. Gendreau walked a few feet behind them, staring down at his smartphone, texting someone. "Back there in the coven's house," Robin began. "I hate to pry, but—"

"My face?" asked Sara.

Robin nodded. "When you were unconscious, you, uhh—"

"Witches eat children," said the illusionist. "I was almost one of those kids. I was in an oven when the Dogs of Odysseus stormed the property and saved us. But they didn't get to me in time—I was already burning. They saved my life, but they couldn't get rid of my scars. So, when they offered me an artifact and a discipline, I chose

Illusion. The witches took my face, but I used their own magic to take it back."

• • •

"My brother would have been real happy to see so many people comin' up this rock," Joel said, indicating the climbers assembled to one side. Twenty-six of them altogether, men and women and a few kids, gathered downwind so as not to sour the rest of the congregation with their sweatiness. Joel sat on a rock at the foot of the promontory, flanked by the framed photos.

Sunlight filtered through the trees, dappling his bare shoulders. "I'm gonna let y'all know, it was a hard-ass climb, but I'm glad I did it. I felt closer to Fish in the last couple of hours than I have in years." His voice broke. He reached up and ground one eye with the heel of his hand.

For a moment or so, he was unable to continue, sitting there on that rock, his eyes wandering across their faces.

"I wish he could have been here to see it," he continued. "He never said anything to me about comin' out here, so this was kind of a surprise. Marissa here is the one that let me know about his extracurricular activities, so if you one of the ones got stuck in the mud comin' up the back road, y'all know who to bring it up with."

Gentle laughter came from the crowd, barely audible over the birdsong. He let a little bit of time pass, listening to the forest around them.

"We had a kind of family feud goin' on, and we didn't talk much. Moms had a bit of trouble in her later years, and Fish moved out to go to college, so it was up to me to take care of her. And at the time, I thought he had abandoned us—abandoned her, abandoned me. I was the only one that lived in that house, only one had to deal with her 'difficulties,' and near the end, the only one clothed, bathed, and fed her. For a long time, I hated him for leavin' the two of us there together.

"But I've had a lot of time to think lately, and I've realized he didn't abandon us. He still helped on the financial side of things—namely, bills—and I know now, this was the only way he knew to help. He could be an inspiration—" And here Joel glanced at Wayne, who sat on a rock at the front of the gathered throng, along with Pete and Amanda.

Adapt and overcome. The boy smiled sadly, raising a power-fist.

"—But when it came to hands-on kinda stuff, ol' Fisher, he just wasn't prepared for that. He didn't know how to handle Mama's particular brand of crazy. Now, he could talk a good game. He could have you believin' you were the strongest, or the smartest, but he wasn't the hustlin' type. So, he helped the best way he knew how: by keepin' our moms and me off the streets." A pause. He looked down, picking a fingernail. "I wish I understood that when we still had time to make up." He gestured at the sky. "But I know in my heart of hearts he's up there in Heaven's comic shop right now, and he knows. He knows I love him. I always have."

"He knew," Robin interjected, from the other side of the promontory. "He knew before all this. He knew you loved him. And he loved you."

When he heard that, the pizza-man's eyes welled up and he took a moment to collect himself, pinching the bridge of his nose. "Anyway," he continued with a deep inhalation, as if he'd awakened from a deep sleep, "Moms is gone, now Fish is gone. It's down to me now. High time to follow his lead and do a little growin' up. Do a little less drinkin'. A little less tokin'. Maybe take care of myself." He flexed. "Get me a gym membership. Get back in shape. It's been a minute since I picked up a weight, y'all."

"We can get you a discount," a man said from the crowd.

"I just might take you up on that," Joel said, pointing. He floundered, glancing at Robin. "Well, this the first time I ever had to do something like this, so I'm running out of words. Help me out here, sister."

Dozens of eyes zeroed in on Robin, and she instantly locked up and went blank. She could talk to a camera smoothly enough, but when it came to getting up in front of people in Real Life™, she was out of her league. "Umm," she said awkwardly, eyes down, smoothing out her dress. Yes, folks, Robin Martine was wearing a dress, a little black T-shirt dress, dark cranberry leggings, and black flats. Feeling like a little choir girl, she spoke down to her hands, trying not to unsettle herself by looking back up at the crowd. "Have to admit I didn't know Fisher well, at least as an adult. But back in the day, my mom used to babysit Fish and Joel. From what I remember of him, he was a good kid. Always quiet. Smart."

"Smart," said Joel. "Goddamn, he was smart."

"Yeah. He had this little computer thing? Looked like an adding machine, had these word games on it: scrambles, missing letters, etcetera. He'd play that thing for hours on end."

"He liked to read *Reader's Digest* magazines." Joel laughed and sniffed back a wet sob. "You believe that? An itty-bitty boy sittin' there, readin' a old folks' magazine. Shit, he read everything he could get his hands on—the newspaper, your daddy's Tom Clancy books, *Field & Stream*, *Highlights*, *Cracked*, *Mad Magazine*, your mama's big red medical encyclopedia, he'd even leaf through a *TV Guide*."

"Started loving the pop culture stuff early. Had a *Ghostbusters* proton pack, I remember. He would run around our house, busting ghosts."

"Oh, my god," said Joel. "Can you imagine if he knew about the dem—" He cut himself off, eyes darting over the crowd. *Demon. Top-secret need-to-know info, indeed.* "Yeah, man, I remember one day he come runnin' into your little tower bedroom and tried to ghost-bust the two of us while we was playin'. We ended up getting in a fight and you got your lip busted."

"Yeah." She laughed.

Felt good to feel her memories slowly come back to her through the haze of time. By now, the medication was completely out of her system. It had served its purpose, the Abilify and the Zoloft, helping to eliminate the psychosis and depression of the last several years. But she was stronger now, tougher, her mind ground down to a hard, stony polish. The grueling brainwashing she had endured at Medina Psychiatric to wipe her mother's hex out of her mind was over.

It was time to move on and remember, to reclaim her stolen past and face the future.

Silence fell over them again. A vivid red cardinal in the trees timed it with an intermittent chirp, like the battery reminder of a smoke alarm. "There are so many of you. I think he loved everybody that came to Movie Night at his comic shop," said Joel. "Wish he could see all y'all up here."

"I expect he can, dear Mr. Ellis," said Gendreau, with a knowing smile. The curandero peered up at him from his seat on a slab of stone, bereft of his bull cane. "I expect he can."

32

Wayne was a zombie. He spent the entirety of Halloween on Joel's couch, mindlessly watching horror movies on television and ignoring trick-or-treaters who rang at the doorbell every few minutes. His cellphone was glued to his hand. In the hours and days since the assault on Lazenbury House had failed to turn up his father, he'd sent dozens and dozens of text messages to Leon's phone, waiting and listening for a response.

WHERE U AT DAD

None came. He refused to go to school, staying in bed until almost lunchtime, and he didn't sleep well at all, pacing quietly around the house until well after midnight, staring out the front window at the lights of downtown Blackfield like a soldier's wife.

They'd put in a missing-persons report at the police station, but Robin knew if Cutty didn't want him to be found, he wouldn't be.

For her part, she drove Wayne around all Wednesday and Thursday night, looking for Leon in all the obvious places—the high school twice, the liquor store three times, the police-taped comic shop once, and 1168 no less than six times—but he was nowhere to be found.

Since it had a spare bedroom, Wayne stayed with Joel Ellis at his mother's uptown bungalow house. Robin kept vigil over the hollow-eyed boy and edited her videos for the MalusDomestica channel while Joel went back to work at Miguel's. *Gotta keep moving,* she thought, staring at the laptop. She marveled at her demon self staring out of the screen with her traffic-light eyes. *Like a shark, you gotta keep moving, you gotta keep putting those videos out there, even if you got your arm chewed off, your mom was inside of a tree, and your orangutan demon father turned you into the third-place entry at the Blackfield High Art Show.*

Since Kenway Griffin didn't have anything better to do, he hung around with her. He and Joel had long conversations about what they were going to do with his brother Fisher's comic shop.

So, except for Wayne, the house was alive with activity. Joel appreciated the company, since he'd finally had time to fully process his brother's death. His decision to go back to work so soon wasn't made lightly. Miguel refused him at first, practically forcing him to go home and rest, and grieve, but Joel had insisted, saying he needed something to take his mind off of things, said he needed to stay busy. Nothing made this more obvious than the way he'd been Wednesday afternoon; Kenway had found him a drunken, sloppy mess splayed out in the kitchen floor, and he would have agreed to just about anything if it meant he wouldn't have to sit in his childhood home alone, listening to the wind lowing in the eaves, waiting for some arcane monster to come finish him off.

Someone knocked at the front door. Robin tore her eyes away from the TV and answered it.

Instead of kids—she figured she'd probably handed out candy to at least thirty Spider-Men, Iron Men, and Batmen at this point—she found the three magicians. A feverish indigo sunset squatted low across the sky behind them, making shadow-teeth of the city.

"Trick or treat." Sara Amundson wore her Murdercorn wig again. Must have rescued it from their demolished Suburban.

Robin was dressed as a witch, of course, green-faced in a Morticia Addams wig. In a fit of pique, she'd also painted her cleavage green to fill out the deep V of her black Lycra gown. "Nice," said Lucas Tiedeman, dressed in an Eastwood poncho and gambler hat, a cowboy revolver gleaming at his hip. "Super hot."

"Thanks," she said dryly. "Come on in." She stepped aside, eyeballing Gendreau's velvet top hat. With his navy waistcoat, he really *did* look like Willy Wonka.

They sat at Mama Ellis's table, all marked up with dozens of *algiz* runes. The only light in the room came from the hood over the stove, casting a dim yellowish light over them. Somehow, it gave the scene a desolate yet warm feel, like a lone streetlamp in a dark alley. Robin busied herself putting up the dishes in Joel's dish drain, and said over her shoulder, "I have a pot of coffee on, if anybody wants any."

"I'll take some," said Gendreau. His voice was the dusty, whispery croak of Death.

Robin eyed him. "How's your throat?"

"Getting better." The magician's pizzle cane looked odd without the pearl on top. "I owe you my life."

She smiled, searching the cabinet for a cup. She settled on a mug with a picture of a smiling macaw in front of a tropical vista. PANAMA CITY BEACH, it said across the bottom in slashy letters.

Sara opened the lid on the gravy boat in the middle of the table and peered inside. "Where's your boyfriend?" Whatever was in there must have been distasteful, because she grimaced and put it back down.

"I don't know," said Robin, pouring coffee. "He's been gone all day. He said he was trying to sell off his signage shop."

Sara grinned crookedly. "I take it he's made up his mind to go off with you, then."

"Yeah. He wants to be my 'cameraman.'"

"If the van's a-rockin', don't come a-knockin'," said Lucas, raising a fist for Sara to bump.

"Pervert." She scowled and opened the gravy boat, showing him the contents.

Lucas sat back. "Ew."

Handing off the coffee to Gendreau, Robin took off her floppy witch-hat and hung it on one of the posts of the fourth chair, then folded her arms and leaned against the stove.

"Thank you," he croaked.

"You're welcome."

"Oh, that reminds me." Gendreau reached into his jacket and took out a pocket watch, handing it to her.

"Is this a heart-road artifact?" Robin held the watch up to the hood-light and studied its cracked face-glass. It was genuine. Power lay dormant inside, pulsing drowsily in time with the ticking clockwork. Helping Annie into the afterlife had won Robin her humanity back somehow, but she was still half-demon . . . and after the catalyzing effects of finally facing Andras, she supposed there were parts of her that were permanently stretched out of shape. She would never be fully normal again.

Screwing open the back of the watch, Robin examined the gears inside, where she found a lock of dark hair. This was where the power originated, a wellspring that darkled weakly but constantly, sending off the eerie staticky signal of a long-dead radio station.

Hair in the watch.

A tooth in the pearl.

What *was* all this?

When she looked up at Gendreau, the question must have been plain on her face, because his own held an expectant solemnity. He looked twenty years older than he had when they'd met in her hospital room Tuesday; his bone-blond hair now seemed more silver than platinum, and his eyes were rimmed in blue shadow.

He produced the tooth that had been inside the head of his cane and put it on the table, sipping his coffee and regarding it as if he could divine the meaning of life from it.

Presently he asked, "Robin, have you ever heard of a 'teratoma'?"

"No, can't say I have."

"It's a type of tumor that contains a piece of organic matter. Some teratomas have teeth in them . . . some contain hair, some bones, some have entire body parts in them like hands and eyes. A few of them have even been entire fetuses. Pale, gnarled little goblins wadded up in a pouch of skin, quietly and insidiously stealing their host's blood supply. Sometimes, they're called 'parasitic twins.'"

"Well, *that's* gross as shit." The concept was terrifying to think about, like something out of a Japanese horror movie.

"Indeed." He picked up the tooth and held it at eye level. "Teratomas are rare but not super-rare. One out of every forty thousand births. Doesn't sound like many, but it comes out to about five a day. Anyway, the witches' *libbu-harrani* are teratoma, usually located around the heart, which is why they're called heart-roads."

"A cancer that channels ectoplasmic energy."

"Pretty much."

"Wait," said Robin, "you mean when they do their ritual, the heart isn't actually replaced? It's still there?"

"You've never looked for yourself?"

She thought about it. "It's kind of hard to do an autopsy on a pile of ashes."

"Ah . . . yeah. I suppose it would be. But yes, the heart is still there. It just beats really slowly. The witch is"—the mage made air-quotes with his fingers—"'undead.' Animated by the heart-road and kept from rotting by the dryad fruit. When the ritual is done to surrender her heart to Ereshkigal, what's happening is, the witch has agreed to lend Ereshkigal her life-force. You know, sort of like when an expatriate working in another country sends money home to their family. And in exchange, the goddess endows them with undeath. They are liches—immortal sorcerers, walking cadavers who are animated by the goddess of death."

Pacing slowly around the kitchen, Robin said, "So, it *is* possible for a demon to completely revert a witch to human form by closing her heart-road."

"And doing so temporarily reverses the liche ritual, yes," wheezed Gendreau.

"Liche-ual," chuckled Lucas.

"With enough caution, skill, and knowledge," continued Gendreau, "it's also possible to similarly . . . 'un-witch' a witch with surgery to remove the teratoma, though it's only been done successfully a couple of times. Normally, the procedure kills the witch, or the witch kills the surgeon. Because, dear Miss Martine, these cancers are not natural occurrences. They are . . . how shall I put this? . . . Attempts. Trespasses."

"Attempts at what?"

"Entry. Something's trying to use our bodies as doorways."

Robin's neck bristled. She stared at the curl of hair nestled inside the watch.

"We assume Ereshkigal. She's trying to force her way into the corporeal world. Teeth. Hair. Bone." His eyes were dark and steely. "She's trying to use humanity to give birth to herself. Each one of these body parts is a link to the whole, a piece of the original." He took a slurp of his coffee and placed it kindly back on the table with both hands, in a meditative fashion. "Consider the watch your enlistment bonus. If you'll join us. You've got the experience. You've got the power—"

"The po-*werrrrrr!*" sang Lucas, strumming an air guitar.

Gendreau eyed him. "—and if you'll accept my proposal, I can guarantee you the arrest warrants you've racked up in your vigilante adventures the past couple of years will . . . shall we say, get lost in red tape."

"Red taa-*aape!*" Lucas power-chorded.

The curandero gave him a disapproving scowl and continued.

"There are arson and murder cold cases out there, Robin. Breaking and entering charges floating in the legalsphere. Carjackings. Missing people—witches, child molesters, rapists, wife-beaters."

Robin's skin went cold.

"The FBI is looking for a Caucasian woman in her late teens, early twenties. You've got millions of YouTube subscribers. You used to *never* use real names in your videos—your operation is going to shake to pieces because you're getting cocky. How long do you think it's going to be before the wrong person finds out about your videos and puts two and two together?" He leaned forward. "We can *protect* you."

Did I think I was going to be invisible forever? Robin sighed, feeling stupid and reckless. *He has a point.* Did she think the goodwill of the beat cops and neckbeards lavishing secret praise on her videos and offering allegiance in her video comments would continue forever?

Could she even be certain they would still be on her side if they found out the incidents in her videos were real?

"I don't do well with leashes."

"Trust me, it would be a long one." Gendreau gave her an earnest smile. "The longest. You get to keep your videos, your van, your life . . . for the most part. Look, you saved my life. I will do everything in my power to make sure yours stays intact and the worst analysis you'll have to endure is a cheek swab. Maybe a urinalysis at the worst."

She swallowed, biting the inside of her cheek. A tin sign nailed to the kitchen wall said, DRINK COFFEE! DO STUPID THINGS FASTER!

"Can I have a couple days to think about it?"

Gendreau nodded. "Of course. It is not an easy decision."

"Speaking of videos," Robin added, "I uploaded my latest video today as a Halloween special. Almost an hour long. People are going apeshit for it. Ten thousand views since breakfast."

The front door opened and closed. Kenway came into the kitchen, his keys jingling in his hand. "Looks like I'm missing a sweet party." He sidled around the crowded table and framed Robin's face with his big hands, kissing her on the forehead. "Hi, you."

Her heart leapt. ". . . Hi."

Gendreau shotgunned the last of his coffee and pushed his chair back, rising.

"Don't let me run you guys off," said the veteran.

"Oh, we were just leaving," said the curandero, leaning on his headless cane. "I'd like to relax and find a good meal before we head home tomorrow. There's a Mongolian grill on the way to the hotel and I've heard lovely things."

"Happy Halloween, by the way," said Kenway.

"Happy Halloween," agreed Robin.

"Happy Halloween," the three Dogs of Odysseus echoed in unison.

"Thank you for the coffee," Gendreau told Robin, handing her the empty mug. As she reached for it, he locked eyes with her. "And again, for saving my life."

• • •

Out front, a white Toyota Sienna waited by the curb. Kenway and Robin stood on the front porch and watched the magicians march down the front walk. Sara wedged herself behind the wheel, grunted something about a "fucking Oompa-Loompa," and readjusted the seat.

"You don't strike me as the minivan type," Robin told Gendreau.

"I'm not," he rasped, tossing his cane in the back with Lucas. "But the rental selection here in Podunk leaves much to be desired. And thank the stars for good insurance, or we'd be *walking* back to Atlanta. Hertz isn't going to be pleased the Suburban's been smashed and shot full of bullet holes." Gendreau slid the side door shut and turned back to them, one hand tucked into a jacket pocket like a Napoleonic dandy. The healer-mage tipped the blue velvet top hat, folding himself into the passenger seat. "I await your answer, Miss Martine."

Robin waved with a halfhearted smile. The Sienna pulled away and rolled down the street, where it flashed its taillights at the stop sign, turned right, and disappeared.

"What was he talking about?" asked Kenway.

"Joining their wizard cabal. Probably want me to be their pet demon-girl or something." She sat on the front stoop, where the wind tugged and swept at her silky black wig. "Where have *you* been all day?"

"I got you a surprise."

"A *what*?" Robin's face burned. "You didn't have to do that."

"I know. But I wanted to."

"What is it?"

"If I told you, it wouldn't be a surprise, would it?"

She screwed up her face. "How *much* was it?"

"Some dollars."

She got up and slap-pushed him in the chest. "That's not a real answer, Hammer Boy."

He laughed and snagged her witch-gown, pulling her in and crushing her against him, and suddenly she was intoxicated, his cologne (Was he even wearing cologne? She wasn't sure) making her dizzy. The wig tumbled down her back as he lifted her face and gave her a deep kiss.

Her hands balled into fists of their own accord, scrunching his shirt.

He broke away, then kissed her several more times all over her cheeks and forehead, slow and methodical. His beard was like being blessed with a loofah. "Come on," he told her, heading into the house to fetch Wayne. "We'll go check out your surprise."

33

They drove slowly up Broad in Robin's utility van. Even after two days, the street was still littered with a rock-concert aftermath of trash and cast-off clothing. The city had towed away Doc Gendreau's overturned Suburban and the water company capped the broken fire hydrant, but the amount of debris in the road was . . . well, the word *excessive* came to mind. Many of the shopfronts near the central plaza were busted out, leaving jagged-toothed mouths plundered of their contents.

Nobody could give the cops a straight answer as to why a riot had broken out in uptown Blackfield. But the prevailing theory, going on hearsay and conjecture, was the car accident that kicked it off—the garbage truck running a red light and causing a Suburban to hit several people and plow through a fire hydrant—started with bystanders pulling the driver of the garbage truck out with the intent of beating him to death, and it escalated through mob mentality and panic into a full-fledged riot.

They never learned who the driver of the truck actually was, or how he'd even gotten his hands on it. But the mutilated body of a man named Roy Euchiss (brother of renowned shitheel Owen Euchiss) had been found in the wreckage of Fisher Ellis's comic book shop, beaten to death. The acid damage to his skin seemed to corroborate Joel Ellis's story of what happened Sunday, and the fact that Michael DePalatis's (partner of renowned shitheel Owen Euchiss) body was found with Joel's stolen car seemed to link the brothers as accomplices. The cops were still processing his fingerprints against prints found in Joel's car, but Robin was sure they were eventually going to agree the guy with the smashed face was the Serpent that had been sending them creepy, taunting letters for the last couple of years.

A deep sigh blew from the little boy beside her. The look of stony misery on his face broke her heart. Robin took Wayne's hand and leaned over, looking into his eyes.

We'll find him.

Kenway pulled into angle parking in front of his art shop, put the van in Park, and turned it off. He sat there so long, even Wayne looked over at him.

"You okay?" asked Robin.

"I sold the shop," said Kenway. One of his big hands came up and he scraped an eye with the heel of his hand.

His face scrunched up and that was all it took to compel her from the van and around to his side. She opened the driver door and took his arm, and Kenway turned in his seat, dropping his face into his hands. He started crying into them, *urgently,* a great shuddering-shaking that elicited deep, hitching gasps, *hup-hup-hup-hup-hup.*

Robin took his wrists. "Hey! What's wrong?"

"I sold the shop, Robin," he said between sobs. He let her pry his hands down. His face had turned a livid red and his eyes were bloodshot. Sitting sideways had tugged the cuff of his left pants leg up, and the prosthetic foot clanked against the rail under his seat. "I sold it early this afternoon over"—*hup-hup-hup*—"lunch."

"Can't say that was the best of ideas," she said, "but why are you crying?"

"Because I'm letting him down again."

"Who? Let—"

Oh. *Ohhhh*.

"Hendry," he said, "Chris. My old buddy."

". . . Ah."

"I made breakfast and I let him d—" Pain flashed across his face. ". . . I let him down, and now I'm sellin' the shop and leavin' town." With the last word, anguish tightened inside him and he squeezed his eyes shut, leaning forward until the steering wheel met his forehead.

Fresh tears rolled into his mustache. "I'm leavin', man. And it's like he's dead all over again."

Seeing this big man crying his eyes out made Robin want to bawl too. She pushed his hair out of his face and held his beard. Veins thumped in his temples. "You're not letting him down, babe," she told him, her own eyes burning, "you're letting him go. You're lettin' him go *on. He's* letting *you* go."

He shook his head.

Wayne got up on his knees, putting a hand on Kenway's back. She caught his eyes over the vet's shoulder and they traded a concerned vibe.

She let him cry it out for a little while.

"I did it because I needed to," he said.

"You did," she agreed.

"I need to quit . . . quit kicking around this town—"

"Quit kicking *yourself*. You've got to stop blaming yourself for what he did." For a change, she took his face in her hands and kissed his forehead. "You did what you could, and he did what he felt like he had to do. None of that was on you. Okay?"

Kenway nodded, scrubbing his eyes with the collar of his shirt. He looked so tired, with the bandage around his head, and his purple eye-sockets. She could have sworn she saw the first hints of gray in his beard.

"I saw his ghost," he said, staring out the window.

By now it was completely dark, and bright, sharp stars glittered through holes in the gray tent of the sky. The Halloween night air was brisk and drafted down the street in damp, heavy canvas waves. Down the street, a troupe of college-age trick-or-treaters walked by on their way to some party, screaming and laughing.

"Saw his ghost in the witches' house that night with Heinrich," he continued.

Jesus, thought Robin.

"That's what scared me off, made me run away. He was all bloated and gross, and his eyes were all blown out, and he had puke all over his fucking shirt." He turned, and the sorrow in his eyes hardened into a hot, red-eyed resolve. "That frontier witch, the illusion one. She made me see him. Hallucination." He chewed his upper lip. "I think that's part of why I want to go with you. To get away from Blackfield, where he died. And to . . . to help you end the kind of cruel monster that could make somebody see shit like that." His fists clenched. "I hate them so much."

When the knot in his chest finally loosened, Kenway dug in the door pocket for a handful of napkins and mopped his face with them. A sodium vapor streetlight cast a dismal, rust-orange light over them. "I'm probably ruinin' your surprise, ain't I?"

"No." She couldn't help but chuckle. "No, not at all."

She stepped back to let him out and he wadded the napkins into a ball, stuffing them into his pocket.

"Come on," said Kenway, taking a shuddery breath.

Georgia heat lightning flickered silently across the dark sky. They followed him down the block to the little side parking lot reserved for the dentist's office and the Mexican restaurant. In the slot where Kenway's truck was usually parked was now a motorhome. It was one of the ugliest, boxiest things she'd ever seen. It resembled an ice cream truck, with a racing stripe down the side that formed a heartbeat W near the front fender.

"Oh, my God," said Robin. "You did not."

"1974 Winnebago Brave. I know a guy . . . he collects stuff like this. You should see his property, he lives on the road goin' south out of town, across from the Methodist church. Old VW Bugs all over the place." Kenway unlocked the door and opened it, and she climbed a tiny set of metal stairs into a wonderland of wood paneling. Inside was a cross between a treehouse and an armoire. "I thought you might appreciate sleeping on a bed," he was saying, "even if it's an RV bed, a lot more than a sleeping bag in the back of a panel van."

Her throat closed up. The sink was full of ice and a champagne bottle.

"For drinking, not for smashing," Kenway said, climbing into the motorhome. The whole thing lurched to one side as he filled the narrow space. "But if you *really* wanna christen it, I got a bottle of Boone's Farm somebody left in my fridge last Christmas after my Army unit party."

Wayne climbed in and sat in the dinner nook. "Cool," he said, listlessly staring around. His eyes were dim, bleak flashlights with old batteries. His hands rested on the table as if he couldn't remember what they were for.

Kenway stood in the galley, gauging him. He opened the cupboard over the stove and took out a stack of clear party cups. "You know what, kid?" he said grimly, but encouragingly. "You need to take the edge off. How about you share this champagne with us?"

"Really?" Wayne stared into the back of the RV. "Okay." He checked his phone for the ten thousandth time.

A few moments ticked by as Kenway stood there with the bottle in his hand. "Shit," he said, "Forgot to get a corkscrew. Be right back." He stepped outside, the motorhome shaking like a wet dog from his weight.

The boy looked up from his phone. "I can't believe you guys are gonna sit in here and drink champagne while my dad's still out there somewhere. With that *witch*."

Totally forgot I was dressed as one. Lycra hugged her slinky, boyish figure so tightly, it made her self-conscious. Sitting down in the breakfast nook across from him, she took his hands with her pasty green ones and looked into his face with deadly seriousness. "We're going to find him. I promise. I've found every witch I've looked for up 'til now. This one won't get away either."

He watched her, the blinds-filtered light glinting on his glasses, the cellphone coloring his jaw a ghastly blue. The windows guttered with lavender lightning.

"You hear me?" she reiterated. "We *will* find your dad."

He nodded, perhaps a bit dismissively, and went back to flipping through the apps on his phone.

"No. Listen." She leaned in and looked up at his face again. He smoldered at her in irritation, but at least he was paying attention. "I will turn every stone, I will burn down every house, I will fight every demon between here and Hell if that's what it takes." She sat back, letting her hands slide away from his. "I've killed to get where I am, and I ain't afraid to do it again . . . . So, don't count me out, little man."

In the reflection on Wayne's glasses, she saw an eerie green gleam in her own silhouette's eyes.

To his credit, he didn't flinch.

Kenway stepped into the Winnebago again. He held up a pair of channel-lock pliers. "Never leave home without 'em."

"You are such a redneck." Robin shook her head.

He picked up the champagne and clamped the pliers on the cork, twisting it like a stubborn bolt, and it came out with a heady *thoonk!*, gurgling white foam into the sink. He filled three cups with it and carried them to the table. Robin scooted over and let him sit down.

Wayne sipped at the champagne and wrinkled his nose. "Tastes kinda like paint." He finished it off. "I think I like beer better, honestly."

"Well, uhh!" Kenway tossed his back and slammed the cup on the table with a feeble clap of plastic. "I had no idea you was a grown-ass man, Mr. Connoisseur!" The vet pushed himself to his feet and started to pour himself another, then decided to drink it straight from the bottle. He gave a shudder. "Aight, maybe you got a point. I got some good local beer in my apartment. And some weird shit, too. You like cocoa?" He pulled the plug on the sink to let the ice water drain.

Robin took the champagne bottle and stood up. Kenway paused in the door to study her face.

"What do you think?" His face seemed to be asking, *Did I do good?*

She smiled widely. "I think you spent a hell of a lot of money and gambled your place away on a girl you barely know, but . . . I do love it." The wooden cabinets and walls glowed a soft cheese-orange in the darkness. "I really do." She slid her arms around his neck and squeezed him tight. The bottle in her hand rolled across his back.

"Thank you," he said, his face muffled by her jacket. "For understanding. For standing there and lettin' me cry it out."

She leaned back and looked him in the face. The laugh lines under his eyes were wet. She scraped them with her thumb. "Of course."

They stepped down out of the Winnebago. Robin stood there, her eyes playing over his broad back, and she wondered what he was thinking. *How did I let this man so easily slide into my crazy life where so many others before him have bounced right off? Am I his ticket out of town?* The random crying jag over his friend and the fact he actually had the money, and the means, to leave Blackfield whenever he wanted, must have meant this was a conscious, deliberate decision on his part. *Am I, though? Am I the means to an end? Am I an excuse to leave?* Robin wrapped her arms around herself, feeling the cold a little bit more than usual. He did seem to have real feelings, but . . . if she let him in, was he going to stay?

"Are you *sure* you want to be my cameraman?" she finally blurted out. *Cameraman*, here, having evolved beyond its original platonic connotation. *Connotations*, she thought, *isn't that where the magic is?*

Hope sparkled in his red-rimmed eyes as Kenway turned. "I don't think I've ever wanted anything more."

She realized it was the first time she'd seen anything like it since she'd met him. The even-keel Zen complacency she'd come to associate with him hadn't been contentment at all, it had been a . . . *lostness*. A sort of bleak one-foot-in-front-of-the-other dormancy. His perceived failure to save Chris Hendry had been a self-imposed prison cell.

"Even after what you've seen?" she asked.

Taking out a pack of cigarettes, he tapped one out and tucked it into his mouth. He produced a lighter. "Yeah. Hell, all that probably did the *opposite* of running me away." He cupped his hands around his face and lit the cigarette, putting the lighter away. They started up the sidewalk to his shop. "Ever since I met you," he said, "it's like . . . it's like . . ." He pincered the cigarette and blew a stream of blue-white smoke. "Well, lemme put it like this: do you have any idea how much body armor weighs in the Army?"

"I can't say I do."

She *did* know, actually—after wearing an IOTV every day for months, she knew quite well—but she really wanted to hear what he was about to say and didn't want to ruin the moment.

"It's a Kevlar vest with ceramic plates capable of stopping assault rifle rounds. The Kevlar by itself is like wearing a leather jacket, but with the plates in, it's forty pounds—more, with extra side plates, codpiece, helmet. Heavy as balls, but if you wear it all day, you get used to it. But at the end of the day? When you take it off? You feel like you're walking on the moon. Your step is *all* spring." His beard parted with a broad smile. "Ever since I met you, it's like I took off my armor. I can breathe again." An anxious hand crept up to rub his face. "And, you know, I don't . . . I don't really want to give that up. You know?"

The corner of Robin's mouth quirked up in recognition.

"I know."

He unlocked the front door of his art shop, the cigarette cherry glowing in the dark shapes smeared across the glass, and pulled it open. The front area presented them with long smears of pale gray: the rollers and spools of his vinyl machines. Robin and Wayne followed him through the shop and into the garage. "I'll have to teach you how to play cornhole," Kenway told him as they started up the stairs to the loft apartment.

Wayne's face was traced in blue by his cellphone screen. She could see he was texting his father again. He grunted noncommittally.

An electronic *bink!* came from the top of the stairs.

Wayne froze. His glasses were white squares, refracting the screen of his cellphone. His thumb danced across the screen and they heard the *bink!* from above again. *"DAD?!"* Frantic, he scrambled up the stairs, almost on all fours.

"WAIT!" Robin lunged for his ankles and missed. *"No!"* she shouted. *"Don't go up there!"*

34

The boy reached the top of the staircase and disappeared over the crest. Robin and Kenway thundered up after him, his titanium foot clanking like a robot, the champagne sloshing in her hand. Rising into the lightless apartment, she scanned the shapes around them, trying to pick out something familiar, something human.

Wayne stood in the open kitchen. The white-eyed shadow snatched up a square of light and waved it over his head. "It's Dad's phone!" He came over, holding up Leon's phone and his own. "Why is Dad's phone here? Is Dad here? Why would Dad be here? He's never even *been* here, has he?"

"Come on," Robin told him, her arms and neck prickling. "We need to get out of here, *now*."

She took his wrist. "Come on, we got—"

"*AAAH!*" screamed Kenway, lurching forward onto one knee. The cigarette fell out of his mouth.

Leon Parkin stood over him.

Both of Leon's hands were wrapped around the Osdathregar, and he had jammed it deep into Kenway's back. Heat lightning blued the clouds outside, briefly turning the windows overlooking the canal into a bank of television screens. A strange silhouette, squat and angular, was outlined by the squares of dim light. The apartment plunged into darkness again.

We're screwed, we waltzed right into this, as Kenway crawled away, the silver dagger jutting from his back. She moved toward the maniacally grinning Leon, clenching her fists and preparing for a hand-to-hand. *Cutty waited for the magicians to leave so she'd have the upper hand again.* She still had the champagne; she'd break it over his head. *I gotta take Parkin out of commission first,* she decided, but Wayne slammed into her chest.

"No!" the boy shrieked. *"Don't kill him!"*

As soon as he shoved her, Wayne ran at Leon. The familiarized man threw his arms wide, his eyes and teeth flashing in the abyss of his face, and Wayne plowed into his father's belly. Both of them plunged backward down the stairs in a sickening drum solo of knees and elbows. Leon snarled. Wayne screamed. The scuffling-smacking sounds of a fight carried up to her, and she started to take off downstairs, but the sight of Kenway with a knife in his back made her hesitate.

Silent lightning illuminated the loft's windows, tracing the strange figure again. "It's so nice to finally meet you," the thing in the wheelchair said, with a voice like dry leaves blowing across a sidewalk.

"Morgan," said Robin.

"Morgan," said the Matron. "Sycorax. Circe. Cassandra of Apollo. Miss Cleo of the Psychic Hotline. I forget. You get to be my age, you forget a lot of things."

Indirect lighting in the kitchen clicked on, bathing the apartment in a soft, slanting glow. Marilyn Cutty stood on the other side of Kenway's chopping block. "Happy Halloween, littlebird," said the witch, coming around the kitchen island at a stately pace.

Tearing her eyes away from Cutty, Robin peered at the wheelchair at the edge of the light and saw a thin, hunched hag swaddled in an old quilt.

The Matron's arms were twigs, hooked into drawn, papery fists. Her mouth was frozen in a gaping tragedy-mask frown. Eyes like manzanilla olives twitched in stretched, drooping eye sockets. One of the holes sank down her face toward the corner of her stiff lips, revealing a knob of cheekbone in a grotesque C. She was the looming specter that had followed Annie down the driveway all those years ago. She was Haruko Nakasone's prophetic ghost-painting. She was the drowned woman in the black bathtub.

Perched in the valley between the Matron's left ear and the knob of her left shoulder was a burden of sweat-slick flesh that writhed like the egg of a giant snake. "Ah, yes," rasped the ancient witch, almost obscured under the tumor. "Happy Halloween, my dear."

"Champagne," said Cutty. "Feeling festive, I see."

Carefully, cautiously, Robin stood the champagne bottle on the floor to free her hands. Her eyes flicked down to the Osdathregar sticking out of Kenway, and out of the corner of her eye she saw Cutty regard it as well.

Blood glistened between the veteran's lips.

Is he dead? Her heart tumbled in her chest. She lunged for the dagger, but she was too late. It leapt out of Kenway's back and whirled across the room, landing in Cutty's outstretched hand. Before she could react, Cutty gestured at her and an invisible force washed her across the apartment, where she hit the bedroom wall and hung there, suspended some eight feet in the air. Paintings tumbled from the wall in a card-flutter of canvas squares, clapping to the floor.

The Matron wheezed laughter.

"Ereshkigal." Cutty smiled as she paced slowly, inexorably, out of the kitchen. She flourished the dagger. "We've been incubating her for quite some time now. It takes time to resurrect a death goddess, you know." The witch casually leaned against the kitchen island and gestured at the Matron and her fleshy, heaving tumor. "Hundreds of years, we've been working to bring Ereshkigal into the material world. Coddling her, feeding her life from the dryads. Mum's been eating for two for a very, *very* long time." The witch scoffed sadly. "Halloween. It's almost too on the nose, isn't it? Hokey. But I kinda like it."

Robin tried to push away from the wall, but no dice: she was glued down. She could move her hands, though, and as Cutty kept talking, she slipped one into her jacket.

"Regretfully, I've missed a few of your birthdays, littlebird," said the witch, emphasizing every so often with the handle of the dagger. "What kind of a grandmother am I? So, after your magician friends left, I thought, why don't I bring Mother to town and make a night of it? Throw you a surprise party. Isn't that *neato-keen*? I wanted you to see her. I wanted you to see what you and Annie missed. Annabelle betrayed us and endangered our family. You refused my generosity and killed my sisters. The time for reunions, and conciliations, and truces is over. Your mentor is dead. Your family is dead. Your little boy-toy is dead. Now you're going to lay eyes on the goddess Ereshkigal and feel the true weight of your failure as she is reborn, and then you are going to die, cold and alone."

"But I haven't seen the last season of *Breaking Bad* yet," Robin said petulantly. "Let me finish that, and then you can come back here and resurrect the Mesopotamian avatar of death in our kitchen, okay? In the meantime, that dagger belongs to me."

"You should—"

Interrupting her, the top of the Matron's massive hunchback split open like a Jiffy-Pop bag—*splutch!*

But instead of popcorn, what volcanoed out was a river of . . . at first, Robin wasn't sure. Looked like crude oil, black and thick—then a nose-burning stench filled the apartment with fish and rotten eggs. Pus and blood and God knew what else sprayed straight up in the air and clattered to the floor around the wheelchair.

Even Cutty was surprised. "Oh, goodness gracious," she said, and tugged the collar of her sweater over her face.

Robin's fingers closed over the prize in the pocket of her jacket. She pulled out Gendreau's watch and flipped it upside down, screwing it open with her thumbs. The backplate came loose with a subtle *click*, revealing a lock of hair.

The shredded skin over the hunchback's colossal tumor spread like lips, and the whole thing tilted forward, spilling its contents.

A great gush of fibrous black matter poured out of the broken hump like a horse giving birth and hit the floor with a surprisingly bony *thud*. The empty sac flopped over the Matron's lap, covering her face with a parachute of loose skin. Soupy slime oozed down her shins.

Robin removed the teratoma and focused on it, seeking the energy lying latent inside. Light spiraled up her arm, her skin glowing green from within, as the heart-road entered her mind and infused it with a strange power. To her bewilderment and horror, she experienced a sensation as if her brain had sprouted fingers, dozens of them, pressing against the inside of her skull. Darts of pain rippled across her scalp as it seemed to stretch.

"Yo, Maude," she said, pointing.

Preoccupied by the nauseating resurrection taking place in front of her, Cutty looked up. Robin put her index fingertip over the Osdathregar and stole it out of Cutty's hands as if she were dragging a file on a computer screen. The dagger whipped upward and hovered over the witch's head.

"The hell is this?" asked Cutty, staring up at it. Robin whipped her hand down in a slashing motion. The Osdathregar arrowed down at the witch but halted in midair as if it'd struck an invisible obstacle.

Concentration on her face, Cutty grinned back at her. "Where did you learn to do *that*, littlebird?"

Turning in the air like the needle in a compass, the Osdathregar trembled as Robin pushed against it. "I get by with a little help from my friends." The dagger had become the ball in a game of will, and the blade point slowly, excruciatingly, rotated toward her.

"The Dogs of Odysseus?" Cutty cackled. "They're a bad influence on you." The witch thrust her finger, overpowering Robin, and the Osdathregar whipped across the room. At the last instant, Robin put up her hands and the dagger pierced her right palm, bursting from the back. The hilt slammed into the heel of her hand and the tip of the stiletto stopped a few inches from her face.

It *really fucking hurt,* the blade grinding between the bones of her hand, lacerating the muscle, her fingers forced apart in a Spock *live long and prosper* gesture. She screamed until her throat was raw and her breath ran out.

"I hate to do it, my sweet little demon, but you've got to be taught a lesson." Cutty selected a fillet knife from Kenway's dish drain. Then she went to the creature writhing on the floor and used it to pierce the caul covering its face.

Taking hold of the Osdathregar, Robin pulled it out of her hand, inviting a fresh round of agony. Blood ran down her arm. She flung the dagger back at Cutty, who looked up and put out a warning hand.

It stopped in midair again.

"You need new material," said Cutty, twirling her finger. The Osdathregar tried to pivot again, but Robin pointed with both hands two-gun style. She howled with effort, tears standing in her eyes, muscles cording under her skin. Cutty's face darkened. "Do you know what the definition of insanity is, dear?"

Vivid red blood dribbled from the girl's clenched fist. "I may not be insane," Robin growled from the wall, her entire body shaking with exertion, "but I'm pretty goddamn crazy."

The witch stepped away from the thing on the floor, redoubling her efforts, her teeth bared, eyes wide.

"Uungh," said a low voice.

At first, the two women thought it was the thing on the floor, but it turned out to be the other thing on the floor—the big blond lunk with the blood running down his back. Kenway stirred, slowly finding his feet, and he got up.

"What are you doing?" asked Robin. "Stay down, I got this."

"We're in the shit, baby." He looked at them, assessing the situation. The man was hunched over in agony. Blood trickled down his chin and across his neck where the wound had leaked over his shoulder. Approaching the dagger hovering in midair, he gripped the Osdathregar with both hands.

"What is this?" demanded Cutty. "Stay out of this, boy!"

Slowly, excruciatingly, Kenway rotated the dagger like a pressure valve, so it was pointing in the other direction—at the witch standing in the kitchen.

Sweat trickled down Cutty's gray face. "No! *No!*"

"I am tired of your bullshit, lady," replied Kenway. "I'm gonna end this if it fucking kills me." He leaned into the dagger, walking it toward her, and he looked so comically, so ludicrously like a mime fighting an invisible wind, Robin almost laughed. Cutty thrust her hands forward and the pommel hit him in the lips, but he let out the most ferocious growl and put his back into it.

Ten feet. Seven feet. Five feet.

The Osdathregar trembled in his hands, and then he was vibrating, like a man gripping an electric fence, still growling, only now it was a shuddering washing-machine utterance: *"GRR-R-R-AAAH!"* Cutty backed against the kitchen island as the blade came within arm's reach.

As if she were Superman launching himself forward from a stand-still, Robin punched with both fists.

Darting out of Kenway's hands, the Osdathregar flew the last couple of feet and caught Cutty in the solar plexus, threading through her, lifting her. Robin brought her fists down as if ending an orchestra piece and the dagger darted into the floor, nailing the witch to the hardwood planks.

Kenway collapsed next to her.

The ear-splitting shriek that came out of Cutty was unbelievable. The oven door, the microwave door, and every lightbulb in the room exploded, raining glass all over the kitchen floor. Every drinking glass in the dish drain shattered. Even the television screen spiderwebbed.

The force pinning Robin to the wall let go and she dropped onto her hands and knees, barking her shin on a nightstand on the way down.

"Uuuuuuuhr," groaned the cadaverous horse-limbed thing on the floor.

Robin crawled to her feet and staggered toward it. An angular shape moved restlessly inside a cloudy white caul. The rubbery sac was clear enough she could see through it. Thick wisps of black hair clouded around pale limbs . . . an elbow . . . a hip . . . a hand . . . a face.

One bloodshot eye gazed through the membrane. A finger poked through and ripped the knife hole wider. Robin jerked away from it in horror and her ankle bumped something.

The bottle of champagne.

Getting an idea, she approached the thing tearing out of its amniotic sac, her heart slamming in her chest over and over, veins rocketing with adrenaline. Robin steeled herself and grabbed the reborn Ereshkigal. Her fingers sank into clammy flesh like cold butter.

A thin, malformed face stared at her, eyes glassy and veiny under a scum of cold, clear mucus. *"EEEEEEEEE!"*

Robin screamed back, terrified, *"Aaaaah!"* but she was already steaming along and there wasn't no stoppin' *this* train. She rose, flexing, and lifted Ereshkigal by the upper arms. The wraith under the flapping caul screeched and kicked like a feral child.

A hard, strange wind skirled through the apartment, rising and howling and stinking of rot and sulfur, and the paintings flapped and clacked in stiff wooden applause. Papers blew off their fridge magnets and swirled in the air, plastering against the couch and cabinets. Robin's sexpot witch-gown flapped madly around her thighs. She muscled the larval Ereshkigal over to the lifeless Matron in the wheelchair, and there she dumped it on top of Morgan, or Sycorax, or whatever the ancient bitch wanted to call herself. Then she turned, grabbed up the bottle of champagne, and . . .

. . . remembered champagne is not flammable.

"Shit. *Shit!*" she shouted into the hurricane.

She dashed to the kitchen, threw the bottle into the sink (where it shattered) and hauled the refrigerator door open.

Inside was a carton with one egg in it, a bottle of ketchup, a half-quart of milk, a box of Mexican leftovers, and enough liquor and beer to stock a tavern. "Thank God for bachelors." She grabbed a bottle of Stolichnaya. Storming around the island (dodging Cutty's reaching hands on the way), she approached the wheelchair-bound corpse of the Matron and the banshee in her lap.

"*Nooooooo!*" roared Cutty. Her face changed, became cavernous with teeth. A fell light shined in her eyes and she bucked ferociously against the dagger's hilt. "*You stupid little shit!*" Wind kicked across the side of the building, howling into the apartment through the broken windows. Cutty snarled in a guttural, blustering roar. "*I'll crack open your chest and eat your heart, girl!*" The witch panted like a winded horse, slavering and coiling around the dagger in her chest. "*Get this thing out of me and I'll show you how to hurt! You'll wish Annie never pushed your sorry ass out of her rotten cunt!*"

"You know what? I'm done listening to your two-faced bullshit." Giving her a wide berth, Robin shut the refrigerator door. Then she braced her foot on the wall and hooked her fingers around the back of the fridge.

Six feet to her right, Cutty looked up, curious.

"Rot in Hell, Mee-Maw," said Robin, pulling.

"What are you d—NO! *NOO!*"

Closing her eyes against the sight of the contorted face of the woman that had helped raise her, Robin pried the fridge away from the wall and overturned it on top of Marilyn Cutty's head. The Kenmore flattened the witch's skull with an impact heavy enough to vibrate the hardwood floor. Gray brains and skull fragments sprayed in a thin starburst.

Thin wisps of energy curled from underneath. Gore sizzled as if the floor were a griddle, and dissipated into black scum. Some part of her regretted having to do that. "I'm sorry, Marilyn," she said, watching the energy fade. She couldn't bring herself to absorb the heart-road lingering in the maimed corpse. *I'm sorry there wasn't any love in you after all. We thought you were a gift, but you were a manipulative box of snakes tied up with a pretty bow. You used our love for you against us, used our family and used me to make your coven stronger. I'm sorry you couldn't have been the grandmother we thought you were.*

But I'm not sorry I had to end you.

She picked up the vodka bottle and turned to face the last two monsters in the room, the ruined Matron and the thing writhing in her lap like a mashed beetle. "Now. Back to business," she said, opening the Stolichnaya and approaching the wheelchair. Clear vodka sloshed inside the bottle as she raised it over the alleged Ereshkigal. "Where were we? You like to party, Gollum?"

Upending the liquor, Robin made the vital mistake of looking down at the wheelchair as she went to pour its contents out.

Gazing back up at her was the gap-faced Matron.

Hard eyes stared out of those hollow, desiccated sockets. Robin flinched. As the vodka trickled down the creature's warped face, the rawhide tongue in its mouth worked and it said, hoarsely, *"Yee-Tho-Rah."*

Dark tendrils burst out of the Matron's shoulder where the fully formed teratoma had birthed itself. Thin pseudopods snaked and slithered like black spaghetti noodles across her terrifying face and down her chest and arm, covering both her and the reborn Ereshkigal, obscuring them in protective roots. The tendrils fattened and hardened as they propagated, developing cracked bark-skin.

"*Yee-Tho-Rah*," the Matron said again, and a wave of pressure exploded from her skull, crashing against Robin in an invisible ripple of distortion and throwing her to the floor. Knuckles banged against hardwood. Forehead bounced off of kitchen tile.

And Robin went away.

35

When she opened her eyes, she was home.

"No!" she shouted, scrambling to her feet. She stood in the front hallway of the Victorian, the front door at her back. It was night.

Soft lamplight tumbled through the door from the living room. Golden dust hovered around her boots. "What is this shit? Is this Illusion magic? You cheating hussy." She automatically reached toward her pocket with her good hand, and the first thing she realized was that her dress didn't have any fucking pockets, and the second thing was she didn't have the aripiprazole anymore.

No more med-bombing to dispel the illusions.

"Shit. Shit-shit-*shit*." She turned this way and that, scanning the house for some kind of sign, somebody else, another person, some crack or divot she could use to peel back the illusion.

Blood trickled down the side of her face from a cut at her hairline and pattered on the floor from the stab wound through her hand. She wrenched the front door open. Outside was inside—beyond the threshold was the very hallway she was already standing in, as if viewed from the front porch. She ran out the front door and into the Victorian's foyer.

Behind her, the front door slammed shut. She rounded on it and flung it open, only to find the Victorian's kitchen as viewed from the back stoop.

She shut the door and stared angrily at the sideboard in the hallway, with its cordless landline phone and framed portraits of Robin and her parents. This house wasn't the one currently being lived in by the Parkin family—it was the one she'd shared with Jason and Annie Martine, the house she'd grown up in. And since (a) the house wasn't real, and (b) there was no Andras, she didn't even have the demon to back her up against the Matron.

Snatching the doily off the sideboard, she dumped the phone and portraits on the floor and wrapped the lacy cloth around her wounded hand, tying it off. As she did, she caught a glimpse of her Halloween costume—her skin was painted green and she was wearing a black Lycra skirt with the hem ripped to tatters, but the makeup was mostly gone from her face, leaving her with a weird green burnish lingering around her nose and in her ears.

"I have to get out of here," Robin growled, heading upstairs, cradling her wound. "I have to get back there before Kenway dies or that weird screaming baby-woman goes full *Akira*. I don't have time for this *It's a Wonderful Life* shit."

In the second-floor hallway was a long, low bookshelf, the one running from the master bedroom door all the way down the landing to the bathroom door. Crammed into it were all of Robin's many books, from her original Stephen Gammell editions of *Scary Stories to Tell in the Dark* to her Stephen Kings and Dean Koontzes. If there was anything her mother allowed her to indulge in, it was the Scholastic Book Fair and the Books-A-Million in Blackfield, and this shelf was evidence. Sliding one of the tomes out—Nora Roberts's *Morrigan's Cross*—she turned it to a random page and started reading it. Another page. The middle of the book. The ending. "Perfect copy," she said, tossing it over her shoulder. It flapped through the balusters and into the hallway downstairs. She slid out another one, Joe Hill's *Heart-Shaped Box*. Random page. End of the book. Beginning.

"Another perfect copy. Fuck," she said, and turned to hurl the book down the landing. *"Fuck! Fuuuck!"*

"You're not going to outthink the Matron," someone said by her left shoulder.

Twitching in surprise, Robin spun to find Annie. Or, at least, most of what she remembered as her mother.

What stood behind her was the suggestion of a shape limned in gossamer light, like an invisible woman standing in the rain. "She's not like most illusionists," said Annie. "She can get in your head and scour the deepest reaches of your memory. She knows every word of every book on that shelf. If there are Christmas presents in this house, she knows what's in them. She knows which of those stairs creak and which ones don't. She knows how much cereal is left in that box of Lucky Charms in the kitchen. She's been doing this for centuries—you're not going to be able to dismantle the illusion by looking for books with blank pages, or by counting the ice cubes in the freezer."

"You scrambled my brains when I was a kid. It's half your fault I ended up in the crazyhole to begin with, and I've been busting my ass all alone. What makes you think you're qualified to come out of nowhere and help me now?"

"I thought you forgave me."

"I did," said Robin, "but I never said I forgot."

Annie frowned. "I was only ever trying to protect you. I'm still trying to do that, if you'll let me. Stop with these cobbled-together, half-assed tactics. Overdosing on antipsychotics. Trying to play her game by looking for inconsistencies in her illusions."

"Then how the hell do I undo this?" she demanded, pacing across the creaky floor. "I don't have anything left in my bag of tricks."

"You *can* teach an old dog new tricks." Annie smiled. "Did you forget?"

"Forget what?" Robin winced as the wound in her hand sent a jolt of pain up her wrist. "I don't have time for riddles, Mama."

"What did you do to Theresa?"

"I devoured her power and closed her heart-road." Robin paused. "Are you saying my demon side can get me out of here?" She looked around, frantic, and asked despondently, "How? I don't have the Matron here, I can't grab her and tap the road."

Throwing her arms wide, the glassy specter did a perfect slow-motion *Sound of Music* twirl across the hardwood floor, her hands open. "You don't need to, honey. You don't need to go to her, she brought the feast to you. Look, you're surrounded by her magic. You're soaking in it. You'll have to drink a river, but nobody says you have to start at the source."

Confused resignation settled over Robin. "So . . . what does that mean? I have to devour the illusion?"

Annie nodded. "I think so, yes."

Kneeling, Robin pulled out another story, an enormous brick of a book, and opened it to the middle. Between her hands was a well-thumbed copy of Susanna Clarke's *Jonathan Strange & Mr Norrell*. She took hold of the top of the first page and ripped it neatly down the spine, then wadded the paper into her mouth as if it were a handful of potato chips. It was dry and tasteless as her saliva soaked into the pages.

"Not quite what I had in mind, baby," Annie said.

Her daughter glared at her, mouth crammed full of fantasy. "Well, you weren't very specific, were you?" she said, voice muffled.

Eyes back down to the book. She'd *seen* something, there, for a moment, out of the corner of her eye. Some faint trace of green luminescence. Ink stained her tongue as the ball of paper in her mouth became soggy. She ran her fingers across the smooth surface of the next page, and a ghostly green St. Elmo's fire traced the path her fingertips made down the paper, brief and otherworldly, static electricity in the dark.

Yee-Tho-Rah, thundered a godlike voice from the bowels of the house.

The glass in the window at the end of the landing crackled delicately, like thin ice. *Yeee. Thooo. Raaaaaaaaah,* the Matron intoned again.

Wood floorboards under her hands flexed and creaked as the house shook—not an earthquake-shake but a subtle vibration. Nailheads twisted slowly up out of the floor. Pain coursed over Robin's scalp and shot needles down her brainstem as her skull seemed to shrink, compressing her gray matter. *Yee-Tho-Rah, Yee-Tho-Rah,* the Matron continued chanting, the mantra coming in waves, a slow three-beat phrase to the tune of Queen's "We Will Rock You," rippling throughout the house.

Invisible knives pierced Robin's eardrums and she doubled over, her forehead pressed into the open book. The words in front of her eyes blurred.

"Don't let her beat you, baby," said Annie, standing over her. The spirit knelt by her daughter. The pictures on the walls danced softly on their hooks. "I didn't mean for you to actually eat our reading material, but if it's working, then by all means, keep going."

Tears dotted the book's pages. "I figured," Robin grunted, eyes scrunched shut against the torture, "that would be where the strongest, and most complex, *uuggh,* part of her Illusion hex was goinnng*gggGGGHH FUCK.*"

YEE. THO. RAAAAAH, roared the house around her, and then the room seemed to *twist.* Sheetrock ripped. The studs in the walls complained, sounding for all the world like a chorus of frogs, and then snapped behind the wallpaper, a series of gunshot *crack*s. The entire house seemed to bend over double. Trying to ignore the chaos all around her, Robin ripped another page free of the book and stuffed it into her mouth with a crackle. So goddamned hard to chew.

"Embrace it," Annie shouted over the noise. "You have hellfire in your heart. Show this old hag how it burns!"

Anger—no, *rage,* blind, violent, seismic rage boiled up inside of her, and the ball of page-paper burst into flames in her mouth. She inhaled through the fire as if it were a cigarette and smoked the witch, filled her lungs with the witch's last energies, filled her body with it, ignited her bones and her soul and everything she was with the paranormal power of the heart-road of the Matron Yee-Tho-Rah.

Littlebird, the girl she had been, the little tomboy that walked around barefoot and kissed pretty softball pitchers, she caught on fire.

Attention-whore Robin, the filthy, half-mad, overmedicated teenager furious at having her childhood stolen and put back in upside down, she caught on fire.

Malus Domestica, the witch-killer with the van full of swords, she caught on fire.

Past and present went up in flames, roiling in her chest, and Robin vomited all this burning pain and anger out in one long stream of dragonfire. A helix of light poured from her mouth, washing across the bookshelf and wall, where books charred and erupted. She turned and blew it all over the floor and banister. Flames rippled across the carpet like blue dominoes.

The second floor of the Victorian folded like a mirror curving inward and she fell, sliding down a runner of embers, as the house tried to turn itself inside out and wad itself into a ball to crush her. She blew hellfire as she went, clawing at the floor, and hit the end of the landing feet-first, somersaulting through the window.

Glass crashed around her, and she fell into nothingness.

• • •

The first thing she saw when she came to and emerged from the mirage was the pale figure standing over her. Robin gasped a ragged breath and sat up. She had been lying against the overturned fridge, the remnants of Cutty's brains soaking into her jeans.

Heat still filled her mouth and eyes, tinging everything with a feverish red. She leaned over, slid the Osdathregar out of Cutty's twice-dead chest with a whetstone sibilance of blade against bone.

Almost knock-kneed in her frailty, Ereshkigal staggered, trying to find the strength to stand. The newborn death goddess was thin, scrawny, her wet hair clinging to her face and chest in sheets. Her skin was still the sickly blue-white pallor of a stillborn colt, her fingers long and spindly as she reached out for balance.

We finally meet, girl, said a whisper in Robin's brain.

To the half-demon witch-hunter, the strange creature should have been a blinding light, an edible mother lode, a font of power to satiate the hungriest of demons. But as the Matron's illusion faded and Robin's eyes focused on the thing in front of her, she briefly saw them: ethereal silver strands, thousands of them, a web of shimmering beams in every direction, flowering out of the central Ereshkigal, pulsing, each softly glowing tendril pulling something out of her.

"All them witches," she said, gripping the dagger in her wounded hand. Blood dripped from the hilt, mixing with Cutty's black rot. "They're still connected."

With time, I will be strong again, whispered Ereshkigal.

Fire still coiled in Robin's chest, etching her nerves into her bones like the flash-shadows of a nuclear explosion. The air smelled of gunpowder and rotten eggs.

I will offer you that which Marilyn Cutty no longer can. What is no longer hers to give. The death goddess extended a supplicating hand, teetering like a drunkard. *Join me, protect me, serve me . . . and I will give you your mother back. Your father. Your friends. You will have a life free of hunting. Free of this transient existence, living on the road, risking your life for nothing. You can be the woman the girl was meant to be.*

"The woman I was meant to be," said Robin.

She plunged the Osdathregar into Ereshkigal's forehead.

"I already am."

The silver blade pierced the soft skull with a sickening *squelch* and sank in all the way to the hilt. Ink ran from the goddess's eyes in four harlequin streaks. "Guck," she said, leaning backward in surprise.

Kicking up one leg, Robin planted a foot on Ereshkigal's chest and breach-kicked her into the Matron's lap, the wheelchair jerking backward.

Yee-Tho-Rah stiffened, looking up with those shriveled green-olive eyes. The arm not pinned by the choking, stunned body on top of her unfolded and reached for Robin. And kept reaching. The Matron's arm seemed to lengthen, growing and stretching, the bones inside twisting and crackling. She was still covered in those squirming black cellar-roots, and they darted out in fine pseudo-pods, sticking to Robin's dress.

Dirty yellow fingernails grazed her face.

Where she expected the dying Matron to offer one last plea for mercy, only an endless shriek of indignation and revenge echoed in her mind.

Opening her mouth, Robin spewed a gout of red hellfire.

The Stolichnaya vodka caught in a bright splash and a *WHOOSH* of flame. Ereshkigal shrieked and thrashed, gabbling nonsense, the handle of the Osdathregar protruding from her forehead like a unicorn's horn. Wind from the broken window caught the fire and whirled it into a tower of flame, reaching toward the ceiling.

Someone came trudging up the stairs and Robin turned to see the Parkins, looking very much the worse for wear. Wayne had one of Kenway's toluene paint markers and a deep scratch on his face. Leon had an *algiz* rune drawn on his forehead and he was cradling a blood-slick cat.

The cat jumped out of his arms as Mr. Parkin gaped at the fire. *"Christ!"*

Rushing at the conflagration, Leon ripped the dagger out of the monster's face, tossed it aside, then grabbed the arms of the wheelchair and ran it backward. Flames licked at his face. His eyebrows roasted, curling into ash. The back of the wheelchair crashed through the remains of the window and somersaulted backward into the dry canal three stories below.

Broken glass and fire rained into the darkness as Robin watched—dazed, exhausted, traumatized, her feet unwilling to propel her any farther.

Stepping over the fallen Kenway, Leon stumbled toward the kitchen, where his iPhone lay at the edge of the carnage, glowing softly in the shadows. He grabbed it and dialed 911.

The three of them watched the thing in the canal burn as Robin polished off the Stolichnaya straight from the bottle. A distant ambulance siren fell over them, growing to a caterwaul. "You look like you need a drink, Mr. Parkin," rasped Robin, and she offered up the vodka.

Hefting Kenway's fire extinguisher, Leon smiled tiredly and sprayed the flames lingering on the floor—which was already blackened from the spider-fire Robin had dealt with a few days ago. "No thanks. I'm done with that stuff."

She shrugged. "More for me."

36

Silence reigned over the Volvo as the Dogs of Odysseus made their way through the streets of Petoskey. The only sound was the steady white-noise *shush*ing of the SUV's tires as they coasted over ghostly swarms of snow-powder.

"Radio?" asked the woman driving.

"I could use a little peace and quiet," croaked Gendreau in the passenger seat. The magician stared out the window at the passing restaurants and summer homes. To their left was a hillside neighborhood of gingerbread houses not unlike Robin's childhood home, their porches swathed in plastic winterization sheeting. To their right sprawled a marina bristling with yacht masts, and beyond that glittered the gray waves of Lake Michigan.

The sunset was a hot red blur on the water, compressed by a thousand layers of pinks, purples, and blues. After a few minutes of introspective solitude had passed, Sara said from the back, "You doing okay, Andy?"

"I just need time," said Gendreau. As had become habit, he touched the scar across his throat.

"And a new relic," said Lucas. "Martine ruined your cane."

"It's okay." The curandero delved into his jacket liner and took out the dead tooth. "Carrying around a penis as long as my leg doesn't suit my image as a man of taste. Once we're home and I've had a little time with my therapist, I'll speak with our quartermaster here and see if there's another item that might match my particular set of skills. And by 'therapist,' of course I am referring to the bottle of Dewar's in the bottom drawer of my desk."

Under a puffy down vest, the driver wore a blue dress covered in black palm-leaf silhouettes. Running across the left side of her chest was a seven-inch surgery scar in the vague shape of a Nike swoosh. She was Asian, fine-featured, with ringlets of raven hair shot through with silver.

"I'm sure you're itching to ask," said Gendreau.

The woman stopped for a red light. "You made your reports." She gave him a glance, eyes quickly back to the road. "But I'd be lying if I said I wasn't curious."

"Your son is doing well. Clever."

She nodded.

"Good-looking kid," Gendreau added. "Takes care of his father."

A wistful smile touched the corner of her mouth.

"We've got a long road ahead of us, trying to find Cutty and Leon," said the curandero. "She's long gone—probably skipped town as soon as Martine got out of the hospital. Weaver likely stayed behind to slow us down and give her coven-sister a chance to escape."

"When I made those rings," said the woman, "I never considered the idea they might react to the protective wards Annie Martine put on the house."

"Goes to show you how sensitive these energies can be." Gendreau slumped in his seat, folding his arms. It had been a long flight, with an exasperating six-hour layover in the Detroit airport.

As much as he enjoyed the McNamara Light Tunnel, he enjoyed his bed considerably more. "I think we can all internalize a little new knowledge from our adventure in the boondocks this week."

The driver shook her head. "Of all the places, a backwoods town in the South. I guess he was tired of the big city after all." The light turned green and she pulled into a small but labyrinthine shopping district.

Two- and three-story brick buildings loomed over the streets, lining their path with clothes boutiques, Mackinac fudge shops, restaurants, fancy furniture merchants. The woman drove them deeper into the maze and eased into parallel parking next to a small restaurant, picture windows framed by a rainbow of coffee mugs embedded in concrete. The sign above the front door read ROAST & TOAST CAFÉ.

Next door was a tiny bookstore. MCLEAN & EAKIN BOOKSELLERS. "So," said Gendreau, opening his door and unfolding his long legs, "pray tell, dear Origo, might you have a suitable relic to replace my broken cane?"

"Not quite as dapper as the one you had, but I think I may," said Haruko, putting quarters in the meter. "How do you feel about rings?"

"I could be convinced."

Across the street, the black greyhound watched the magicians file into the bookstore from his vigil on the corner.

Even though they couldn't perceive him, pedestrians gave the Beast of Gévaudan a wide berth as they bustled long the sidewalk. The church-grim looked up, hollow eyes traveling the face of the bookstore, past the windows on the second floor, and the third floor, to the roof and beyond, to the hidden tower only he could see, the Ithacan Library, reaching invisibly into the sky over the lake.

Alaskan summer was in full swing as a 1974 Winnebago Brave trundled into the parking lot of Cap'n Joe's Tesoro gas station. Emerald mountains crowded around the town, their peaks thrust into the low clouds as if jostling for a drink of rain.

Wincing in anticipation as the vehicle's brow slipped under the eaves, Robin angled the RV underneath the awning and parked by the pump at the end.

Satin-gray ocean lapped at the shores of the bay across the road. She sat for a moment, gazing absently, not really thinking. Eventually, she unclipped the seat belt and climbed out of the driver's seat. A trash bag full of clothes sat on the floor under the breakfast nook. She opened it and her lip curled at the coppery stink of blood. She tied it shut and carried it outside.

Graffiti was spray-painted on the side of the dumpster—WELCOME TO ALASKA in two-foot-tall letters. What concerned her was that the middle *A* in ALASKA was the witch-rune for

378 · S. A. HUNT

homelands, the sideways Jesus-fish. Clomping across the parking lot in untied combat boots, she lobbed the bag of clothes over the rim of the dumpster, then went into the gas station. A few minutes later, she came back out with a little bag, glass clinking inside.

Wind rolled in off the ocean as she pumped gas, giant tides of air that pushed waves across the puddles and made the awning's aluminum sheets thunder. Her Mohawk blew in the gale.

"Morning, love." The shape of her mother Annie coalesced from the cool air.

"Hi, Mom."

Only Robin could see and hear her. Annie's AM-radio voice was tinny and hollow, but her diction was razor-sharp. She wore a flowing sundress, or at least that's what Robin thought it was; the ghost was mostly diaphanous and gauzy. Ever since she'd pulled Annie out of the dryad, she appeared from time to time, as if checking in. She supposed she carried Annie in her heart now, or at least in some room of her mind.

A red pickup truck angled in, paused as if in indecision, and then pulled up to the next pump. In the back was a bundle of fishing poles, nets, a tackle box. Mashed beer cans.

The door opened with a rusty *crack* and the driver got out, dressed like some kind of farmer, dirty chambray shirt and even dirtier jeans. His face was a wild bristle of salt-and-pepper scruff. Instead of opening his mouth to reveal grungy chompers and a *Howdy, y'all,* he smiled with flawless eggshell teeth and said, *"Guten Morgen. Schönes Wetter, nicht wahr?"*

Good morning. Lovely weather, isn't it?

"Uhh . . . ja. *Wenn Sie eine buh—Beerdigungen, v-vielleicht."* Yeah. *If you like funerals, maybe.* It was the best she could remember from Heinrich's books. *Probably sound like I have some kind of brain damage.*

The German laughed. "What brings a beautiful young woman like you out here to the middle of nowhere by herself?" he asked in a heavy accent. His eyes were hooded but clear. And they were gravitating to her ass.

"Creepazoid," murmured the ghostly Annie.

Robin smiled and whispered confidentially behind her hand, "*Ich bin hier, um eine Hexe zu töten.*"

Laughing even harder, the German unscrewed his gas cap and looked back at her. Something in Robin's eyes made his smile fall cold. If it were possible for a man's ears to lie flat back like a dog, Herr Fisherman's would have. He got back in his truck without putting the gas cap back on, cranked it, and pulled around next to the store.

His doors locked. *Clunk!*

Robin laughed. "You're gonna be waitin' a while for *me* to leave, sucker." The meter on the pump had climbed to nineteen dollars. "The Brave is thirsty today."

She engaged the auto-cutoff and climbed into the Winnebago. Her MacBook sat on the breakfast nook table. She opened the laptop and woke it up to find a couple of new emails buried in a mess of spam and Malus Domestica fan mail. The first was from Anders Gendreau, asking her how Alaska was treating her. She typed up a quick answer and fired it off:

> *Hey Andy,*
>
> *It's beautiful up here but hard to sleep with it always daytime. I'm done here for now, but I might spend a couple more days here in the mountains before I take off back to the Lower 48, if you don't mind—I could use a little more nature in my life. Looking forward to getting back. Let me know if you guys want to get together for the Fourth.*
>
> *—Robin*

The second email was from Wayne Parkin.

Hi Robin!!!!!

I hope you're having fun. Dad and I love the pictures you've been posting in Alaska and Canada. That moose you saw on the freeway was crazy!!!! I hope her and her baby are okay!!!

Miss you here. Dont know if you saw the pictures we put on Instagram but Joel and me fixed up the comic shop real good and with Marissa's help, we got it running this week. Its doing great. I guess Fisher made a will a couple years ago and left the shop to Joel. Him and Marissa are sharing ownership and thanks to all our ideas . . . especially Marissa . . . Joel says the shop is out of the hole, whatever that maens.

Turned out Miguel was the one that bought Kenway's art shop and turned it into another pizzeria . . . the Rocktown Cafe . . . since they're right down the street from the comic shop we share alot of business!!!

Anyway I wanted to say hey and tell you I'm doin real good in school. And thank you for kicking that demon out. We sleep good now. Dad had that symbol tattooed on our shoulders. At first the tattoo guy didn't want to do it but then Dad showed him your videos and then the tattoo guy was all about tattooing a kid. It hurt real bad but I didn't cry at all. Dad was proud of me.

Dad hasnt had a drink since we moved here. He misses Mom sometimes and he gets this look on his face when Mr. Johnson messes up and offers him a beer but he never takes one.

Love you Ms. Martine. Come see us when you get back.

PS. Joel decided to try his brothers "keto diet" after all. He had a hard time with it at first he got real sick for a

few weeks but now he's doin alright. He still cheats some-
times but he says he feels better than he has in a while.
Also he's taking self defense classes with Marissa.

Robin closed the MacBook, digging through the bag for a can of green tea. She opened it with a *snick!* and sat in the nook, slurping and staring out the window.

"Get up, you lazy bastard," she called. "I've been driving all night. It's your turn."

A groan came from the bedroom loft.

"Get uuuuup." Robin slurped tea.

"Uuuuuhhng."

She got up out of the nook and went into the back. Kenway was sprawled facedown on the bed in his underwear, the sheet sideways like a toga. She pulled the sheet off and smacked him hard on the ass.

"Yo!" he shouted, scrambling to roll over. Grabbing her wrist, he dragged her into the bed and held her down until she was forced to pinch him and it turned into a tickle-fight. He won by forfeit when he took her face in his hands and they kissed, an intoxication of slow gulping and lip-biting and tongue-licking.

"My devil-girl," said Kenway, her cheeks cupped in his bear paws.

He got up and pulled an elastic sock over the end of his leg, then strapped on his prosthetic foot. Lumbering through the Winnebago, he pulled a can of coffee out of her bag and slugged half of it back, then put on some clothes and went out to put away the gas nozzle.

While they'd been necking in the back, another car had pulled up to the other side of the pump. A young woman fed gasoline into a raggedy station wagon, her shoulders bunched up against the damp wind. Dark circles of insomnia ringed her eyes.

Sitting in the back was a little boy. He seemed to recognize Kenway and rolled down his window, but what he said was so low,

Robin couldn't make it out. The woman—his mother, assumedly—gave him an earful. He frowned and rolled the window back up. Before any further words could be exchanged, the boy's mother got in the car and drove away with a squeal of tires.

"What was *that* about?" asked Robin as Kenway tucked his bulky self behind the wheel of the Winnebago.

"Kid asked me if I was the guy from that show on YouTube." He buckled his seat belt and started the engine. "Told him I was. He said there's a witch living in the woods near his house. Almost got his sister and now she's been prowling around all night trying to get *him*. They call her 'the Qalupalik,' the Old Woman of the Sea."

"I take it his mom told him to shut up about the witches."

"Actually, she told him to shut up, shut up, *shut up about the goddamn witch*." He was already fording the parking lot, chasing after the station wagon. Robin staggered across the listing deck of the RV and plopped into the passenger seat.

Seagulls sliced the sky over the road. She leaned over to turn on the radio, and static brought her to a station playing Halestorm's "Daughters of Darkness." Rock 'n' roll filled the Winnebago with sound and fury. Annie stood behind the transmission hump, her hands on their headrests, smiling. As Robin watched, the shade vapored into nothing.

"Thought you were gonna take a nap," said Kenway.

"Promises to keep, babe." Robin picked her nails with the Osdathregar. "And many witches to kill before I sleep."

Acknowledgments

At the end of the first book in this series, I thanked my mom, my agent, my editor, and of course the Outlaw Army—my stalwart supporters from the very beginning.

Here I thank them again, but this time, I'd also like to thank Callum Plews, the producer for the series' audiobooks, and the narrators he's set to task. It's going to be an amazing experience hearing my characters speak for the first time.

I would also like to take this opportunity to thank my boon companions here in Petoskey. Moving a thousand miles away from my rural hometown in Georgia to an unfamiliar Michigan tourist trap where I knew nobody could have been a lonely experience, but the friends I discovered here made me feel welcome and safe. Kate and the BBC, the Richey sisters, the D&D gang, the three Zachs (Sheppard, Matelski, & Fischer), Bob and Esther, the Meyers, the Michelsen family, Jake and Sherry, McLean & Eakin Booksellers, the Roast & Toast crew, Steve and Gary at Ruff Life, Jeanine—you guys became my second family. You made this town a home for me.

*Turn the page for a sneak peek at
the next Malus Domestica novel*

THE HELLION

Available September 2020

Intro

Then

Her first night in Heinrich's compound was a long one. The teenager lay under a wool military blanket in the deepening twilight, listening to the silence of the desert and rain drumming on the tin roof. The man slept hard, his breath a steady susurration barely audible under the rattle of the rain. Occasionally, heat lightning flashed across the ceiling, throwing her makeshift bedroom into ghastly ghost-story detail.

An incredible crash of thunder shook the room.

Terrified, Robin sat bolt upright and threw the curtain aside, preparing to run for the door.

"Good morning," said Heinrich.

As always, he wore all black—jeans, boots, a thermal henley draped on his broad shoulders. The witch-hunter sat on a stool at the kitchen island, tall and lanky, with an expressive mouth and hard eyes, and his skin was the cold, steely kind of black, like he'd been carved from the night itself.

One of the many things she would pick up from him: the paranoid gunslinger tendency to sit against the wall, so she couldn't be shot in the back. Or have her throat cut, how the witches liked to get you when your guard was down. Simple and effective.

"What time is it?" She put on a pair of the fresh new socks she'd bought on the way through Mississippi. Reaching under the cot, she dragged out her new boots and wriggled into them.

"About six." Heinrich beckoned her over. "Come on, I made food."

The teenager joined him at the kitchen island, where he'd made omelets and bacon on a big plug-in griddle. French press half-full of coffee. A cookie sheet rested on a towel, loaded with several flaky biscuits. Nearby, a radio quietly played a morning drive-time show.

"Boy howdy, you know how to do breakfast." Robin poured a big cup of coffee, dipped a spoonful of sugar into it, and made herself stir it before gulping half the cup in one go.

He watched her. "Most important meal of the day."

Caffeine clawed the sleepiness from her brain. "Been so long since I had a good cup of coffee," she said, downing the other half. She poured another cup and took an omelet, along with bacon and a biscuit, and ate ravenously. "Don't let you have it in the psych ward."

"We'll need the energy." The man peeled open a biscuit and spooned jam into it. "Today you start your training. Sleep okay?"

"Slept like shit." She ground the back of her wrist into one grainy eye, her fingers shiny with grease. "Thanks for asking."

"Yeah," he said into his coffee cup, "I know the feeling." He grinned. "You gonna sleep good tonight."

• • •

According to the man, the building they lived in had been used by the Killeen Fire Department as a training structure. The lower floors were devoid of furniture or decoration—just bare cinder-block walls and cement floors. Heinrich led her all the way down and around the back of the bottom staircase to a rusty steel door.

This he opened, and he shined a flashlight into a closet full of junk: two sawhorses on which hung a pair of flak jackets, a plastic trunk, and leaning in the corner was an assortment of PVC pipes pushed through foam pool noodles and wrapped in duct tape.

"Here, put this on." He took one of the flak jackets and handed it to her.

The instant she took it from him, the heavy jacket hit the floor. She gathered her arms inside and lifted it over her head. Two slabs of armor in the front and the back, and one pressed against each hip. Heinrich meticulously fastened all the buckles and straps, pulling them tight until the vest fit her like a turtle shell. He rapped his knuckles on her chest, the flashlight shining in her face. "This is called an IOTV. It's a military—"

"Flak jacket?"

"A flak jacket is something different. Vietnam gear. This is desert shit. I don't remember what IOTV stands for, but the ceramic plates can repel small arms fire. It's current military issue. Weighs about forty pounds."

Robin's face went cold. "You ain't gonna be shooting at me, are you?"

"Lord, no." Heinrich smiled. "This is just for weight training. Bought 'em for emergencies, but they make good weight vests." He didn't specify what constituted an "emergency." Instead, he opened the plastic trunk and dug out a pair of things like icepacks. Velcro ripped open and he slipped them around Robin's ankles. "Ankle weights."

"What is all this for?" Her feet felt like they were made of lead.

"Like I said, weight training. Come on." He grabbed one of the pool-noodle swords and a burlap sack, and led her back upstairs. "Want you to wear 'em for three hours today, and every day from now on. Toughen you up, get you used to carrying extra weight. Trust me, you'll see where I'm going with this after that three hours."

By the time she had climbed back up the three flights of stairs, the teenager was huffing and puffing. "Jesus," she wheezed, leaning against the wall of their den as Heinrich stepped over to the record player and put on a Fugees album. The speakers banged out "Ready or Not," and Lauryn Hill sang about playing her enemies like a game of chess.

"Tired already?"

"No," she sighed.

"Good," said the man, and he threw her a padded stick. She barely caught it, almost fumbling, and when she looked back up, he had heavy pads strapped to his hands. "Let's work off that breakfast, kiddo."

• • •

The rain worsened into a downpour—bad enough Heinrich had to let down the tin-sheet awnings covering the windows. They spent the entire time in the "lair," as he called it, beating each other with the pads and the boffer. Plenty of room there, an open space some thirty or forty feet square, the furniture pushed out of the way, with that dusty Oriental rug in the middle of it.

Their sparring session was soundtracked by everything from Ray Charles to Ol' Dirty Bastard to James Brown to twenty different heavy metal bands. "Nine times out of ten, once you're face-to-face, they gonna try to claw you with their fingernails," he said. "Like fightin' a wildcat." She tried to bat his padded hands aside, but somehow he kept managing to shrug past it and deliver a volley of body blows. "But it's a last-ditch effort. They'll try to keep you from even getting close in the first place."

Frustration twisted around her chest, binding her even tighter than the IOTV. She couldn't seem to move fast enough to get through his hands. "They'll use tricks, try to appeal to your empathy. Lie to you. Offer you riches, immortality. They'll make you see things. Terrible things. Wonderful things. Things that make no goddamn sense. They'll make familiars, like they did with your daddy, send those after you. When all else fails, they fall back on the claws."

He slapped her across the face. "You paying attention?"

Heat and ice surged across her skin as a shot of adrenaline hit her, pissed her off, made her see red. Santa Esmeralda crooned in the background, *I'm just a soul whose intentions are good.* She swung the boffer overhead—"Urrgh!"—and caught him across the wrist.

"Good one," said Heinrich. "Time to come down. Get out of that vest and go get some water."

Dropping the boffer, Robin staggered toward the kitchenette, clawing at the IOTV's straps. Clutching the counter, she used her foot to hook a stool and drag it over to sit on. As soon as she got the armor off and let it slam to the floor at her feet, every muscle in her body screamed out in relief.

● ● ●

December in Texas. Humidity made it unbearably chilly outside, cold right down to the bone, but their lair was heated from underneath by a furnace.

In hindsight, the structure and exertion were probably what cured Robin of her torpor and cleared her head, focused the thoughts scattered by the death of her mother and the breaking of her spell, and fended off her depression, more than the psych medication. First thing every morning, they got up and ate breakfast, then sparred each other until lunch whether they felt like it or not. Heinrich went out to chop some wood while Robin made lunch, then they ate together and spent a few hours poring over old books. Case studies about witches, occult encyclopedias, language trainers, German, French, Chinese, and Icelandic magic tomes, books of hieroglyphs and runes, and other esoterica.

This is where she learned more about the ways and methods of how witches were able to use cats to scry and to control people. She learned the radius from which a *nag shi* dryad could draw life-force, what factors could alter that reach, and the properties of its accretion disk, such as how running water could dampen it; she learned fire was just about the only thing that could kill a witch older than at least forty years, and bullets were useless other than slowing them down. She learned the various forms witches who held the Gift of Transfiguration could choose to take—beasts and self-augmentation only, no doppelgängers or inanimate objects; she learned how elaborate witches could make their illusions, from simple visions of insects to artificial realities; she learned the range and strength and dexterity of the Gift of Manipulation, which you might know as *telekinesis,* and ways to defeat it, such as blinding the witch, because they could only manipulate objects they could see.

After study time, Robin went outside in her vest and brought firewood up the two flights of stairs to the third floor, whether they needed it or not. By Christmas, she had filled the entire eastern wall of the furnace room with chunks of oak and pine, and Heinrich had to cut the loads from five to two per day.

Then it was suppertime. The weekends were downtime, and they made big, heavy meals on Saturday and Sunday like slow-cooker Italian meatball soup, chicken enchiladas, steaks and baked potatoes, and pizzas of all shapes and kinds, and during the week, they nibbled the leftovers for supper.

After dinner, they crashed on the couch with a little bowl of ice cream or a soda float and watched TV or a movie out of Heinrich's collection. DVDs and VHS tapes covered one entire wall of his den. Robin lost count of the number of times she fell asleep on the couch watching Zatoichi annihilate a gang of troublemakers.

"Wherever I go," said the blind swordsman, "I'm the god of calamity."

• • •

By that summer, their sparring looked like something out of one of those movies. The teenager worked him around the den with the boffer, and he juked and jitterbugged out of the way like Sinatra, the both of them swashbuckling up and down the stairs, from the window and through the kitchenette. Whenever he managed to parry the boffer and go in for the kill, either he'd get kicked in the leg and staggered, or Robin would twirl the boffer over her head and down across his forehead.

One day, she backed him into the kitchen and he managed to pin the boffer with a cabinet door. Out of some kind of instinct, Robin snatched a barbecue fork out of the dish drain and tried to stab him with it, but Heinrich shielded his face with his free hand, and the fork jammed deep into the hard foam of the punch pad.

Pulling out the fork with a wince, he tossed it in the sink, then slid his hand out of the pad. Two neat puncture wounds vampired the back of his fist.

She gasped. "I'm—"

Heinrich gathered himself, standing. "It's okay."

"I'm so sorry."

"I said it's okay." Blood dripped on the kitchen floor between their feet. "The apprentice has become the master," he said, backing away to the first-aid drawer. He dug out a roll of gauze and wrapped it around his injured hand. "Maybe," he began, as the girl ripped a handful of paper towels off of a nearby roll and wiped up the blood, "maybe it's time to finally show you something."

She gave him a confused look.

"Come with me," he said, grabbing a combat knife off his bed and clipping it to his belt.

They clomped down the stairs to the bottom floor of the fire tower and into the closet where he kept the pads and boffers. In the back of the room was a steel rack with cardboard boxes. In one of them was an orange case, and inside the case was a flare gun. He handed it to Robin.

"What do I do with this?"

"Stick it up your ass? I don't care. Just don't lose it."

She shrugged and jammed it into the back of her jeans.

Outside, Robin followed him through the broad main avenue

running through the middle of Hammertown. Spaghetti-western shopfronts loomed over them on either side, their façades welcoming them inside with signs in Arabic. He stepped down one of the side alleys, cutting between a tin shack and a two-story building. Left, around a corner, through a chain-link gate with a *Beware of Dog* sign in Arabic.

Brazen sunshine baked the dirt under their feet. Before them spanned a seemingly infinite vista of Texas desert and, in the distance, a backbone of vague gray mountains.

Between here and there was a lone bur oak, with a short thick trunk and branches stretching in every direction. This tree draped shade over a dilapidated barn with a high, pitched roof and a broad door. Strung through the handles was a strong new chain, secured with three padlocks. The man took out a keychain and unlocked all three, tossing the chain aside. Then he opened the door, pulling both panels aside.

Inside, a ragged, filthy woman in a tattered dress stood tied to one of the support posts under the hay loft, her tangled hair over her face. Ripe body odor hung in the air, along with some pungent, fruity undercurrent Robin couldn't quite identify.

"Oh, my God!" she cried, pushing past into the room.

Before she could free the man's captive, one hand shot out and grabbed the drag-handle of her vest, stopping her in her tracks. Heinrich pulled her gently backward, pointing at the ground.

"Icelandic containment ward."

On the dirt under her feet was an enormous circle etched with salt, an elaborate runic diagram comprised of a dozen concentric circles. Between each circle was an unbroken sentence of hundreds of sigils. With his bandaged hand, Heinrich directed Robin's attention to the walls and ceiling, where dozens of *algiz* protection runes had been painted on every visible surface. Then he pointed at the woman tied to the support beam in the center of the runic bullseye. Glinting in the woman's chest was the handle of a dagger.

"Is that a witch?" Robin struggled to make sense of the scene.

Nothing witchlike stood out about this scrawny woman, whose face was pale with abject terror and exhaustion and misery. The woman peered at them through a curtain of matted hair. "Oh, God." Her voice was kitten-weak. "Are you here to save me? This man has had me trapped here for months."

A burst of anger gave Robin the words she needed. "You mean you've had a witch out here the entire time? Like eighty feet from where we sleep? Are you high?"

"Please help me," said the woman. The silvery dagger was buried in her chest right up to the cross guard, and a stain ran down her belly in a banner of dull brown. "I think I might be dying."

"You ain't dyin', Tilda," Heinrich said mildly.

Writhing in her bonds, Tilda stared at him with wild, baleful eyes. The man stepped across the outermost circle of the containment ward toward her, taking care to disrupt the runes with his foot.

"What are you doing?" asked Robin, her heart beating a little faster.

"Been a couple of months since I been around to see my good friend here." Heinrich stepped inside another of the concentric circles. Dry dirt gritted under his boot as he disturbed another ring of symbols. "Thought we could stop in and say hi before lunch." The woman's eyes didn't leave Heinrich's face. Terrible eyes, the washed-out blue high beams of a dope fiend, glaring from under thick eyebrows. Heinrich stepped into another of the circles and a slow smile spread across her face, revealing jagged teeth in ink-black gums.

"I don't think that's a good idea," said Robin.

Fear gripped her. Shivers ran through her like a stampede of wild horses, and her face and hands became cold. The sound of her mother's last words, echoing in the back of her mind as Annie Martine lay broken on the floor—*Cutty. Witch.* The sight of her father writhing on his back next to her, blood gushing out of his mouth and nose. *Witches aren't real witches aren't real witches aren't real*—but they were, weren't they? They were real. And here was one, right in front of her, large as life and dark as death, glaring at the both of them as her mentor crept closer and closer.

"Nothing is a good idea, except in hindsight." Heinrich stepped into another circle, scuffing the diagram again. "Every decision we make is a Schrödinger's Box. D'you know what that is, Robin Hood?"

"Sure. Yeah. The cat in the box."

"The cat in the closed box, both alive and dead until you open it and find out which it is. Every decision we make is a Schrödinger's Box—both good and bad. We never know which until after we make it."

The woman's breathing came quick and fast, blowing streamers of her hair out in front of her face, *huff huff huff huff* like birthing breaths in a Lamaze class. She laughed under her breath, casting all pretense aside. "You're a pretty little one," she croaked, her cheek meeting her shoulder in a bashful sort of way. "A little older than I like, but that just means I'll have to cook you a little longer. You're still ripe."

"Cook me?"

"Yeah, Robin Hood," said Heinrich. "They eat virgins, remember? They're pedophages? Didn't your mother ever read you the story of Hansel and Gretel?"

"You mean that's *real*?"

"Yeah, it's real. We been reading the same books up there in that tower, ain't we?" The man took another step into a smaller circle, dragging his foot through the salt symbols. "Remember that one I made you read about witches in medieval Russia?"

She winced. "I'm sorry. It was long-winded as shit and really badly translated. I only made it about halfway through."

Dust shook out of the witch's clothes, hanging in the sunbeams coming through the hayloft, as she thrashed violently in her bindings. Rope bound her wrists and elbows behind the pole; rope kept her neck pinned. "It's been so long since I've eaten," said Tilda, grinning with those gnarly brown teeth.

"Anyway, who the hell said I was a virgin?" asked the teenager.

Halfway through scuffing another of the circles, Heinrich shot her an incredulous look. "You were involuntarily committed in your sophomore year, and you've been in there ever since. Your mother was about as religious as you can get in the South without mailing your paycheck to Billy Graham. You trying to tell me you got laid in the nuthouse?"

"Well, you did just call it the 'nut' house."

If he'd been wearing glasses, he would have peered over them at her.

"No, I didn't get laid." Robin scowled. "I was too busy going through the Ludovico technique, sleeping through HGTV reruns, and eating spaghetti with a plastic spoon to care about sexual intercourse. Besides, antidepressants make it hard to orgasm, apparently."

"TMI, kiddo."

At this point, the man was only a few feet away from the witch. Her mouth opened, and kept opening, and her tongue uncoiled, fattening, lolling from between her teeth like a purple python. Lengthening, sharpening, Tilda's teeth bristled in her cavernous mouth. "Come a little closer, Heinie," she said, grinning.

"Heinie?"

Despite herself, Robin couldn't help but laugh.

The man stepped inside the last circle, a ring of runes some six feet across. Reaching out with her serpentine tongue, Tilda could almost reach him—close enough, in fact, for Heinrich to lean backward to avoid getting licked in the face. As he did, he moved around the witch, sidling around the inside of the innermost rune ring.

"What are you doing?" asked Robin.

"Oh, nothing." Heinrich's hands rose in that *don't mind me* way.

The witch watched him, her tongue curling around her own upper arm. "What *are* you doing?" she asked, as if she couldn't believe what she was seeing either.

Then Tilda looked down at her feet. Robin looked down as well, and realized the Icelandic containment circle had been disturbed in a straight line from her own toes to directly in front of the witch. The witch's eyes came back up to Robin's face, grin widening. In one swift motion, Heinrich slid the combat knife out of its sheath and cut the ropes.

Looking back and forth between the two of them, Tilda seemed to be indecisive about who to go after first, but she turned toward Robin and lunged forward, reaching—

—the teenager flinched in terror, falling—

—but Tilda was immediately halted by the silver dagger in her chest, doubling over around it. *"Gurk—!"*

"What the hell, dude?" said Robin, sitting on her ass in the dirt. She reached behind her back and pulled out the flare gun he'd given her earlier, pointing it at Tilda.

"The Osdathregar." Heinrich stepped away from the witch, standing by the innermost rune ring. "In the Vatican Archives, documents call it the Godsdagger. Secret verses of ancient Hindu texts refer to it as the Ratna Maru." Tilda reached up and grasped the hilt of the Osdathregar, trying to wrench it loose. The man paced around the perimeter of the ring, his hands clasped behind his back. "Nobody knows who made it; nobody knows where it came from. All we know is that it's powerful enough to stop a witch cold in her tracks."

Hollywood had conditioned Robin to expect the eldritch and the ornate: a wavy flambergé with a pewter-skull hilt, cord-wrapped handle, and a spike for a pommel, a Gil Hibben monstrosity from a mall kiosk. But the real Osdathregar was a simple main gauche with a gently tapering blade a little wider than a stiletto. The guard was a diamond shape, the handle was wrapped in leather, and the pommel was only an unadorned onion bulb. The diamond of the guard contained a small hollow, and engraved inside the hollow was a sinuous scribble.

"See that symbol there?" Heinrich pointed at the hilt. "That means *purifier* in Enochian, the language of the angels. Regardless of where it came from, this is a holy weapon. Which means even if it can't outright kill a witch, she can't remove it from where it's embedded. Deep magic, baby. You stake her into the floor, or a wall, wherever, she'll be there until the end of time, or until you come along and pull it out."

With the flare gun's muzzle, the teenager gestured to the diagram that filled the barn floor. "What about this, then? And the ropes?"

Heinrich shrugged. "In my line of work, I've learned to appreciate redundancy."

"What *can* kill a witch, then?"

A wry smirk. "Come on, Robin Hood. That's Mickey Mouse kindergarten shit. You *know* what kills a witch."

". . . Fire?"

"Ding ding ding!" cried Heinrich. "We have a winner! Now, listen—I've brought the anger out in you, Robin. Made a fighter out of you. You finally cut me. Now I need to get rid of the fear. A knife ain't nothin' but a worthless piece of steel unless you're willing to use it!"

With that, he pulled out the dagger.

Now nothing stood between them.

"Guns can't stop me, child," said the witch, marching resolutely through the gaps in the ward and out of the barn. In broad daylight, she was even more disgusting, a crusty ghost wrapped in shit and rotten fabric. Blood running down her chin looked like hot black tar, dribbling all over the ground. Her fingernails were yellowed spades. Her hair was the woolly, filthy mane of a lion, and her eyes were fiery red and yellow, with pinprick pupils.

A shout from the man in the barn: *"Fire, you idiot!"*

The flare gun in her hand. Robin pointed it at the witch and pulled the trigger, but the safety was on.

Tilda didn't even flinch. "Nice shootin', Tex," she cackled, and charged, tongue snaking, harpy talons extended.

"Fuck!"

Panic made a live wire out of every nerve in Robin's body. Stones dug into her knees. She aimed the flare gun with both hands and fired. The flare hit center mass.

Waves of incredible heat washed over the little barnyard as the creature erupted into flames ten feet tall, a tornado of smoke and light. Tilda shrieked madly, staggering toward the teenager, flaming hands outstretched.

"Grain alcohol," said Heinrich, coming outside to join them.

Blackened fingers combed through dim orange whorls of light, cupping and clawing, searching. The rest of her was obscured by the column of fire. The teenager shuffled sideways along the fence, trying to keep the flaming witch from grabbing her. "I see you burning, Robin Martine," gurgled the thing in the flames. Collapsing on her knees, and then kneeling prostrate in the shade of the giant bur oak, Tilda laughed through a mouthful of fire. "One day, your enemies will trap you, and you will burn just like me." She fell over and lay motionless, a black wraith shrouded in light. "You will burn," she said in a strained hiss. "You will die."

The last syllable seemed to stretch on forever, becoming the soft rustle of the bur oak's leaves, until it faded into silence, broken only by the warp and woof of the flames biting at the wind.

They stood there and watched her burn until she was a coal sculpture, twisted into a fetal position in the dust.

"That wasn't pleasant," said Heinrich.

"Wasn't a fucking birthday party, that's for sure."

He looked over at her, genuinely surprised. "It's your birthday?"

"Yeah," said the teenager, and she walked away, still gripping the flare gun in one trembling hand.

"Happy birthday," he called after her.

"Stick it up your ass."